Caylen's Quest

by

Robert B Marchand

Argus Enterprises International, Inc.
Book Publishers
North Carolina~*~*~New Jersey

Caylen's Quest

Argus Enterprises International, Inc.

For information:
Argus Enterprises International, Inc.
Post Office Box 914
Kernersville, North Carolina 27285
www.a-argusbooks.com

ISBN: 978-0-9819075-6-7
ISBN: 0-9819075-6-3

Book Cover designed by Dubya

Printed in the United States of America

Caylen's Quest

In The Beginning

The year was 1919, and the war machines that had ravaged all Europe ground to a halt. The Great War was, at long last, now finally over. Bodies of the dead, those that could be found and identified, were being shipped home to grieving loved ones. Millions of soldiers, those who had survived—both maimed and whole—returned only to find that any employment was difficult, if not impossible, to find. Entire families were hard pressed just to survive The war had taken great toll on virtually every family, and had left many widowed mothers without support. Making ends meet on the scant pay that was available to women during the early part of the twentieth century was difficult at best.

Throughout all of Canada, rumors of gold strikes drew hundreds of thousands of gold prospectors seeking the promised riches, only to find the rumors were, for the most part, just rumors.

Other rumors across the countryside alluded to things much less pleasant than gold mines. Creatures of strange being were supposed to inhabit parts of the magnificent forests and mountains that were so prevalent across Canada: lean, hungry, furry man-eating monsters were reportedly seeking prey. Sightings of huge black wolves silently stalking through the woodlands were claimed, but never substantiated

Not the least of these rumors was those regarding an old Indian medicine man that possessed mystical powers beyond belief. This 'Shaman' was reportedly seeking a specific individual, an individual to whom great powers had been promised.

In reality, not one of the rumors had been verified and, in fact, all had been dismissed as being caused by ingesting too much of the fine Canadian whisky distilled with the pure mountain water that was easily available.

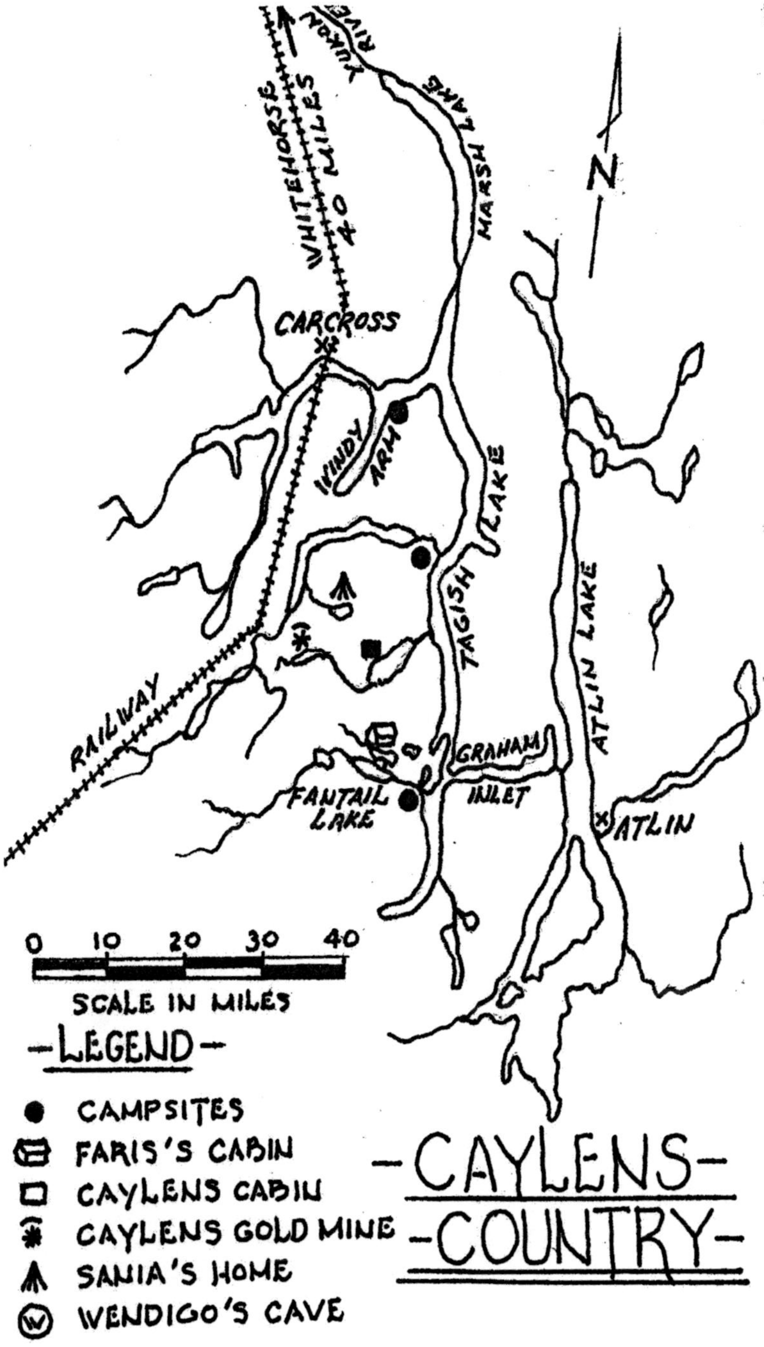
YUKON RIVER
MARSH LAKE
WHITEHORSE 40 MILES
N
CARCROSS
WINDY ARM
TAGISH LAKE
ATLIN LAKE
RAILWAY
GRAHAM INLET
FANTAIL LAKE
ATLIN
0 10 20 30 40
SCALE IN MILES
-LEGEND-
CAMPSITES
FARIS'S CABIN
CAYLENS CABIN
CAYLENS GOLD MINE
SANIA'S HOME
WENDIGO'S CAVE
-CAYLENS-
-COUNTRY-

Chapter 1

The Letter

Caylen Helms had just reminded his mother, Lora, for the third time within just a few days, that his birthday was now only a mere three weeks away, and that there was a certain something extra special the local Greenwood, British Columbia General Store was displaying in its show window.

"A pretty nice fishing rod and reel on sale for just four dollars and eighty nine cents, Mom."

His mother responded to him quite sharply, saying, "That's just four dollars and eighty-nine cents more than we can afford right now, Caylen. You should know that." As a part time teacher in the Greenwood elementary school, Mrs. Helms made barely enough money to pay the rent and to purchase sufficient food and clothing for herself and her ravenous, growing young son. The small pension she received from the Government of Canada for the ultimate sacrifice her dead husband made in the Great War helped a little but they still struggled each and every month to eke out an existence.

Caylen had only recently shown any real interest in the sport of fishing or of any other outdoors sports. He spent much of his time over the past two years immersing him in the local library children's books. He was, once he had learned to read reasonably well, taking an inordinate interest in the adventures of gold prospectors, fur trappers and Northern Canadian pioneers. His mother had begun to become quite concerned about his open lack of interest in any form of outdoors physical activities. This lack of interest on Caylen's part began to show shortly after she had received word in early Nineteen-seventeen that her husband, George, had been killed in action in France. Her young son, Caylen, was only four years old when his father had gone off, with his Canadian rifle regiment to fight the Germans in Europe. As a result, he couldn't remember clearly any real details about his father or of his father's past.

What Caylen did somewhat remember, however, was the many exciting stories that his father told him before he had gone off, as had many other young Canadian men, to fight the Germans in far away France. He remembered his father telling about his personal experiences and his many adventures in the Yukon Territories of Northern Canada, where he once spent three years in the Whitehorse area, trapping and prospecting for gold, as had many other young Canadian men during the early twentieth century. These stories related by his father and impressed into the mind of an attentive young boy were all that he could still remember of his father except for what his mother related to him.

What Caylen did not, or could not tell his mother, was the fact that he dearly loved his father and the memories of him, and that he fully intended, once he was old enough and physically able, to follow in his father's footsteps and explore the wild Northern regions of Canada. Further, he couldn't, or wouldn't, tell her just how proud he was of that tall, handsome, uniformed soldier who had hugged him so tightly just before his departure, telling him how much he loved him and that he, Caylen, had to be the man of the house and that he was to look after his mother until he returned from the war.

He still clearly remembered his mother reading to him, repeatedly, the many long letters his father wrote to them from the muddy trenches and the battlefields of war torn France. He remembered his father saying, in many of those letters that he wanted, to return one day to the far North that he loved so dearly where he once prospected and explored.

Caylen also could easily recall the looks of worry and concern that he could see on his mothers face when the letters suddenly stopped arriving. His and her entire world then come crashing down on that late summer day a few weeks later when the long black Government car pulled into their gravel driveway. He could still remember the look of abject terror on his mother's pale, white face when she saw the Military Chaplain approaching them, carrying a large brown envelope in his hands.

Caylen's entire world, for the following two years, consisted of inquisitively questioning his mother, and gathering as much information and knowledge as was possible from the small local Greenwood library about the Northern wilds of Canada where his father once freely roamed.

He now felt, after exhausting every possible local source of information that the time had come, for him to practice the skills that he would need in order to follow in his father's footsteps, and to survive in the far Northern reaches of Canada.

As the little gold mining town of Greenwood did have a small stream flowing that was nearby and within easy walking distance, and contained both trout and small amounts of powder gold, Caylen was certain that he could, given the proper equipment and sufficient practice, soon teach himself how to fish and to pan for the gold his father once told him, lay about, nearly everywhere in the far north, just waiting to be picked up.

~*~

Three weeks later, on the morning of his eleventh birthday, Caylen was awakened by the late spring morning suns warm rays as they caressed his young cheeks. It took him just a few minutes to finally realize that it was now morning and that it was his birthday. Once this realization had fully sunken in, he leaped out of bed, quickly dressed and rushed out to the kitchen where his mother was cooking the usual mornings breakfast of hot oatmeal porridge.

"Happy Birthday, son," she said, as Caylen's eyes raced about the small kitchen in eager anticipation.

"Where is my present?" he finally blurted out.

"Before we talk about presents," she replied, "We need to think about your father. We should spend a little time remembering him and to send him a small prayer, as he is probably watching over us right now."

With that, she went out of the kitchen and into her bedroom, coming out a moment later carrying a small brown box in her hand.

"Is that my birthday present?" Caylen asked.

"Well," his mother replied, "It's not a birthday present from me, but it is a present that your father wanted you to have, and it's not just for you, it's for both of us. It seems," she continued, "that the Army was keeping it for him but as he is no longer with us, they now want us to have it."

She then opened the box and Caylen could see that it contained four smaller, thin, embossed boxes. Taking each of the smaller boxes one at a time out of the larger one, Lora opened each box in turn and placed them on the table, so that her son could see their contents. Each of the four boxes held a round silver medal, inscribed on their edges with his father's name and military serial number, and to each was attached a multi-colored ribbon, with a small brass pin fastened to the ribbon.

As Caylen looked in wonderment at these four small symbols of his father's ultimate sacrifice, his mother, with tears in her eyes, said,

"These are medals that the Canadian Government has given to us to honor your father's service, his bravery and his sacrifice for Canada. They are now yours, Caylen, as I know your Dad would want you to have them. Your Dad also sent us a letter just before he was killed, a letter that he wanted me to read to you only when I felt you were ready. Well, my son," she said, "I think you are old enough and are now ready."

She picked up a small, dirty and tattered tan envelope that she had obviously opened to read many times before this particular occasion. Removing a two-page, well-worn letter from the envelope, she began to read in a soft, low voice.

> *"My Dearest Wife Lora and my beloved son Caylen, As I scribble this quick letter to you, I am sitting in a dirty, smelly, muddy foxhole somewhere in France. I am not allowed to tell you exactly where I am and I do not really know for certain, but I can say that we are going to attack up a large hill that is right in front of us, at first light tomorrow morning. There are many crack German SS troops holding this hill and we have been told that they have been ordered to fight to the death to keep their position. We have also been told that they may try to use poison gas on us to prevent us from winning this fight. It will not be an easy battle for us to win as this hill is very steep and very high and they have machine guns everywhere. I do not want to frighten either of you, however, I thought that I should tell you that I have had some bad dreams lately and have been thinking a lot about God and of the possibility of death. I have lost a lot of really good friends lately and am getting just a little concerned about my own safety. It is not that I am afraid of dying,*

> *It's that I am afraid of what my dying, (if I should get killed) will mean to both of you and to your futures. I first want to tell you both that I love you with all my heart and soul and that you are my life. You both are all I ever wanted from this life. In addition, if I should die over here, I will die knowing that you also love me. What more could I ask for? I will now have to close this letter as our Corporal has just given us an order to load up and make ready. Before I do close, I want to again tell you both just how much I love and care for you both. To you, Caylen, my dear son, I want to ask you to be strong for me and to look after your mother, and to respect and obey her in all things until I return. If it should happen that not return to you, Lora, know that I have loved you from the first moment that we met. Love to you both, forever and ever, Dad. "*
> *"P. S. Lora; If I do not make it back, please read this to Caylen when you think he is ready, and give to him, my old prospectors pack."*

Caylen's mother then said to him, quite emotionally,

"There is one other thing that I have to tell you, son."

Caylen replied quite quickly, in anticipation,

"What's that, Mom? What is it that you have to tell me? Is it about my birthday present?"

"Well, no, it is not about your birthday present, I don't quite know how to tell you this, but as you know, we are barely existing here and the Company has told me that they will be raising our rent next month. What I wanted to say was that I have been writing letters to a nice man whom lives in Northern British Columbia, and he has been writing me back. He is coming down to meet us next week and he might ask us to move up north to live with him."

Caylen said nothing for about five or so minutes and then he suddenly blurted out. "But what about Dad, Mom?"

His mother took Caylen into her arms and whispered softly to him,

"Your Dad will always be your Dad, Caylen, and he will always be with us, no matter where we go or what we do." She continued, "But even though you might just think of me as your mother and still married to your dad, your dad is in heaven and I am still quite a young woman with my whole life ahead of me. I also believe that you need an older man in your life to show you, and to teach you the man things that all men need to know about as they grow."

"But I don't need anyone but you to show me all those things, "Caylen replied." You can show or help me learn everything I need to know 'because you're a teacher and teachers are supposed to know everything. "

"Teachers certainly do not know everything," his mother said. "I need a man in my life and so do you. Now, for my sake, I want you to be nice to this man when he gets here."

Caylen could see that his mother had made up her mind and that he could do nothing to dissuade her from doing as she had planned.

"Okay, Mom, "Caylen mumbled. " I will be nice to him.

"Alright, son. Thank you." His mother said. "Now let's go up to the attic and see just what good things are in your Dads old prospectors pack?"

With that comment, Lora and Caylen climbed the narrow wood stairwell up and into the dark spider and cobweb filled attic.

"Now, just where could it be?" mused Lora.

"Is this it, Mom?" Caylen asked, pulling a long, heavy canvas sack out from under a pile of cardboard boxes.

"I think it just might be," said his mother. "Let's take it downstairs and see what's in it."

They soon had the dusty heavy pack down the stairs and onto the living room floor, where Caylen eagerly tugged at the straps that held the big pack closed.

"Just hold on a minute, young man," said Lora, "Let me open it and take everything out, one thing at a time."

Lora then undid the two buckles that, along with the thick leather straps, held the pack tightly closed. Tugging on the straps, she finally managed to get the cover open. She then reached in and pulled out a three piece, sectional, steel fishing rod, to which was attached a casting reel filled with a heavy braided linen line.

"Wow! That's just what I need, Mom. Is there anything else?"

"Give me a minute and we shall see," his mother said, reaching deeper into the sack. "Oh, here's a metal box, and from the sounds it is making, I would bet that it is full of fishing hooks, sinkers and lures that belong with that fishing rod. "

Taking the box on his lap, Caylen opened it wide to display, as his mother had guessed, numerous fishhooks, sinkers, lures, floats and a spare spool of braided linen fishing line.

"Look, Mom, now I have all I need to go fishing! I bet I can catch lots of big trout with this stuff."

"Don't be so anxious, young man, I think there are quite a few more things in here," Lora said. Digging back into the bag, she soon pulled out a large spool of braided wire, a cast iron pot and frying pan, and, in addition, a flint and steel fire starter, a small axe and a folding spade, and a large gold pan. There was also a coiled length of rope, a large knife in a leather sheath, a rolled canvas tarpaulin, and a heavy, long, oily, cloth wrapped object.

"Here," she said, handing it to Caylen. "Unwrap this, but be careful, it's quite heavy."

Suspecting what this oily rag wrapped object might be, Lora watched closely as Caylen slowly and carefully unrolled it, turning it over and over on the floor so that whatever the object was, it could not fall out of it's oily wrapping. As he neared the end of the roll, Lora could see Caylen's eyes growing wider and wider as he realized just what that roll of oil-soaked cloth contained. As the last fold fell away, she heard him give out a small gasp of delight as he saw the little blued barrel and the shiny walnut wood stock of a Canuck, single shot, twenty-two caliber rifles.

Reaching over, she took the little rifle from Caylen's trembling hands and quickly re-rolled it in the oily cloth.

"You're still too young to have this." She said, "You can have it when you reach your fourteenth birthday and not one day sooner."

"Aw, Mom", replied Caylen, "Can't I just look at it?"

"I will let you clean it and look at it once a month." His mother relented. "But you can only have it when I am watching."

Looking deep into the sack, Lora discovered one last box. Feeling quite confident as to its contents, she left the case of five hundred twenty-two caliber long rifle bullets in the bag, replacing all of the removed items except the fishing gear and the gold pan. Re-securing the bags straps tightly, she said to Caylen.

"Now, we are going to put this bag in my bedroom closet, and you are not to go into it unless I say you can."

"Okay, Mom. Now can I go out and show the guys my birthday present?"

"Get out of here, "Lora said with a smile, "And don't be late for lunch."

"Oh yes, one other thing ", she said as Caylen raced out the door. " Don't forget, that man from up north, Mr. Fariss Lubak is going to be visiting us next week."

~*~

Lora had seen an article in the monthly publication of the Greenwood Newsletter telling of all the lonely wealthy miners living in the Northern reaches of Canada's wilderness who were looking for wives that would be willing to move to the North to live with them. The article included the names and locations of some of these lonely men. It also asked that any interested ladies should write to the address shown in the article so that the newspaper's northern contact could forward their letters to some of these men who would then hopefully respond directly to the writers.

It had taken over two months, but Lora finally received a written response to her letter. It came from a man who described himself as being a mid-thirties, wealthy prospector who owned a large waterfront home located not too far from the major Northern City called Whitehorse. He also indicated that he was the owner of a rich gold mine that was located quite close to his home. His descriptions of himself and his home was well enough to her likings for her to continue corresponding with him, And, in addition, to eventually invite him to visit her and Caylen in their Greenwood home.

Chapter 2

The Meeting

The following week went by quickly for young Caylen. He spent much of his time cleaning and oiling his fishing reel, practicing his casting skills and reading about fishing, fishing techniques, types of fish and just about anything he could find about fishing at the Greenwood Library. He also made queries to some of his neighboring young male friends as to the fishing possibilities in the local stream that ran nearby. He gave little thought to the upcoming visit of his mother's gentleman friend other than to, at one point, ask her,

"Mom, do you think that Mr. Lubak knows about fishing, gold panning and guns?"

"I'm sure that he knows quite a bit about all of those subjects and much more," she replied. "He lives in the North where just about everyone hunts and fishes. Why don't you ask him yourself when he gets here?"

"Ah, he probably won't want anything to do with me, I'm just a kid." Caylen replied. "I bet Dad would have known about all those things if he was here. I just bet he would sure show me."

Lora, with a tear in her eye and a small catch in her voice, replied.

"Yes, Caylen, my son, I'm certain that he would. Now go out and play, while I make us some supper."

~*~

A few days later, in the early afternoon, as Caylen was practicing his casting skills on the front yard, a tall, heavily muscled, good looking man wearing a red-checkered shirt and sporting a full facial beard, walked up the lane towards Caylen's and his mother's home. He stopped and stood watching Caylen practice casting for a moment or two before saying with a broad smile,

"Hey there, young lad, you ain't going to catch nothing here, fish don't live in the grass, they lives mostly in the water cause they had finds it too hard to swim in the grasses."

With that opening statement, he laughed uproariously at his own joke for a Moment or two, then crossed his heavily muscled arms over his chest and said,

"Would you'd be young Caylen Helms, boy, and is this here the Lora Helms's place?"

"Mom!" yelled Caylen. "There's a man out here to see you."

Lora soon appeared at the front door of their little house, wearing what Caylen knew were her best clothes. She smiled at Caylen, and then said to the man,

"And who might you be, Sir?"

The big man gaped wide-eyed at Caylen's quite attractive mother for a long moment before speaking. He then uncrossed his arms and quickly removing his hat, said,

"I be Fariss Lubak from up North, ma'm. Might you be Lora Helms, the lady I's has been writing to."

"Yes, Mr. Lubak, I am Lora Helms, and that boy you just spoke to is my son, Caylen. Now, may I welcome you to our home?"

"Is you the Lora Helms I's been writing to then?" he asked once more.

"Well, unless you've been writing to another Lora, I am indeed the Lora Helms you have been writing to." she replied. "Now, please come in and I will make us a cup of tea."

As Caylen watched, the man and his mother entered the house and closed the door.

After an hour or so had gone by, Caylen's mother opened the door and called out to him.

"Caylen, please come into the house, Mr. Lubak wishes to meet you."

Caylen, full of curiosity about this big rugged-looking man, went up onto the veranda, put down his fishing rod and entered the house where he could see the large man, Mr. Lubak sitting at the kitchen table, sipping hot tea out of a saucer.

"Why are you drinking your tea from the saucer, Mr. Lubak? Did you spill it?" he asked.

Mr. Lubak roared with laughter and said, "I pours the hot tea into this here saucer because it helps to cool it off a bit, boy. You sure ask funny questions. Come over here, boy, and sit down and hear what I have to say."

"My name is Caylen sir, it isn't 'boy'," Caylen replied.

"Okay, Caylen, boy, c'mon over hear and talk to me."

Caylen, beginning to not like this big rough speaking man, sat down at the table beside his mother.

"What do you think of comin on up to the North to live in the bushes wit me in my house," asked Mr. Lubak.

"Are there any fish up there?" asked Caylen.

"They are fishes everywhere in all the waters, theys big ones and theys small ones and theys are in between ones."

"Did you know my dad?" asked Caylen. "He used to live up North, when he was a trapper and a gold prospector."

"No, I didn't know your pa, but that's what I is, a gold prospector," said Mr. Lubak. "I's also does some huntin fer meats and such."

"Wow!" said Caylen, "Have you found any gold yet?"

"Theys are lots of gold where I am at, boy. It just needs to be dug out of the ground."

"If we came up to live there, would I be able to help you dig it out?" Caylen asked.

"Fer sure, Caylen boy. Der's lots of gold fer everybody to dig up there. I's will even gets you yer own pick and shovel."

"Can we go, Mom? Can we go?" Caylen asked.

"We will see." His mother answered. "We have a lot to talk about and a lot to think about before we decide. Where exactly do you live, Mr. Lubak, and what does your home look like?"

"I live not too fer from one of the biggest cities in the North," replied Mr. Lubak. "Its name is Whitehorse. It's a big house and is close by, and it has lots of room's fer living in and fer storing things in."

"Mr. Lubak tells me that he has made a lot of money from his gold mine In addition, that he can look after us so that I will no longer have to work outside our home ever again," said Lora, looking at her son.

"Tell me more about the fish where you live, Mr. Lubak," asked Caylen. "Are there any real big ones up there?"

"Big fish? Well, boy, there is fish up there as long as your leg and twice as heavy!" exclaimed Mr. Lubak. "You can catch one every time you throw's out your line in the waters."

Caylen thought for a moment before he said,

"Will I be able to take my Dad's old prospecting bag with me if we go? It has lots of good stuff in it that I will need."

"You's can take whatever you wants wit you," Mr. Lubak said.

"You sure do talk funny, Mr. Lubak." Caylen suddenly blurted out.

"Caylen! You apologize to Mr. Lubak right now!" said Caylen's mother; her face reddening in her embarrassment as Mr. Lubak's face also began to redden in sudden anger.

"That's okay, Mrs. Helms, the boy just proble don't know much bout things like that, it's not his fault and he doesn't have to apologize at all. Just so's you both knows, I was born and raised in a place in the East of Canada, out bout four t'ousand miles or so. Dat's pretty much the way most of us people from backs there talks. It's cause we never got the chance to get much schooling like you'd all did," Mr. Lubak said.

"Well, thank you for explaining, Mr. Lubak; I am certain Caylen will not embarrass me by asking such foolish questions like that again." Lora said. "Will you, Caylen?"

"No, Mom, and I am sorry, Mr. Lubak. I didn't mean to be rude." Caylen responded "When are we leaving, Mom? Can I start packing now?"

"Not just yet, young man. We have a lot of details to work out. It is a big move and it's a long ways away from here, and besides, we do not have enough money saved to pay for that kind of move right now." Caylen's mother said. With that, Lora asked Mr. Lubak if he would return for supper that night.

Mr. Lubak readily agreed and left only to return a few hours later to consume enormous quantities of the large smoked ham, cabbage and boiled potatoes that Caylen's mother had prepared. After finally eating his fill, Mr. Lubak belched loudly, pushed himself away from the table and said,

"As good a meal as I's ever et, Mrs. Helms, I tanks you is a dam fine cook!"

"Well, thank you, Mr. Lubak," said Caylen's mother. "I appreciate the compliment."

"You's don't have to keep callin me Mr. Lubak, ma'm. You can call me by the name Fariss, that's the same name me mother gave to me."

Mr. Lubak then rose and thanked Mrs. Helms again for the supper and excused himself, saying that he would return the following day for another visit with them. After he had gone, Caylen's mother asked Caylen what he thought of Mr. Lubak and if he would like to move to the North to live with him. As she had expected, Caylen was quite excited at the prospect of going to his father's beloved North. He had, as she could see, been also quite impressed by Mr. Lubak's vivid description of his home, the fishing and of his gold prospecting.

Fariss Lubak, however, had not as greatly impressed Lora as he had her eager young son. While she did find Fariss quite physically attractive in a rugged sort of way, she kept having moments of doubt and fear that she could not explain or shake. There was just something about this big man that, at times, did not seem quite right to her, but then she would think to herself, *You're being foolish and just a little too picky, Lora. He's a good man who will be good to you, will look after you and Caylen and give you both a good home and a good life.*

She still had many questions that needed to be answered before she was willing to commit herself and Caylen to such a life-changing move. She realized that Caylen had been quite taken by, and impressed by, Mr. Lubak's colorful stories and that he would only be too eager to move to his birth-father's beloved Northlands.

~*~

Mr. Lubak appeared at the front door of the Helms residence about ten a.m. the following day. Caylen's mother again asked him in to have another cup of hot tea. Much to Caylen's amusement, he again immediately poured some of it into his saucer and began to sip from it with loud slurping sounds.

Caylen then, to Mr. Lubak's amusement, attempted to imitate this action by pouring some of his cold milk into his saucer, and sipped it as he had observed the visitor doing.

"Caylen!" his mother said sharply, after giving their guest an embarrassed look. "Drink your milk properly from your cup."

"But Mom, Mr. Lubak drinks his tea that way," said Caylen.

At that statement Mr. Lubak laughed out loudly and said,

"That's okay, boy, but likes I's said before, I only does it to cool off the tea so's I can drink it witout burnin me mouth. Your milk is already cooled so's you don't needs to do it to something that's already cooled." He them turned to Caylen's mother and said,

"One other ting I wants to tell you's both once more, you's don't have to always be callin me by Mr. Lubak, you's can cal me Fariss, me given birth name."

Lora found herself becoming more and more at ease with Mr. Lubak as the days went by. She was beginning to be won over by his seemingly easy going, down home mannerisms. She had pretty much decided that her initial apprehensive feelings were unfounded. He also seemed to always have the right answer to any of the many questions she posed to him. He definitely seemed to have won the support of Caylen, as he continued to regale him with his broken pronunciation of words and sentences, and his never-ending stories of the North and his many fishing and hunting adventures.

~*~

Just minutes before four a.m. on the fifth day of Mr. Lubak's visit, Mrs. Helms was awakened suddenly by loud screams of terror and the sounds of Caylen thrashing about in his bed as he slept. She jumped up and raced to his bedside, thinking that something terrible had happened to him only to find him, still asleep with his arms waving about as he yelled loudly,

"Don't hurt me, please don't hurt me."

"Wake up! Caylen, wake up. You're having a nightmare!" she said.

Caylen woke, sitting up and sobbing as his mother held him in her arms.

"It was only a bad dream," she said, "Just what was it about that scared you so much?" she asked.

"I was being tortured, Mom. A big ugly man that looked a bit like Mr. Lubak had me tied to a tree and was burning my arms and legs with a steel poker. But then, just before I woke up, a really old Indian man came out of the bushes, chased the other man away, and was untying me when I woke up."

"Well, it was only just a dream." his mother tried to reassure him.

"But it seemed so real, Mom. The old Indian even spoke to me, he called me 'Adahy'. What does that mean, Mom? What does Adahy mean?"

"It doesn't mean anything, Caylen. It was only just a dream. Now, try to get some more sleep, son. It will soon be morning and you need your sleep as Mr. Lubak said he would be here to visit early today."

~*~

Mr. Lubak stayed in the little village of Greenwood for three more days before leaving on the train to return to his northland home. Caylen's mother had decided that she would follow him North in a few weeks, to become his wife, and to live with him and her son in Lubak's northern home. Lora had thought long and hard about what she was about to do. She was more than just a little nervous and unsure that moving so far away was the right thing for her and Caylen to do and she was still a little unsure about Mr. Lubak. She had no one to discuss her decision with as her parents had both died some years earlier and her nearest relatives, a distant Aunt and Uncle, whom she had never met, were located on a farm somewhere in Northern California.

She could, however, see no specific reason, other than the distance to be traveled, for her not to take Mr. Lubak up on his offer. She would have a good home, security for her and her young son and more importantly, a father figure for young Caylen as he matured, and a man who seemed to love the North and the outdoors life. She knew that she did not love Fariss Lubak as she had loved her precious George, but Lubak seemed quite personable and she felt that she could, with time, grow to care for him.

Mr. Lubak had given her, before he left for his home, sufficient money to get her, Caylen, and their personal effects via trains and ships, to a village called Carcross, in the Yukon territories, where he would meet them. This village was, apparently, the nearest railway stop to the northland home where he lived. Lora had given him a long list of items along with hers and Caylen's clothing and shoe sizes so that he could purchase these needed items for them in the City of Whitehorse before they arrived. Lora wondered for just a fleeting moment why Fariss did not just take her and Caylen into Whitehorse so they could assist in these and other purchases of items that they might need.

She then spent the following two weeks preparing, packing and then repacking hers and Caylen's personal effects for the long journey into a strange land that they were about to undertake.

Caylen was quite adamant that they bring the entire contents of his fathers prospecting pack with them. Nothing his mother could say could convince him to leave any of its contents behind. His mother finally relented and the entire pack and its contents were included in the materials to be shipped.

She had been quite concerned for a few days about Caylen's nightmare and its apparent terrifying effect on him. The nightmare had not recurred but, over the next several days, Caylen seemed quite troubled by it and kept asking her if she knew just what the word Adahy was or meant. She had just finally convinced him that it really meant nothing, when he again had pretty much the same nightmare where once again, the old Indian, who again called him 'Adahy', rescued him from the torturing. It took Caylen's mother another week or so to again, convince Caylen that his nightmares meant nothing and were caused only by the excitement of their upcoming trip.

Chapter 3

Ocean Voyage

The big day Caylen was waiting for had finally arrived. He and his mother watched closely as their personal effects were loaded onto the back of the truck that Mr. Lubak had previously arranged. The truck was to transport Lora, Caylen and their personal effects over the primitive rough roads that led from Greenwood to the city of Vancouver, where they would then board a steamer, the Prince John. This ship was to take them by sea to the Northern coastal town of Prince Rupert where they would then board another smaller coastal steamer that would deliver them and their effects to the gold rush town called Skagway. From Skagway they would travel via a narrow gauge railway called the White Pass and Yukon Railroad to the village of Carcross where they were to be met by Mr. Lubak.

The White Pass and Yukon Railway, a narrow gauge railway, had been constructed in eighteen hundred and ninety-eight during the Klondike's mad gold rush days so that the eager prospectors would not have to make the climb over the steep and dangerous Chilcote pass. The narrow gauge railroad would, over the years transport thousands of avid gold seekers from Skagway to Whitehorse. From Whitehorse, the gold seekers would then travel by homemade boat down the Yukon river to Dawson City and other remote areas where rich beds of placer gold had been discovered in the many streams that fed into the Yukon River.

After two long days of bumping and bouncing about in the old moving trucks cab on the rough primitive old wagon roads that led Westward from Greenwood, Caylen and his mother finally arrived in the big bustling city of Vancouver on th lower mainland. Their driver apparently had been in the city before, as he knew exactly where to deliver them.

As they drove up to the city docks, they could see a large coal fired steamship with a single stack tied to the dock that was emitting a small trickle of smoke. A large steam-operated crane on shore beside the tied up ship was loading boxed and bagged supplies into a cargo net that lay spread out on the on the dock. Once the big cargo net had what the cranes operator considered a load, he would signal the dockworkers that would secure the net to the cranes lifting hook. The crane operator would then lift and swing the load into the open deck hatches of the ship where the deckhands would quickly remove and stow the cargo below decks.

Before long, their driver had their personal effects off-loaded and on the dock, where they soon joined the other goods being loaded and stowed on the ship. They could also see a tall man dressed in a uniform that had gold stripes on its shoulder epaulets standing near the steep stairwell that led up to the ships deck. Assuming that he was one of the ships officers, they walked up to him and asked if he knew where they could purchase the required tickets to Prince Rupert.

This man introduced himself as the ships purser and advised them that they could board the ship and shortly thereafter, could purchase their tickets directly from him for the sum of forty-one dollars and fifty cents. He also told them that the ship would be sailing early the next morning and that it would be best if they spent the night on board in their cabin.

Caylen and his mother were soon settled down in their little cabin, which was, according to the purser, on the starboard side of the ship. They were both happy to see that their little room had a porthole that allowed them to look out over the Vancouver harbor.

Caylen could see two heads of animals that looked like dogs swimming about in the harbor about fifty feet from the ship. As he watched he saw the two animals suddenly dive under the water, disappear from sight for about five minutes and then reappear some distance away.

"Mom, come and see these funny animals that look like dogs swimming and diving out in the ocean," he said to his mother.

After a quick look out the porthole, Caylen's mother replied, "Those are seals, Caylen, they live in the ocean and eat fish for food, we will likely see lots of them on this voyage and may even see some whales, if we are lucky."

Caylen and his mother were wakened suddenly at about six am the next morning by the sound of the ships horn as it pulled away from the Vancouver pier. They dressed quickly and raced out to view the scene as the steamship belched black smoke from its single tall stack and made its way out into the open passage that led to the waters of the Pacific Oceans Inland passage

"Say goodbye to the South "said Caylen's mother, "It may be some time before we see this part of British Columbia again, if we ever do."

"This is going to be a great trip and a great adventure, "Caylen said, with a happy smile. " I can't wait to get up there."

"Well, I am sure that you are quite correct when you say that it will be a great trip, Caylen, and I certainly hope you are correct when you say it will be a great adventure. We will just have to wait and see though."

"Oh, Mom! How can it not be a great adventure? We are moving to the North to live in a big house with a man who has lots of money and who knows everything there is to know about gold mining, fishing and hunting." Caylen replied.

"Let's just wait and see, "his mother answered, "Let's just wait and see."

~*~

The next few days were quite exciting for Caylen. The ship seemed to stop at every little port that existed on the mainland, the coastal islands, and the Eastern side of Vancouver Island and on the Queen Charlotte Islands. On each of these stops, the ship unloaded and loaded both passengers and cargo bound for these and other ports along the long British Columbia coastline.

Caylen would spend hours each day on deck observing all that occurred. On more than one occasion he saw large groups of what the ship deckhands called porpoises. On one other occasion, he saw what they called 'killer whales' circling about, killing and eating some of the many seals that also were in abundance.

"Thems are som bad fish," one deckhand said to Caylen. "You don't wants to fall in the water if they's nearby, or you'll be done for, for sure."

Caylen was unsure if the man was telling him the truth or just teasing him. But just to be safe, he stayed well away from the ship's railings whenever he observed any of these beautiful but fearsome-looking ocean predators swimming and cavorting nearby.

While Caylen and his mother found the nine-day trip, for the most part, quite exciting, the ship made one stop that sickened both him and his mother. This stop was at a whaling station called Rose Harbor, on the southern tip of the remote Queen Charlotte Islands. During this ten-hour stopover, the ship unloaded many tons of supplies, foodstuffs and empty oil barrels, and then loaded into the ship's hold, hundreds of barrels of rendered whale oil. The Rose Harbor whale blubber-rendering plant was operated twenty-four hours each day when they had whales as they now did. Caylen could see four dead whales tied up along the pier and another halfway up the steep ramp that led to the rendering plant. The terrible stench that emanated from the plant was overwhelming, and permeated everything downwind of it. Needless to say, Caylen and his mother were quite elated when the ship finally sailed off towards their next port of call.

On the ninth and last of this, the first leg of their ocean voyage, the ship landed at the Port of Prince Rupert, where they had a three-day wait before boarding the much smaller ship that was to deliver them to the village of Skagway.

Caylen and Lora checked in at the only hotel in Prince Rupert, the "Rupert House" for this three-day wait. Trying to keep from being bored during this wait, they made their way about the small fishing village, examining the seemingly endless quantities of native Indian goods and carvings that were for sale at what they thought were ridiculously low prices. Caylen was quite taken by the shiny black argillite totem poles that had been hand carved by the Haida natives of the Queen Charlottes and placed for sale at quite a reasonable price in one shop.

"Do you think I could buy one of those?" he asked his mother.

"Well, how much is it?" his mother asked.

Caylen asked the shopkeeper the price of the particular argillite totem that had drawn his eye. It was about five inches tall and quite intricately carved with a wolf's head at the very top. It had then been polished to ebony black sheen, and had the initials of the Haida carver scratched into the base.

"That piece will cost you exactly one dollar and fifteen cents," said the shopkeeper.

"What does it mean?" asked Caylen.

"It represents a Warrior's Spirit and was carved by a famous Haida chief long ago."

"I just have to have it, Mom. I really need to have it." Caylen said.

"Well, alright young man, but consider it as your Christmas present for this year," said his mother, as she reached into her handbag.

"Gee, thanks a lot, Mom. This will be all I want for next Christmas. Thanks, Mom!" Caylen said, as he wrapped the small totem in his handkerchief and carefully tucked it into his pants pocket.

The following afternoon they boarded the little steamer that was to take them from Prince Rupert up the coast through the many islands to Skagway. This trip was on much quieter waters than their earlier voyage and proved to be uneventful except for the sighting on one beach of what the ship's steward called a "spirit bear."

They landed at the bustling town of Skagway in the early morning and were fortunate to find overnight accommodations in a small hotel near the terminal of the narrow gauge railway that had been constructed in eighteen ninety-eight to transport the thousands of gold seekers over the steep Chilcote pass and on to the town of Whitehorse that was located on the banks of the big Yukon River.

At ten a.m. the following morning, after ensuring that her and Caylen's supplies and luggage were placed on board the baggage car, Lora and Caylen boarded the train for the next phase of their journey. This portion of their trip was the shortest of the three phases they had undertaken so far, as the train ride was normally only about seven hours long. It was, however, quite a spectacular trip as the route wound its way through some of the most beautiful scenery in North America. They could see, from their window, huge snow-capped mountains, glaciers, rushing rivers, mountain goats and in one small, weedy pond, a huge bull moose feeding hungrily on the ponds many lily pads. Caylen was so taken aback by all of this that he could only, for most of the trip, utter only one word, "Wow!" over and over.

As the little train chugged across a trestle and into the village of Carcross, they could see that the majority of the village's buildings were quite small, constructed of logs and were quite low to the ground. Seeing their puzzled looks, a nearby passenger asked them why they were looking so curiously at the little houses.

"Why are all of these houses so small and so low to the ground?" asked Lora.

"It's because they are so much easier to keep warm in the winter when the temperature gets down to forty or fifty below zero." the man said. "Sometimes they dig down into the ground four or five feet because the ground helps to insulate the house from the cold."

As the train pulled up and stopped beside a little cabin with a wood board sign that read "Carcross," Lora and Caylen could see the beaming, bewhiskered face of Mr. Lubak smiling up at them from the platform. When they stepped down off the train, he rushed up and hugged both of them, saying,

"I's is sure glad to see you's guy's." I's been waiting here for two days for you's."

"Well, we are now here," replied Lora. "What's next?" she asked.

"We needs to gets yer boxes and trunks from the baggage car and then we needs to see the marry'in man. We's needs to gets us married first thing in the morning so's we's can pack up every'ting and gets off to our home." replied Mr. Lubak.

Fariss then took Lora and Caylen to a small cabin where he had arranged for them to stay the night. After he had accompanied them to their night's lodging he started back to his makeshift camp that he had established on the shores of the lake beside his canoes. As he passed by the little Carcross bar, he saw two large Native men watching him as he neared where they were sitting just outside the bar's entrance. They stood as he came up to them and one of them said,

"Is you Fariss Lubak, the miner from down south on Tagish Lake?"

"I be him," Fariss replied, belligerently. "Who's be you two and whats you wants wit me?"

"We is blood-brothers of Wildflower," said the same man. "And we want to know what you done with her after you took her away from here."

"Git away froms me 'fore I cuts you's both with this here knife." Fariss retorted angrily, as he pulled a long, sharp hunting knife from the sheath that hung from his waist-belt.

The two Indian men looked at each other, turned and strode away, saying as they left,

"This not be the end of this, Mister. We will, one day, find out what you done with our sister."

~*~

Early the following morning, after a much too short of a night's sleep in the small cabin where Mr. Lubak had taken them, Lora and Caylen found themselves standing beside Fariss as the local Justice of the Peace that Fariss had found recited to Lora and Fariss their marriage bonds. As soon as they were married and had signed the marriage register, Fariss said,

"Okay, we is done here so let's git go'in down to the lake."

Puzzled, Lora asked, "What do you mean by 'down to the lake', Fariss, and why were ours the only names in that man's marriage register?"

"Our house is down the lake a bit is whats I means." said Mr. Lubak. "We's got a bit of a canoe trip to gets there, so we's needs to load up yer stuff and git go'in."

"What about that Justice of the Peace and his marriage register?" Lora asked again.

"I'se doesn't know." replied Fariss." Maybe his other books was full."

Fariss did not give Lora or Caylen any of the details of his buying trip to the city of Whitehorse. But, as he alone knew their destination, he had purchased all of the items on Lora's shopping list and much, much more. In addition to her big list of items, he had purchased three hundred pounds of flour, two hundred pounds of salt, one hundred pounds of sugar, two hundred pounds of beans, thirty pounds of tea, seventy-five pounds of lard, a ninety-pound round of cheese, a sack of turnips, a sack of cabbages, ten boxes of ammunition, a long gill net, matches, ropes, wire, files, nails, tools, wooden kegs of salt pork, spices, animal traps, seeds, pots and many other miscellaneous items.

It had taken him quite some time to stow this entire foodstuff and articles in his canoes in as waterproof a manner as was possible. His purchases had cost him fourteen ounces of his precious gold dust. He had also had a jeweler fashion a gold wedding ring for Lora from two small gold nuggets that he had found. He did not, of course, even consider informing them of his drinking and fighting of the previous three nights in the Carcross bar as he awaited their arrival.

~*~

As they prepared for their water voyage, Caylen thought about his meeting with the four Carcross boys the night before. It happened as he was strolling about the small village. He had encountered them on the narrow gauge railroad bridge, as they were attempting to catch some of the fish that Mr. Lubak had identified as Arctic grayling that were resting in water that lay in the shadow of the trestle. Seeing this strange boy watching them, one of the quartet asked.

"Hey, you! Who are you, and what do you want here?"

"My name is Caylen Helms, and me and my Mom are going to live with Mr. Lubak in his big house." said Caylen.

"You mean Loony Lubak?" Another of them said, looking at Caylen in a strange manner. "Who would want to live with old Loony Lubak?"

Caylen didn't reply, but hurried off to their cabin. He decided that it would be best not to inform his mother of his encounter with the boys or what they had said, at least for the time being.

Chapter 4

The Canoe Trip

Fariss led Lora and Caylen down to the water's edge, where they saw the vessel in which they were going to be traveling. Pulled partially up on the sandy shore of the channel connecting Nares Lake and Bennet Lake were two large canvas-covered canoes. The larger of the two canoes was about twenty feet long and had a small wooden mast mounted about a third of the way back. The second, smaller canoe was about eighteen feet long and tied to the stern of the larger one with a rope of about twelve feet in length. The smaller canoe was piled high with supplies that were, in turn, covered by a protective canvas cover. Lora and Caylen's packs and suitcases were piled on the beach beside the two canoes.

"Let's git your stuff loaded up so's we can be on our way," said Fariss, as he began to stow their supplies in the two canoes. "I's already been to Whitehorse to git our supplies fer this winter," he added.

"Wow!" said Caylen. "Are we going to paddle these boats to our house?"

"Thems are not called boats, thems are canoes." said Fariss. "And, yes, we is goi'n to paddle these canoes to our home down the lake."

"Just how far down the lake is our home," Lora asked.

"Just a bit," said Fariss. "We should be there in no time at all, exceptin there be a storm or two that we might have to wait on."

"Can I paddle too?" asked Caylen.

"Yer dang right you's can paddle, boy. This here is your own paddle and you even got a spare one if you breaks this one." said Fariss, handing Caylen a well-polished spruce paddle. "We's even go a couple fer your Mom."

"Do you expect me to paddle also? " asked Lora.

"If we has to go agin'st the wind and can't use the sail, it will take all of us to keep these here canoe's movin down the lake." Fariss replied. "Now, git aboard so's we can git on our ways."

Fariss soon had Lora and Caylen aboard the large freighter canoe with Lora on the front seat and Caylen on the center seat just behind the little mast. Fariss then pushed both canoes off the beach and climbing onto the rear seat of the freighter, picked up his paddle and said,

"Now, you's two can paddle just likes I is, but I's is the one who steers from back here, and as soon's we gits out into the lake, we's will put up the sail. If the winds be right, we's can just sits back and enjoys the ride."

Lora and Caylen both tried their hand at paddling the canoe. They found it quite easy at first, as the channel had a definite current that assisted their movement downstream and out into the huge Nares Lake. They were beginning to tire but as they entered the big main lake, Fariss told Caylen how to raise the small, dirty-grey canvas sail so that it would collect the stiffing westerly winds that soon had them moving towards the East much faster than the paddling had done After about five hours of cruising down the wide expanse of the lake, Fariss raised his paddle and pointed it towards a point of land far in the distance and slightly to their right.

"They are where we are stopping and making camp to-day," he said.

"Is that where our house is located?" Lora anxiously asked. She was much too embarrassed to tell Fariss that her bottom was beginning to feel the effects of sitting on the hard wooden seat of the canoe for five long hours.

"No, it's a bit further yet." Fariss replied. "We has a ways to go."

Lora said nothing in reply but thought to herself, *I wonder just how far it is to this house that he said was close to a big town?*

Roughly an hour later, just as the sun was beginning to cast the shadows of the three canoeists on the water ahead of them, they beached the canoes on a sandy beach in a small hidden cove on the eastern side of the point. Lora and Caylen could see, at the edge of the thick spruce forest, the pole framework of a small structure. Beside this framework was an obvious fire pit with a small stack of wood piled beside it.

"This is where's we be spending this night." Fariss said. "This spot be the edge of what be called 'Windy Arm'. This Nares Lake be one big lake," he said.

Pulling a large folded piece of canvas out of the smaller canoe, Fariss draped it neatly over the framework of poles that stood at the forest's edge. He tied each corner with a piece of rope firmly to the base of the poles and left the front of the now canvas-clad frame with a loose end hanging down to act as a doorway.

"Here be our house for tonight." he said, smiling at Lora. "Here be our wedding house." With that statement, he went back to the canoe, and as Lora and Caylen watched with some apprehension, took out an axe and another smaller piece of canvas and quickly constructed a much smaller but similar shelter immediately beside the larger one.

"Now, Caylen, lad, here be your house for tonight." he said

"But why can't I stay in your tent?" asked Caylen, looking first at Fariss and then at his mother.

"Cause this is our marry'in night and we wants to be alone." said Fariss, smiling and winking at Lora as he spoke.

"You'll be alright, Caylen. It will be nice for you to have your own little house." Lora said. "And besides, we'll be right here beside you." she added.

Caylen appeared to be satisfied with this answer so Lora assisted Fariss as he spread out their bedrolls and retrieved a bag full of cooking pots and tools from the canoe.

"Well, Caylen, boy, now's we has to go round that corner there to the crick and catch us some supper whil'st yer Mom gits the fire lit." Fariss said." So, git's yer fishing gear and come along," he added

Before long, Caylen found himself standing with his father's old fishing rod at the outlet of a small bubbling stream that ran happily out of the forest and over the rocky bank down into the lake. As he looked into the clear, cold aqua waters of the lake, he could see the sandy bottom and the many shapes of the Arctic grayling as they darted to and fro, catching and gorging on the multitudes of emerging insects that the creek's current had carried from the forest out into the lake.

Caylen, unsure of just what to do next, watched as Fariss fastened a small spinner and a small rock to one end of his hand-line. Placing his foot on the opposite end of the line, he laid some ten neatly piled coils of the line on the ground in front of himself. Taking the lure, the rock and about three feet of line in his right hand, he began to twirl it about and over his head. When the lure was spinning about at what he considered an appropriate speed, he let go of the lure and rock. The momentum of the spinning lure and rock carried the lure out over the surface of the lake about thirty feet, where it landed with a splash in the midst of the milling, feeding fish. Picking up the loose end of his line, Fariss began to draw it towards himself with small jerking motions. As Caylen watched in wonderment, a two-pound grayling flashed out of the school and rolled over, as it gulped down the small lure.

"Wow!" said Caylen, as he prepared to toss out his little spinner. "Do you think I can catch one, too?" he asked.

Before Fariss could respond, Caylen's rod bucked and jerked, as a second grayling of about the same size as the first impaled itself on his lure.

"Oh, boy!" he said. "This is great! Are there any really big fish in this lake, Fariss?" he asked, as he reeled in the brightly colored little fish.

"They's some fish called gray trouts out in the deep waters that's about maybe ten times that big or even bigger," said Fariss. "We's will see if we can't git a big one fer our breakfast." he added.

Before long, they had four more of the beautifully iridescent colored grayling lying on the shore beside them. As Caylen watched the dying fish, he saw their brilliant iridescence colors slowly fade away until they were only a drab grey with no evidence whatsoever of their spectacular coloring remaining. He watched closely as Fariss gutted and cleaned the six grayling before grabbing them and running back to camp to show his mother, who by now had a small cooking fire burning merrily and a bucket of tea water boiling.

In a few minutes, they were all dining on the freshly caught roasted grayling, boiled navy beans, and hot tea.

"Boy, this is great, Mom. Fariss is going to show me how to catch a really big fish next, aren't you, Fariss?" said Caylen, still excited about his fishing exploits.

"Yes, boy, we is go'in to give her a try in just a bit." said Fariss." But, you's needs to calm down now, afore you's gets a heart attack and falls over dead!"

After relaxing with a mug of hot tea for about an hour, Fariss rose and told Caylen,

"Now, Caylen, you go catch me a little grayling and tries to keeps it alive. When you gets it, yell fer me and then I's will show you how's to maybe catch a real big gray fish."

Caylen, after catching and releasing four larger grayling, finally landed one that was only about nine inches long. Leaving it hooked on his line, he left it in the water and returned to camp where Fariss said,

"Dat's a perfect size for whats we wants." He then rose, picked up his hand-line and tied on a much larger hook. He then secured a baseball-sized rock to the line about three feet back from the hook that he had jabbed through the tail section of the little grayling. Walking down to the waters edge, he fastened the hand-line's opposite end to a small flexible tree trunk about five feet from the ground. He then took the line and laid it out in large, neat loops along the water's edge. Taking the rock and hooked grayling in hand, he then hurled it out as far as he could into the lake's cold deep blue waters. Caylen looked on in utter fascination until Fariss had thrown out the bait and rock sinker before he said,

"I figured out just why you did everything but I don't know why you tied the line way up on that tree. A big fish will bend that tree and might even break it off, "he added.

"No he won't," said Fariss. "That there tree be a mountain ash and it be really tough so's it will only bend and dat big fish can't bust the line cause the tree's bending will takes up the shocks of his pullin on the fishin line."

"How big of a fish do you think we will catch? asked Caylen.

"Well, we's just can't say fer sure until we sees it." replied Fariss. "Sometimes we don't gits nothin at all, and sometimes we gits a monster," he added. "We'll just have to wait until mornin to see. Now, it's startin to git dark so's we best git back to camp and git bedded down before yer Mom starts to worryin bout us."

In a few minutes, they were bedded down in their respective tents.

~*~

Caylen had left his door flap up so he could observe the clear night sky and the bright night stars. He could hear Fariss's gruff voice and his mother's soft whispers easily in the still night, as they discussed the day's events. He could not quite make out what was being said, but he could detect some anxiety in his mother's voice as she and Fariss lay together for the first time. After a short period, he heard what sounded like a gasp from his mother, a loud grunting from Fariss, and then a sudden silence. As the long tiring day finally brought him to the edge of sleep and his eyes were just beginning to close, he was brought fully awake by a sound that made every hair on his head stand upright.

"Arf, Arf, Arf, Arooooooo," he heard. The long drawn out mournful howl of the Arctic timber wolf was soon followed by another even longer wailing howl and then another and yet another until the sound seemed to Caylen to be the devil's own orchestra playing a song just for him.

Caylen, afraid at that moment for his very life, but not wanting to reveal his fright, pulled the tent door flap fully shut and covered his head with his woolen blanket. In a few moments, the howling stopped and, after such a long tiring day, he was fast asleep even as the cool evergreen-scented night air of the North woods drifted a light fog out over the big lake.

~*~

The next morning, Caylen was roughly wakened by the loud voice of Fariss yelling at him through his tents door flap,

"Hey, boy, gits yerself out here and pull in this here fish before it busts off this tree!"

Quickly pulling on his pants and sweater, Caylen rushed out into the early morning grayness to see Fariss standing by the tree to which he had fastened his fishing line. It was waving back and forth so much that it seemed to Caylen it would surely break.

"Well, you goin to see what's on the other end of this line or is you just goin to stand there gawkin at it?" Fariss asked, as Caylen stood gaping at the waving little tree.

"You mean that you want me to pull it in?" asked Caylen.

"Fer sure, Caylen boy. Pulls it in so's we can see what's we's got hooked on the other end." Fariss replied.

Grasping the heavy line in both hands, Caylen began to pull it and whatever was fastened to the other end shoreward. As the line tightened, he was suddenly nearly jerked off his feet by the struggling fish. Quickly regaining his composure, he began to slowly bring the huge fish closer to the shore. Suddenly, as it drew closer, the monster trout broke the surface of the lake only a few feet in front of where Caylen was standing, splashing both him and Fariss with cold lake water.

"Hey! You's had better be careful or dat fish be pullin you's into the lake instead of you's pullin him out." Fariss said, laughing at Caylen's antics.

It took Caylen another five minutes to get the huge fish up into the shallow water, where he could see just how big it was. It looked to him to be about three and one-half feet long and nearly one foot deep at the thickest point of its body. He had managed to get it within a few feet of the shore when Fariss waded in towards it. Reaching down with both arms, he scooped the monster fish up in his arms and stepped ashore.

"Here you is, boy, your first gray trout. I's seen bigger, but dis here's not bad for yer first one." said Farris, grinning at Caylen. "Now's you got to guts and fillet it out so's there be no bones in the meat." he added.

"Mom! Come over here quick and see what I caught. What do you think it weighs, Fariss?"

Caylen was so beside himself with excitement at catching such a huge fish that he took little notice of how red his mother's eyes were from crying and how she would not look at Fariss at all.

"That's great Caylen. Now, get Mr. Lubak to show you how to get some of it ready for the fry pan and breakfast." Lora answered.

"I'd guess it would weighs bout forty or so pounds, boy. Now gets your knife and I's will tell you whats to do." Fariss said.

With considerable guidance from Fariss, Caylen soon had two huge slab-like fillets of lake trout removed from the big fish. He sliced these into large pieces and gave them to his mother who immediately began roasting them on forked sticks that she had stuck into the sandy beach so that the forks were in the direct heat of the fire.

She salted and wrapped the remaining pieces of fish in a piece of oiled cloth for storage and later consumption.

Fariss, Lora, and Caylen all were soon sitting comfortably on the log in front of the campfire feasting on the freshly caught fire-roasted trout.

"This be good fish, Mrs. Lubak," said Fariss, smacking his lips.

"It sure is, Mom. Can I have some more?" asked Caylen.

"Eats all you can gets in you, boy. This goin to be a long day on the paddles." Fariss said.

"Are we not nearly there yet?" Lora asked.

"We be there when we gets there and no sooner, woman!" exclaimed Fariss, suddenly angry. "Now don't be all the time askin when we is goin to git there," he added with a frown. "Now lets gits this here camp togedder and gits on down the lake. I's don't likes the looks of that black weather from the West that's comin in."

Caylen and Lora both drew back from this sudden unwarranted outburst of anger from Fariss. Lora looked at Caylen and could see that he was about to respond in kind to Fariss, so she caught his attention and subtly shook her head, as she felt that any kind of dissention on hers or Caylen's part would only serve to infuriate Fariss further. She was, as she watched Fariss staring at her, suddenly very, very afraid. She had, in the pit of her stomach, the same sickening feeling that she had felt when she first saw the Army Chaplain coming up the lane to inform her of her beloved husband's death during the Great War. She also knew that, given their current situation and their remote location, they were quite powerless and at the mercy of Fariss Lubak and his peculiarities. She thought to herself, *Oh my God! What have I gotten us into? This man is not what he seemed to be.*

"Hurry up, Caylen. Let's get this stuff loaded so we can be on our way." she said, smiling bravely at him and Fariss in an attempt to lighten the moment.

Caylen had seen the funny odd look his mother had given him. He had also seen her red eyes earlier and now, sensing Farris's obvious anger, did as he was asked without questioning either her or Fariss. He deduced, correctly, that not everything had gone exactly as Fariss had wished on his first night alone with Lora.

Caylen wasn't entirely sure of what really went on during a wedding night, but he was confident that it had something to do with how babies were made. Even though Caylen did not quite know how babies were really made, he felt sure, for some reason, that was what had caused Mr. Lubak to get so angry at him and his Mom.

What Caylen didn't know, and what his mother could not tell him, was that Fariss had forced himself on her without any consideration for her feelings. As a result, her first sexual encounter with him had been quite painful and not at all enjoyable for her and she had, following the act and unfortunately for her, and also Caylen, tearfully expressed her hurt to Fariss, along with her displeasure with him. She now realized, much too late, that Fariss did not take kindly to criticism or advice of any kind, on any matter.

She also knew that she needed to get Caylen alone long enough for her to attempt to explain to him Fariss's temperament, how easily his anger could be triggered and his obvious displeasure at any attempts by anyone to tell him anything that might vary from or disagree with his own ideas or directions.

As they broke camp and repacked the canoes, Fariss thought to himself that while Caylen appeared to appreciate him, and was quick to both learn and to follow his advice and orders, that it was obvious that his new wife, Lora was going to present a problem for him in the future.

"Oh well, " he said to himself, "a few smacks on da head and maybe a beatin or two, and she'll be okay, and if I has to, I'll smack her kid a little to git's her attention."

His thoughts then went back to Wildflower, the Dene woman that he had purchased from her drunken common-law husband in Carcross about three years before. He recalled how she always, without too many punches from him, did everything that he told her to do without question, and how she had always greeted him with downcast eyes and a warm bed. He now felt that he had probably been just a little bit hard on her on that cold winter day when he had come home early, cold, hungry and wet from a long day at his placer mine and found no warm food or drink waiting for him.

He thought to himself, *Maybe's I shouldn't have locked her outside that night as punishment; at least she wouldn't have froze to death. After all, she weren't all that bad and it weren't really her fault I come home early that day.*

He thought for a moment about how he had found Wildflower the following morning. He had opened the cabin door, expecting to find her, huddled and cold lying against the door. Instead, when he opened the door, he saw her lying dead, as though she were asleep, on her back and in the snow about ten feet from the cabin, with her arms folded over on her chest. She was frozen solid, and it took him only a few moments to comprehend that she had deliberately ended her own life quickly and painlessly, by lying on her back in the deep snow in the forty-below-zero night.

His new problem was to now figure out just how to dispose of her solidly frozen body. His first thought was to simply bury her somewhere in the forest but he knew that this disposal method would take days of hard work as the ground was, like her body, also frozen solid. He then contemplated, for a moment before rejecting the idea, of dragging her body far out into the woods where the forest carnivores could quickly take care of her. He even considered wrapping her stiff corpse in a blanket and hanging her by her feet from a high tree branch where the animals could not get at her, and waiting for the ground to thaw before burying her body.

He had finally resolved his disposal problem by carefully excavating a deep hole about thirty inches wide by about sixty inches long and about four feet deep in the hard packed but unfrozen earthen floor of his cabin.

Once the grave had finally been excavated, Fariss had wrapped Wildflower's frozen body in a blanket before gently placed her in the excavation. He then quickly refilled the grave with the excavated earth, packing it down with his feet as he went. Finally finished, he softly said to himself as he smoothed off the floor, "There you's be, Wildflower, I's really feels bad that you's froze up, but at least you's will be warm now."

~*~

The three canoeists were soon again out on the broad, windy expanse of Nares Lake, and by noon they were about half way across the wide entrance of Windy Arm. The already cloudy sky darkened even more and the North Westerly winds began to blow even harder from behind them. Fariss knew quite well that if they didn't make it to the shelter that the West shore of Tagish Lake would provide them, they would be in deep trouble and in danger of drowning, if the coming gale caught up to them.

"Caylen, see's if you's can git a bit more sail up that pole. We needs to go's faster afore dat wind catches up wit us." he yelled over the splashing noises the two canoes were making as they cut through the ever rising lake waves.

Caylen, hearing the concern in Fariss's voice, looked quickly back at Fariss in a attempt to determine just how concerned he really was before tugging on the small sails lashings. He managed to tighten the rope enough so that their forward motion increased noticeably.

"Is that okay Fariss?" he asked. He had detected what appeared to be a concerned look on Fariss's face but he did not want Fariss or his mother to see that he was beginning to get just a little worried himself about the increasing wind and the rising waves. He added, "We are sure moving along really fast now. Would it make these canoes go any faster if we had a bigger sail?" he asked.

"We is goin plenty fast enough now, boy," said Fariss. "We needs to be able to keep control of these here canoes and the directions they's goin in. We has to makes it behind that point of land and onto Tagish Lake afore sunset, cause we's will be in big trouble if we don't."

Caylen guardedly watched his mothers white hands as she tightly gripped the large canoes gunwales. The canoe cut cleanly through the majority of the rising waves but the waves that did splash over the bow were increasing in size and in numbers. On at least two occasions he observed her become ill and deposit at least some of her breakfast over the side and into the turbulent waters of the lake. He decided that the wisest thing for him to do was to maintain his silence, for his mother sake, stay calm and say nothing.

Fariss could see that both of his passengers were more than a little concerned about their safety. He smiled to himself and thought, *this will gives them someting to talks about tonight, if we's makes it to tonight.*

"There she be!" suddenly yelled Fariss. "There be the point we's been lookin fer," he added, pointing with his paddle at a blurry shoreline some distance ahead and slightly to the right of their course. "We's will be okay now," he added, muttering quietly to himself, *I sure hopes so, anyways!*

Upon hearing Fariss's yell, Lora finally opened her tightly closed eyes for a good look around. What she saw terrified her even more. The swiftly moving canoes were now traveling faster than the following waves, causing the large freighter canoe's bow to rush up the three foot wall of water, and to then crash down over the top, causing the canvas and cedar craft to shudder and shake, splashing the cold lake water over the bow and into the canoe itself.

Caylen could barely hear Fariss sudden loud scream but he did understand what he had yelled. Grabbing the tin bucket that lay beside him, he began frantically bailing water out of the canoe as if his life depended on it, which of course, it did. Too occupied with his bailing of water to notice anything else, he suddenly became aware that the canoe was suddenly riding along much smoother than it had been a few minutes earlier. Looking out to right, he could see much calmer waters and a row of tall pine trees behind a smooth sandy white beach.

"We's be safe now," said Fariss. "Now's we needs to get a camp and a fire goin so's we can dries ourselves out."

It was nearly dark by the time they had set up camp for the night and had a cooking fire going. They soon had their fill of roasted trout and boiled beans. Fariss, knowing that the remaining slabs of trout would not last much longer in the warm weather decided to stoke up the fire so as to provide a good quantity of hot coals. He then cut a few forked sticks on which he impaled the trout fillets. Jabbing the ends of the sticks containing the fish into the soil by the fire, he tilted them so that the heat and smoke of the fire would drysmoke and preserve the trout, ensuring that they would have unspoiled fish for at least a few days.

"These will be smoke cooked and will keeps for four, maybe five days without spoiling," he said, as Caylen looked on curiously.

"How long do you need to smoke them?" asked Caylen.

"You's can smokes them until they's real hard dried and they will keeps safe to eat fer a long spell. You's really needs a proper smokin house to do's it proper, tho." replied Fariss.

"How much further to your house, Fariss?" asked Lora tentatively.

"We's goin to stay puts here tomorrow, and gets us dried out 'fore we goes on." Fariss replied, avoiding Lora's question. "We's needs to keeps our gear dried out or it's will spoils."

Early the next morning, following a leisurely breakfast, Fariss, Lora and Caylen emptied both canoes completely, spreading all the foodstuffs, blankets, household goods and the personal items that Lora and Caylen had brought, out on the sandy beach so that the breeze and the warm September sun could dry them out. Fariss then told Caylen,

"See's if you's can catch a few more's of them graylings for supper tonight, they's lots better tastin than that there gray trout." He then lay down on the warm sand and almost immediately, went to sleep.

~*~

When Lora was confident that Fariss was sleeping soundly, she walked over to where Caylen was busy casting a small spoon as far out into the big lake as he could and said,

"Caylen, we need to speak about a few things now that we have a chance to do so without Fariss hearing us.

"Okay, Mom. What is it?" Caylen asked.

"Well, I know you like most of what Fariss does, what he says and what he shows you," she replied. "But I am really afraid of him and I don't really trust him at all."

"But why not, Mom, he seems to like us a lot and he sure knows a lot about stuff like camping, fishing and canoeing." Caylen said.

"Yes, he does, Caylen. But I just have a bad feeling that he isn't very truthful, and that he has lied, and continues to lie to us about many important things." Lora replied. "For instance, he has told me three times what his house looks like, and each time he describes it differently. He also told us that his house was close to Carcross but it is now two days since we left Carcross and he still won't tell us how much further we must go to reach it. I am starting to be more than a little afraid of him," she added.

"Don't you worry, Mom. I will protect you.," replied Caylen, as he pulled a small, brightly colored grayling up onto the sandy shore.

The remainder of the day went by smoothly and quietly with Caylen and Lora enjoying each other's company as they talked about their adventure so far and of what could possibly lay ahead. The only disturbances were the sound of Fariss's loud snoring, the splashing of feeding fish and the occasional croaking of passing ravens as they flew over the camp to eye the beach for any possible signs of food.

The third day of their journey dawned brightly and was clearly going to be a great day for traveling as the morning breezes were from the Northwest and were light enough to provide great sailing. The three canoeists were soon paddling south, along the west shore of the huge Tagish Lake with just a little help from the light breezes that were coming down the lake. Fariss preferred to keep the canoes as close to the shore as was reasonable and safe. After the stormy day on the rough open waters of Windy Arm, Lora and Caylen both very much appreciated this safer route and really enjoyed the spectacular mountain scenery that surrounded them. Other than startling a huge mother grizzly bear and her two young cubs that they suddenly came upon when they rounded a wooded point on the lake, the day was thankfully, quite uneventful. The bears had been attempting to catch and eat some of the salmon that had swam up the Yukon river from the ocean to spawn in the small feeder streams of Tagish Lake. The third day of their journey ended when Fariss suddenly steered the canoes towards another sandy beach beside quite a large stream that raced over and around large boulders to splash down into the lake.

Lora and Caylen could see many huge silver and reddish tinged salmon leaping over and around these boulders as they made their upstream journey to eventually spawn in the same waters where they had been born. They could also see, on the shore, a wood pole framework quite similar to the one they had used at their first night's camp. It was apparent that Fariss liked, if at all possible, to utilize the same overnight areas each time he made the long canoe trip to Carcross. They were all quite tired, and were soon abed and fast asleep, having first fed on the smoke-cooked trout and some leftover beans from that morning's meal.

They had all been quite exhausted from that long day's efforts and slept quite soundly with one exception. Caylen was again suddenly awakened from a deep sleep by the loud mournful wailing of a timber wolf that was obviously quite close to their camp. As he lay listening in fear and wonderment to the eerie howling, he recalled the odd dream that he had been having just prior to his awakening. It was very similar to the nightmare that he had prior to leaving the village of Greenwood, with the exception being that in this dream he was not being tortured, but was being spoken to by an old wrinkled Native Indian man, whose appearance reminded Caylen a little of a wolf, and who again called him Adahy. Caylen, before he drifted off into sleep once more, murmured to himself, *I must tell Mom about my dream, and ask her again if she knows what Adahy means."*

The next day of their trip was very similar to the last. They spent the day sitting, paddling and gazing in wonderment at the never-ending beauty of their mountainous surroundings. Fariss had little to say other than to yell the occasional command at them. Lora and Caylen both laughingly decided, on this fourth day of sitting on a hard, polished wooden seat, that they both must have incredibly huge blisters on their bottoms and that, if they were given the choice, they would never ride in a canoe again. Fariss simply smiled at their good humored bantering and then suddenly said, much to their surprise,

"Just one more day, and we's will be home."

Lora and Caylen had noticed that the cold waters of the lake had gradually changed color. Instead of the clear emerald color that had pretty much been the norm until then, the waters were rapidly attaining a pearly white hue. Caylen finally got up enough nerve to ask Fariss about this change in the water, saying to him,

"Fariss, how come the water here is a different color than before and why can't we see into it very far, anymore?"

"It's cause we's be gettin close to the head end of this lake and this here waters comes from all that melting ice over there." he said, pointing at the glacier-covered mountains just to the west and the south. "The glacier ice be full of silts and such that settles out as the waters goes down the lake until it's finally gets clear."

Their fourth night was again spent in a previously used camp at the mouth of a much larger and slower-moving stream.

"This be where's we leaves this here lake and goes up this here river." Fariss said.

Their fifth day of travel began early the following morning after a rather harrowing night for Caylen. He had been quite tired after another long day of paddling the canoe without much help from the wind, forcing the three travelers to paddle for the better part of the day. He had retired to his hastily set up shelter without trying his hand at the fishing of the local waters, as was his usual routine.

He was soon fast asleep, dreamless and unmoving, until he was, in the early hours of the morning suddenly again awakened by the eerie howl of a northern timber wolf. This time, the wolf's howl sounded so loud to Caylen that he thought to himself, *It must be really close*. With that thought and hoping that he might be able to catch a glimpse of the creature, Caylen pulled open the door flap of his shelter. It took only a second or so for him to realize that what he was seeing in the bright moonlit night was in fact real, and that he was awake and not still asleep and dreaming. Laying on the sandy beach about ten feet in front of his little shelter and looking directly at Caylen with huge luminous emerald-green eyes, was a huge, jet-black timber wolf. The animal made no sound whatsoever, but simply stared unblinking at him for two or three minutes. Petrified with fear, Caylen laid there, staring back without moving or speaking. The wolf finally stood, stretched, and with one last look at Caylen, turned and trotted off into the blackness of the spruce and pine forest. Caylen lay in his shelter in fear and wonderment, not able to sleep until just before the early morning's sun began to peek over the trees of the far distant shore of the lake.

Caylen said nothing to his mother or to Fariss about what he had seen during the night. He could not understand why they had not been wakened by the wolf's loud howls as he had. By the time they were packed and paddling up the wide river, he had nearly convinced himself that it had all been a dream. Then he recalled that he had indeed seen the large paw prints and the impression in the soft beach sand where the animal had lay and watched him. He thought to himself, *They would never believe me, so I better not say anything about it.*

After only about an hour of paddling up the river, the trio entered another large lake that ran off to the west. Paddling up that lake for another hour bought a comment from Fariss.

" We goes off to the left up another river soon." he said.

It was only a few more minutes when he steered the canoes towards a sandbar that jutted out into the lake. As they passed around the end of the peninsula, Caylen could see that they were entering another river, which was not quite as large as the one they had passed through earlier that day. Another three hours of hard paddling brought them to yet another huge lake, where they pulled ashore for a badly needed rest and a small lunch.

"This here be called Fantail Lake, and we's is almost home." Fariss said. We's will be sleeping in our own beds this night." he added.

After a quick lunch, the trio were back in the canoe, paddling along the north shore of Fantail lake. Before long, they found themselves in yet another river. This river, while navigable, was much smaller than the previous one had been. After another two hours or so, they entered another lake, the smallest of the lakes they had traveled through. It took them only two hours to reach the west end of this lake. As they neared the small, fast-running rocky stream that fed the lake with icy glacial meltwater, Fariss finally uttered two words that Lora had been thinking that he would never utter.

"We's here, you's two, we's home!"

They pulled the two canoes well up onto the sandy beach and looked about themselves at the overwhelmingly beautiful scenery that surrounded them. To their north and northeast, all they could see in the foreground was a dense spruce and pine forest. They could though, see a small opening in the trees that was obviously the beginning of a trail. To the northwest, they could only see massive glacier-covered rocky mountains that appeared so close that they looked as if they could come crashing down on them at any moment. To the west and the south, they could see in the distance even more towering mountains that were also laden with glaciers and snow

"My God!" exclaimed Lora, as she stood, gazing about in awestruck wonder. "This place is so beautiful! Caylen, have you ever seen anything like this?"

"No, Mom. Is this where we're going to live?" Caylen asked.

"Just up the trails a bit." Fariss said. "We's gots to get this here stuff ups to the house and stowed befores it gets dark, cause they's lots of bears round here that will get into it ifs we leaves it here." With that, Fariss picked up as much as he could carry and started up the trail that led into the forest. Grabs some of that stuff and come on." he said. "It's not far."

Lora and Caylen hurriedly picked up some of the supplies and followed closely, as Fariss led the way up the gradually rising trail to where their new home was located. Lora began to feel more and more apprehensive with each step up the trail, fearing what she was to soon see. They had only traveled for two or three minutes when the trail opened onto a small clearing about seventy-five feet in diameter. Standing at nearly the exact center, towards the rear of the clearing, was a small structure, about twelve feet wide and about twenty feet long, constructed of vertical logs that were about five to six inches in diameter. These logs had been stripped of their bark and had been dug into the sandy soil to support their vertical positioning. The nearly flat roof was only about six feet up from the earth and was also constructed of spruce logs closely spaced. These roof logs crossed the width of the building and rested on other logs that rested atop the vertical wall members. These logs were in turn, covered with smaller axe-flattened logs that spanned the entire length of the roof. This entire roof had then been covered with what appeared to Lora and Caylen to be mud and soil to about one foot in depth and had grass, weeds and small shrubs growing out of it. The walls that they could see from where they were standing, contained only a door about three feet wide by about five feet high and a single, shuttered window about one foot high by two feet long. A stone fireplace and chimney at one end of the building appeared to be its only redeeming feature. About mid point of the roof stood a small metal pipe that Lora took to be a chimney.

Lora's heart plummeted as she stared in dumbstruck awe and bewilderment at this tiny wilderness structure as she thought to herself, *This can't be our house. Lord, please let this be just an outbuilding and not our new home."*

"Well, there she be, Lora. There be your new house." Fariss said as if in answer to Lora's thoughts. "Should I's be carryin yous in, wife?" he asked grinning broadly.

"I really don't think that will be necessary." replied Lora. "Besides I don't think that you could get me through that little door unless you broke me into two pieces."

"Wow, that sure is a neat place!" said Caylen, adding further to Lora's disappointment. "Do I get my own room?"

"Only ifs you wants to build it." said Fariss, laughing loudly at his own dry humor.

"Can we have a look inside?" asked Lora.

"Course you's can, it be your own house now." Fariss answered. "Go's on in, there be no locks on the door, they's not needed out here."

Lora went tentatively up to the low door and undid the stiff wire hook that held it closed. She swung the door in and opened it as wide as she could to enable her to see the dark interior of the cabin clearly before she entered. To her great surprise, there were three steps down from the door threshold to the hard packed dirt floor. Also, much to her surprise, the interior of the cabin was quite clean and neatly laid out. Besides the small iron cookstove that had cost Fariss two trips from Carcross and three precious weeks of his time, there was a homemade wooden table and three handcrafted chairs, shelving along one wall and a hanging bunk that would serve as a sleeping area for Caylen. She could also see another door that she guessed probably led to a bedroom for her and Fariss. She went down the three steps to stand on a caribou skin rug that lay on the floor at the foot of the stairs. At that point, she realized that the floor of the cabin had been dug down into the earth some two and one-half feet. While this gave the appearance from the outside of a very low to the ground structure, its inside ceiling height was well over seven feet. She could also see clearly the large stone fireplace and oven that covered nearly all of the end wall of the cabin.

"What's you think?" asked Fariss. "I'se spent nearly two weeks fixin this here place up real nice fer you's all."

"I think that it looks really nice, but it needs a woman's touch," replied Lora, afraid to express her disappointment. "It is certainly not what I had expected. Well, let's get our food and our gear inside and stored so we can all get a good night's sleep." she said, with a sigh of resignation, relief and acceptance of hers and Caylen's situation. She found that her mind was in complete turmoil, and that her feelings of dread were increasing at each revelation.

Chapter 5

Winter Preparations

Fariss, Lora and Caylen spent the remainder of the day hauling the supplies and their personal goods from the two canoes up the trail and into the cabin. They soon discovered that besides the inside door that was visible, there was a second, unseen and smaller door in the rear wall of the cabin. Upon opening this door, they observed quite a large room behind it that had been excavated out into the earth that was piled high against the back wall of the cabin. This room was about fifteen feet long by six feet wide, with shelving and bins on all the walls and was, not surprisingly, noticeably cooler than the cabin and the outside temperature.

"This be our cold storage room," Fariss proudly stated. "I's built it myself to stores my foodstuffs in. It don't never freeze in the winters and it don't never overheats in the summers."

In a little more than two hours, they had all of the gear and food in the cabin and stowed away in every possible space. Fariss and Caylen then pulled both canoes well up and away from the lake to a spot where Fariss had placed poles between trees to hold the inverted canoes. Taking all of the paddles with them, they returned to the cabin where Lora was still rummaging about and looking into everything, so as to acquaint herself with everything in and about her new home.

"Why are you putting the paddles in the house?" she asked.

"Cause if we leaves them outside, the porkies will eats them for the salt." Fariss replied. "The porkies eats anything that mights be salty from our sweaty hands." he added.

It was a few moments before Lora actually comprehended what Fariss had just said.

"Oh, you mean porcupines," she said, for Caylen's benefit.

"Dat's what I said," Fariss replied. "Porkies."

After a cold supper of partially smoked trout, Fariss announced that it was now time to "git ourselves bedded down, as we's got lots of works to do before snow flies." As it still was quite light outside, Lora asked if Fariss knew what time it was.

"It be nearly ten at night," he replied. "Summer days be really long up here in the North and summer nights be real short." he added. "And it is just opposite in winter. We's got to gits ourselves ready for winter, starting right away tomorrow."

~*~

Early the next morning, the loud yelling of Fariss rudely awakened Lora and Caylen.

"Times to gits up and gits to work!" he yelled. "We needs to git the nets out and catch us some fish for smokin and dryin and we needs to git loads and loads of firewoods in or we's will freeze to death this winter. We also has to gets some dry alder for the smokin." he added. "And we's got to gits us a moose or two for dryin and maybe a fat bear and some caribou's soon's we can. We's also gots to get out and picks some cloudberries, blueberries, cranberries and some of dem tasty wild mushrooms for dryin and eatin in the winter's months." he added.

"And just how do you suggest that we do all of that?" Lora asked.

"We's just has to gits ourselves started cause snow will be here soon enough," Fariss replied. "Caylen and me will gets the nets out fer the fishes whils't you'se collects some alders fer the smokin. One'ct we gits the nets set, me and the boy can get's to work gitten some heatin and cookin wood in." he added.

Following a quick breakfast meal, Fariss led Lora and Caylen out along the small stream to a rocky area. The ground along the stream was covered with waist-high bushes that were loaded with large red berries.

"These be cloudberries," Fariss said. "And these low bush berries on the rocks are blueberries. We needs lots and lots of both of dese kinds to dry and keep the scurvy away this winters. We also needs as many of those here cranberries as we kin gets," he added, pointing at some bushes further out towards a swampy area. He also showed Lora and Caylen a large mushroom growing on the forest floor, saying.

"These is also good to eats and can be dried, so we's should pick them whenever we can."

Fariss then showed Lora and Caylen what dry alder looked like and told them, "Fore you does anyting else, Lora, we needs lots and lots of this here dry woods brought up to the smokehouse fer the smokin of our fishes and meats."

They returned to the cabin where Fariss got out the fishnets and paddles, while Lora found some containers for the berries and mushrooms before heading out to gather the dry alder.

"Now, don't be goin too fars from the crick," Fariss said. "And makes lots of noises so's the bears will stay away," he added. "They's eatin the crick fish this time of the year and we's don't wants them to be eatin on you's."

Fariss and Caylen were soon in the smaller canoe, paddling along a sandy shore just to the west of where the stream entered the lake. Fariss explained to Caylen that there were ocean run salmon in the lake but that he was really after the big resident lake trout because the salmon were now quite soft-fleshed, and not very good eating after their long fresh water journey from the salt water of the ocean. Caylen was quite taken with, and impressed by all of the wood lore that he was absorbing from the woods-savvy Fariss. He was excited and eager to learn all he could about life and survival in this remote and isolated land, but he was also just a little hesitant to reveal his ignorance of wilderness life to Fariss by asking too many questions. He soon, however, forgot about his hesitancies and was asking about everything he could think about. Fariss finally had to say to him,

"Listen boy, why don't you saves all your questions until you sees what we's does and then maybe's you's won't have to ask so much."

Fariss had actually enjoyed answering Caylen's rapid-fire questions at first, but soon found that the boy's constant chatter was beginning to annoy him. Before long, they had the long net stretched out from the sandy shore into the lake, and suspended by rock weights so that the bottom of the nets were just off the sandy bottom of the lake trout's spawning grounds.

"These here trouts likes to lays their eggs in the sand close to the shore." Fariss explained. "They lays their eggs in the fall like the salmon, but not in the streams. They likes the quieter waters of the lake."

Caylen could see the nets' floats moving about in a jerky

manner even before they were fully set out. He was about to tell Fariss when Fariss said,

"See them floats bouncin about, boy? That means the trouts are here and already gittin caught in this here net. We's will check them later today." he added, as they went ashore. "I thinks we's will have lots of fishes to guts out afore dark tonight. Now's we's goin to check the gold mine and then starts gitten some dry wood in." Fariss said.

About thirty minutes later, they passed Lora, who was singing loudly and busily collecting the cloudberries and blueberries just off the creekside. She waved at them as they passed by, and Caylen quickly informed her of their mission.

"We are going to check the gold mine and get some wood." he yelled.

After a few minutes of walking up a trail, Caylen could hear a distinct change in the sound of the rapidly running stream. The sound became much louder and was quite obviously the result of a much faster flow of the water over the gravelly, rocky streambed. As they rounded a corner he could see where the stream came over a steep embankment. He could see where a diversion channel had been dug to one side of the stream so that some of the stream's water would flow into a long wooden trough that had been constructed in the dug out channel. As they neared this roughly made contraption, he could also see a wooden gate at the opening to the channel that could be opened or closed to control the amount of water flowing into the wooden trough. He could also see wooden slats across the bottom of the trough spaced about one foot apart. This entire contraption was about twenty-five feet long and set at a thirty-degree angle with a wider top and a bottom section that was much less steep than the top section. Fariss could see the puzzled look that Caylen was giving him as he looked at this carefully constructed, self-feeding sluice box. Before Caylen could ask, Farris began to explain its operation to him.

"I shovels the gravels and sands that I thinks might have gold into the top of the sluice and then opens the gate to let in the water." he explained. "The fast water moves the gravels and sands down the sluice and over the slats. The gold in the gravels be much heavier than the sands and gravels so's it sinks to the bottom and gits caught and held by the slats until I scrapes it out at the end of a day. I also puts a wool blanket at the bottom that catches the real fine gold dust." he added.

Caylen had many more questions about this operation but thought it best to wait and see for himself before asking for any further explanations from Fariss.

"Well, everyting seems okay up here so let's git some wood." Fariss said.

They returned to the cabin, collecting and stacking bundles of the dry and semi-dry alders that grew in profusion along the stream. As they neared the cabin, they both carried large bundles with them to what appeared to Caylen was a large, mud-covered hut with a small hole in the roof. This structure was located behind and to the left of the cabin. A small, heavily stained moose-skin flap served as a door, and on one side of the exterior a fire pit of flat stones was positioned so that any smoke generated entered the structure through a short piece of metal pipe.

"This be the smokehouse." Fariss said. "It be takin up to three days smokin to gits the fish so's they won't rots and five or six days for the moose, caribou and bear meats," he added.

For the next few hours, they continued to collect and pile alder. They also limbed and dragged out many dry log windfalls of pine and spruce and some that Fariss had fallen earlier in the year so as to permit them to dry out. He said these dead logs would make great firewood for the long winter that lay ahead. By the time the sun was about three hand-widths above the mountains that lay to the west, Caylen was exhausted and said as much to Fariss.

"What you mean, you's tired?" Fariss said. "We's still gots to gather the trouts, cleans them, splits and hangs them, gits the smoke-fire goin and keeps it goin till we's done wit the fish smokin. We's don't have no times to gits tired until all the works done with." he added for both Caylen and Lora's benefit.

Lora had picked berries and mushrooms all day and had spread them out over the hearth of the fireplace so as to permit them to dry for storage. Sensing that Fariss was close to losing his temper, neither Lora nor Caylen said anything further about the long workday. After another hasty supper, Fariss and Caylen returned to the lake and were soon removing large lake trout from the long nets mesh. After emptying the net of about twenty-five trout of ten to thirty pounds each, they replaced the nets and paddled to shore, where Fariss showed Caylen how to fillet the trout and prepare them for smoking. They then packed the filets of fish in a wooden keg that was filled with salt-water brine that just covered the fish. Fariss had mixed this brine and put it in the keg before they placed the fish into the keg.

"There." exclaimed Fariss. "Now we wait till morning and then we rinses off these here fishes and then we hangs them in the smokehouse and gits the smokin fire goin." "Now we can gits to bed and gits some rest."

~*~

Early the following morning, Fariss showed Lora and Caylen how to rinse off the now salt-brined fish fillets, and how to hang them properly on the wooden rods that crisscrossed the smokehouse interior. He then demonstrated how the smoke was generated in the firebox using the smoldering alder wood by limiting the amount of combustion air available to the alder. He explained in detail, that alder was the only wood available in the North that could be used, as any other local wood would impart an unpalatable flavor to the fish making them inedible. He also reiterated that the smoke had to continue to be generated steadily until the fish was completely smoked or it would soon spoil and be inedible Fariss and Caylen then returned to the lake and again emptied the nets of another large catch that required filleting and brining. Once they had this load of fish ashore, Fariss turned and said to Caylen,

"Now, boy, you's seen yesterday what to do next, so gits to it cause I's got to gets up to the mine and gets some more gold. And when you's is finished with that jobs, you's can gets in some more alders and dry firewood."

Lora, back at the cabin, decided that she should, now that she was alone, look about the cabin and storeroom and make herself more familiar with everything in it. She knew that Fariss had quite a short temper and that he expected both her and Caylen to assume much of, if not all of, the responsibilities of the household, and its daily operations such as the daily cooking, washing, cleaning, the collection and storage of foods, as well as the gathering and storing of the upcoming winter's heating and cooking fuels. She first looked about to ascertain just what was available to her with regards foodstuffs, utensils and cooking facilities. She soon located and rejuvenated with some flour and water, the sourdough starter that Fariss had placed inside a wooden box in the cool storeroom. She was quite pleased with the large stone oven that Fariss had constructed above the open fireplace. It even had a hinged flat stone door that fit quite nicely across the oven's opening to seal in the heat, when required. The little iron cookstove also looked quite capable of performing its intended function, although it had only a flat cooking surface and did not contain an oven of any sort.

Looking about the cool storeroom, she noted a number of large empty wood boxes that were obviously to be used for the longer-term storage of foodstuffs. The boxes' odors told her that at least one of them had been used as a container for salted fish with another smelling like smoke. As a matter of fact, she thought the entire storeroom smelled like alder smoke, a not entirely unpleasant odor. There were also a number of oak kegs that looked as though they would hold liquid without leaking. Rows of shelving filled with the goods they had brought with them from Carcross lined two of the storeroom walls.

Lora felt quite happy with what she had found, although, as she told herself, *This will not be an easy life for Caylen or myself, but it will certainly be an interesting adventure for us!*

Having familiarized herself with her new surroundings, Lora went outside to look at the areas around the exterior of the cabin. The stream was only about fifty feet from the cabin, and formed a large oval pool in which Lora could plainly see a school of large grayling resting in the crystal clear water near the pool's sandy bottom. A narrow log bridge across the stream above the pool provided easy access to the far bank and to the trail that led to the berry patches that she had picked from on the previous day. On the opposite side of the cabin and about fifteen feet to one side stood a small toilet constructed of peeled wood poles stuck into the ground in a vertical position. It had a sloped roof of flattened logs and a caribou skin flap of a door. The smokehouse stood right behind the toilet and Lora could see Caylen busily feeding the smoker fire. She could also see and smell the pungent white smoke that seeped through the roof opening and the many cracks that laced the mud walls and roof of the hut.

After assuring herself that Caylen was okay, Lora gathered her berry picking baskets and headed off to find more of the wild fruit that she knew was essential for their health during the long upcoming winter months.

As she walked along the pine and spruce needle covered pathway, she again thought to herself, *I surely hope and pray that I have done the right thing for Caylen and myself.*

She attempted, as she walked along, to convince herself even further that she had done the correct thing by coming to the North with Caylen to live with Fariss. She found, however, that the more she thought about it, the more uncertain she felt about her decision. While Fariss had only demonstrated his anger on one occasion, early on in their canoe trip, she couldn't help but think that the unwarranted, sudden display of wrath on his part was or could be nothing compared to what he might be capable of. She felt her entire body grow icy cold for a moment at the thought of what he might do, should he really lose control of himself.

~*~

As Fariss neared his mining creek, his excitement grew until he was almost at a run. In the days before he had left for Greenwood to meet his bride, he had dug into what appeared to be a extra rich pocket of gold-bearing gravels. At the end of one long day of shoveling the heavy materials into the sluiceway, he had recovered nearly four ounces of black, gold-bearing sand and two solid gold nuggets of about one-half of an ounce each. After panning the black sand and picking out the gold dust, he found that he had over three and one half ounces of pure gold, counting the two nuggets. At the current rate of ten dollars per ounce delivered to the gold buyer in Whitehorse, he had made thirty-five dollars in that one day. He felt certain that his prior averages of about one-half to one ounce per day were now history and that his luck had finally changed and that he had now gotten into the mother lode.

I'm rich, he thought. *About one more summer or two and I's can retire to the south somewher's , one'ct I gits about one t'ousand or so ounces. I's will just gits me out of here to somewheres warm.*

He thought for a moment or two about his new family but quickly discarded any ideas of what would become of them.

They's kin stay here when I's leaves, he mused, *"I ain'st goin to let thems have my gold. No way's that's goin to happen. I's will make them both works extra hard at the home so's I's can spend all's my time gitten gold out of this here mountain."*

~*~

A few days later, as the three were all sitting at the table finishing their evening meal, Lora said to Fariss,

"Are we going to get any other kind of meat to eat besides fish? I think we will soon get tired of having nothing but fish to eat." she added quietly.

By Lora's rough estimate, they had, over the past few days, smoked, dried, salted and stored over two hundred pounds of lake trout, grayling and whitefish.

"You's will soon gits lots of meats for eat'n," Fariss replied sharply, scowling at Lora. "I's got to git out and shoot a moose and maybe a bears or two and some caribou wens't they comes down from the north."

"How do we keep all that meat from spoiling?" Lora asked.

"Well, we's dries it first and also salts some and soons it turns cold, we's just lets it freeze solid." Fariss said. "I's will takes the boy out tomorrow morning and see's if we can git somting good fer eaten."

At first light the next morning, Fariss and Caylen were in the smaller of the two canoes, paddling quietly along the lakeshore. Fariss had taken his hunting rifle and a handful of cartridges with him, after telling Caylen that he was not to touch it or even to speak unless spoken to. Caylen was quite astonished at the size of the bullets that went into the big lever-action rifle, and was also full of questions about the gun. He was, however, aware that Fariss would only tell him about such things when and if he was ready to, and that if he questioned him too much or too often, that such questions might only serve to anger Fariss.

After they had paddled for a few moments, Fariss laid his paddle quietly down and, cupping his hands over his mouth, gave three short deep grunts.

"Uhh, uhh, uhhhh."

While the grunts were not overly loud, they seemed to Caylen to reverberate off the surrounding hills with the deep grunting sounds bouncing back almost instantly. It was a moment or two before he realized that the sound that he thought was an echo was, in fact, a similar sounding reply from something that was hidden in the alders that grew in profusion along the shoreline of the lake.

"Uhh, uh." Fariss grunted again.

Almost immediately, Caylen heard a loud crashing and snapping noise coming from the brush along the shore. These noises were quickly followed by the appearance of a huge bull moose that charged out of the alders to stand on the beach, looking around and out over the lake in an effort to determine where his challenger was located.

Caylen could only stare in wonderment at this magnificently large antlered animal as it stood in the cool morning light, with steam rising from its warm body. His open mouthed awe was almost immediately interrupted by the thunderous roar of Fariss's rifle, as Lubak triggered off two quick shots at the huge animal. The moose quickly turned as if to return to the forest, taking only two short steps before collapsing in a heap on the shore of the lake. Caylen could see its body shudder and quiver for just a moment, as the life forces of the animal left its huge body.

"There you's be, boy," Fariss said. "They's enough meat there for most of the winter. Now's we's got work to do gitten that animal gutted, skinned and cut up. Then we's got to gets all that meat back home and into the smokehouse for curin and dryin."

It took Fariss and Caylen the remainder of the day to skin and butcher the huge bull moose. They boned it where it had fallen and loaded the rich, dark meat into the moose's own hide that they had placed, fur side down, inside the canoe. It took two canoe trips to get all the meat back to the cabin where Lora was kept busy slicing the chunks of meat into thin strips that she first rubbed with a mixture of salt and pepper, and then hung over the poles and rods inside the smokehouse. Fortunately there was still a goodly supply of dry alder remaining to fuel the smoke drying fire.

"We's gots to make sure this here moose meat be dried real good or its will turn bad," Fariss commented. "This be real good food for travellin light when we go on trips.

"How long will it take before it's dried just right?" asked Caylen.

"Dat depends on lots of tings," said Fariss. Depends on the heat, how thick the meats is and how longs you wants to keeps it. You's has gots to keep checkin on it until its done right. Now why's dont you two gits back to work and quits askin so many dang fool questions!"

Lora and Caylen looked at each other after this loud outburst from Fariss, but said nothing.

Fariss then told Lora and Caylen how to make what the natives of the north called 'pemmican'.

"You's takes some really dry, chopped-up meats and berries and then you mixes them with some cooked down caribou fats. It be really good and lasts a long time if you's keeps it cool."

It took nearly a week of Lora and Caylen tending the drying fire and moving the strips of meat about on the drying rods before the meat was dried to Fariss's satisfaction. They rarely saw Fariss during this time, as he was usually on his way to his placer mine before dawn and not back until nightfall. Lora quickly learned to have his breakfast and supper meals on the table and waiting for him whenever he arose from bed or appeared for his afternoon meal. The cursing, ranting and raving that came from him on the one day that he arrived home early only to find his supper meal not quite ready had its desired effect. After that she always had some freshly baked sourdough bread and cold meats ready for him to eat on the table in the event he was early. She also always had a loaf of sourdough bread and some dried meat or fish in his pack and ready for his lunch at the mine.

She and Caylen continued to gather and dry the berries and mushrooms that she knew would stave off the ever-present threat of scurvy during the long northern winter days.

~*~

Lora could now easily sense that Fariss was not to be completely trusted and that he was easily angered, at times for no apparent reason. His demeanor and attitude towards her and Caylen seemed to be rapidly worsening as the days passed. As the days passed she feared more and more that his sudden outbursts of anger could easily lead to his harming herself or Caylen. She decided that she should speak to Caylen of her fears before any such harm took place, but she was also just a little apprehensive about conducting this discussion. She felt that he might be beginning to look at Fariss as a father figure and might not believe that her concerns about their safety were at all justified.

It was about mid afternoon on the following day that Lora decided the time was right for this talk. She asked Caylen to walk down to the sandy lakefront beach where she, and he, would not be overheard, should Fariss approach them unexpectedly. She found a large fallen tree that they could both sit comfortably on before she began to speak.

"Caylen, son, I want to have a really long and serious talk with you and to ask you to be really truthful with me and tell me just what you think of this life in the North so far, and what you think of Mr. Lubak and the way he has been acting since we arrived here."

"I am really learning a lot about living up here," Caylen said, in a slightly evasive tone. "I can catch, clean and smoke fish, dry moose meat, find good eating berries and wild mushrooms, paddle and sail a canoe and find my way about easily in the bush."

"Yes, yes, you can," Lora replied. "And I am really proud of what you can do. You are really a good, hard worker, and I am positive your dad would really be proud of you too, if he were here."

"I kind of like Mr. Lubak at times," Caylen said, in response to her questioning gaze.

"But?" questioned Lora, sensing that he wanted to say something more.

"Well, whenever I talk to him, I always feel like he's going to hit me." Caylen said, looking at Lora in a manner that told her he was quite afraid that she might not believe what he was saying.

"Caylen, I know that you're telling me just what you believe is right and I want to tell you that I feel much the same way. I'm afraid that if we do something that Mr. Lubak doesn't like that someday he just might harm us," Lora said. "Now, we must talk about how we can make sure we are safe as long as we live here, and how we can protect ourselves from Mr. Lubak should it be necessary."

"I will protect you, Mom." said Caylen. "Fariss said that he is going to show me how to use my rifle."

"Oh, Caylen. Please be really careful with that thing, I don't ever want to see you pointing it at anything you don't wish to kill." Lora replied, a little shocked at his statement.

"Well, if Fariss ever hurts you, Mom, I will shoot him dead, just like he shot that moose." Caylen stated in a matter of fact way.

"Oh, Caylen. Don't ever let me hear you say such things. But, thank you. And please remember that I love you dearly."

" I love you, too, Mom.," replied Caylen.

For the next hour, Lora and Caylen discussed Fariss and his increasingly moody outbursts and what they could possibly do to minimize them and their effects on their welfare. They decided that about all they could was to attempt to not antagonize Fariss and to comply as much as possible with his directions and his orders. Directions and orders that they both agreed were becoming each day more and more aggressive, demanding and threatening in tone. As they concluded their discussion and strolled back to their cabin, Lora asked,

"Caylen, have you seen what Fariss does all day long up at his mine?

"No, Mom, he has never let me spend more than a few moments up there before he tells me to get back to the cabin, but I think he shovels gravel and sand into the sluice box all day."

"Well, have you ever seen him get any gold from his sluiceway?" Lora asked.

"No, but he told me that he cleans it out every night before he comes home," Caylen replied. "If he gets gold, I don't know what he does with it."

"Well, he must be getting some gold as it wouldn't make sense for him to keep going up there and working at it if he wasn't," Lora said.

"I could sneak up tomorrow and watch him to see what he does," said Caylen.

"No, don't do that!" Lora replied. "If he saw you spying on him, he would really get mad at you."

Caylen didn't reply but thought to himself, *That's just what I'm going to do and I won't get caught.*

~*~

A few days later, Lora and Caylen heard the sound of Fariss's big hunting rifle in the distance, firing rapidly three times late in the morning. He had taken to carrying his rifle with him on a regular basis when he had begun working his claim. He had also decided to say nothing to Lora or Caylen about his increased findings of gold in the sluiceway, and he had begun to get quite paranoid about his ever-growing hoard of gold dust and gold nuggets. He did not want either of them to know how much gold he had found or where he had hidden it.

About two hours after they heard the three shots, Fariss appeared at the cabin, yelling at Lora and Caylen to bring their knives, come out, and help him butcher the bear he had just killed. It took the remainder of that day and the following day to skin and butcher the huge fat grizzly bear that Fariss had shot near his claim. They ended up with approximately two hundred pounds of rich pork-like bear meat, preserved with salt, in the wooden boxes that were kept in the cold room. Lora cut all of the thick layers of pure white fat from the meat and rendered it down to where it looked quite similar to the pails of lard that they had brought with them.

"This fat be good for lots of ting's," Fariss replied to Caylens query as to its use. "Specially for rubbin in dry skins and makin leathers soft and nice and for waterproofin boots."

~*~

As the fall days became shorter and shorter and the nights longer, the temperature began to fall to below the freezing point every night, and they began to experience occasional falls of snow. Lora and Caylen could see the snow levels on the surrounding mountains creeping ever further down the slopes until the morning arrived when they opened the cabin's door to find about six inches of snow carpeting the ground.

"Well, winter be here." Fariss said. "The caribou deers be here soon and we's will have lots more fat meats for freezin."

About a week later, Caylen spotted a small herd of strange looking deer-like animals on the shore of the nearby lake. Later that evening he told Fariss of what he had seen and Fariss said that he would "gits some deer meats tomorrow."

The next day he rose as dawn broke and as he left the cabin carrying his rifle, said to Lora and Caylen,

" Get's your stuff ready fer butchering cause this won't takes long."

About fifteen minutes later, Lora and Caylen heard about seven shots in fairly quick succession. In a short time, Fariss appeared at the door to say to them.

"Git goin, they's four deers dead, bled out and ready fer butcherin down by the lake. Jest foller my tracks on the snow to gits to them. You's two knows what's to be done, so gits to it."

It was to take Lora and Caylen three full days to fully process the four caribou. They first had to eviscerate and skin out the carcasses before quartering them and carrying the meat back to the cabin. Once there they followed Fariss's instructions and wrapped the now frozen sections of meat securely in the animals' own skins and suspended each of the pieces high in the branches of the surrounding trees. This, according to Fariss, would keep the meat frozen and well preserved for their use until the spring thaws, with the frozen animal skins keeping the frozen meat safe from hungry marauding animals and the ever present ravens and jays.

"We's now got lots of meats fer this here comin winter," Fariss said. "And we's can always catch us more fish through the ice holes in the lake if'n we runs short." he added.

A few days later, Caylen's almost constant requests that he be permitted to use the little twenty-two rifle that his father had left him, were finally met with success. Fariss got the little rifle out and showed Caylen how to load and fire it, unload it and then how to clean and care for it. He insisted that Caylen perform the cleaning tasks over and over again until Caylen felt sure that he could perform them in his sleep. Caylen, as Fariss observed and told Lora, appeared to have a definite talent insofar as the handling and use of the little weapon. He could load and fire it with amazing rapidity and accuracy as Fariss soon discovered. Caylen, from the beginning, and to Fariss's chagrin, outshot him at every attempt. It was not long before Fariss declared to Lora, that Caylen was, "Full trained and a better shot than I's be."

Chapter 6

Fariss Revealed

The winter was to prove to be extremely long and cold. Fariss had not been able to impress upon Lora and Caylen just how cold forty and fifty degrees farenheight below zero really was. They soon discovered that any day that dawned with a cloudy sky usually meant that the outside temperature might at least be tolerable enough for them to go outdoors to search for the always needed dry firewood or to venture down to and out on the frozen lake to try their hand at ice fishing. These ice fishing trips always proved quite adventurous to Caylen, who loved to do anything that broke up the dreary monotony of cabin fever. (As Fariss called it)

Lora also quickly discovered that her husband, her son and she consumed much more food in the cold winter months than they had during the warm summer and fall seasons. She was kept quite busy, constantly preparing and cooking breads, soups and meats for herself and her two ever-hungry cabin mates.

As the nights grew longer and the days grew shorter, the creek and the gravels surrounding Fariss's gold mine had also frozen solid. While some enterprising northern miners would use huge bonfires to thaw the frozen gravels and hand pan the placer gold from them, Fariss had long ago decided that this method was just to much work, and besides, he was quite confident that his newly discovered "mother lode" would, come spring, soon make him wealthy beyond his wildest dreams. His new, earlier rich find, that he had been unable to fully explore before having to go to Greenwood to meet Lora, had given up, on his return, over one hundred and thirty ounces of gold dust and nuggets before winters onset had forced him to stop his operations.

As the long winter slowly passed, Fariss found himself becoming more and more impatient with Lora and Caylen. The confined space of the little house did nothing to alleviate the caged-in feelings and the impatience he felt at not being able to work his claim and extract its riches. His brooding, short temper and long periods of silence did nothing to ease Lora or Caylen's fearfulness of any possible actions towards them that he might attempt. On more than one occasion she found herself attempting to calm outbursts of anger from Fariss that seemed to erupt from him for no apparent or obvious reason.

~*~

As Christmas day neared, Caylen and Lora had decided to erect and decorate a small spruce tree in one corner of the cabin. They had quietly discussed doing this amongst themselves without telling Fariss of their plans as they hoped to surprise him. They waited until Fariss was out checking on his snowshoe rabbit snares that he had set in a attempt to supplement their other meat supplies. They had just completed decorating the tree with some pine and spruce cones and small strips of white rabbit fur when Fariss returned. Throwing his catch of two solidly frozen snow-white rabbits on the cabin floor, he stared for a moment at the prettily festooned tree and then suddenly screamed at them.

"Jest what in the name of all that's holy does you's thinks your doing to my house?"

"We just thought. Fariss, that we would surprise you by making the house nice for Christmas," Lora replied quietly.

"I's really don't give one hoot's what you's thot," Fariss replied, grabbing the little tree and stuffing it into the fireplace where it and its decorations were consumed by the hot flames in less than a moment.

Caylen looked fearfully at his mother, afraid to say anything that might provoke Fariss any further. He was also awaiting his mother's reaction to what seemed to him to be a wholly unwarranted outburst.

" Now, Fariss, why did you have to do that?" Lora asked. "We went to such a lot of work to try to make the house nice just for you."

"I's don't has to explain anyting I does to you's two," Fariss retorted. "I's the man here and this be my house, so's I will do whatevers I wants to, whenever I am wants to."

After this unwarranted sudden outburst by Fariss, Lora and Caylen just looked at one another and wisely said nothing more.

Fariss continued to glower at them for another few minutes. It was obvious to Lora that he was looking about the neatly organized cabin for something additional that he could rant and rave about.

"Look, boy," he yelled, "The wood piles is gitten down. You's git out right now and tops it up befores we all freezes to death in here!"

Without saying anything in response, Caylen wisely got up, pulled on his coat and proceeded out into the cold to fetch more firewood for the already nearly full woodboxes. As he waded through the ever-deepening snow towards the stockpile of firewood, he saw, in the snow, the tracks of a large animal. He was able to follow the tracks until they took him completely around the cabin and onto the hard-packed snow path that led to the outdoor toilet. Once the animal had left the soft snow and trod on the harder snow of the trail, he could easily make out their shape and size. He quickly realized that the tracks had been made within the last few moments, and that their maker had been a very large, heavy timber wolf. Feeling terror beginning to well up inside of him, Caylen returned to the woodpile, grabbed an armful of wood and raced back to the protection and warmth of the little cabin.

Caylen wisely thought that, given the previous and recent outbursts by Fariss, he would say nothing about the fresh wolf tracks to Fariss or his mother. The fresh wolf tracks in the snow brought back to Caylen memories of the dreams he had experienced on the long canoe trip into these northern wilds. He also recalled his other similar dreams and his early morning sighting of the huge black wolf with the shiny green eyes. He wondered for a moment if it were possible that all of these dreams and sightings meant anything, or if they were connected in any way.

It was only three days later that Caylen awoke during the early hours of the morning with a start. The warm cabin was still and quiet except for the occasional snap and cracks coming from the burning wood in the fireplace and the wood stove. He could tell that the weather outside was extremely cold, as he also heard the sound of tree trunks in the nearby forest exploding like rifle shots from the extreme cold.

As he lay in his warm cozy blankets, he thought of what his dream had been that caused him to waken so suddenly. His memories of his previous dreams were rapidly lessening but he remembered clearly just what had awoken him on this particular morning. In this dream, he was standing, alone in the snow at the edge of the nearby frozen lake, when out of the forest ran the huge black timber wolf with the green glowing eyes that he had seen in his previous dreams. Alongside the running wolf was the old wrinkled Indian man that Caylen had also seen in his earlier dreams. The old man was also running and keeping up with the wolf. He was also shouting as he ran alongside the huge animal.

"Adahy! Come with us, Adahy! Come with us."

Caylen lay in his cot until morning, thinking and wondering about what his dreams were really about and what they might mean. He decided once more that he wouldn't tell or worry his mother about his recurring dreams until he had time to consider them and their meaning himself.

Later that day, Caylen tromped through the newly fallen snow down along the frozen lake to the area that he had seen in his dream the previous night. When he reached the spot that he approximated was the same as was in his dream, he was astonished to see, coming out of the forest that was only about fifty feet away, the tracks of something quite large. He waded over to them and stared down at the large imprints of a heavy running wolf. Beside the wolf tracks were also the tracks of a running man. Caylen looked in wonderment and confusion at these two sets of tracks in the snow. He followed them with his eyes as they circled about on the lake's frozen surface and then re-entered the forest quite close to where they had come out.

His first reaction at the sight he had just seen was to say to himself. *I must still be still asleep and dreaming, I need to wake up*!

It took a few more minutes for him to fully realize that what he had just seen was, in fact, real, and that he had not dreamt it, and that he was indeed fully awake. Caylen's next thoughts, on realizing that the tracks in the snow were real and not a figment of his dreams, was that he should rush back to the cabin and tell Fariss and his mother.

As the penetrating cold of the winter day began to penetrate his thick clothing, he thought, *I wonder what they will think when I tell them of my dreams and what I saw on the snow today? They will probably think I have gone crazy!*

It took Caylen only a moment longer to decide that he wouldn't reveal what he had dreamt or he was now seeing on the snow to anyone for the present. He decided that he would wait and perhaps tell only his mother at some later time. As he turned for one last look at the two sets of imprints in the snow, his jaw dropped open and his eyes opened wide as unbelievingly, the human tracks gradually faded from sight, leaving only the deep imprints of the wolf's paws in the snow. He stared at the remaining tracks for a few more minutes, wondering if he really had seen the human footprints in the snow alongside the wolf's tracks or if his imagination was running amok. He finally decided that he should get back to the cabin and that he was definitely not going to reveal to anyone what he had just seen, at least for a while.

~*~

As the long cold months slowly went by, Lora and Caylen both found that Fariss was withdrawing into himself more and more, and that the majority of his communications with them were sudden outbursts of unreasonable anger or uncalled for comments such as:

"How's comes you's only made three loaves of bread today?" "Why's don't you's scrapes the frost from the window?" "Who's do's you thinks ate that last piece of fish?" "Git's up and helps yer Mom clean the house." Git's yerself up and puts more wood on the fire." "Get you's out and gets some more snow fer meltin into drinkin water." "Don't be talkin to me lest I's talks to you's first." "Dis here cup of tea be cold, git me some hot teas." "Did I's say you's could do that?"

Lora and Caylen quickly realized that any overt reaction or response by them other than to their agreeing or complying with him would only result in even more anger and further outbursts from Fariss. They soon began to fear that his vocal outbursts would turn into real physical abuse towards them. On more than one occasion, when Fariss was away from the cabin, Lora and Caylen would discuss Fariss's ever-worsening behavior, and how they could protect themselves from him, should he become physically abusive towards either of them.

"If we see that he is angry, we must not do anything to make him any more angry. We must do whatever we can to calm him down." Lora said.

"It seems that no matter what we do or say, he just gets madder and madder every day." Caylen replied.

"When that happens, we must not say anything at all, we should just answer him in a way that might calm him down."

"But, what if he gets really mad and hits us?" Caylen asked.

Lora did not respond to this question by Caylen. She had begun to fear that exact thing but she didn't have any idea of what she could or would do if Fariss did eventually become physically abusive towards either or both of them. There were no neighbors or friends living nearby that they could go to. Their nearest outside contacts were, to the best of their knowledge, over five days travel away, over the frozen lakes that lay solidly under the minus thirty to fifty degree below weather. Their choices in any event were quite limited. They would have only their own skills and wits available to them should their situation with Fariss become intolerable.

Some two weeks later, early one cold morning the situation regarding Fariss's increasing morose and sullen behavior appeared to take a distinct turn for the worse. The main fire that the cabin depended upon for its heat was the huge fireplace on the end of the cabin that Caylen was required to keep well fueled, day and night. Caylen would pile three or four logs on this fire prior to his crawling into bed for the night. This amount of wood normally kept the fire burning quite well until he arose early the following morning to refuel it.

On this particular morning, the fire, during the night, consumed most of the fuel that was available to it and had burned down to where just a few glowing embers remained. Fariss, awakening early than was usual in the winter morning's chill, quickly noted that the fire was nearly out. Caylen and Lora were soon made fully aware that Fariss was not happy having to climb out of his warm blankets and dress in the cooling morning air. His roar of anger shook the cabin's walls and brought the pair of them fully awake in less than an instant.

"Caylen, you stupid, careless little idiot, you's has let the fires go nearly out! Now gets you'r stupid self out's of bed and gets your jobs done fore I smacks you one on yer fool head!" Fariss screamed.

Before Caylen could come fully awake and before he could comprehend what was occurring, Fariss had torn the blankets from him and yanked him from the bed by his arm and onto the cabin's floor. Caylen rose groggily from the floor, shaking the sleep from his eyes and looking about in panic, not fully awake and expecting Fariss to strike him at any moment with the huge fist that he was waving about in front of his face. Lora, also awakened by Fariss's loud ranting, could see that Fariss had completely lost control of himself. She feared, at once, for the safety of her son and immediately rose and placing her hand on her husband's arm, said to Fariss in as calm a manner as she could,

"Now, Fariss, dear, I'm sure that Caylen didn't intentionally let the fire go down, he probably just slept in and, besides, there are still lots of hot coals left."

Fariss responded to Lora's calming voice almost immediately by lowering his waving arms, looking at her and replying in a much quieter voice,

"I's dont's really cares just whats he intended to do, the fires is his job, and he didn't do his job and I's is gettin cold!" Fariss retorted.

"Well, Fariss, do you really expect him to stay up all night to keep the fires going? Lora asked.

"Ifs that's what he's has to do, then that's whats he's has to does," responded Fariss. "That's his job here and he's ain't been doin it."

After this exchange, Lora felt that she should probably refrain from antagonizing Fariss further, so she said quietly, "Caylen, why don't you stoke up the fire, make Fariss a nice cup of hot tea and apologize to him for your forgetfulness."

"Okay, Mom." Caylen replied quickly, realizing what his mother was doing. "I'm sorry about the fire, Fariss. It won't happen again."

"It better not." mumbled Fariss.

The behavior displayed by Fariss improved over the next few days to where he was again simply ignoring the presence of Lora and Caylen except when he wanted something from them or wanted them to do something. There was absolutely no idle conversation initiated by him . He would, if spoken to by Lora or Caylen, respond for the most part with a simple grunt, an 'okay', a 'no' or a 'yes'. It appeared to Lora and Caylen that he had lost the ability to complete a sentence that contained more than one word. His new personality, while much less hostile than before, soon began to again frighten them. Lora again felt that she should discuss Fariss's strange behavior with Caylen at the first opportunity. That opportunity arose when Fariss announced to them one morning that he was going to go over the lake to Atlin for a few days. When Lora asked him," Where and what is Atlin?" He replied,

"It be a place out there, a couple days to the East over the lake ice ."

Further questioning by Lora was answered by Fariss with vague waves of his arms or a "never mind" or a "you's don't needs to know." So Lora finally just gave up questioning him and waited for him to leave on his planned trip. Fariss finally, three days after he had first announced that he was going to go to Atlin, loaded his large backpack with supplies, slung his rifle over his shoulder and, without further comment to Lora or Caylen, left, wearing his big snowshoes, for the long trek to Atlin.

Once Fariss had been gone from the cabin for about an hour, Lora asked Caylen to get warmly dressed, as she did likewise. She then led him down the trail to the lake and looked out across the snow-covered lake's surface at the small distant speck that they knew was Fariss trudging along towards the Eastern horizon.

"Come on back to the cabin, Caylen." she said. "We need to talk about Fariss and the way he's been behaving towards us lately."

~*~

They were soon back at the cabin, shedding their outdoors clothing and warming them by the open fire. Lora made herself and Caylen a hot cup of tea and they both settled down at the table before Lora began to speak.

"I really don't know how to explain what I have to tell you other than to tell you just what I'm feeling," she began. "Fariss is starting to really frighten me with his odd behaviors, and I just don't know what to do."

"Yes, I know Mom. He really scares me, too, at times," Caylen replied. He seems to get really mad for no reason at all sometimes.

I just try not to get him any madder than he already is when he gets like that. I try to go away from him."

"Yes, that's probably the best thing to do, but he seems to be getting worse all the time," Lora said. "He talks a lot when he is asleep, and keeps saying he is sorry and also that he can see wildflowers." she added. "I don't know why it bothers him so much, but when I asked him one morning about his dreaming of wildflowers, he got really angry at me and shoved me out of bed and onto the floor."

"Well, maybe he won't come back from Atlin, wherever that is." Caylen said. "Maybe the wolves will get him or maybe he'll fall through the ice and drown."

"That's not a nice thing to say, young man!" Lora retorted, "I don't ever want to hear you say anything like that again!"

"I'm sorry, Mom. It's just that I'm really scared of him sometimes and I don't know what to do." Caylen replied.

"Well, when he gets back, let's both of us try to be nice to him. Spring will be here soon, and he'll be working up at his gold mine again. He seems to be much calmer when he is out of the house and is working at it." Lora said.

Fariss was gone for nearly two weeks. Caylen and Lora spent a lot of time talking and discussing ways to appease Fariss and ways to make their life in the Northern wilds easier and more pleasant. They both had decided that the wilderness life was, with the exception of Fariss's angry and mean spells, quite enjoyable. Neither of them really missed the furor and hubbub of the life they had endured in the bustling little village of Greenwood.

Caylen also discussed at length with Lora his ever-increasing dreams of the huge black wolf, the old Indian and the word Adahy that he could recall from his dreams. He also told his mother, with some apprehension, about seeing the wolf and the man's tracks on the lake the previous week. When he told her about the man's tracks and how they had disappeared from the snow before his very eyes, she looked at him strangely for a moment before replying.

"You probably really only saw the wolf's tracks but then you let your imagination get carried away. You know just how vivid your imagination can be." she said.

"Yes, I guess that's what it probably was," Caylen replied, not for one minute believing what she had just said, but thinking that he shouldn't pursue the matter further, at least for the time being.

During the next week, the cold north winds began to relent a little, and the two pioneers could, during the daylight hours, detect a definite warming of the air. The sun's warm rays began to soften and even began to melt some of the heavy layers of snow that blanketed the forest, lakes and surrounding mountains. Spring was definitely just around the corner. When Lora eventually checked her homemade calendar, she estimated that it was probably about mid April.

~*~

Fariss took the better part of four days of hard snowshoeing across the lake snow and ice and through the low mountain pass to reach the village of Atlin. In past years, he usually made this trip at least three times a year during the long Northern winter. He found that it certainly helped to break up the monotony of lonely cabin life in the wilderness. It also permitted him to sell and trade his summer's find of gold dust and nuggets for much needed winter supplies. He usually spent a week or two enjoying the rough strong whiskey that the gold rush community served up in its many bars and saloons. His rough tough manner and his excessive drinking usually managed to get him involved in a few brawls, and on this particular trip a knife fight that resulted in a serious injury to his unfortunate opponent. This man required surgery and stitches at the Atlin first-aid station to repair the deep knife slashes and the two punctures to his abdomen that Fariss had inflicted on him.

Fariss spent one long night warming a small uncomfortable cot in the town's little log jailhouse where, on the following morning, he was questioned at some length about his role in the nearly fatal attack. The town's only law enforcement, at that time, consisted of one member of Canada's Northwest Mounted police force.

Constable Frank Whitman was on the final year of his first tour of duty in Canada's Northlands with little prior experience of any kind in frontier law enforcement. As the victim of Fariss's vicious attack, for fear that Fariss would seek revenge, chose to not to register a formal complaint against Fariss, and with no witnesses about to come forward to testify against him, Constable Whitman had no choice but to release Fariss with a stern warning.

"Get out of Atlin or I will lock you up until you rot." The Constable did not say anything to Fariss about what else he had learned during his questioning of Fariss's drinking partners of the previous night. They had informed him that Fariss had, in a boastful manner, said to them.

"I's finally gots rid of my squaw girl fer good and gots me a new lady and a readymade son to do's all the works round the cabin."

The Constable wondered to himself just what Fariss had meant when he said that he had "gotten rid of his squaw" so he decided to include in his report of the incident that would eventually end up in Whitehorse, all of this information, but as he couldn't see any relevance of that subject to the stabbing incident, he pursued it no further.

~*~

Fariss, after this episode, packed his gear and headed west for his cabin. His two weeks away from his cabin had permitted him to, after the fourth day, sleep soundly, without having his usual dreams or nightmares about the native girl, Wildflower, and her ghost that he kept seeing in his sleep.

Being a very superstitious person, Fariss had recently begun to believe that the spirit of the dead Wildflower just might be in the cabin and that she could be the cause of his terrifying dreams. He had really begun to get concerned about these dreams when Lora asked him why he was seeing wildflowers in his sleep. He knew now that he should never have buried her under the cabin's dirt floor, but with Lora and Caylen now living in the cabin, he knew that there was little that he could now do to remedy that error.

Chapter 7

The Gift

Fariss, after his return from Atlin, appeared rather quiet and subdued as compared to his terrible behavior prior to his two weeks absence. Lora and Caylen were both quite pleased with him, as he seemed to be his old self once again. He would initiate conversations without prompting and even displayed a little of his quiet humor by teasing them about their fastidious insistence on washing up each and every day.

"You's two is goin to rub the skins right offs yer faces," he said, with a grin. "They's enuff skin in that there wash water to makes us up a nice meaty soup fer supper."

"Oh, Fariss, you are such a tease," Lora replied, hoping to keep Fariss in this rare, new-found humorous good nature.

"Fariss, can you take me out ice fishing today?" Caylen asked, knowing that Fariss took great pleasure in doing out of doors things and that he also enjoyed displaying his many outdoor skills to Caylen or anyone else who would listen.

Everything seemed to go quite smoothly for Lora and Caylen over the following weeks. Spring's approach seemed only to add to Fariss's good humor, as he now began to think of his gold claim and that he would soon be able to resume his extracting of gold from the rich find that he made late last summer. He decided, wisely, to not tell Lora any details of his trip to Atlin or that he sold all of his last summer's find of gold to Atlin's gold commissioner. He had walked out of the commissioner's office with over two-thousand dollars in cash. He spent only about seventy-five dollars of this money on lodgings, food and drink while there, allowing him to return and hide, in his secret cave, two thousand and ninety dollars in Canadian currency. Added to his already stowed money, his stash totaled nearly six thousand dollars, which was lodged in a metal box hidden under a pile of rocks on a ledge in his little cave.

Caylen's dreams and visions of the huge black wolf and the old Indian who kept calling him Adahy slowed, so that he was only occasionally experiencing them. One night after Lora, Fariss and he were abed after watching an extremely vivid display of the spectacle commonly known as the Northern Lights, Caylen did experience a recurrence of the dream. In this particular dream, the old Indian was standing with the black wolf beside him. The old man was looking at Caylen with his piercing black eyes and softly addressing him in his dream, saying,

"*Adahy, I have asked that you come to me but you have not yet obeyed me. I am, therefore, as a sign of my sincerity towards you, about to send you a gift that you will call Cheveyo.*"

The old man then added, *"You will take this gift as your own and you shall love and cherish it as you would a blood-brother. You shall bring this gift that I have given to you with you when you decide that the time is right for you to come to me."*

When Caylen woke the following morning, he could, as was normal following these dreams, remember quite clearly everything that he had dreamt about. He did, at the first opportunity, tell Lora of what he had seen and what the old man had said to him.

"He said that he was going to send me a gift and that I was to call the gift 'Cheveyo'. What does Cheveyo mean, Mom?" asked Caylen.

"I have no idea, son." Lora replied, "Perhaps Fariss can tell you."

"I don't want to tell him about my dream." Caylen replied. He will make fun of me."

"Well, you don't have to tell him of the dream, just ask him if he knows what Cheveyo means." Lora said.

Later that evening, following their evening meal, Caylen, observing that Fariss appeared to be in a relatively good mood, said to him.

"Fariss, do you know what Cheveyo means?"

"Where's did you's hear dat word?" asked Fariss.

"I read it in one of my school books," Caylen answered. Lora had, as the opportunity presented itself, been continuing with Caylen's schooling as best she could. She had brought a number of her instruction books from Greenwood with her and was having Caylen read through many of them as part of his studies.

"Well, I thinks it be an Indian word and I thinks it might means 'spirit warrior'." Fariss said.

As Fariss appeared to be receptive to Caylen's questioning, Caylen decided to ask him about one more thing that was bothering him.

"Would you also know what the word 'Adahy' means?" he asked.

"You's sure has lots of questions tonight," Fariss answered. "I tinks that it means somebody living in the woods."

Later that night, after Fariss left the cabin for his evening toiletries, Caylen said to Lora.

"What kind of gift would you call 'spirit warrior'?" he asked.

"I have no idea," Lora answered. "I guess you will just have to wait and perhaps you'll find out in your next dream." she added, with a smile.

"Oh, Mom, now you're making fun of me." said Caylen.

"Well, I think this whole matter is really quite humorous," said Lora. "You have been having all these dreams and now you seem to be acting as though they really happened and were not just part of your dreams."

"Yes, I suppose I have," replied Caylen. "But they all seemed so real at the time. It was like I was really doing and seeing all those things."

"You should just try and forget them," said Lora. "You have a very vivid imagination and I think you just get confused sometimes about what is real and what is not real."

Caylen thought about what his mother had said to him about his dreams and their lack of any connection to reality for some time. He knew that she was not really making fun of him but he also knew that she didn't take his dreams as seriously as he did himself.

~*~

The next few weeks of spring went by quickly. The surrounding snows soon disappeared with the lake's ice following fast behind. The stream that ran by their cabin was the last to clear itself of its winter's ice and was soon overflowing, as the mountain snows that lay high above them drained their icy meltwater down the slopes and into the full and overflowing streams, rivers and lakes that lay below.

Fariss began to make daily trips to his placer mine to scrape any thawed gravels from the long pit that he had dug the previous summer. He was able, each day, to obtain some "colors" from his sluiceway, but the small amounts of gold-bearing gravel that he was able to collect from the slowly thawing pit seemed to him to not be nearly as rich in gold as it had been the previous summer. His anticipation grew as each warm spring day released more and more thawed materials to his pick and shovel. The results at the end of each day's work, however, failed to match his enthusiasm or his previous takes.

Early one morning as he was having his breakfast of gruel and dried fish, Fariss suddenly said to no one in particular.

"I's would sure likes some fresh fried eggs fer a change."

"Now where on earth do you think we would be able to get fresh eggs way out here?" Lora asked.

"Well, you's two gits dressed for the wet's places outsides and I's will takes you's out and show you's," Fariss replied.

In a few moments, Lora and Caylen were following Fariss down to and along the lakeshore. They could hear, coming from the marshy bay they were approaching, the honking and quacking of the many Canada geese and the many different varieties of wild ducks that come to the North, and were now utilizing that particular area as nesting grounds. Many of these birds had already constructed their nests and were now in the process of laying their eggs. Fariss soon located the nest of a large pair of Canadian geese who, at first, didn't appear to want to leave their nest. The mate of the female was also standing nearby, honking wildly at the trio as they approached the nest.

"Okay," said Fariss. "First things we does is to chase thems birds away from here so's we can see's into their nests."

He then rushed at the nesting pair; waving his arms about until the two wildly honking geese flew off and circled about, high over the three intruders' heads. As they came up to the nest, Lora and Caylen could see two large eggs resting on the nests bottom.

"We cannot take these eggs," she said. "They may not be fresh and won't be any good to eat.

"We's dont wants these ones," said Fariss. "Just watch what I's does."

Fariss then took a piece of charcoal from his pocket and after marking an "x" on each of the two eggs, placed them carefully back into the nest.

"Now," he said, handing the charcoal to Lora and Caylen, "You's two find about ten, maybe twenty more nests like this one and puts a marks on all the eggs you's finds in them. You's then gots to remembers where all those nests are at."

"But how is this going to get us fresh eggs? " asked Lora with a puzzled expression on her face.

"Dat's simple," Fariss responded with a grin. "You's just comes back here tomorrow and every day after, to all these here nests with these marked eggs in them and you's takes out for us to be eatin, all those eggs that don't have no "x" on them."

"Well, my goodness." said Lora. "What a good way to get fresh eggs. However did you think of this, Fariss?" she asked.

"Wildflower showed me," said Fariss, without thinking.

"Who is Wildflower?" asked Lora.

"Just a old Indian gals I's knew who's lived in Carcross," said Fariss, thinking quickly as he realized he had said too much already.

Lora decided from the way Fariss reacted to her question about Wildflower that it would be best if she said nothing more about the matter. She and Caylen were to collect many fresh goose and duck eggs over the next few weeks. The family feasted for a time on fried eggs, boiled eggs, poached eggs, omelets and any other egg dishes that Lora could concoct from the foodstuffs they had on hand or could find in the surrounding forests. She also preserved about two hundred or so fresh eggs in barrels that she first filled with a solution of potassium silicate and water. Fresh eggs would remain fresh and edible for months in this solution before spoiling.

Early one warm spring morning a few days later, Caylen awoke from a deep sleep with a start. He had been having another of his weird dreams about the old Indian and the big black wolf. In this particular dream he saw the big wolf sitting just outside the cabin's door. He could also see a small, round black object lying on the ground between the wolf's huge front paws. In Caylen's dream, the big wolf simply sat panting, with his red tongue hanging down from his open jaws, for a few minutes before turning and loping off into the forest.

Caylen lay abed for another five or so minutes, wondering just what this, his latest dream could possible mean, or if it meant

anything at all. As he could hear Fariss and his mother beginning to stir, he decided that he should get out of bed to tend the fires and perform his morning toiletries before the early-rising Fariss yelled at him. Caylen quickly pulled on his shirt, pants, socks and shoes, threw a couple of logs of firewood on the fire and prepared to head off to the outdoor latrine located at the edge of the forest clearing. He grabbed his light jacket to ward off the early morning's chilly air and exited the cabin. Not really noticing exactly where he was placing his feet, he hurried down the short path to the lavatory. As he walked along he looked to the east at the morning sky and commented to himself,
"Another nice day, I wonder what will happen today."

He had no sooner made this query under his breath than he felt his foot hit something on the trail. The object that his foot had struck emitted a loud protesting squeak and, before he could stop himself, he had fallen forward to land flat on his stomach on the hard packed trail. He lay unmoving for just a moment, gathering his wits about himself before realizing that he was unhurt. He then rolled over and looked to see what had tripped him, and what had made such a funny noise. Caylen looked, and then looked again, with his mouth falling wide open in utter astonishment and disbelief as he realized what had tripped him.

Sitting on his little haunches with his tiny head cocked off to one side, his ears standing erect with what could only be described as an amused look on his face, was a perfect little miniature of the huge black wolf that had so often inserted itself into Caylen' dreams. The animal was an exact, tiny replica of his dream-wolf. Even his bright little eyes were emerald green. He sat, looking at Caylen, with what appeared to Caylen to be a grin, seeming to say.
"*Well, what are you looking at clumsy?*"

The little puppy then came forward and then, as Caylen lay in astonishment, licked his face and mouth with his warm wet little tongue.

~*~

The huge black timber wolf lay quite still under the thick canopy of fir trees at the edge of the cabin clearing. He was now fully rested after the long journey from his den, carrying his young son in his massive jaws. While he had not been overly pleased with the taking of his favorite son away from his den and his mate, the choice was not his to make. He had long ago discovered that, once his master entered his mind that he was unable to fully control his own thoughts or his actions. The sound of his mate's mournful howls had followed him for some distance, as he carried his son to the human's den. As he watched his son being tripped over and then picked up by the human, his apprehension grew and he rose to his feet, prepared to protect, with his life, his defenseless son. It was only after he saw the human cuddle his son to his chest and turn to re-enter his den that he turned and loped off towards his homelands, his mate and his master.

As he crested a small hill, he stopped and, turning his huge head back towards the human's den, gave a loud, long mournful howl as a final goodbye to his son

~*~

Caylen finally, after the little wolf pup decided that he had licked his new friend's face clean, picked the little animal up, finished his toiletries and then carried the pup into the cabin to show his mother and Fariss. As he neared the cabin with the squirming little puppy in his arms, he heard, far in the distance, the long, eerie howling of a mature timber wolf echoing throughout the forest. He entered the cabin to find Fariss and his mother both up and about, preparing to go out to the latrine.

His mother, as she began to say good morning to Caylen, spotted the little black pup in his arms.

"Caylen, what on earth do you have there? Oh, my goodness, it's a little puppy!" she exclaimed. "Where did you find it?"

"It was lying just outside our door." Caylen replied. "I think its parents must have left it there. It's too young to have traveled on its own. He really likes me, Mom." he added, "Do you think I can keep him? I will feed and water him, and train him to do lots of things that will help us."

"That there animal isn't no puppy, he's be a wolf." Fariss growled. "He's will grows up real big and be eaten alls our foods up and maybes he be eatin us too. You's should be takin him down to the lakes and drowning him."

"Oh, Fariss, that would be cruel and besides, he's only just a baby. You can't expect Caylen to drown such a cute little baby puppy that is obviously so young and helpless."

"He's wont's be young and helpless fer too long," was Fariss's reply. "Before you's know's it, he's will be grown up, real mean and eatin all our foods and then us too."

"I'll catch extra rabbits and extra fish for him." Caylen almost yelled in his sudden fear for the little puppy's life. "I can shoot my rifle now, and I can shoot other kinds of food for him, too. Please, Fariss. Please, Mom. Let me keep him." Caylen looked pleadingly at both Fariss and his mother as they, in turn, both looked at each other in a questioning manner. He could feel the tears beginning to well up in his eyes, as he imagined having to destroy the quivering little bundle of fur that he now held so tightly in his arms.

"Well," said Fariss, beginning after a moment to relent a little. "I don't tinks it be's too good an idea, but I has seen some of them there wolf dogs thats turned outs okay. Buts, it be's up to yer Mom to say yes or no," he added.

Caylen looked at his mother expectantly. He knew immediately what her decision would be. He also knew that she would relish giving him a bit of a hard time before she gave her final answer, so he allowed her to tease him just a little more.

"It's going to mean a lot more work for you, son." she said. "Are you positive you can manage?"

"I will work extra hard, Mom." he answered; now quite sure that she would soon give in.

"Okay. We will let you keep him for two weeks to see if you really do look after him," said Lora." If we see that you are neglecting him in any way, we will have to get rid of him," she added, knowing quite well that in two weeks the little puppy would have become a permanent part of the family, and that she would, by then, love the little puppy just as much as Caylen already did.

Caylen knew that her last statement was intended for Fariss's benefit and that his mother could no longer resist the little wolf's bright green eyes, wet tongue and friendly manner. He thought for a moment and then blurted out.

"Thanks, Mom, and thanks Fariss. I know exactly what I'm going to name him. I'm going to name him 'Cheveyo', but I'll call him by what Fariss said that word means, it means 'Spirit Warrior' but I'll shorten that name and just call him 'Warrior'."

"Dat's a good name," said Fariss. " When he gits bigger we's can teach him to fights other dogs and then we's can makes lots of money making bets on him in Carcross and Atlin."

Caylen knew better than to comment on Fariss's last remarks but Lora, having no such reservations, responded quickly.

"I do not think that teaching Warrior to kill other dogs is a very good idea. If you taught him to attack other dogs, that kind of training would just make him so mean that he might also attack people."

"I's has told you's before, and I's will tell you agin," Fariss growled in anger at Lora's contradiction of him. "This be my house and you's will do what I say's, not what you's says!"

Lora and Caylen looked at each other, saying nothing, as they knew immediately that any further comments from them would only provoke Fariss even more.

Chapter 8

Warrior

The next few weeks were some of the happiest days of Caylen's young life in the wilderness. His new-found friend, little Warrior, kept him quite busy and entertained with his comedic antics and playful nature. The little wolf pup needed absolutely no encouragement whatsoever from Caylen to initiate some kind of play between them. He would pick up small twigs or pebbles and bring them to Caylen, dropping them in front of him and then happily sitting down beside the dropped article, waiting expectantly for Caylen to throw whatever he had brought so he could "fetch" it and start the game all over again. He followed Caylen around wherever he went, bouncing merrily along behind him in obvious ecstasy at all the attention he was getting. If Caylen, for any reason, did not allow the pup to accompany him, Warrior would sit, with his head cocked back and his little green eyes gleaming, and give off his best imitation of a grown timber wolf's eerie howl. These imitation howls, at least for the first few weeks, never failed to set Caylen, Lora and Fariss off into gales of laughter at his funny sounding puppy attempts. Before long, however, his voice had deepened to where he began to sound like any other wild wolf. He even, on occasion, prompted a response from the pack of wolves that claimed that particular local territory as their own.

Warrior also, for some reason that Caylen found quite puzzling, seemed to always avoid one area of the cabin's floor. It was as though an invisible fence had been erected around that specific area that kept him from entering it. On one occasion, Caylen picked the puppy up and put him down in this area that Warrior always avoided. To Caylens surprise, the pup let out a loud yelp and ran as fast as his little legs could carry him back to Caylen's arms, where he lay shivering in fear for a few moments before returning to his normal playful self.

When Caylen believed that Warrior was about three months old, he began to train him to obey his verbal commands. Warrior had, from the very first, been extremely fast to respond to anything that Caylen asked of him. He would walk beside Caylen, just to his right and slightly behind him. He would come immediately to Caylen whenever Caylen called him by name or said, "Warrior, come."

It seemed odd to Caylen that his pet would respond almost immediately to his commands but would never pay any attention whatsoever to Fariss or to Fariss's commands. It was as though he could not hear anything that Fariss said to him or that, for him, Fariss didn't even exist. Warrior's reactions to Lora's commands were only marginally better. When she would give Warrior a command, the wolf would look at Caylen as if to say.

"Is it okay for me to do what your Mom wants?"

Only if Caylen said "It's okay, Warrior" would he react to her commands. If Caylen failed to acknowledge Warrior's look when Lora gave him a command, Warrior would simply go about doing whatever he had been doing and totally ignore her.

When Caylen had Warrior trained so that the animal would do pretty much as he was told, he felt that the next step in the training should be to teach Warrior about guns and hunting. Caylen was more than a little unsure as to how his wolf pup would behave or react when he was faced with a wild animal or heard the sound of gunfire for the first time. He began this phase of Warrior's training by taking his twenty-two-caliber rifle and letting him examine and smell it thoroughly. He then accustomed Warrior to the sound of gunfire by doing some target practice with Warrior standing beside him so that he could relate the loud noise to the weapon.

Warrior appeared to grasp and understand all of these lessons with ease. It seemed to Caylen that Warrior was saying to him,

"Okay, okay! I get it. Now let's get on to the next lesson."

~*~

As spring turned into summer and the sun's warming rays thawed the mountain slopes enough so that Fariss could begin to work his small open-pit mine, he began to spend nearly all the long days toiling at his claim. It seemed, to Lora and Caylen that he was becoming more and more obsessed with his placer mine on each passing day. He would barely speak to them except to tell them to do or get something for him. He was, as Lora said to Caylen one morning, becoming "much as he was last summer when he was so miserable and mean to us."

Late one evening, after Caylen and Warrior had fallen asleep on his cot, Lora asked Fariss how his work at the mine was getting on. She normally didn't ask him anything about his gold mining ventures, as he had, in the past, always seemed to resent or take offence to any questions she asked about his gold claim. This time his response was no different and possibly even worse. He seemed to explode with anger at her quiet query as to how his work was proceeding.

"What's business is it of you's?" he screamed angrily at her, awakening Caylen and causing the five-month-old Warrior to growl menacingly at him from where he lay by Caylens cot.

"Is you's spyin on me? Why's you askin those questions of me?" he yelled, slamming his metal teacup down on the plank table. "Why's don't you's two jest leaves me alone and tends to your own dam things, and I wants you's to keeps that there dam wolf quiet." he concluded, storming into his and Lora's bedroom, leaving her, Caylen and Warrior to stare, unspeaking at each other.

Lora placed her fingers to her lips, signaling Caylen not say anything, as she feared if Fariss heard them say anything at all, he might get even angrier. This was, by far, the worst display of anger from Fariss that Lora had seen since the previous year.

What Lora didn't know, and what Fariss wasn't about to reveal, was that his rich gold find of the previous summer was not apparently as large as he previously estimated and was now giving out. His sluice box had only given up about three ounces of small nuggets and about twelve ounces of the valuable yellow dust since spring. This meant, according to Fariss's rough calculations, that he was now averaging less than one-half ounce per day, as compared to the three to four ounces per day the claim had given up during the latter days of the previous year. Fariss knew, but would not admit to himself, that the claim had probably given up the majority of its richest ore to him and that his daily take would likely only decrease even more as the days went by.

To worsen matters even further, his dreams and nightmares

concerning Wildflower were beginning to recur again. He was beginning to see her accusing face nearly every night in his sleep. She would appear to him as he slept, and stand over the spot in the cabin where he had buried her, and point her finger at him accusingly, saying only two words over and over.

"Why, Fariss? Why, Fariss? Why?" she would say again and again to him until he would come wide awake with warm, wet perspiration completely covering his entire body and soaking his and Lora's bed through and through.

As a result of these nightmares and the ever-diminishing gold that his claim was giving up, Fariss was noticeably losing body weight as well as his temper. His outbursts at Lora and Caylen were now occurring on a daily basis. They became so rabid that Lora again began to fear for her and Caylen's safety. She, once again, felt compelled to discuss her concerns with Caylen before any serious incident or harm came about.

Before Lora had her opportunity to discuss Fariss's worsening behavior with Caylen, Fariss announced that it was again time for them to make their annual supply trip to Carcross and Whitehorse. Fariss decided, due to his recurring nightmares about Wildflower, he would make this long journey earlier than in previous years. The poor results of late from his placer mine also contributed to his decision.

He knew that if he left the cabin his nightmares would, at the very least, lessen and the long trip would give him time to consider his options regarding his current placer mine's location. He had, a few years earlier, found other promising areas nearby that had given up some good color and now felt that perhaps some of these other areas deserved further exploration. He felt that a three-week break from his nightmares and his mining was well deserved.

He also knew that Lora and Caylen would welcome such a trip to civilization, giving them the opportunity to purchase new clothing and much needed household items.

~*~

Warrior's training was progressing much faster than Caylen had anticipated. The wolf pup, now nearly six months old, could hardly be called a pup. He now stood almost eighteen inches high and weighed about fifty-five pounds. He seemed to understand completely everything that Caylen or anyone else said to him. He would respond without hesitation to any verbal or hand command that was given him by Caylen. The only real problem insofar as Caylen was concerned was the fact that Warrior would not, under any circumstance, react in any way to anything that Fariss said. He would if Fariss gave him a command, simply look first at Fariss and then at Caylen, waiting for Caylen to say "Okay, Warrior," before complying. He would now, if Lora spoke to him, respond to her verbal directions if Caylen simply nodded to him following Lora's commands. Warrior, on many occasions, astonished Caylen by seeming to anticipate what Caylen was about to do or ask him to do. He would rise, for example and go to the cabin's door if Caylen was even thinking of going out. He followed Caylen everywhere, refusing to be left behind. He would eat nothing unless Caylen or Lora had given him it. He would touch nothing that had the scent of Fariss on it. This behavior towards Fariss by Warrior was worrisome to Caylen, as he knew that Fariss didn't take kindly to being ignored by anyone or anything.

~*~

As they prepared for the long canoe trip to Carcross, Fariss explained gruffly to Lora and Caylen that they had to be prepared to leave at any time of his choosing. As he explained to them, paddling the two large canoes over that great a distance without the assistance of the winds would take the three of them more than two weeks. He explained that they should wait for the winds to blow from the opposite direction that they wished to travel in so as to make the trip much easier and faster.

They only had to wait two days for this to happen. On the third day following Fariss's announcement of the trip to Carcross, Lora and Caylen were awakened by Fariss before dawn. He yelled at them.

"Gits yerself's movin, the winds be from the South and dat's whats we wants, so's let's be gettin on our ways afore it changes round agin and comes from the wrong direction."

The trio, accompanied now by one half-grown wolf, were soon on their way down the first small lake and its outlet river, headed at top speed for the huge open waters of Tagish Lake.

Warrior, as Caylen quickly noted, appeared to be immensely pleased with his position in the large freighter canoe that they towed behind them. He sat mid-ship, with his head turned slightly towards the shoreline, with his long, red tongue hanging out, and what could only be described as a huge grin on his handsome black wolf's face.

~*~

The trip to Carcross took them seven long days. They were forced to spend two days paddling the canoes when the wind completely stopped blowing, and then one full day ashore when the wind shifted to the Northwest, causing them to actually lose ground. Other than for the wind's direction, the good warm weather stayed with them during their entire journey.

When they finally arrived at the little village of Carcross, Fariss and Caylen hung the heavy canvas tarpaulin between two trees to form a small tent-like enclosure. They then dragged the two canoes out of the water and inverted them alongside the shelter. Fariss then, to their utter and complete surprise said to Lora and Caylen.

"Okay, you's two is all set up now. I's will rides the train into Whitehorse and gets our big supplies fer next winter."

"But, I thought we would all be going into Whitehorse," said Lora.

"No, I's is goin alone. You's two needs to stay here and watch our tings in case they's gets took." Fariss replied.

"Who would take them?" Lora queried.

"They's lots of bad folks round here that would robs you as soon as look ats you. Sides, it costs lots fer us all to rides on dat train and I's has not dug up much gold this year."

"Oh, I didn't know that you were not having much luck at the mine." said Lora. "You never speak to us about your mine so we didn't know." she added.

"Dat's cause it be my business and not yours," Fariss retorted, sharply. "Now I be gone fer five, six days fore I's gits back, so's you's two jest stays put and watch our stuffs. Now here's be some money fer you's two
to buy sometings you's needs."

"Okay, Fariss." said Caylen. "Warrior and I will guard

everything. I'll catch some grayling and trout for us to eat while you're gone."

Early the next morning, Lora and Caylen watched Fariss board the little Yukon and Whitepass railway train, as it passed through from Skagway on its way to Whitehorse.

"Well," Lora said, to no one in particular," I guess we're on our own for a few days."

~*~

"We can explore the town and maybe meet some people who knew Fariss from before we met him." Caylen said, thinking of the boys he had met as he had passed through on the way to Fariss's cabin. He wanted to see if he could find out more about the background of this strange brute of a man whom his mother had married.

The two spent the remainder of that day preparing their little camp for the five or six day wait that confronted them. They dined that evening on some of the many tasty grayling that literally fought each other for a chance at Caylen's fishing lures. As they were quite exhausted from their long journey, they were abed and sleeping soundly before the evening sun had dropped below the western horizon.

The next few days went by quite rapidly as Caylen and his mother explored the little community. They thought it best to have Warrior stay in camp and guard their few possessions while they did their roaming about. Fariss had given Lora a few dollars to spend as she pleased, so they examined, in detail, all of the limited merchandise available in the few local shops, purchasing nothing other than a little salt and some lard to supplement her cooking supplies. She did want to purchase much more but her fear and apprehension at what Fariss might say or do about her using some initiative and purchasing needed supplies without his permission caused her to buy nothing more at all, except for a length of fishing line and a few fishhooks for Caylen.

They met and talked with many of the local folks, who brought Lora, more or less, up to date with the outside world's news. She was quite happy to talk to everyone she could, after her year of speaking to no one other than Fariss and Caylen.

On the fourth day of their camping stay; as they were relaxing by their noonday fire, they observed two big native men approaching their camp. As they neared, Warrior stood and moved between Lora and Caylen and began a low, throaty growling that was barely audible.

As the two men neared, Caylen could see the jet black hair on Warrior's neck and shoulders begin to stand erect; his growling deepened and grew much louder. The two men stopped dead in their tracks when they heard Warrior's loud growls. The newcomers called out to Caylen.

"Is that animal yours? Is it a wolf?"

"Yes, it's mine, and yes, it's a wolf. And I don't think you should come any closer without permission. That is, unless you want to be bitten." Caylen said." It's okay, Warrior, you can let them come closer." Caylen allowed, after watching the two strangers for a moment.

In response to these instructions, Warrior grew silent and immediately lay down beside Caylen, keeping a close watch on the two native men as they neared the small camp.

"We want to talk to you, if are you Fariss Lubak's woman." one of them said, obviously addressing Lora.

"No, I am not Fariss Lubak's woman; I'm his wife, Lora. And this is my son, Caylen. And that wolf pup is called Warrior." Lora replied.

"Okay then, you is who we wants to talk to," the first man said. "I am called Lokni, my brother here is called Kosumi and our sister is called Wildflower by you whiteskins."

"What do you want to ask us about?" asked Lora, "And where is the sister you call 'Wildflower'?"

"That's what we wants to know." said Lokni. "Where is our sister? What have you done with her?"

"What do you mean by asking us what we have done with your sister? We don't even know anyone by the name of Wildflower and have never known anyone by that name." Lora replied, not quite truthfully as she did recall Fariss saying that he had known someone by that name.

"Why would you ask us where your sister is?" Caylen queried.

"Because Fariss Lubak took her away with him in his canoe many years ago and we have never seen her since that day." said Lokni.

"Well then, why don't you ask Fariss where she is. He has

never spoken to us about her." Lora responded.

"We have asked him many times of our sister's whereabouts and each time we ask, your Fariss does not reply except to threaten our lives." Kosumi said.

"I'm sorry, but we can't help you." said Lora.

"Then perhaps you can tell us where you live so that we may visit your home and speak to Fariss Lubak ourselves in his own home." said Kosumi, obviously growing quite angry that they weren't getting the answers that they had hoped for.

"No, my mom will not tell you where our home is and neither will I." Caylen spoke up suddenly, as he detected a growing anger in the pair. As he spoke, Warrior, sensing the alarm in Caylen's voice, stood, his low growling beginning again and his long fangs exposed.

"I think you had better leave us now as my wolf does not like you very much." Caylen added.

At this, the two men strode off, leaving Lora and Caylen to discuss at length what had just occurred. They had no idea whatsoever where this person called Wildflower was, or just what the connection she and the two native men could have with Fariss, or even if what they had said was true. Lora and Caylen could only wait until Fariss's return and ask him about the incident, its cause and what it meant, hoping that he would be willing to talk about it with them.

~*~

It was another four days before Fariss returned from his Whitehorse buying trip. He seemed, now, to be in much better humor than before he left and seemed quite anxious for them to be on their way home.

"Let's gets this stuff loaded ups and gits goin," he said. "I's needs to gets back and starts a new diggins at me sluice box."

It took only a few hours to break camp, haul the supplies from the train station and load up the canoes. With a few hours of daylight remaining, the foursome pushed off from shore and were soon headed east toward Windy Arm. They weren't able to use the small sail on this first day, as the winds were non-existent. The three had been paddling along in silence for about an hour when Caylen happened to glance back at the towed freighter canoe to see how Warrior was doing. Much to his surprise, he could see, to their rear, a small green canoe that was being paddled by the two native men, Kosumi and Lokni, that they had met at their camp a few days earlier.

The two men were in a much smaller and faster canoe and were closing rapidly on them.

"Mom," he said to Lora. "Look behind us."

Lora turned and, recognizing the two men, said to Fariss,

"Fariss, those two men behind us were asking us about their sister who they called Wildflower. They said that you took her with you when you left Carcross a few years ago, and they wanted to know where she is."

Fariss turned, and also recognizing Wildflower's brothers, said,

"Those two men's are bad ones and all they wants is to robs us from our supplies and our gold." Without saying another word, Fariss lay down his paddle and picked up his heavy 45/70 Winchester rifle that lay directly in front of him. Swiveling his body toward the rear, he levered a cartridge into the chamber and, to Lora and Caylen's astonishment, he shouldered the weapon and fired it at the two men.

Lora and Caylen could see the waterspout that the heavy bullet caused as it struck the water just to the right and behind the oncoming canoe. They again heard the roar of the big rifle as Fariss triggered off a second shot. This time, they both clearly saw the heavy lead bullet strike the leading paddler in his right shoulder. The puffing out of his shirt, the sudden raising of his arms, the dropping of his paddle and his falling back into the canoe verified instantly that the four hundred grain solid lead bullet had found its mark. The rearmost paddler in the canoe reacted instantly by swinging the canoe about and paddling furiously towards the shore that lay only a few hundred feet to the south.

"Fariss! What are you doing? " Lora screamed.

"Shuts up yer mouth, woman, and keeps paddling or theys will kills us all!" exclaimed Fariss.

"But why did you shoot them? All they wanted was to ask you about their sister." Lora said.

"I's don't have to tell you's nothin bout why's I shoots at them ceptin to says that they's would kills us all iffen they gots the chances." Fariss retorted angrily. "Now gets back to paddling fore

I'se really gets mad."

Lora and Caylen both knew that any further discussion about what just occurred was useless and would only serve to infuriate Fariss further. They continued to paddle eastward until Fariss decided that their followers were no longer behind them, and that they could now make landfall and set up an overnight camp.

The remainder of the trip back to the cabin took another four days. Strong following winds made the remainder of their journey down the huge Tagish Lake easy and quite pleasant for the paddlers, who were now only required to steer the swiftly moving watercraft with their paddles.

Unfortunately, the shooting incident early in the journey weighed heavily on the minds of both Lora and Caylen, causing them to wonder again about their own safety and about the irrational, ever-changing behavior of Fariss.

Fariss didn't mention either the shooting or the woman called Wildflower again, seeming to act as though the incident had never occurred. His ignoring of what occurred and its potential seriousness only served to cause Lora and Caylen to become even more fretful about their own safety.

~*~

Once they arrived back at their little cabin home in the wilderness, it took only a few days for them to get back into their normal day-by-day routine. Fall was again approaching with winter foodstuffs and firewood waiting to be gathered and prepared for storage. The smokehouse fire was again soon smoldering away, causing many delicious and mouth-watering odors to permeate the little clearing and the surrounding forests.

Caylen's training of Warrior continued, with the rapidly growing animal seeming to get smarter and stronger each day.

Lora made—from a caribou skin that she first scraped clean of all hair—a pair of saddlebags that she presented to Caylen as a gift on his thirteenth birthday. Caylen had supposed that she must have completely forgotten about his birthday but, to his surprise and glee, she hadn't, and had placed the saddlebags along with a homemade birthday card at his bedside while he slept.

It took him only a moment to figure out what the saddlebags were for and how they were to be used. He could see that his mother had fashioned them so that they could fit an animal of Warrior's current size and yet could also be easily expanded to fit him, as he grew larger. He soon, much to Warrior's disgust, securely fastened the empty bags over the wolf's back. Warrior spent only a moment or two expressing his displeasure over the unfamiliar weight but he soon forgot that they were even present and before long was ignoring them completely.

Caylen left the packs attached to Warrior for three full days, leaving them empty during this entire time. On the fourth day, he placed in each of the two bags a small, equal amount of beach gravel. As he began with only about two pounds per side, Warrior barely noticed the difference in weight. Within two weeks, Caylen could easily load the packs with more than ten pounds in each pack before Warrior would complain. Warrior would tell Caylen exactly when he felt that the weight was too much for him to bear by simply laying down and looking up at Caylen with an expression that quite clearly said,

"It's much too heavy, and I'm not moving until you make it lighter!

~*~

Fariss, since their return, had barely spoken to either Lora or Caylen. He was quickly returning to his moody old self, expressing himself in outbursts of rage and anger at the smallest of incidents. His nightmares, visions of Wildflower and his periods of sleeplessness had returned. His placer mine was again giving up only minute quantities of dust each day.

In addition, he was now haunted by the thought that he might have killed one of Wildflowers brothers. It was not the thought that he might have killed Wildflower's brother that troubled him the most. It was the fact that he missed out on killing them both that really troubled him. The native brothers of Wildflower, until the time he shot the one brother, had only their suspicions to base their actions upon. They now, after his shooting and possibly killing of one of them, could present actual evidence to support their claims if they chose to go to the Northwest Mounted Police. He believed that, if he could have gotten rid of both of the brothers, no one, save Lora and Caylen, would ever know what happened to them. He also felt that Lora and Caylen presented no real danger to him and that if they ever did become a problem, they could easily be gotten rid of and placed beside Wildflower in her cold, damp grave.

As winter again approached, Lora became more and more apprehensive about Fariss's increasing sessions of depression, his nightmares and his outbursts of anger for no apparent reason. Any attempts by her to open a dialogue with him or to comfort him were met with even more outbursts of rage and irrational behavior from Fariss. At times he seemed oblivious even to her and Caylen's presence in the cabin. She and Caylen both found him, on more than one occasion, carrying out lengthy conversations with himself or with some unseen and unidentifiable entity. He began to leave them alone in the cabin for days at a time before suddenly appearing, cold and hungry, with no explanation at all as to where he had been.

On one occasion, just after the New Year had passed, Fariss was crossing the cabin floor and approaching Warrior, who was now nearly full-grown and weighing about one hundred and twenty pounds. Warrior, who had never, even on the rare occasions that Fariss showed kindness towards him, ever warmed to Fariss, raised his big head and uttered a low, deep growl. Fariss, reacting in a vicious manner, stepped over to him and raised his foot as though to kick him in the stomach.

Caylen, hearing the low growl from Warrior, began to yell a warning to Fariss, but before he could say anything, Warrior had jumped to his feet and grabbed Fariss's upraised foot in his huge mouth, tripping him up so that Fariss immediately fell hard, toppling hard over onto his back on the cabin's floor. In the next instant, before anyone could react or say anything at all, Warrior was standing astride Fariss with his huge, snarling, dripping jaws and his long bright fangs only inches from Fariss's exposed throat. Fariss lay unmoving where he had fallen, knowing without any doubt, that even the slightest movement on his part would probably result in his throat being ripped open by those enormous exposed fangs.

Caylen hesitated for only a brief moment before saying.

"No, Warrior! Back! Back!"

Warrior instantly moved over to Caylen's side and slumped down onto the dirt floor, his green eyes fixed intently on Fariss's every move as he rose from the floor and returned to his seat by the fire without saying a word.

Lora, who had been standing and watching in stunned horror as this scene unfolded before her, breathed a long sigh of relief, sat down and murmured to herself. *Fariss will now kill Warrior, and possibly Caylen.*

She knew that if she did not do something soon that Fariss would probably go completely mad and could try to kill them all. She knew that she could no longer avoid, as she had been, discussing with Caylen all the events that had occurred during and since their Carcross trip earlier that summer.

Chapter 9

Confrontation

Everything was calm in the Lubak home for the next few weeks. Fariss said nothing at all to Lora or Caylen regarding the incident with Warrior. He scarcely spoke at all, and anything he did say was as brief as could be.

He continued his lengthy absences with no explanations as to his whereabouts to either of them. Lora could see that he was also losing weight and that he was still bothered by his dreams and nightmares. He would awaken her in the night with his loud cursing and yelling, that would continue until she would finally be able to shake him awake.

Lora's apprehension increased each day to the point where she began to lay in bed, awake, listening for Fariss to begin his nightly ranting. As the long winter nights began to shorten and the days became longer, Fariss was able to spend more time out of doors and his demeanor seemed to improve slightly. He would now, at least respond to any questions they put to him with a grunt, although just an 'okay' or a 'no'.

As spring approached and the days became increasingly warmer, Fariss would, to Lora's chagrin, take his big 45/70 Winchester rifle down from its wall rack and disappear for hours at a time. Her queries as to just what he was hunting for were met with silence, a grunt or sometimes a "none of yer business." She began to fear more and more for her and Caylen's safety, and begged Caylen to stay inside the cabin with her whenever Fariss went out with his rifle.

It was a beautiful spring day with the air temperature at about thirty degrees farenheight and with the sun shining brightly on the melting snows. Early that morning, Caylen had decided he would take Warrior out on the lake and try to catch a nice fresh lake trout for their supper.

Fariss had taken his rifle and left the cabin before daylight, saying nothing to Lora or Caylen as to where he was going. The winter's snow had now begun to melt in the day's warm sunshine, causing the remaining snow on the lake ice to crust over and reflect the bright sunshine so as to almost burn one's eyes if they weren't wearing some form of eye protection.

~*~

Caylen had fashioned himself a pair of wooden goggles that had only a small slit over each eye that quite nicely reduced and prevented the sun's glare from affecting his vision. While he was once reading a book about Eskimo life, he saw a drawing of an Innuit wearing such goggles and made himself a reasonably good copy of them out of a dry cedar board and some leather lacing.

He chopped a hole in the ice about two hundred yards from shore and had been fishing for less than an hour when he suddenly saw, right beside his left leg, the snow and ice spray up and outwards, as something hit hard and cut a long narrow groove in the icy surface. At nearly the same instant, he heard the loud 'ka-boom' of a heavy rifle shot coming from the distant shoreline. He spun about and looked toward the shoreline, where he could see Fariss, kneeling at the edge of the forest and preparing to fire his big rifle at him again.

"Warrior, go!" Caylen pointed out over the lake to send Warrior out of rifle range, and at the same time, dropping to the lake's icy surface with his feet pointed towards the shore. A moment later, he heard the whooshing sound of the heavy caliber lead bullet as it sailed over his head to eventually plop onto the ice far out on the lake. An instant later the second 'ka-boom' echoed out again, as the sound of the fired rifle's next shot passed directly over his head.

Caylen lay perfectly still for a few moments more before he turned about to see if Warrior was safe. It took him only a second or two to spot the wolf, sitting and waiting for Caylen to recall him, about two hundred yards further out on the lake. He turned to look for Fariss, but could now see no sign of him whatsoever.

He waited about five minutes more before getting cautiously to his feet and waving Warrior in. Watching the shoreline closely for any sign of movement, Caylen gathered in his gear and raced diagonally across the lake towards the protective shelter of the spruce forest. Within a very few minutes he and Warrior were resting safely under the sheltering branches of a large spruce tree. He waited, still trembling, under the tree for at least an hour, and then, hearing and seeing nothing, rose and headed straight for home, looking about fearfully as he proceeded.

Caylen thought long and deeply about what had just occurred. He knew now, without any doubt whatsoever, that Fariss, in his present state of mind, would not hesitate to kill him and Warrior both, if he were given the opportunity. He also knew that if he told his mother of the attempted shooting, she would quite literally tear into Fariss and damn the consequences to her. He decided that he would wait and see what, if anything, Fariss would do or have to say about the shooting.

~*~

When Caylen arrived home, Fariss was already there, sitting in his big chair in front of the fire, cleaning his rifle. As Caylen entered the cabin, Fariss looked up at him and Warrior, but said nothing . Caylen took off his outerwear and boots, waiting a few minutes before saying to Fariss,

"I see you're cleaning your rifle Fariss. Did you get a shot at something?"

"We could use some fresh meat, for a change." Lora interjected, not having any idea of what had just occurred.

"It be none of yer business, but I's did get's a couple of shots at some wolves runnin past out on the lakes," Fariss responded, without looking up.

"Yes, I think I heard both of the shots." Caylen said. "Did you hit any of them?"

"Is you's that stupid?" Fariss asked. "Iffen I's did hits them I's would be skinnin theys hides out now, woudn't I?"

Caylen didn't immediately respond to this statement by Fariss. He knew that it would be best for him to say no more as it would only result in more anger and denials from Fariss.

A moment later, he, changed his mind and decided that he must now, without any further delay, confront this dangerous situation head on. He walked over to the rifle rack and, picking up his little twenty-two-caliber rifle, placed a long rifle cartridge into the rifle's chamber.

With his mother watching in obvious horror and total disbelief at what she was seeing, Caylen, with Warrior close by his side, walked over to stand directly in front of the frowning Fariss, who had been closely watching Caylen's every move.

"What you thinks yer doin, boy?" he asked. "You's knows yer not to be havin a loaded rifle in the house."

"You know and I know just what it was that you shot at twice out on the lake, and we both know that it certainly was not wolves." said Caylen, tilting his little rifle so that its muzzle was only about two feet from Fariss and pointing directly at the front of his head. As Fariss watched, he placed his forefinger lightly on the trigger of the fully cocked weapon.

"Turn dat rifle away boy, fore I gets really mad." Fariss said, with cold perspiration beginning to bead up and run down his forehead.

At this point, Warrior appropriately began the low guttural growling that Fariss knew was intended just for him and was the prelude to an attack.

"I think perhaps I will wait until you move outside before I 'accidentally' mistake you for a wolf and shoot you. Or, maybe I'll just give Warrior permission to attack you where you are." said Caylen. "I don't want to get Mom's good furniture all wet and bloody." \

"Caylen! My God! What do you think you're doing?" Lora exclaimed, horrified at what she had just seen and heard.

"Just wait, Mom. I'll explain all this to you in a few minutes when I'm finished dealing with Fariss."

"Give Mom your rifle, Fariss. Give it to her right now!" yelled Caylen, as Warrior moved even closer to Fariss, growling even louder.

"Okay, okay. You's is crazy, boy! Fariss said, handing Lora his rifle.

"Now go over and get all the bullets for his rifle, Mom." said Caylen.

"What's you's goin to do, Caylen boy? I's needs dat rifle and those there bullets for hunting foods and fer protections." Fariss whined.

"I'll keep it safe, but you won't be able to have it unless I say so." Caylen replied, as his mother took from Fariss the box of bullets that sat on the floor beside his chair.

"Now Fariss," added Caylen. "I'm going to tell you something and you had better listen to me very carefully because I will only say it once, and your very life depends on you hearing and understanding me. Now, are you sure you are listening?"

"I'se hearing you boy." Farris said, glowering at him a Lora stood, her mouth agape in amazement at what her young son was doing.

Lora did not fully understand what the reasons were for Caylen's current actions, but she knew that something quite serious must have occurred while he was outside on the ice. She finally sat her shaking body down at the table, deciding to wait until the currant situation was concluded before asking for details

"I'm going to be watching you every moment that you are awake and Warrior will be watching you whenever you are asleep or outside," Caylen said. "And if you ever do anything to hurt Mom, Warrior or me, either Warrior or I will surely kill you and feed your rotten carcass to the ravens and foxes."

At this, Fariss slumped back in his chair, muttering to himself but saying nothing intelligible that anyone could hear or understand. Seeing that he was totally in charge of the situation, Caylen decided to press his advantage just a little further.

"Do you understand everything I just said?" he asked. "I want to be sure that you completely understand that if you ever try anything like that again, that I will surely kill you!"

Fariss just looked at Caylen and nodded his understanding. Satisfied that he was now well in control of the situation, Caylen put his outdoor clothes back on and took from his mother Fariss's big rifle and cartridges. He then turned to Warrior and said to the snarling wolf, pointing at Fariss.

"Watch him Warrior. Don't let him move until I return."

Aware that Warrior understood his instructions perfectly, Caylen knew quite well that until he returned, and released him from his orders, Warrior would ensure, with his life, that Fariss did not stir from his chair. Caylen also knew that Fariss understood quite well that his life would be in extreme jeopardy from the wolf should he attempt anything that might provoke Warrior into attacking him.

Caylen went out of the cabin and walked a few feet into the

forest until he was hidden from sight. When he was confident that he could not be seen from the cabin, he quickly stripped down the big Winchester rifle, removing the hammer and mainspring from its mechanism. Placing these items in his pocket, he returned to the cabin and leaned the weapon against the doorframe. He then went to the smokehouse and retrieved a handful of bear fat from the tin that was stored there. Taking a rag from the pile that his mother kept next to the tins of goods in the smokehouse, he covered it with the bear fat and then wrapped the rifle's trigger and spring tightly in the rag, before placing it inside an empty can. He then went into the forest a few feet and buried the can beside the trunk of a large spruce tree.

Returning to the cabin, Caylen took the big rifle inside, and with Fariss glaring at him, placed it back on the wall rack. He also returned the two boxes of ammunition that he had taken. Turning to Fariss and his mother, he said.

"Now Fariss, what I have done has made your rifle incapable of firing. I have removed all of the parts that set off the bullets so it can't be used unless I get those parts back from where I have hidden them, and put them back into your rifle."

"How's you's spects me to gits meat fer eaten?" asked Fariss.

"We don't need any big animals for meat until next fall." Caylen replied. "Our spring and summer foods are fish, bird eggs and dried or smoked meats from last year, so you don't need your gun for a while."

"Whats about if we needs it fer protectin?" Farris asked.

"Well, you're just going to have to make do without it." Caylen said. "I'm not letting you have those parts back until I'm sure that it's safe to do so."

"Why don't you's calls off yer animal so's I's can gets about my works?" Fariss said.

Caylen could see that Fariss was calmed down considerably, and seemed to be his normally quieter self for the moment, at least. He looked at his mother, who was still sitting, wide eyed in wonderment, at the table. She was completely lost for words over what had just occurred. Her pride in Caylen's actions was so great that she thought her heart would burst right out of her chest. She stared at him, realizing that he was rapidly becoming a man, even though he was just thirteen years old. Her pride in him was, to some degree, offset by the realization that he had been forced by circumstances into maturing at a much earlier age than was normal, and that this early maturing was entirely the result of her own previous actions.

"Okay, Warrior, you can relax now," Caylen said. "But I want to tell you once more, Fariss, that we will be watching your every move from now on, and that Warrior will also be watching you, so you had best behave yourself."

"I'se will be good." Fariss said, in as meek and chastised manner as Caylen or Lora had ever heard.

Caylen then, with Fariss listening, gave Lora all of the details about what had occurred out on the ice. Lora's first reaction was to take Caylen out of Fariss's hearing and tell him that they must immediately leave and get back to civilization as soon as possible.

After she had calmed down a bit, the pair decided that, as the lake's ice was getting quite thin in the warm spring air, it would be unsafe for them to attempt the long trek to Carcross at this time, and that it would be better to wait and to reconsider their options at a later time. Especially as they had no real idea of where Carcass was relative to their current location.

~*~

Lora and Caylen's day-by-day lives became much less disturbing following Caylen's confrontation and laying down of the rules to Fariss.

Fariss came and went quite as usual but without his big rifle. As the winter snow and ice rapidly disappeared under the warming rays of the sun and the warm westerly winds, he began to spend more and more time at his placer mine. He rarely spoke to Lora and only spoke to Caylen through Lora, never directly. As Fariss had decided to not contribute to the gathering or catching of the springtime foods, Lora and Caylen were kept busy replenishing their food stocks with Arctic grayling, lake trout, whitefish, spring mushrooms, goose and duck eggs and the forest's edible greens and roots.

Things remained quite calm over the next few weeks. Caylen had another of his dreams, in which he saw the old Indian and the big black wolf again. In this dream, the old Indian asked him if he had received his gift, and asked anew why Adahy had still not come to live with him. Caylen, when he awoke during the night of this dream, realized that the gift the old man was speaking of was, in fact, Warrior, but he was still puzzled as to why the Indian kept asking him to come to him.

Caylen and Lora discussed Fariss's behavior at every opportunity. Lora knew that Fariss's seemingly rational temperament he was currently displaying would not continue, and she feared greatly for Caylen's life. Caylen had, a few days following his confrontation with Fariss, given her all the details of the shooting incident on the ice. After considering and then rejecting the idea of leaving their home for the distant village of Carcross, they formulated a plan whereby Caylen, who assured Lora that he would be okay, would leave the cabin and construct himself a shelter far enough away so as to be safe. Lora knew that Caylen was in possession of all the skills that he would need to survive on his own in the wilds, and that he could and would remain in contact with her whenever Fariss was away from the cabin, and that Caylen could do so without Fariss's knowledge. She was also quite confident that although Fariss hated Caylen with a vengeance and would kill or attempt to kill her son at the first opportunity, he would not, at least for the present, harm her in any way.

It seemed to Caylen that winter had disappeared overnight. The lake that had been frozen completely over one day, was now suddenly wide open, while the alders that grew along the stream were covered with the green leaves of summer. Warrior, now slightly more than a year old, stood a good twenty-eight inches high at the shoulder and exceeded one hundred and fifty pounds in weight. He had still not attained his full adult weight and would easily put on another twenty-five or more pounds before he reached full maturity. It wasn't unheard of for a male Arctic timber wolf to reach or exceed one hundred and seventy pounds weight, and it now appeared that Warrior was to be one of those animals who would match or even exceed that weight. When Caylen allowed him to run freely in the forest as he usually did each morning, Warrior would strike out in whatever direction the winds were blowing to conduct a regular patrol, marking is territory as he traveled. He would often pick up the scent of a hare, a caribou, a moose or some other animal that had trespassed into his personal territory. When this happened, he would pursue the unfortunate animal and chase it completely out of his area, or, if his hunger got the best of him and the animal was not too large for him to handle on his own, he would take it down, kill it, and then consume it , or part of it. He could, as could other timber wolves of his size, easily consume between ten and fifteen percent of his own body weight at one meal. He would also carry back to the cabin, portions of whatever he had killed to share with Caylen.

Caylen, at first, had no idea what he was supposed to do with the fresh, bloody pieces of meat that Warrior brought to him. He was quickly made to understand, by Warrior, however, that if he didn't not accept the gift of food, Warrior would be deeply insulted and would then sulk for the remainder of the day. Caylen soon realized that it was much better for Warrior and his personal relations if he gratefully accepted these gifts from Warrior, even if he later disposed of them or, at a later time, gave them back to the ever-hungry, still growing wolf to consume.

It was about three weeks after Caylen's confrontation with Fariss that he decided to take Warrior and explore the cliffs that lay to the Northwest of their cabin. He announced his intentions to Lora and Fariss the prior evening, and packed some food and small items in his small backpack.

Fariss, on the morning of Caylen's exploratory trip, had risen and as was normal, disappeared from the cabin even before Caylen's early start.

Caylen was soon picking his way along the steep and, in some areas nearly vertical, cliffs that ran along a deep canyon that had been formed over thousands of years by running water from the melting glaciers that lay further to the West. At one point, he sat, with his back resting against a vertical rock wall that extended hundreds of feet above him. His position permitted him a spectacular view of the canyon and the lake that lay beside Fariss's remote cabin home. He could even see, on the Eastern horizon the wide expanse of the huge Tagish Lake.

As he was finishing his smoked trout sandwich, he could hear the ever-present black northern ravens high above and behind him, calling out excitedly to each other. He knew that these birds often followed forest travelers in anticipation of finding food. He stood and began to move away from the rock wall to see if he could see what the ruckus was about, when suddenly several large granite boulders came crashing down over the side of the cliff to land on and flatten the very spot where he had been sitting only a moment earlier. He looked up to see if he could see what had caused the rockslide that would surely have crushed him, had he not moved at the sound of the ravens' squawks. As he scanned the cliff's rim, he suddenly saw the head and shoulders of Fariss peering down at him from the point where he was sure the rocks had originated. When Fariss saw Caylen looking up at him, Fariss quickly pulled back and disappeared from sight, leaving Caylen shaken but unhurt.

Caylen decided quickly, that he would return home and await Fariss's arrival so that he would immediately confront him about what he had just tried to do. There was no question that Fariss had just attempted to kill him for the second time. He also knew that if he didn't confront and deal with Fariss immediately, Fariss would continue in his attempts until he was finally successful and Caylen was dead. He didn't relish having to tell his mother of the incident, but couldn't see how he could avoid her finding out about it and still confront Fariss.

When he arrived home, he found Fariss already there, sitting in his chair by the fire. He looked up as Caylen and Warrior entered, but said nothing.

Lora, totally unaware that anything unusual had occurred said to Caylen,

"Your home early. I thought you were going to spend the entire day exploring the cliffs."

"Yes, that's what I started out to do." replied Caylen. "But something unexpected happened and I decided to come home early."

" Oh? What happened?" Lora asked. "Did you get your feet wet?"

"No, I was nearly hit by some falling rocks and figured it was just too dangerous for me to be out there." Caylen said, watching Fariss's face as he spoke.

"Yeah, dem loose rocks up there on those cliffs can falls on you's just about anytimes." Fariss said, with a smirk.

"Especially if they're pushed by someone!" retorted Caylen. "Where did you go this morning Fariss? Were you perhaps following me?"

"I'se wents fer a walk up my gold creek lookin fer more places to digs." replied Fariss. "I'se was no place nears you's ."

"Well then, I guess you must have a twin brother that you don't know about who lives up on the cliffs, because I saw someone who looked just like you and was dressed just like you, looking over the edge just after those rocks came down and nearly hit me." Caylen said.

At that, Fariss said no more, but slumped down in his chair and stared into the brightly burning fire.

"Are you serious, Caylen? Are you okay? You're not hurt, are you?" Lora anxiously asked, coming over to stand by him.

"No, I'm fine, Mom." Caylen responded. "But I'm not to sure just what I should do. Maybe I should tell Warrior to kill Fariss." he added loudly, so as to ensure that Fariss could hear him.

Fariss said nothing in response to this statement by Caylen, but continued to stare into the fire.

Lora then signaled quietly to Caylen that they should wait until Fariss was out of earshot to further discuss the matter .

The following day, after Fariss had gone up to his gold claim, having said nothing further about the incident, Lora and Caylen talked at length regarding what they could possibly do about Fariss and his very obvious hatred toward Caylen.

"We should just pack up and leave as soon as we can." stated Lora . "Before he goes completely mad and kills us."

"But, it's really just me that he hates enough to kill." said Caylen. "He really doesn't hate you, Mom."

"I'm still terribly afraid of him, and I'm really afraid for you." Lora replied. "Perhaps we could take the canoes and go back to Carcross."

"We can't do that." Caylen answered. "Fariss has hidden the paddles somewhere in the bush and, besides, I don't really know how to get to Carcross from here."

"Well, we have to do something before Fariss does manage to kill you." said Lora. "Do you remember what we discussed doing a while back?"

"Yes. Perhaps that's what we should do. It's spring, so I'll have lots of time to find a good place to build a warm shelter, and get food for winter."

"I'm certain Fariss will want to go out for supplies soon, so that would be the best opportunity for you to go. I'm sure he won't mind if we tell him we would rather stay here and let him go out by himself." Lora said.

"Okay. Let's do it that way, then. I'll start looking for a good spot to build on, and I'll sneak some supplies and equipment out that he won't notice are gone. Then, when he goes, we can build a cabin for me." Caylen said.

"But, how will we keep in touch with each other if you are living somewhere else?" asked Lora." I will be really concerned about you if I am unable to see you very often."

"I'll sneak up to the cabin, and if I see the window curtains open, I'll know that Fariss is out. Then, I can come in and visit." said Caylen. "Warrior will stand guard and let me know if Fariss is returning, so I can leave before he arrives. Warrior will also protect me from Fariss if he does sneak up on us. I'll have my rifle, and besides, I'll take Fariss's big rifle and his bullets too.

Over the next several weeks, Caylen managed to gather a good supply of tools and preserved foods together. He also began traveling much further abroad than he usually did. He knew that he had to find a secluded site that was accessible to food supplies and water, yet the site needed to be within a day's walk to Fariss's and Lora's home, and still be not easy to see or find. On his third exploratory trip out to the Northwest, Caylen found a medium-sized stream that he followed down to a large lake that ran off to the East. At the point where the stream entered the lake, he could see, in the clear, deep water, large lake trout hovering just off the bottom, while numerous rainbow-colored grayling flashed about them, feeding on the many emerging insect larva. He explored the surrounding area extensively, finally determining that it was good a spot as he would probably find. It was about seven miles from Fariss's cabin, in an area that Fariss seldom traveled. and the route to the site was through a gap that, from its approach, appeared impassible. It was only after arriving in the narrow entrance that one could see that the opening led through to a large valley, which that contained streams, rivers and the lake.

Caylen decided, once he found this spot, to begin working immediately on his home-to-be. He located, near the site, a rocky area that contained a large number of flat rocks of three or four inches thickness. He toiled for three days, hauling large numbers of these flat rocks to his chosen building site, as he knew they would be invaluable in his construction efforts. His selected site was on a small knoll located only fifty feet or so from a large pool on the big stream that flowed into the lake that was only about one hundred and seventy feet downstream. The site was well hidden from the lake by a thick stand of tall black spruce and the ever-present alders. The surrounding forest was comprised of more of the closely spaced, slender black spruce trees that extended skyward forty to fifty feet before their branches completely blocked out the sky. Caylen felled over eighty of these straight and easily peeled trees with the axe and saw that he had taken from Fariss's tool supplies. He was able, before Fariss's departure to Carcross, to stockpile on the site, most of the natural forest materials that he would need to construct his new home.

It was early morning in the month of June when Fariss announced to Lora that he was leaving, by himself, for Carcross that very morning. This announcement was quite surprising, as she had really expected him to insist that she travel with him. She had anticipated that he would not want Caylen along, but his saying that he was going by himself was, while welcome, not at all expected. He did, however, ask her to give him, before his departure, a list of items and foodstuffs that she felt would be needed over the following year. This request by Fariss also surprised her as she really expected him to continue acting in a odd manner. To her astonishment, however, his behavior towards her and Caylen during the days just prior to his departure showed considerable improvement, to the point where he was almost pleasant toward them both.

Once she had prepared and given Fariss her shopping list that she had supplemented with some additional items she knew she would need for her household after Caylen took what he needed from her current supplies, Fariss immediately paddled off up the lake without further ado, raising his little sail as soon as he was clear of the sheltering shoreline.

Lora and Caylen both sighed with relief as they watched Fariss sail off down the lake. They knew that the trip would take Fariss, traveling alone, three weeks or more. Lora was elated, as they were to now have at least those three weeks of relief from Fariss's angry outbursts and mood swings. It also gave them a three-week window for Caylen to get himself a new home built and get relocated to it.

Chapter 10

Alone

Once Lora and Caylen were confident that Fariss was really gone and that they would have about three weeks of uninterrupted time alone, they began, in earnest, to move supplies and materials to Caylen's new home site. After they had all of the essential items relocated and a temporary shelter constructed, Lora packed a few personal items of her own and they both moved into the shelter at the site where Caylen planned to build his cabin . Lora figured that before Fariss returned, she could stay at the site and assist Caylen as much as she could to construct his new home and get relocated.

They began their construction by clearing and leveling off a twelve foot by fourteen-foot pad on top of the little knoll that Caylen had selected as a building site. Caylen then excavated this area down about two feet into the ground and leveled off the bottom that was to be his floor. He then began to place the flat rocks that he had previously carried to the site side by side to form, at one end of the hole, a rock fireplace that would serve as a cooking fire, and also heat the little cabin during the cold winter months.

Caylen used, at Lora's suggestion, some of the sticky red clay that they found in the feeder creek as a sealing and bonding agent between each layer of the fireplace rocks. He soon realized that this clay would not only bond the rocks together, but also provided, once it had dried, an impenetrable seal against the outside winds, weather and insects. As Caylen constructed the all-important fireplace, Lora carried multiple pails of dry beach sand from the lakeshore to the excavation, and layered it about two inches thick over the entire floor area to provide a dry, porous surface for the soon-to-be little home.

Caylen, while using the sticky red clay on his fireplace, gave some consideration to mixing some of the clay and the dry sand together and then leveling the moist mixture over the floor area and allowing it to dry. His idea, as he explained to Lora, was that, once the mixture dried, it would provide him with a hard, level floor for his cabin that could easily be kept neat and clean. They discussed this idea for some time before deciding hat it could be easily be done later on in the construction process, if time permitted, but their priorities should be to just get the cabin built.

Once the fireplace was completed to Caylen's satisfaction, he began to cut and place his previously cut logs in a horizontal fashion, rather than vertically as many builders of the North did. He felt, and Lora agreed, that they would be much easier to chink and seal against the cold winter winds than would the more common vertical method of building.

It took them only four days to erect the cabin walls. Caylen took Lora's suggestions regarding the roof construction and made the front wall about three feet higher than the back in order to provide a goodly drainage slope to the roof. Once the walls were in place, the pole roof took another two days to install. The hardest work of all was now just ahead. They had to carry hundreds of pails of dry earth to the roof and layer it completely over. When this was done, they went down to the lakeshore where Caylen, earlier in his exploratory trips, had discovered a small, grassy meadow. Using his spade, he carefully cut long, narrow strips of the grassy sod into manageable pieces that he and Lora then carried back to the cabin on a stretcher-like device they constructed of two poles and a piece of canvas. and placed, grass side up, on the earthen roof. They carried many pails of water to encourage the freshly planted roof sod to take root in the soil and stabilize the roof against erosion .

Cutting the door and little window opening was the final chore. Once he hung the caribou skin flap over the door and window openings, the cabin was complete and ready to move into. Some minor finishing touches remained but, as Caylen explained to Lora,

"I can finish it off myself, Mom. I'll wait until the wall logs dry out more before I chink them, and I can build my furniture as I need it. Now, let's celebrate by cooking some trout on my new fireplace."

It had taken them fifteen days to construct Caylen's new home. It took them another three days of traveling back and forth, carrying supplies and foodstuffs, from the home cabin to the new one before they could claim to be ready. Even Warrior was beginning to show signs of tiring, as he was required to carry more than his share of heavy items in his backpacks.

Caylen also retrieved the trigger assembly for Fariss's rifle; re-assembling the big weapon and then taking it and all it's ammunition with him back to his new home.

He was now completely prepared and ready to move. Lora, as the expected final departure of Caylen neared, was beginning to get quite emotional about his leaving, and began to express to him, quite vocally, her concerns.

"What will you do if you get cold this winter? What are you going to do for food? I won't be there to cook for you. What will you do if you get sick or hurt yourself? Do you think you can catch enough fish and meat for both Warrior and yourself? What if you get attacked by a grizzly bear? Do you have enough salt? Do you have all your socks? Do you think perhaps that I should go with you? I'm really afraid for your safety!"

Caylen allowed Lora to vent her feelings and frustrations completely before gently admonishing her about her concerns over him. He had earlier given some serious thought to asking her to move with him, but reasoning had finally negated this idea. He knew that Fariss, upon his return, would be quite happy to find out that Caylen had left, but that he would not be able to tolerate or to permit Lora to leave him. He would stop at nothing, should she leave him. He would kill them both should he find them, and Caylen knew that, should he really want to, Fariss, with all his wilderness skills, could easily track him down. He also knew that, while Fariss might initially be very angry about Caylen's taking his tools and supplies, his elation at Caylen's departure would soon cause him to forget any idea of revenge that he might have.

They waited as long as they dared before Caylen took his final goodbye

Giving his mother a warm hug, he promised her that he would return as often as he could to visit and assure her that all was well. He had previously varied his route each and every time that he and Lora traveled back and forth from his new cabin in order to leave as little trace as possible for Fariss to follow. On this, his final departure from the home cabin, he again chose a different route that took him far to the west of his new home. In addition to concealing his trail, he also wanted to explore this area and locate the source of the large stream that flowed past his new home. He climbed far past the stream on which Fariss's sluice box was located, noting the many new "digs" that Fariss made in his most recent unsuccessful attempts to find again his lost gold source. The stream finally petered out at the base of a steep hill that Caylen decided to climb over, heading even more westerly to where he could see the rocky terrain falling away far in the distance. Once he finally reached what seemed to be the highest point of land in that particular area, he climbed atop a large rocky knoll to where he could see for miles around. To the South and Southeast, he could see, far in the distance, over the heavily treed green of the spruce forest, the lake on which Fariss's cabin was situated. Away to the North and Northwest, he could see huge snow-capped peaks that appeared to block the entire horizon. To the Northeast, however, all he could see was rolling forestlands and the big lake where his new cabin was located. He could also see, to the West of his cabin's location on the big lake, another much smaller lake. Reasoning that this lake probably drained into the bigger lake , he decided to head for it and follow its outlet stream, hopefully, home to his cabin.

He reached the smaller lake late in the afternoon. Deciding that it would be unwise to continue after darkness had fallen, he quickly constructed a small night camp and consumed the cold meal Lora had stowed in Warrior's pack.

When Caylen awoke, it was around two in the morning. The night was quite cold, still and bright under the northern skies . The nearly full moon added to the beauty of the night, as he lay abed, recalling his dream of a few minutes prior. He had again seen the old Indian and the huge black wolf that looked so much like Warrior. In this, his most recent dream, the old Indian had spoken again to him, saying,

"Adahy, my son. You have finally begun to find your own way on this earth. Now, you must continue on your quest until I send for you."

The dream vision had then faded away only to return again a few moments later with the old Indian speaking to him further .

"You must wait for two moons to pass, and then you shall return to your mother's side for two days and two nights, during which time you shall find Wildflower and give her peace,"

Caylen lay awake for over two hours, pondering this last dream and wondering just what on earth it could mean. He wondered about Wildflower and her brother's search for her. He wondered about her connection to Fariss and where she could possibly be found. He also wondered what connection there could possibly be between the old Indian of his dreams, himself, Fariss, Lora and Wildflower, wherever she was. As sleep began to finally deaden his senses, and Warrior had again snuggled close by his side, he heard, or thought he heard, the deep, long, mournful wail of a mature timber wolf in the distant moonlit night.

The following day broke bright and clear, promising to be a great day for exploring the surrounding thinner, more open forest. The dense forests had, at this higher elevation, given way to the occasional green, grassy meadows that were, at times, frequented by the huge mountain grizzly bears. These big animals loved to come out and simply bask in the warm sunshine and graze on whatever green grasses and edible roots they could find in the meadows. They probably would have also enjoyed dining on young Caylen, had they been given the opportunity. Warrior's presence, however, and his constant vigilance, never failed to alert Caylen to the grizzlies' presence and to provide him with the warnings he needed to avoid becoming lunch for one of the big bears. He did catch a glimpse of two of these animals and gave some consideration to using Fariss's big rifle to collect one for its useful fat and quite edible meat. His unfamiliarity with the area and his not knowing exactly how far distant his cabin was, however, stayed his hand.

Maintaining his direction of travel for three hours brought him to the edge of the clear blue waters of the small lake he had observed the day before from atop the high point of land. Following the shoreline around, he eventually reached a small stream flowing down a steep embankment from the north side of the lake. Continuing on down, past many rocky rapids and small waterfalls, the little stream entered a much larger, slower traveling stream that continued downwards over a gravelly bottom. This stream meandered along ever downwards, but also formed numerous large pools in which Caylen could see the many small and large shapes of fish darting about and laying on the bottom. He soon began to recognize the area where he had built his cabin and was, within a very few minutes, resting comfortably on the floor of his unfurnished little home .

Caylen spent the next three weeks constructing furniture, a small smokehouse and a toilet. He also found nearby, a small cave that would serve him well as a cold storage area for his foodstuffs. The cave was approximately forty feet deep into a rocky cliff near the stream that flowed past his new home. He had even found, still frozen solid at the rear of the cave, rear, a solid wall of clear ice. He quickly took possession of this natural refrigerator for the cold storage of his food supplies . He fashioned a log door that would keep small animals from raiding and eating his stored food supplies. Bears were about the only animals that he feared might still be able to remove his door and loot his food stocks .

His next project was the gathering and preserving of his next winter's foods. Since he had no gill nets or even a canoe from which he could use to set the nets if he had any, he fashioned three long, weighted lines with two hooks spaced about ten feet apart and a rock weight on each line.

Using his fishing rod, he then caught a number of small grayling from the stream and cut them into pieces for bait. Hooking a piece of grayling to each hook, he threw the rock and baited hooks far out into the lake and fastened the shore end of the lines to a tall, flexible, slender willow tree. These set lines produced at least two large lake trout for his smokehouse each day and occasionally four or five. In addition, while waiting for the trout to bite, he kept busy gathering and drying the many cranberries, mushrooms and other edible berries that grew in profusion along the nearby streams. He also, for entertainment, food and bait, spent many hours catching the multicolored grayling that frequented the nearby streams.

Warrior, during all this time, seemed to be having the time of his life. Caylen now permitted his wolf pet much more freedom than he had when they resided with Fariss. He had always been apprehensive about what Fariss might do to the animal, should he catch him outside and away from Caylen. He had also been much reassured about his own safety when Warrior was nearby whenever he was in Fariss's presence. Caylen knew that Warrior could easily protect himself, should Fariss attempt to harm him, but he also knew that his wolf pet could still be shot or speared or stabbed, should Fariss catch him unawares. Now on their own, he had no such fear for Warrior's safety so he permitted him to roam about freely during the daylight hours. To his surprise, he found that, while Warrior seemed to appreciate this new found independence, he seldom left Caylen alone for more than two or three hours at any one time. He seemed perfectly content to follow and assist Caylen in whatever he was doing. This helping proved, at times, to be more of a nuisance than an aid, especially when he would drop a mouthful of saliva-covered berries into Caylens collecting pail! He was, however, quite helpful in the gathering of wood and the packing back to the cabin fresh-caught trout.

These summer days and weeks spent on his own, in just the company of his pet Warrior were some of the most enjoyable times that Caylen had spent in the North. While he was compelled to work harder than he ever had before, he was working for himself, his pet wolf and no one else. While he did miss his mother's presence very much and thought about her constantly, he found that his new-found freedom of movement very calming, as compared to his previous tumultuous life with Fariss constantly attempting to control his every move.

As summer passed, Caylen filled his cold storage cave with smoked and dried fish, dried berries and mushrooms. He also began to think about procuring bigger game such as moose, caribou and bear. He felt at first that he would forego the moose and just get caribou and bear meat, but then reconsidered, as he recalled Fariss saying that the caribou didn't always show up. He decided that it would be better to have too much meat than not enough, so he intended to get at least one moose and possibly two caribou, as well as fat bear, later in the fall.

He continued to explore his new home area in every direction save South where Fariss and Lora resided. He did not wish to accidentally leave any indication of his presence that Fariss might find. He knew that Fariss had considerable tracking skills and should he find any sign of Caylen, he just might, out of curiosity, track him back to his new home. He usually explored off to the North across the stream that flowed past his cabin and into the big lake. He had soon located, about one-half mile from his home, a large willow meadow that was home to a small herd of moose that Warrior thought looked quite tasty. Caylen, however, to Warrior's chagrin, felt that they should wait another month or so before harvesting one of the yearling bulls. He also found signs here, within a reasonable travel distance of his cabin, where some of the migrating caribou had spent previous winters. On one occasion, he swung off to the Northwest and came upon another lake that appeared to be about half the size of the lake he had constructed his cabin on. It was here that he encountered, fishing in the stream that drained this lake, a large black bear. This animal, although it still had at least two months before it would den for the winter, showed huge rippling rolls of fat on its sides and back.

"Perfect," Caylen whispered to Warrior who was expectantly waiting for Caylen to shoot. "This bear will do fine for us in about one more month , so you'll just have to wait a little longer, Warrior."

Recalling his last dream in which the old Indian had told him to return to see his mother, he realized that he had not seen her for nearly two months. Packing a few supplies, he decided that he should trek South and visit her. Wanting to ensure that he could not be back-tracked by Fariss, he traveled North, then West, before heading for his objective. Although Fariss's cabin was only about seven miles as the crow flew, his trip took him nearly two days and over twenty miles of difficult traveling. He arrived at Fariss's cabin just as the sun was dropping behind the Westerly Mountains. As he lay hidden in the trees, he could see that the single window's curtains were drawn tightly closed, Lora's signal to him that Fariss was home. Moving quietly away, Caylen set up a small night camp about a mile down the lake from the cabin. He slept soundly until the morning sun's warm rays woke both he and Warrior. Leaving his gear in the camp, he made his way quietly to his hiding place near the cabin. He had waited only a few moments when he observed Fariss leaving for his placer mine with a brand-new rifle slung over his shoulder. He then saw his mother looking out the small window as she drew back the curtains.

Lora, when Caylen had left to live on his own, had wept off and on for three days. She felt completely responsible for everything that occurred since they departed Greenwood over two years earlier. Caylen, although he seemed for the most part, to enjoy his life in the North, had been forced to mature much sooner than he should have and had missed a huge part of what could only be called a normal upbringing." She realized now that she had made a terribly wrong choice when she chose to marry and relocate into the wilds of the North with Fariss, but could not now conceive any means by which she could escape from her current situation and return her life to some form of normalcy . She thought for a time that she should leave with Caylen and try to live on their own, but in her heart, she knew that such a life would, in the long term, be impossible. She wondered if she and Caylen could have taken the canoes without the paddles and attempted to sail to safety, or if they could have made some paddles on their own. A million thoughts and ideas crossed her mind over those few days but none seemed to provide her with anything but a deeper sense of dread over what might transpire in the near future. As the days passed, she carefully opened and fastened back the curtains of the cabin's single window so that Caylen, should he wish to visit, would know it was safe to do so. As time went by and neither Caylen nor Fariss appeared, she grew more and more depressed and unhappy with her situation. She grew more concerned about Caylen' welfare each day until, on the afternoon of the seventh day after Caylen left, she spotted the sail of the big freighter canoe as it raced along, ahead of a stiff following north wind toward her .

Fariss, as he came ashore, appeared to be quite alright and in good humor. Lora had already observed from previous trips, that his temperament seemed to take a dramatic turn for the better whenever he was away from the cabin for any length of time . This improvement usually lasted a few weeks before he would gradually return to his normal dysfunctional self, and again begin to have his nightmares and to torment anyone near him.

As Fariss stepped out of the canoe, he greeted Lora with a huge smile and a hug and looked about for Caylen and Warrior. Seeing neither, he worked at unloading their supplies for a few minutes before asking.

"Where be Caylen at? He shoulds be here's helping to's unloads these here supplies."

"He decided that he should leave your house, so he has gone away to live on his own " said Lora, not wishing to give any more information to Fariss than what he asked for, but also not wanting Fariss to think that she was trying to hide anything from him.

"Why's he done that for?" asked Fariss. "He's too little to be's out on his own"

"He felt that he was causing you and I too much trouble and that it would be best for us if he left. And so did I." Lora said, choosing her words carefully so as not to anger Fariss. "I gave him some of your tools and supplies to help him out, as I knew you woudn't mind." she added.

"Jest whats did you's give him?"

"I let him take one of your axes, one of your saws, some salt and some of last year's left-over food supplies." Lora said. "I also told him to take your big rifle, as I knew you would buy another one while you were in Whitehorse." she added, fearing this last personal item of Fariss's that Caylen had taken would really set him off.

"Well, all dats okay," Fariss responded. "I'se did gets me a brand-new rifle. Where bouts did he goes to?"

"I'm not sure exactly where he went. I have not see him since he left and I am quite concerned for him. He is not even fourteen years old yet and shouldn't be on his own at that age." Lora said, quite surprised at Fariss's seemingly good natured reaction and concern.

"He's be a big lad and he's be real good in the bush fer someone young as he be." Fariss said, "He's got more smarts than most all grown mens I'se has met. "

Lora thought that Fariss seemed to be accepting Caylen's departure with considerably more graciousness than she had expected. She was unsure if he was actually being sincere about Caylen's departure, or if he were simply leading her on by saying what he knew she wanted to hear. She decided to test his display of sudden generosity and apparent benevolence by asking him a few questions about Caylen's departure and possible return.

"Fariss, how would you feel about Caylen coming back to see us once in a while?"

"Dat's okay, long as he leaves that mean wolf dog of his outsides the house. " Fariss replied.

"Perhaps he'd give you your rifle back if I asked him." Lora said, thinking that she might as well broach that touchy subject.

"No, he's should be keeping it fer himself case he's be needin it fer big animals." replied Fariss. "Sides, I's got me a brand-new 38/55 repeatin rifle that's lots better than that old 45/70 that he's took."

Lora was quite astonished at Fariss's easy going acceptance and forgiveness of all that had occurred prior to and during his buying trip. She did, however, acknowledge to herself that this sudden change in his behavior was quite typical of him and that he could just as easily, and probably would, soon revert back to his old mean, miserable self. She realized that he must be suffering from some kind of mental disability and that something specific or perhaps many things could set him off into one of his rages or spells of depression. She also realized that, for some unknown reason, whenever he left his wilderness cabin for any extended period, he would usually be quite okay for some time following his return.

Fariss had had a good trip to Carcross and Whitehorse. The North winds had been quite cooperative and, for the most part, he had only to steer his canoes during his long journey. He had, fortunately, not encountered Wildflower's brothers in Carcross, but he had heard that one of them had been shot and seriously wounded during the previous year, and that he barely managed to survive. It had, all things considered, been as pleasant a trip as he had ever had. His bad dreams had ceased almost immediately after he departed from his wilderness cabin, permitting him to once more get a good sound night's sleep. The ceasing of his terrible dreams and his visions of Wildflower affected him, his temperament and his day to day living much more than even he realized. Fariss could not, had he wanted to, even begin to explain to Lora the sudden shifts in his temperament. All he knew was that, for some unknown reason, he did not, when away from his cabin, suffer the nightly dreams and nightmares about Wildflower. He only knew that he always felt much better about himself and everyone else when he was not at home. He was quite sincere, and meant what he said about not minding that Lora had given some of his things to Caylen Nor did he see anything wrong with Caylen's striking out on his own. His recollections of his cruelty toward Warrior and his attempted killing of Caylen were now only vague memories, memories that he was not entirely sure were even real. If someone had questioned him about the particulars of those incidents concerning Warrior and Caylen, his response would most probably have been,

"I'se don't remembers nothin bout dat." And, in reality, that response would have probably been the truth. His short-term memories were just that--very short term. His long-term memories, however, were still quite vivid and clear in his mind. He easily remembered pushing Wildflower out of the cabin on that frigid winter's night long ago. He also clearly remembered placing her stiff cold body in the trench he had dug in his cabin floor. Her serene, solidly frozen face was etched clearly in his mind. It seemed, for all time, never to give him any peace or to allow him a quiet night's sleep again in his cabin. He even remembered placing some of Wildflower's personal belongings alongside her and then again, every few inches above her, as he covered her body with the cabin's soil. He also seemed unable, or unwilling, to relate the death of and his burial of Wildflower to his persistent nightmares and bad dreams of her.

When Caylen observed Fariss leaving for his daily mining trip, he knew that he had at least an eight hour period during which he could visit his mother. Telling Warrior to "stay and watch for Fariss," he entered the cabin, greeting his surprised, elated mother with a "hi, Mom. How have you been?"

Lora dropped the dishrag she had been holding and grabbed Caylen, hugging him tightly and saying,

" Oh, Caylen, I've been so worried about you. Are you alright? You're not hurt are you? Is Warrior alright? Are you hungry? Sit down and tell me everything, while I make us some tea and get you something to eat."

"Slow down, Mom. I'm okay, Warrior's okay, everything's fine. Yes, I'm a little hungry and yes, I will sit down." Caylen responded happily, glad to see his mother was doing well, and even gladder to taste her excellent cooking again.

"I see Fariss is back and that he's gotten himself a new rifle."

"Yes, but he seems to have forgotten pretty much everything that occurred between you and him before he left for Carcross." Lora said. "It's quite odd but he didn't seem to mind at all that you took those tools, supplies and his old rifle."

" I wouldn't trust him, or anything that he says," Caylen answered.

"I don't blame you at all because I find his present manner quite surprising and puzzling." Lora said. "I think that if he walked in right now, he would greet you and would probably want to hear all about your adventures since you left. He actually seemed quite concerned about your welfare when I told him that you had left to be on your own." she added.

"Well, I still don't think that I want him to find me here just yet." Caylen said. "Let's see what happens when you tell him I came for a visit today. You can tell me about his reaction to finding out that I visited you on my next visit."

~*~

Caylen and Lora spent the next five or six hours bringing each other up to date about what had happened since Caylen's departure almost two months ago. As the late afternoon sun began to cast its long shadows across the cabin's clearing, Caylen arose and promised his mother that he would return again in about two weeks. Giving her a hug and a kiss, he exited the cabin and hurried off through the darkening forest, whistling for Warrior, who was already bounding along beside him.

When Fariss returned home that night, Lora told him all the details of Caylen's visit.

Fariss, as she had anticipated, seemed quite okay with the visit and even asked how Caylen was doing on his own and why he hadn't stayed for supper and for the night.

The following two weeks went by quickly for Caylen. He was anxious to get back again to see his mother and to taste her "home cooking" once more. He had not realized until he visited her just how much he had missed her company, and her cooking, during that first month away.

Chapter 11

The Freeing of Wildflower

What Fariss didn't know was that the two brothers of Wildflower, Lokni and Kosumi were aware all along that he was in Carcross that summer. Kosumi was completely recovered from the bullet wound that Fariss had inflicted on him the previous year, but his shattered shoulder still ached enough on occasion to cause him many a sleepless night. The two brothers vowed to themselves that they would find their sister Wildflower even if it took the remainder of their lives. They reported her disappearance and the wounding of Kosumi to the Northwest Mounted Police detachment in Whitehorse, but as they could give no specific information as to Fariss's whereabouts, the police were unable to do anything but transmit a "wanted for questioning" poster regarding Fariss to other Northern communities.

When Fariss returned to Carcross and then left for home with his winter's supplies, the two native brothers watched him leave from their hiding place without confronting him. They knew that if they gave him a day or two lead, they, with their considerable wilderness skills, would, in all likelihood, eventually be able to find his home's location. It would take every bit of their tracking skills and might take considerable time, but they knew that they, given sufficient time and reasonably good weather, could, with a little luck and a lot of perseverance, locate Fariss's wilderness home and, hopefully, their lost sister, Wildflower.

Lokni and Kosumi waited two full days before they set out on Fariss's trail. They knew they might be away for some time, so they packed their canoe for a long trip, taking plenty of supplies. Each of them also took along their big hunting rifles and plenty of ammunition, in the event they needed to protect themselves and for shooting food animals. As their canoe was not equipped with a sail, they were obliged to rely on their own paddling efforts to propel the craft down the lake. This meant that Fariss's trail, wherever it led them, would probably take them much longer than it had Fariss, assuming they could even find signs of his passing.

It took the two brothers two and one-half days to find Fariss's first campsite on the point of land that marked the start of Tagish Lake and the East end of Nares Lake. They easily spotted the framework of poles that Fariss utilized for his shelter when he stayed at this location. It took the a further five days to reach and locate his last camp at the mouth of the river draining Fantail Lake and the smaller lake that Fariss's cabin was on. Not knowing that Fariss's route was up this river, the pair continued to explore further down the huge Tagish Lake for another three days before returning to this last camp. As they had found no sign of Fariss south of this camp, they correctly assumed that he had entered the river, and proceeded upstream toward Fantail Lake. Once they reached Fantail Lake, the pair spent another frustrating two days examining this lake's southern shoreline and its western feeder stream, finding nothing.

As they returned, searching the northern shoreline, they happened upon the small, deep stream that entered the lake quite near its outlet river. Realizing that unless they had, during their previous few days' searching, completely overlooked any signs of him, that this had to be Fariss's route, the duo began, at this point, to be extra cautious as they moved silently up this stream and into Fariss's home grounds. Once they encountered the smaller lake they wisely decided to hide their canoe, make camp and proceed to search the north shore on foot. It was about noon when they found the first signs of human occupation.

As they passed through a small stream that entered the lake, they could see where someone had excavated a number of holes along the creek's gravel shore. As this was quite obviously someone's digging efforts where they were searching for gold along the creek, the two brothers knew that they were likely closing in on Fariss Lubak's wilderness home.

Fariss had already left for his placer mine and his new "digs" when Lokni and Kosumi stumbled into Caylen's hideout campsite about a mile East of Fariss's cabin. It was almost exactly two weeks since his first visit and he had promised his mother that he would return in two weeks.

Caylen had traveled the entire distance from his cabin on the previous day and had not arrived at his little camp until well after dark. As a result, he was extremely tired and had slept in much later than he would have liked. The low rumble of Warrior's warning growls and his pet's cold nose nuzzling at his face awakened him. As he came quickly out of his deep sleep, he could see that the sun was already well up and that it had removed the dampness of the night from the forest air. As he roused himself out of his bedroll, he grabbed his big 45/70 rifle and changed its safety from the off to the fire position. He signaled Warrior to be still as he waited, silently, at the ready for whatever or whoever it was that had caused Warrior to waken him with his low growls.

It took only another moment or two for Lokni and his brother to find Caylen. The wood smoke scent of his little fire of the previous night led them directly to his camp. The pair entered into Caylen's area with very little noise or warning. They were so quiet as they moved through the thick forest that, if they not come directly into his camp or had not Warrior sensed their approach, Caylen would not have ever known of their presence or their passing. As Lokni and Kosumi came into Caylen's camp, they could see a huge black timber wolf standing beside a well built young boy, who sat, holding in his hands, a very large rifle that was pointed directly at them.

After a long moment, during which no one spoke, Lokni said to Caylen.

"I know you, we spoke to you and Fariss Lubak's wife last summer, just before you shot my brother." said Lokni.

"I also know you, but it was not I who shot your brother. If it had been me who shot him he would not be here now, he would be dead. It was Fariss who shot him." Caylen replied, his rifle steady.

"We meant you or your mother no harm." Kosumi said. "We just wanted to find Wildflower, our sister."

"Well, why don't you put your rifles over by that tree and then sit down so we can talk." Caylen said, beginning to relax and wanting to hear more about "Wildflower."

"Is that animal there a wolf?" asked Lokni.

"Yes, I think so." Caylen replied. "I found him on our doorstep when he was just a puppy. He won't harm you unless I ask him to, or if you try to harm me."

Upon hearing how Caylen had come to possess Warrior, the

two native men looked wide-eyed at each other and then they both, in nearly one voice said to each other.

"Cheveyo, he is a Cheveyo!"

"How in the world did you know his name?" Caylen was puzzled. " Do you know what that means in English?"

"Yes, it means Spirit Warrior," Lokni spoke, "That wolf, he has many powers that only a powerful Shaman could have given him."

"Whats a Shaman?" queried Caylen.

"A Shaman is a powerful native medicine man, who has many great and magical powers." Lokni replied.

"Can they make someone dream?"

"They can make you dream, they can give you nightmares, they can make you crazy if they so wish. It is said that they can also leave their bodies and travel inside the animals and birds of the forests." Kosumi responded.

"Well, I don't know any Shaman, so why don't you tell me about your sister." Caylen said, laying down his rifle.

Lokni and Kosumi spent the next hour explaining to Caylen how Fariss had, four years earlier, purchased their sister from her abusive, drunken, common-law husband in Carcross. All they really knew, subsequent to her purchase by Fariss, was that she had packed her meager belongings, said goodbye to her relatives, and then paddled off down the lake with Fariss. The two brothers also knew that Fariss conducted an annual trip, each summer, to Carcross, so they expected to see their sister accompanying him the following year. When Fariss finally did show up on his annual trip, however, he was alone. What really began to arouse the brothers' suspicions, and caused them to fear that some kind of harm had befallen Wildflower, was Fariss's refusal to even speak to them about her. Their questions to Fariss about their sister and her welfare only seemed to enrage Fariss to the point where he would physically attack them if they even attempted to speak to him. Fariss's obvious reluctance to discuss Wildflowers whereabouts had eventually led to his shooting and the near killing of Kosumi last year.

Hearing this information about their sister from these two men explained to Caylen much of what he had seen of Fariss's attitude towards them, and his apparent reluctance to even speak about Wildflower. What it did not explain or reveal to him, was just what had happened to their sister and where she had gone. He had heard Fariss inadvertently say the name "Wildflower" on a few occasions, but until Lokni and Kosumi told him and his mother that someone named Wildflower was their sister, he had no idea who she was except that she was someone whom Fariss had known.

"Well," he said, after hearing their story. "Knowing Fariss Lubak like I do, perhaps she just left him."

"Wildflower was real good in the bush," Lokni said. "She would have found her way back to Carcross even if it took her a year."

"She may have tried and gotten hurt or drowned." Caylen said.

"Lots of things might have happened." agreed Lokni. "But we think that Fariss be knowing what happened to her and thats why he won't talk to us. We will not be leaving here until we know what happened."

Caylen said nothing more for a few minutes as he pondered all of this new information. He realized that he believed completely everything that Lokni and Kosumi had told him. He could also sense their sincerity and felt that he could trust them completely. As he sat, thinking over just what he could possibly do that would assist these two in their quest for their sister. Warrior suddenly rose from where he had been lying by Caylen's side and walked over to the two native men. As the huge wolf approached them, the pair shrank back in fear for their lives at this sudden move. Warrior, however, as he neared the two men, simply flopped himself down onto the ground in front of them and then laid his big head across each man's legs in turn, giving both of them what could only be described as a huge smile of acceptance.

Seeing this friendly move by Warrior, who didn't normally trust anyone this quickly, convinced Caylen that any doubts he might have about these two men were completely unwarranted.

"Why don't we go to the cabin and see my Mom so you can tell her why you're here." he said.

"What do we do about Fariss?" Kosumi asked. "He will try to kill us again."

"We'll make sure he's not home before we go in. I'll go first and tell my mother you are here, so she'll not be afraid of you." Caylen said. "We'll get much closer to their cabin and then you can wait in the bush until I come and get you."

They were soon standing in the trees at the edge of the cabin's clearing. Caylen could see that the curtains were drawn back, indicating that Fariss had left for his mine workings and that Lora was alone. Taking Warrior with him he quietly entered the cabin and greeted his mother, who was, as usual, elated to see him and Warrior. Before she could say too much, however, Caylen informed her of the presence of the brothers of Wildflower. He also gave her a quick version of what they told him of their sister leaving Carcross with Fariss, never to be seen or heard from again. He advised Lora that he believed completely in what they told him and that he wanted to assist them in whatever way he could. Lora, trusting fully in Caylens and Warrior's instincts, readily agreed to listen to, and speak with Lokni and Kosumi.

In a very few moments, the two native men were sitting at the little table, slurping away at cups of Lora's hot tea and relating their story of Wildflower and their concerns to her. When they finished their story, Lora looked first at Caylen and then at the two men before saying,

"Well, now, that certainly explains a lot of things, now I know what his nightmares were all about and I'm just a little afraid that something bad may have happened to your sister." she added.

"Why do you think that?" asked Kosumi.

"I just do, I don't know why. But I just do." replied Lora. She then told the two men about Fariss's nightmares, his speaking in his sleep about a "Wildflower," his reluctance to discuss her and his anger whenever the name "Wildflower" was mentioned. She went on to tell them of the changes that seemed to occur to Fariss whenever he was away from the cabin.

"It's almost as if this cabin or something in this cabin can control Fariss's temperament." she said. "It's as though it's haunted." Lora didn't, at first, wish to offend her guests by saying everything she now believed, especially after hearing their story, but she finally blurted out,

"I believe Wildflower's spirit may be here in this cabin and that her spirit is, at times, speaking to and frightening Fariss, even causing his nightmares. I believe that her spirit has remained here so that the truth of what happened to her can be revealed."

"But, how can we ever know what has happened unless Fariss tells us?" Caylen asked. "Wildflower only speaks to him and never anyone else."

"Have you asked your Cheveyo?" posed Lokni.

"Cheveyo? Oh, you mean Warrior." Caylen said. "I would, but Warrior can't talk. He can do lots of things, but I've never heard him talk."

"He is a Cheveyo," Lokni said. "He can do many more things than you can even imagine. Ask him about our Wildflower and we'll soon see if he understands."

"Okay," said Caylen, with a smile, attempting to humor him. "Warrior, tell us where Wildflower is, where is she, boy?"
At this command, Warrior jumped to his feet and padded over to the area of the cabin's floor where, until this point in time, he had refused to walk. There, he began vigorously digging up the dirt floor. Puzzled by what was happening, the four humans could only watch as the brown soil quickly began to pile up behind Warrior. It was not until a small flat round metallic object flew out of the growing hole that anyone moved. Spotting this metal object as it flew from Warrior's paws to land on the floor, Kosumi reached over , picked it up and examined it closely before exclaiming loudly,

"This is Wildflower's amulet that she always wore. She would never leave it behind."

Lokni, Kosumi, Lora and Caylen looked at each other in wide-eyed horror, not wanting to even consider openly or admit what each of them was thinking. Finally, Caylen spoke the obvious.

"Look," he said. "Warrior's still digging for something."

Warrior had dug down to a depth of nearly two feet in the hard dry floor before the foursome could hear his hard claws scratching on something much harder than the soil. He suddenly stopped his clawing and digging and sat up at the edge of the hole, looking expectantly at the four people, who were in turn looking at him. Caylen was the first to react to Warriors sudden stop. He rose and went over to look into the excavation that his wolf pet had so industriously made, following his request as to Wildflower's location. All he could see at the very bottom of the hole was what appeared to be a row of small logs lying on the bottom. He turned to Lokni and Kosumi and said.

"I'll get a shovel so we can dig out whatever is down there."

"I surely pray that it's not what I think it is." whispered Lora to no one in particular.

Caylen was soon scraping the logs clean of the dry brown soil.

It took him only a few moments to uncover what looked like a log floor about two feet wide and five feet long. Once he had them scraped clean of most of the soil, he turned to Lokni and Kosumi and said, handing the shovel to Lokni,

"That's all I'm going to do. You two can do the rest."

Lokni glanced at his brother, took the shovel and began to pry up the logs. He soon had them all free and out of the hole, where the foursome could see what lay beneath. It appeared to be the dried flesh side of a caribou skin, lashed and wound tightly about something quite heavy. As they all stood about the excavation, looking at this object lying on the bottom, they all knew instinctively what the tightly rolled hide contained, but they also sincerely hoped they were wrong. After what seemed like an eternity, Lora was the first to quietly speak.

"Please take that thing outside before you open it. Please, please take it outside."

The two brothers, now being, as were Lora and Caylen, quite sure of the hide's contents, lifted the bundle tenderly out of the excavation and carried it out of the cabin's door and into the clearing. Laying it softly down, they untied the lashings and unrolled it to reveal Wildflower's badly decomposed body. Lokni and Kosumi stood silently for a few moments before beginning to shuffle in a circular motion around Wildflowers remains As they shuffled around her body, they began chanting with quavering voices that raised every hair on Caylen's neck and sent chills up and down his and Lora's back. They continued their moving and chanting for about five minutes before stopping. As Caylen and Lora watched, they then constructed a small fire, removed all of Wildflower's remaining clothing and then, one piece at a time, threw them into the fire until all of it was consumed. Then, using their belt knives, they cut each other's hair completely off and burned that also.

Completing these rites, the two mourning brothers rolled Wildflower's body back up in the dry caribou skin and carried her down the trail to the beach, where they carefully placed her and went off to retrieve their canoe. When they returned, they placed Wildflower gently in the canoe's center. Returning once more to the cabin to speak with Lora and Caylen, Lokni said,

"We will wait now for Fariss to return, and then we shall kill him. We must avenge our sister and then we must take her home and place her with her ancestors so that she may travel with them in the spirit world and find eternal peace in the afterlife.

"No! You must go now." Caylen stated. "We cannot permit you to take your revenge on Fariss here. You must go back to Carcross and speak to the Redcoat Police there. They will accompany you back here to question and arrest Fariss, and then take him back for a trial in the white man's court. They will see to his punishment."

"The white man's laws do not care for our people," Kosumi argued. "They will not punish him."

"But nobody except Fariss knows for certain what happened to Wildflower, or what caused her death." Lora injected.

"We shall easily find out the truth of what happened." Lokni said. "A few minutes of roasting his feet in this fire and he'll tell us everything we wish to know."

"No. We will not permit you to torture him, either." Caylen said. "You will have to kill us also, or do it in our way."

"You and your mother are good people." Lokni said. "We wish you no harm, so we will do as you say. We will take Wildflower home to be with her ancestors, and then we will return with the Redcoats to seek the white mans' justice."

"We go now," said Kosumi. "Before the evil Kachada returns, for if he were to return and find us here, we would be forced to kill him."

"What does Kachada mean?" the ever-curious Caylen asked.

"It means white man." said Kosumi.

With that statement, the two native men strode down to the lake, closely followed by Lora and Caylen. In a few minutes they were paddling East, down the lake, beginning the long trip back to Carcross with their dead sister lying between them in their canoe. Before they had gone far, they both turned to wave their thanks to Lora and Caylen one more time.

After they were out of sight, Lora and Caylen went back into the cabin, refilled and packed down the hole in the floor, disguised the disturbed soil with a caribou skin rug, and then discussed at length the day's exciting events. After much talk, they decided that it would be best for all concerned that they not inform Fariss of the day's happenings, as they were unsure of what his reaction might be. They felt that it would be better for them if they waited for the native brothers, Lokni and Kosumi, to return with the police, in the likely event that Fariss became violent. They then hugged and said goodbye to each other after setting an approximate date for their next visit.

Neither Lora nor Caylen, as they parted, said anything whatsoever to each other about the day's extraordinary events. As Caylen walked slowly back to his night camp, he could only shake his head in utter disbelief over what had occurred.

Chapter 12

Calming Fariss

Fariss, when he returned from his placer mine workings that night, didn't notice the recently disturbed soil of the cabin's floor. Lora and Caylen had done a excellent job of compacting the loosened dirt and then covered the entire area with soft caribou skin rugs. It was over three weeks since his return from Carcross, and he expected that his bad dreams and nightmares of Wildflower would soon resume. While he had not yet been able to totally connect her dying and her subsequent burial under the cabin's floor to his recurring nightmares, he did suspect that the cause of his nightmares might just be her lost spirit haunting him. He suspected that her spirit, unable to find eternal peace, still might reside in or near the cabin. He had given some thought to rebuilding his home in a different location, but when he considered the amount of work involved, he discarded those thoughts in favor of simply leaving home for extended periods of time whenever possible. He quickly recognized that his bad dreams and nightmares would disappear whenever he left the cabin or its vicinity so this option made perfect sense to him.

What Fariss and Lora didn't, and couldn't, know was that the spirit or ghost of Wildflower was now no longer in or about the cabin or the surrounding area. She was no longer inserting herself into his thoughts while he slept. She was no longer giving him bad dreams and nightmares to harass and craze him over what he had one to her to cause her early demise. Wildflower had, since her birth, been taught to believe that her spirit, once her physical body had ceased to function, could not ever find peace or move on to a higher plane until her mourners had performed certain traditional rites over her body and disposed of it in traditional native methods. Once her brothers Lokni and Kosumi had removed her body from the cabin, her spirit had chosen to accompany them back to

Carcross, where they then performed those traditional native funeral rites over her and laid her to rest with her ancestors in the little Carcross cemetery. It was only then that Wildflower's spirit was able to rid itself of its earthly connections and to finally move on to find eternal peace in the afterlife with the Great Spirit.

As time passed and fall began to color the surrounding forests and the salmon could be heard splashing their way upstream in the little creek, Fariss was well aware that he had finally begun sleeping soundly and that his cursed nightmares had disappeared. His newest diggings on his mining claim had proven to be quite generous in giving up its valuable yellow dust. He was now averaging over one ounce per day and even more on the days that his sluice box gave up the more valuable nuggets The nuggets often fetched more money than did the gold dust, as the local jewelers liked to set the raw nuggets in rings or pendants, and sell them "as-is" to the many wealthy southerners who loved to openly display their wealth to others.

Lora could also see that Fariss's temperament appeared to be much better than it once was, and even seemed to be improving as time passed. He now discussed with her, his efforts and the yields of his mining endeavors on nearly a daily basis. She also was quite aware that his nightmares had not returned and that he was sleeping much better than previously. Fariss's apparent new lease on life and his freshly acquired good nature did not, however, deceive her for one moment. She had wanted to discuss with him, the possibility of Caylen visiting them both, but still didn't have the fullest confidence that Fariss's new good-natured behavior would continue. She felt that she should wait just a little longer before discussing Caylen's previous aggressive actions with Fariss, in order for her to get a sense of how he would react to Caylen's presence before allowing the two to meet face to face again.

Fariss's purchases in Whitehorse were also quite surprising to Lora. In light of what had ocurred between Caylen and Fariss, she didn't really expect him to purchase anything on this trip, other than the barest essentials in foods and supplies. She had anticipated that, once he took the time to read her shopping list and saw what she had asked him to purchase, that he would tear it up and purchase just what he thought was needed To the contrary. He had not only purchased everything that was on the list, but he had even gotten extra luxury items for her. Some new pots and pans, a new set of dishes, many yards of heavy cloths and flannels and even a few small decorative trinkets for the cabin. She even found, much to her astonishment, a large bottle of scented hair soap and a small flask of perfume. When she found these last two items, she thought to thank Fariss for his thoughtfulness, so she left them sitting on the rough plank table where he normally sat when he returned from his diggings. When he finally sat for his evening meal, the first thing he saw was the bottle of hair soap and the perfume flask sitting directly in front of him.

Lora, watching his face closely when he saw the two articles, could see his bewhiskered cheeks redden with embarrassment at being faced with his gifts to her. He sat for a few moments, too flustered by the occasion to say anything. Lora finally thought that she should probably open the conversation so she said.

"I love the hair soap and the perfume. Fariss. It was so thoughtful of you to buy those for me."

"I's is glad you's likes them." mumbled Fariss, his cheeks reddening even more.

"I think it was wonderful of you and I do thank you.?" Lora said.

"Well, you's works pretty hard round here's and I's ain't the easiest feller to gets along with sometimes." said Fariss.

Astonished even more by this open, forthright admission by Fariss that he was difficult to live with at times, Lora found herself speechless and in open wonderment and disbelief at this new and "improved" magnanimous Fariss Lubak. She began to think again about having Caylen visit them while Fariss was present, as he now appeared to be taking much more of an interest in both her and Caylen's welfare and often spoke of wishing to see him again.

Lora had no idea what actions the brothers Lokni and Kosumi might eventually take, or even if they would take any actions over their sister's death. She didn't know if or when they would bring the Northwest police out to investigate Wildflowers death. She had no idea how Wildflower had died or if Fariss had been the cause of her death. All she knew for a fact was that Wildflower had died; that Fariss had interred her under his cabin and that his demeanor had dramatically improved since the removal of Wildflower's body. Because she didn't know the circumstances of Wildflower's death, her fear of Fariss was still the overriding emotion that she felt. Even though the new "improved" Fariss seemed totally open to discussing any subject with her, she couldn't bring herself, as of yet, to discuss Wildflower's death with him.

Caylen stayed near his little cabin over the following weeks. His only major excursion of any distance was the trips he made back to where he had seen the fat black bear. It took only one well-placed bullet from Fariss's big 45/70 rifle to send this big bruin off to bear heaven. Caylen was able to obtain nearly one hundred pounds of pure white lard and over two hundred pounds of rich pork-like meat from this unfortunate beast. He also smoked and dried over four hundred pounds of moose meat and one hundred and fifty pounds of fat caribou meat. Before the first September snowfall, his cold storage cave was to contain almost fifteen hundred pounds of bear, moose, caribou, lake trout and grayling, as well as a large assortment of dried berries and mushrooms. Unless some wandering wolverine raided his natural refrigerator, his stored foodstuffs would last him well into the following spring and summer.

Once he was satisfied that he had sufficient food stores, he began to plan his next visit to see his mother. He had no knowledge that Fariss was now a different person, so he planned this trip as he had the previous one and made a long, roundabout trip that was nearly fifteen miles in length. When he finally observed Fariss's cabin, he could see that the curtain was fully drawn, so he and Warrior entered straightaway.

Lora, as usual, was quite happy to see Caylen and Warrior, greeting them both with warm hugs and a kiss on Caylen's cheek. Caylen quickly detected that the tenseness and suspicion that usually pervaded the cabin was now gone, and that his mother was quite alert and excited over his visit. Even Warrior detected the changes in the cabin's atmosphere and, to Caylen's surprise, was soon fast asleep on the fur rug that lay directly over the very spot where Wildflower had been interred.

What's going on with you, Mom? You look really happy for a change." Caylen probed.

"Well, that's because I am much happier now than I was before." Lora replied. Fariss appears and acts like a different person now."

"I wonder why he's changed. Are you doing something differently? Or is it because I'm no longer living here? Caylen asked.

"No, Dear. The only thing different that I've seen is that his luck at the mine has improved, and his nightmares seem to have disappeared altogether. We actually have real back and forth conversations now, and he even seems to care about how you are doing." Lora replied.

"I wonder if Lokni and Kosumi taking Wildflower's body away could have had something to do with Fariss's sudden change in behavior." Caylen commented. "Perhaps her ghost was haunting him in some way to avenge what he may have done to her when she was alive."

"I really don't know if I can believe that, but something has certainly made him act very nicely since his return. I almost asked him straight out, last night, how Wildflower had died." Lora rejoined.

"Well, I don't think that would be too good an ideal." Caylen refuted. " I wonder when the police will get here."

" I don't know, but I do think it would be safe for you to stay for supper tonight and possibly even stay the night." Lora replied.

" Staying overnight might be a bit too much." Caylen said. "But, I would like to stay for supper and I'll put Warrior outside when Fariss comes home."

Caylen wasn't about to admit to his mother that he really missed her cooking, her sumptuous meals and the generous helpings of the after meal desserts he knew she would prepare for him.

"Good!" Lora exclaimed. "I shall make us all a nice big blueberry pie for dessert!"

Caylen and Lora were quietly discussing the upcoming winter and the preparations that still needed doing when Warrior lifted his big head and growled a low warning to them.

"That must be Fariss coming. I'll take Warrior outside and come back in about five minutes, once Fariss is inside." Caylen said, rising from his seat and heading for the door with Warrior close behind. As he exited the cabin, Caylen could see Fariss coming down the trail and into the clearing. From the expression on his face, it was quite obvious that Fariss had also seen Caylen exiting the cabin.

"Hey, Caylen boy, it be good to be seein you's! How you been? How's do's you likes living by yourselves and is you's stayin fer supper? Fariss seemed pleased.

Surprised at this unexpectedly warm and friendly greeting, Caylen could only stand with his mouth open as Fariss grew near.

"What's the matters, boy? Cans't you's speak?" Fariss asked.

"Yes, I can speak. How have you been? Did you have a good trip to Carcross?" Caylen said, not quite believing this "new" Fariss.

" Why's don't you's leave that there wolf outsides and come into our house and visits fer a spell?" replied Fariss. "I's would likes to hear how you's has been gettin on while you's been out on yer own."

"Okay, I'll be right in as soon as I find Warrior something for him to do out here," said Caylen. He soon had Warrior lying out in the fall day's warm afternoon sun. A simple "stay Warrior" and the wolf would remain wherever Caylen asked him to, until released from that position by Caylen, and Caylen alone. Only if he sensed that his master was in immediate danger would Warrior stir from where he had been ordered to stay. He was now a mature, fully grown, fully developed, Arctic timber wolf weighing approximately one hundred and eighty-five pounds, and who was afraid of nothing.

Caylen re-entered the cabin as Fariss was placing his new rifle on its rack beside the fireplace. He turned towards the still apprehensive boy and said.

"So tell me and your Mom how you been doin out on your own."

"I've been just fine," Caylen said. " I pretty much have all my winter food preserved and stored. I found a cave near my cabin that still had ice in it in late summer so I'm using it as a storeroom."

"Dat's real good as longs as you's can keeps the bears and wolverines outs of it." said Fariss.

"Yes. Well, I built a log door over the entrance and then I have Warrior put his scent on the door every time I go there;" Caylen replied.

"Where ever did you's get that idea from?" asked Lora.

"Fariss told me last year that wolf pee would keep other animals away from wherever the wolf pee'd." Caylen said. "Apparently they smell it and know that any area marked by pee belongs to the animal that the pee came from, so they leave it alone. Nothing has bothered my stuff yet so it must work."

"Dat was a real good idea," Fariss said. "Did you's gets lots of meats and such in fer the winter?"

"Yes" Caylen replied, trying to change the subject. "I got lots of fish and berries in too." He was feeling just a little uncomfortable talking about big game as he thought it might lead to discussion about the rifle that he had taken from Fariss.

"How's you likes shootin that old 45/70 gun," Fariss asked. "Did you knows that it shoots bullets bout two inches to the left at bout one hundred or so yards?"

"I adjusted the sights so it hits exactly where I aim now." replied Caylen.

"That's enough talk about shooting things." Lora said. "Would you like to see what Fariss bought for me in Whitehorse, Caylen?"

"Okay, let's see it, Mom." Caylen said, thankful for Lora's changing the subject.

The remainder of the afternoon went by quickly with the trio discussing winter's approach and their preparations for the coming of the cold north winds. Lora had roasted a tender fillet of Caribou and sautéed some wild mushrooms for their supper. This repast was followed by huge helpings of freshly baked blueberry pie and hot tea.

As the sun's rays began to cast long, darkening shadows over the little clearing, Caylen, his hunger more than sated, said his goodbyes and promised to return again to visit before the onset of winter and the snow season.

"Jest a minute, boy." Fariss said, as Caylen prepared to leave. I am got you somethin from Whitehorse, too." With that, Fariss went over to his pack and pulled out a brand new hunting knife in a leather sheath. Approaching Caylen, he handed it to him saying.

"This be fer you, boy. It be a real good handmade knife. It be made from some kind of new steel that don't never rusts."

As he made his way back to his overnight camp, Caylen wondered at the extreme change in Fariss's behavior. He did not, for one moment, believe that Fariss had forgiven him for shaming him and taking his rifle. He could not understand how Fariss's current state of mind had come about or if it would remain. He was glad that his mother was okay and seemed to be actually enjoying herself for a change. As he lay, nearly asleep, later that night, he finally gave up trying to understand just what made Fariss Lubak the person that he was.

I guess all I can do is accept him at face value for now. he mused to Warrior as he nodded off.

The next few months went by quickly. Winter set in with a vengeance, freezing the lakes and rivers completely over within a very few days. Caylen found his little cabin warm enough but quite confining during the really cold spells, and managed to escape its dark interior at every opportunity. Warrior seemed to love romping and playing in the deep cold snow drifts, running and play attacking Caylen whenever he thought Caylen wasn't looking at him. They made two more visits to see Fariss and Lora before and on Christmas day. Both of these visits went by uneventfully for all concerned. There were no arguments or irritating incidents of any sort other than on Christmas day when Lora presented both Fariss and Caylen each with two pairs of warm woolen socks that she had knitted.

"What's this!" exclaimed Fariss, his cheeks reddening, "I's didn't gets you nothing so's how comes you's got me these here socks?"

"Because you need them," Lora said, seeing his not Christmas presents, you just needed them."

"Well, yes I does needs more socks all the times." Fariss said, happy to be given this out.

After Christmas and New Years day had passed, the weather again turned really cold, confining Caylen to his little cabin and its immediate vicinity.

The short winter days also passed quite uneventfully for Fariss and Lora as well, although they did have each other for company and each other to speak to.

Caylen, on the other hand, had only Warrior for company, and while he often spoke to Warrior, Warrior's only responses were looks of concern, the occasional whimper and a loud yelp when he wanted out.

Caylen's dreams of the huge black wolf and the old man recurred only once, late that winter. In this dream, he saw again the old Indian standing with the big wolf sitting beside him. The Indian as before, spoke to him, saying,

"Adahy, you have done well, you are becoming a man. And your Cheveyo has also done well. You must now prepare to come to me when I send for you. You shall, at once, prepare for yourself a pack of items that will sustain you for a long journey."

Caylen didn't know what to make of this dream. He did know that this dream, as had the others, been more realistic than a dream should have been. He felt that whatever the old Indian asked of him, he should probably do, so he prepared a small pack of tools and foodstuffs that he felt would sustain him for a long period of time, should he have to go away from his little home in the forest.

Chapter 13

Good Times

The remainder of the long winter passed by quite uneventfully for Caylen. He spent the warmer days exploring the surrounding area on the long webbed snowshoes he had made in late fall from the tough mountain ash found along the streams in his area. He fabricated the webbing and straps from the moose hide that he first scraped clean of fur and then, with his new razor sharp hunting knife, sliced into hundreds of feet of leather lacing. On the days that he didn't go exploring, he either did some ice fishing or snowshoe hare hunting with his little twenty-two rifle. He did continue to visit with, and check on his mother every couple of weeks. He now always found his mother and Fariss getting along much better than they had before the two native brothers had taken Wildflower's body away with them to Carcross. He was beginning to believe more and more that Wildflower's lost spirit had, in fact, been the reason for Fariss's terrible behavior and that her spirit, in its anger and loneliness, had been entering Fariss's dreams and frightening him so that he could not sleep. On one of his visits, late in the winter, when Caylen, his mother and Fariss were sitting and discussing some trivial matter, Caylen, observing that Fariss seemed to be in really good humor, burst out with,

"Fariss, we know that Wildflower used to live here with you and that you refuse to speak with her brothers about her, but could you at least tell us what happened to her and where she is now?"

Fariss did not speak for the longest time and Lora gave Caylen a look that said quite plainly, *I wish you hadn't brought up that subject.*

"It's just that if we knew what happened to her, then we would feel better ourselves." Caylen added, hoping to keep the discussion friendly and to keep Fariss calm about the subject.

Fariss, after giving both Caylen and Lora long searching looks, finally spoke, saying,

"I'se has told you's before that she's don't concerns you's two."

"But, we think that whatever concerns you also concerns and affects us." Lora said.

Fariss again sat, saying nothing for the longest time, mulling over in his mind just what, if anything, he could say that would satisfy their curiosity without incriminating himself. He finally thought out what he would say and said,

" Well, I'se hired her off another miner in Carcross to come outs here to looks after my house and cooks my foods fer me."

"But where did she go?" asked Caylen.

" I'se came home one day from ice fishin and found her out in the snow, frozen solid and dead. " Fariss said.

"But why couldn't you just tell her brothers that?" asked Caylen.

"Cause they hates me fer takin her aways from Carcross and they thinks I'se was responsibles fer her dyin."

"Well, it seemed to Caylen and I that all they really wanted was to know the truth of what happened to their sister." Lora said.

"But's they's is blaming me fer her death now." Fariss said. "Now they's jest wants to kill me."

"Perhaps you should go and see the Northwest Police in Carcross this summer and tell them everything that has happened." Lora suggested.

"I'se don't knows bout that." said Fariss. "They's might jest lock me up."

"Not if you tell the truth about what happened. If you have spoken the truth, then you're not to blame for her death." Lora said.

Fariss did not reply. What he had told them was only partly true. He knew that he was responsible, at least in part, for Wildflower's death, but he also felt quite sure that, had she asked, he would have permitted her back into his warm cabin on that long ago cold winter night. He also knew that he had missed her and that he, in many ways, had cared for her.

He also knew that the Police, if they were to question him about her death, would insist that he give them logical, truthful answers to their queries, and that they would find him, as he knew he was, partially guilty of her death, and that they would hold him over in Whitehorse for a trial.

Thinking that the subject had been discussed sufficiently, Lora decided it was time to change the topic of conversation before Fariss became belligerent or lost his temper. She felt that they had accomplished quite a bit, just in getting him to talk about Wildflower and her demise. Both Lora and Caylen thought it best to not ask Fariss at this time, how he had disposed of Wildflower's body.

As the days grew longer and warmer, Caylen's exploratory trips also grew longer. The ice and snow disappeared quite quickly under the warm spring sunshine, with newly sprouted plants and greenery soon blanketing the countryside. The creeks, streams and rivers gurgled, splashed and roared their way down to the big northern lakes before rushing down the Yukon river to the far away ocean. Caylen's frequent visits to his mother and Fariss also increased as the snow disappeared and the forest traveling became easier. He was even invited by Fariss to come up to his new sluice box location and was even permitted, under his close scrutiny, to assist in removing the valuable nuggets and gold dust from the riffles of the sluiceway. Caylen found that he quite enjoyed this task and decided that he too would do a little panning of his own on some of the many creeks and streams that flowed by and through his territory.

He dug out his father's old gold pan and, using some fine quartz sand from his stream, soon had all the rust removed and the gold pan shiny clean. He then, over a smoky fire, blackened the pan's interior so any gold dust would show up easily against the black of the pan.

He began his gold hunting ventures right outside his cabin. His first few attempts produced nothing but a few easily recognizable yellow iron pyrites in his pan and a backache for his troubles. On his second day of panning, he moved upstream to where a small creek entered the main stream. He followed this little stream to where its waters tumbled over a rocky ledge and down into a small, sandy-bottomed pool. Reaching as far as he could into the pool with his spade, he dug it deeply into the sandy bottom and removed a shovelful of sand and pebbles that he dumped into his gold pan. A few minutes later, Caylen had his first gold strike. The gold dust in the bottom of his pan was hardly sufficient in quantity to get excited about, but it was gold and Caylen was elated over his find. He toiled industriously on this little find for the next three days as the flecks of gold in his pan grew fewer and fewer, until he eventually found nothing more. He calculated his total take of gold for three long backbreaking days of hard labor at about three quarters of an ounce or about seven dollars worth. A little dejected by the results of his hard work, he waited for a few days before setting off to try and find more productive waters.

After resting up from his three days of hard, excruciating labor at his barely productive initial gold find, Caylen decided to set off towards a mountainous area that lay to the northwest of where his cabin was situated. He had, on his earlier journey to find his new cabin's location, traveled through this remote area and recalled seeing many streams and creeks that might contain the precious gold. Preparing himself and Warrior for a two or three day trip, he set off early one warm spring morning. He walked steadily northwest for nearly six hours, following the small stream that joined the larger one that passed in front of his cabin. He crossed many small tributary creeks where he stopped to sample pan, without any luck whatsoever. As the sun began to set, he finally reached the shores of the lake that was the source of the stream he had been following all day.

He quickly set up a small overnight camp, ate a cold supper and was soon fast asleep. Rising even before the morning sunrays had burnt off the cool nights mists, Caylen was soon on his way along the unexplored north shore of the lake. He estimated that this lake was about two or three miles long and perhaps one quarter of a mile wide. He could see that there were at least two canyons sloping down from the northern mountains towards the lake and figured that these canyons likely contained feeder streams that might, with a little luck, contain gold. It took him nearly an hour to reach the first of these fast-running little glacier-fed streams. After about an hour of panning upstream and downstream on this first creek with no positive results, he headed off to the next that was only about one quarter of a mile distant. As the lake's immediate shoreline in this area was clear of trees and was quite sandy, he was able to travel west directly along, and close to, the open shoreline. He came upon the stream, noting as he approached that it seemed to be a rather insignificant little creek with its waters spreading out into many little rivulets as it entered the lake. Nearly disregarding this stream's potential, Caylen was across it and about two hundred feet west along the lakeshore before he realized that Warrior was not beside him. Looking back, he could see that his pet had obviously decided to take a well-deserved rest and was now lying to one side of the little stream just above where he had himself crossed. He could see Warrior lying there, with a pleased look, on the warm beach sand, with his long pink tongue hanging out from his smiling jaws.

"Okay, boy. We'll stop here for a rest and a bite to eat." he said to the animal, as he returned to the creek. Caylen paused only a moment to loosen his and Warrior's packs and lay them out on the beach. Stretching his aching arms and shoulders he decided to walk upstream a little and make his toilet before having lunch. He followed the little stream up about two hundred feet to where it formed a pretty little, perfectly clear, sandy-bottomed pool. The pool was about thirty feet long and about fifteen feet wide and was immediately below a long, rocky rapid that stretched off to the north. Lying on his stomach, he thirstily sucked up a long quenching drink of the stream's pure, ice-cold water. As he was about to stand, something lying on the pool bottom caught his eye. Reaching out into about ten inches of the icy water, he picked up the shiny heavy rock that had just caught his attention and examined it closely. What he could see in his cold wet open palm was a solid gold nugget about one inch thick by about two inches long.

Gaping in disbelief and awe at this totally unexpected find, Caylen, after a moment or two of pure astonishment, sat down to study his find. Bouncing the nugget in his palm, he guessed that it would weigh about five or six ounces and from its well-worn deep yellow color, he thought that its purity was assuredly close to one hundred percent. Caylen then stood and again studied the pool of water and its upstream source in detail. He estimated that the pool was no more than three or four feet in depth at its deepest point. Its source was a small rocky feeder stream that tumbled down and out of the northern hills, through a narrow rock gulley about four hundred feet upstream.

As he studied the big, clear pool of water intently, Caylen began to see other gleaming pebbles strewn across the pool bottom. As he stared intently into the depths of the pool in total awe, he began to tremble as he realized that the bottom of the pool, at its deeper points, was almost solid yellow in color from the numerous small and large gold nuggets that lay there.

In utter disbelief, Caylen quickly shed his moccasins, socks and pants and waded out into the icy waters of the pool. Reaching down into its cold depths, he grabbed two handfuls of the bottom gravels and sands. As the cold water drained from his handfuls of creek bottom, he nearly fell over into the stream. He opened and closed his eyes two or three times, and shook his head vigorously to ensure that he was, in fact, awake and not dreaming. In his two hands, he found he was looking at two handfuls of nearly solid gold sand and gold nuggets. Now in total shock, he opened his hands and save for three or four half inch to one-inch nuggets, dumped the remaining sand and gold back into the pool. He then waded ashore and sat down on the warm sand to mull over what had just happened.

After sitting for about five minutes contemplating what his next move should be, Caylen rose and placed the new nuggets in his pocket with the larger one he had originally found. He then, still shaking with excitement, returned to the lake, retrieved his and Warrior's packs and brought them back to the pool. The pool's location was, conveniently, just above the line of spruce trees that grew in profusion along the lake's sandy shoreline but it was invisible to anyone that might come along the shore, either by boat or walking along the beach. Even the streams outfall into the lake, as spread out as it was, would give the impression to a passerby that the stream was quite insignificant and not worth checking further upstream.

Caylen spent the next hour or so looking about for a more or less permanent campsite, trying to quiet his racing mind so that he could rationally think out what his next move should be. Reckoning that it was about a five to six hour walk from his gold find back to where his cabin was, Caylen estimated that it would take him about three round trips back to his cabin to retrieve sufficient supplies to enable him to set up a summer camp and to remain at the pool site for a few weeks at a time before having to return to his cabin for additional foodstuffs. As he only had enough food with him for three or four more meals, he knew he could only spend one more full day at the pool before returning, unless he shot some small game animals or lived on fish. He turned to Warrior and said to him,

"Well, boy. It looks like we might have a 'glory-hole' here, so we may as well get busy and just see how rich we are."

With that, he stripped down once more to his shirt and, taking his gold pan, waded out to the approximate center of the little pool. Reaching down into the cold water, he dragged his pan across the pool's sand and gravel bottom until it was full of the heavy bottom materials. Unable to tolerate the icy waters for long, he then waded ashore and began to swirl out his gold pan's contents. In a very few moments, he stopped and looked into the pan. Protruding from the course yellow gold gravels and fines in the pan were at least ten gold nuggets varying in size from one quarter of an inch up to two inches, with one that was about three inches in diameter. Caylen hand picked out, all the nuggets that he could see with shaking fingers and laid them in a little heap on a piece of bark that he found on the shore. Finishing the removal of the more obvious nuggets from this first pan of creek bottom, he estimated that it still held at least eight ounces of gold sand and dust. Adding this eight ounces to his estimated thirty ounces of nuggets that he had already removed and the approximately nine ounces that he had grabbed with his hands from the stream, he realized that he had, in less than five minutes, taken roughly forty-seven ounces of gold from the pool. At ten dollars per ounce, he had just earned himself about four hundred and seventy dollars.

With the sudden realization of just how rich his find was, Caylen again began to tremble in excitement. He was once more, forced to sit and calm himself for about thirty minutes before proceeding. As he sat staring at his little pile of gold, Caylen, hearing a loud splash, turned to see Warrior wading out into the icy waters of the pool. As he watched, Warrior ducked his head into the shallow water and picked up something before returning to stand proudly in front of his master for just a moment before dropping a three-inch nugget of solid gold onto Caylen's pile of ore.

Over the remainder of that day and the next, Caylen estimated that he removed nearly fifty pounds of gold from the little pool. He filled Warrior's saddlebag packs to the maximum that he thought the wolf could carry and placed the remainder in his own backpack. He was on his way home the following morning before the sun had fully risen over the snowcapped mountain peaks that filled the eastern horizon.

Arriving home around noon, he unloaded his gold dust and

nuggets into a large empty keg that had previously held some of his last winter's supply of salted fish. He then carried the keg out to the cave that he had fashioned into a cold storage room and, placing it at the very rear, draped a bear skin over it to at least partially conceal it. Returning to his cabin, Caylen then put together sufficient supplies and foodstuffs to last him for a full week. He also gathered together a few tools that he thought would make his mining efforts just a little easier and was back at the 'gold pool', as he called it, by noon the next day.

Before resuming the extraction of more gold from the rich stream sands, he soon constructed himself a little lean-to shelter with a rock-lined cooking pit a few feet in front of it. He also gathered sufficient dry wood for heating and cooking the meager supplies that he proposed to supplement with the many grayling and lake trout that swam in the nearby lake.

It wasn't until the following morning sun had burned off the morning mists that Caylen finally resumed his mining ventures. He had fashioned himself a long-handled rake-like tool that held four-inch raking spikes that was spaced about an inch apart. He could drag the rake across the pool's bottom without having to wade into its icy cold waters.

This ingenious handmade rake, with its long tines spaced about one-half inch apart, would pick up any nugget or pebble of any size over one-half inch in diameter. Caylen concluded from what he had previously found, that the pool's bottom might contain many nuggets of that or greater size and that this method of extracting them would reap the greatest benefit with the least amount of effort in the shortest time.

Shedding all his clothes save for his wool undershirt so that he could enter the water if necessary, Caylen's first attempt at raking the pool's bottom, produced seven gold nuggets and nine rock pebbles. Caylen found that when he did wade into the pool that he could only bear the cold for three or four minutes before he was forced to wade ashore and warm his cold shaking legs. This proved to be more than enough time to fill his rakes tines with nuggets and pebbles that he could pick over once he waded ashore. He also found, after three or four attempts, that he needed more and more warming time between his forays into the pool. Having started at the bottom, shallower end of the pool, Caylen found himself, after about two hours, just too cold to continue and only about seven or eight feet further upstream in the pool with the water getting much deeper.

Noticing that the gold nuggets appeared to be increasing in size as he moved up in the pool towards the head of the pool, he decided to make his last raking just below where the water entered the pool before taking a much needed long warming break. As he waded out into the cold water, he felt his right toe, numbed by the freezing water, hit a large rock on the pool's bottom. Figuring to throw it aside so it wouldn't hamper his rake or stub his toe again, he reached down and broke it free of the pool bottom's grip. Lifting it out of the water he was about to toss it ashore when its gleaming shine stayed his throw and caused him to look a little closer at what he had just picked up. When he looked he found that what he was holding in his hand was not a rock. What he had just lifted from the now disturbed and discolored water was a solid gold oval shaped nugget about four inches long and three inches in diameter. With his cold, numb, trembling legs barely able to keep him upright, Caylen waded ashore, gaping in disbelief at what he had just found. He walked over to where he had previously spread out, skin side up, a caribou hide and placed this huge nugget alongside the pile of smaller gold pebbles that he had already placed there. After a few minutes of warming his shaking body, he decided that he should assess what he had just gathered. The one large nugget alone must have weighed at least eight pounds. He placed it on top of the smaller nuggets and lifted the gold-filled hide in an effort to estimate its weight. His eyes wide in amazement, Caylen found that he needed both hands and considerable effort to raise the bundled hide full of nuggets and gold gravels from where they lay. Subtracting the approximate ten-pound caribou skin from the bundle's total weight, Caylen guessed that he was holding at least fifty pounds of gold in his two trembling hands. A rough estimate of his find's value thus far, would, he thought, exceed seven thousand dollars. Seven thousand dollars for only about five hours work, thought Caylen. Seven thousand dollars worth of gold in only five hours meant that he had just made himself about five or six years wages for one morning's effort, with no obvious end to the gold in sight.

Caylen spent the remainder of the day warming himself, catching a few grayling for his supper and contemplating his good fortune. He wondered what his mother would say when she found out about his find. He also thought about what the fortune could mean to them. He knew his mother would probably wish to return to a nicer climate further to the south and that she would prefer to reside in an area where there were other people living. While she had never really complained about the remoteness of where they now lived, he knew that she really missed the company of others and the conveniences of living in a community that had shops and services available. He also wondered, just for a moment, what Fariss might do if he knew of his find, but quickly rejected those thoughts, as he knew that he would never, ever tell him about his good fortune.

Over the next week, Caylen continued with his raking of the pool bottom. As he had thought, the slowly moving current of the pool had moved the smaller, lighter nuggets and gold fines further downstream in the pool than it had the larger, heavier nuggets. The result was the closer he got to the head of the pool the larger the nuggets were becoming. The second result was that while the nuggets got larger, there were fewer of them. By the end of his fourth day of mining the pool, Caylen estimated that he had accumulated well over fifty thousand dollars worth of gold nuggets and he had yet to even begin panning for the smaller nuggets and gold dust that lined the pool bottom.

Caylen took the following week off from his mining ventures and made six trips back to his cabin and his cave storeroom, carrying all his newly found wealth to his secret storeroom. His thoughts kept returning to what he could do for his mother with all his new found wealth but Fariss always seemed to be a problem no matter what route his ideas took. As long as his mother was married to, and living with Fariss, Caylen knew that she would never consider breaking her marriage vows in order to leave him and return to the south. Lora was having the best summer that she could have under the circumstances. Fariss seemed to nearly always be in relatively good humor; her son seemed to be doing fine on his own, and even her little garden of cabbage, peas and spinach seemed to be doing fine. She had been quite surprised when Fariss had produced these seeds following his last trip to Whitehorse. She had put the seeds on her shopping list but, knowing Fariss, she hadn't expected him to purchase them for her.

Caylen was visiting them about every second week and even stayed overnight on one occasion. Fariss and her son seemed to be getting along quite well with Caylen even assisting Fariss on his placer mine with none of the usual arguments occurring between them.

Fariss had really been feeling good about everything as of late. His temperament had been showing a gradual, yet noticeable improvement ever since his last summer's trip to Carcross and Whitehorse. He hadn't had any recurrence of his nightmares about Wildflower and was sleeping really well. His mining claim, while not as productive as it once had been, was giving up a better than usual amount of gold dust. He estimated that he had averaged about one full ounce per day since spring breakup. He even found that he was able to get along with, and converse with Caylen, whereas in previous times even seeing the boy had irritated and angered him for some unknown reason.

~*~

Before returning to his gold find, Caylen decided to visit his mother and inform her of his good fortune. He thought that he should make sure that she, at least, should be aware of his good fortune and besides, he thought, *If I don't share this good luck with someone, I will surely burst!*

He felt that, since he was now quite wealthy, he would make his mother a gift of the largest nugget that he had, so he retrieved the eight-pound nugget from his storeroom and stowed it away in his backpack.

Caylen arrived at his mother's, and Fariss's, cabin just before noon. Bursting with the news of his recent find, he was quite pleased to see that Fariss was away working at his claim, so he didn't have to wait to tell his mother of his good luck.

" Mom, I have a small present for you," he said, "but you mustn't show it to or even tell Fariss that you have it." He then pulled the big nugget, which he had wrapped in a rag, out of his pack and placed it on the table in front of Lora.

"Oh, thank you, Caylen," she said as she picked it up. "My, it is quite heavy. What on earth is it?"

"Why don't you unwrap it and see?" said Caylen excitedly.

"My goodness, Caylen!" exclaimed Lora. "Is this what it looks like? Is it real? How much does it weigh? Where on earth did you get it? Does Fariss know you have it? Did you take it from his claim?"

"Whoa! Slow down a bit, Mom. One question at a time!" replied Caylen.

Caylen spent the next hour telling Lora about his gold find. He told her about having between fifty and seventy thousand dollars worth of gold already stored away and that he felt that this astonishing amount was nothing compared to what still remained to be taken from the little stream.

"We're really quite rich, Mom. I would say that we might even now be millionaires." he added.

"What are we going to do?" Lora posed. "If we tell Fariss, he might just take it all for himself."

"I think we should just keep it between us for now." Caylen said. "Kosumi and Lokni may be back with the police soon, and they might arrest Fariss and put him in jail."

"Well, you should probably take this nugget back with you, in case Fariss finds it." Lora said.

"Okay, but I wanted you to have it." Caylen said. "But, you're right, so I'll take it and keep it safe for you. Then I'll go back and find some more." He said confidently.

"Just where did you find it?" Lora asked.

Caylen explained in detail where his gold strike was. He told his mother that it was on a small feeder stream that drained into a lake that, in turn, drained into a larger stream that then fed into the lake his cabin was situated on. He explained to Lora that he felt that the big lake that his cabin was built on drained eastward and into the huge Tagish Lake. He recalled seeing a large, slow moving stream that drained into Tagish Lake at the location of their third campsite out of Carcross. He also felt that, if he owned his own canoe, his cabin could be accessed easily by water from Tagish Lake.

"I wonder if Fariss would let me buy my own canoe if I went out to Carcross with him this year?" he asked.

" I don't know," Lora replied. "I do have some money that I could give you so it wouldn't cost him anything, and you wouldn't have to reveal to him anything about your gold finds."

"I think that a seventeen foot freighter would cost about sixty dollars or so. I can pay you back with gold." Caylen said.

"Don't be foolish, that nugget you gave me is probably worth over a thousand dollars." Lora said.

"I could take some gold with me and use it to buy a canoe, but if Fariss found out I had some gold, he might think that I stole it from him.' Caylen commented.

"I'll give you one hundred dollars in case it costs more, or if you need some more supplies." said Lora.

"Okay, thanks, Mom." Caylen replied.

~*~

When Fariss returned from working his claim that night, he was in a good humor. His claim had given him a better than average return that day, and he had also found a small nugget of about one half ounce that he proudly displayed to Lora and Caylen.

"Jest look at this here gold nugget." he said, proudly dropping it on the table in front of Lora.

Caylen smiled to himself smugly, thinking to himself that he would have loved to see Fariss's facial expression if he were to drop his eight-pound nugget on the table beside Fariss's little half-ounce.

"Fariss, would you like some company and some help when you go out for supplies this summer?" he asked.

"Dat would be okay, I suppose." said Fariss, in reply. "I'se were goin to take Lora, too, if she were wantsing to goes."

"No," Lora responded. "I'll stay back and take care of things here, and look after my garden and Warrior until you get back." Lora knew that, while he didn't mind taking Caylen along with him, he would not permit Warrior to accompany them.

"Then, that's settled." said Caylen., "When do we leave?"

"Any times you wants to," Fariss said. Turning to Lora he added, "You's needs to gets your buyin lists together fer me and we's can goes in the morning if the winds right."

~*~

It was late the following morning before Fariss and Caylen departed on their long boat trip. Caylen found himself missing the company of Warrior almost immediately, but knowing that his mother and Warrior would take good care of each other while he was away, gave him much comfort, so he decided to enjoy the trip as much as possible.

The trip took them only four days of leisurely paddling, as they had a good following wind for most of the way. Fariss left Caylen in Carcross as he went into Whitehorse to do the biggest part of his shopping.

Caylen enquired about and soon found an unlucky prospector who was leaving the North and who was only too happy to sell him his nearly new eighteen-foot freighter canoe for the sum of fifty-five dollars. Caylen then located a storekeeper who was able to sell him four iron-strapped wooden kegs for two dollars each. These kegs, thought Caylen, would make excellent storage containers for his cache of gold nuggets and gold dust. He estimated that each keg would hold about three hundred pounds of gold, so these added to the keg he already had, he could store away at least fifteen hundred pounds of the yellow ore. By his rough calculations, this amount of gold would have a value of about two hundred and forty thousand dollars. Just the thought of that much money was beyond comprehension, he thought, until he remembered that he already had up to seventy thousand dollars worth stored away.

Caylen looked about Carcross for Lokni and Kosumi, but they were not to be found. He didn't want to risk drawing attention to himself and Fariss by making enquiries about them, as he felt that the next move was up to them.

Fariss and he soon arrived back home with all three canoes loaded to their maximum. Fariss had been very generous on this trip and, for whatever reason, had purchased a lot of new tools, supplies and a more than normal amount of canned and dried food stuffs. His only comment about Caylens purchase of the kegs was to say,

" You's must be goin to puts up lots of dried and salted eats, that dang wolf dog must be eaten lots of foods."

Caylen's only response was to smile broadly and continue his paddling.

Chapter 14

The Summons

Caylen accompanied Fariss back to his and Lora's cabin to collect Warrior and to say goodbye to his mother. He also, before departing, fashioned a small mast for his canoe, similar to Fariss's, while Lora sewed together a little canvas sail to attach to it. He was, soon after rigging this little sail, on his way back down to Tagish Lake and then northward until he found the campsite on the mouth of the stream that he felt sure drained the lake on which his cabin was located. He was only able to utilize his little sail for part of the journey, but it did save him considerable effort over the two-day trip. He camped at the mouth of the stream in the same camp that he and Fariss had used only a few days earlier on their journey back from Carcross. Early the next morning, he began his trip up this river that he hoped would lead to his home. Finding only a few minor rapids that he was able to line his way through, he entered a large lake in mid afternoon where he could see, far to the West, the familiar mountain peaks that lined the horizon just west of his cabin. He camped on the lakeshore that night, and was home by noon of the following day. Two days later he was back at his "glory-hole" with his new canoe hidden in the forest just below his camp. While he had never seen any other prospectors on this lake, he didn't wish to chance any passing miners stopping to investigate his camp, so he had decided to hide his canoe and wipe any signs of his presence off the sandy beach.

Caylen stayed at his mine site for only fourteen days. During this time he dug and panned an estimated twelve hundred pounds of smaller nuggets and gold sand out of his pond. Added to the approximate five hundred that he had previously gathered, he realized that he was really quite wealthy and that he could now do whatever he wished.

His next thought was that he should get his gold out to one of the big banks in Whitehorse in order to ensure its safety. He loaded his canoe with all four of the gold-filled kegs and a minimum of supplies, and set sail for Carcross. His canoe was really quite overloaded with all of this heavy gold and Caylen was quite fortunate that it was not swamped and sunk as a result. He was quite lucky to have mild weather with only light following breezes to assist him on his way North. He made Carcross in four days, where, in trade for five dollars of his mother's money, he hired two native Indians to help him load his kegs onto the Whitehorse bound train. The banking of that amount of gold could easily have caused him a lot of trouble, and quite likely a stampede of eager prospectors, but after he displayed his eight pound nugget to the banker, the banker agreed to carry out the depositing business in the privacy of his office. When Caylen finally left the bank, late in the afternoon, he possessed a statement from the banker that said he had two hundred and sixty seven thousand dollars in his account.

What no one other than Caylen himself knew was that he had also buried about one hundred pounds of gold nuggets under a huge spruce tree about a mile out of Carcross on the south shore of the lake, as he approached the little village. He thought that it would be wise to "not put all of his eggs in one basket," as his mother had often said. He fully expected to recover even more of the yellow gold, but felt that having some resources near his main shopping area was probably a good idea.

Caylen returned to his cabin feeling quite proud of himself. He had managed to get his fortune in gold into a safe place with no one other than the banker knowing about it. His biggest fear had been that someone would find out about his rich hoard and rob him of it, or that it might even cause a gold rush stampede, where he would be harassed and followed wherever he went. Fortunately, no one suspected or even considered it possible that this young fourteen-year-old boy could have had a fortune in gold in his possession, so he was left alone to do as he wished during his banking trip.

Pleased with his accomplishments, Caylen decided to enjoy a couple of weeks doing nothing but relaxing, fishing and putting up winter stores. He had purchased plenty of supplies with the two hundred dollars cash that he also had taken in exchange for some of the gold from the banker in Whitehorse.

~*~

Caylen's days of relaxation were interrupted on the ninth day by a recurrence of his nearly forgotten dream. His newest dream was again a very real vision of the old Indian standing tall, with the huge black replica of Warrior lying beside him. In this dream the old Indian again, spoke clearly to Caylen, saying,

"Adahy, it is nearly time for you to come here to me, I shall soon send my Tohopka to bring you to my home in the forest. You must begin to prepare yourself for a long journey, as I will not permit you to return to your home until you are ready."

When Caylen woke, in a cold sweat from this dream, he immediately rose from his bed, dressed and began loading his and Warrior's packs. He was unsure of just why he was complying with the old man's instructions but he knew that he must do as the old man directed. He packed sufficient gear and equipment so as enable him to survive indefinitely, should he have to do so.

He wasn't entirely sure that he should be doing as his dream had directed him, but he couldn't seem to help himself. It was as though he was being controlled and he couldn't easily manage his own actions.

It wasn't until he felt fully prepared for a long trip away from his cabin that he was able to relax and contemplate his next move. He sat for nearly two hours that same day, waiting—to no avail—for a sign or instruction of some sort that he could interpret or follow. The longer he sat and thought, however, the more ridiculous he began to feel at having blindly followed instructions that he had received in his dreams. He thought to himself, *How stupid can you be? You dream of something and you think it's reality? Boy, you are dumb!* "The more he thought about it, the stupider he felt, until finally he decided to just give up on any such thoughts and carry on with his normal routines.

The next morning, Caylen loaded up his already packed supplies and headed off to spend a few more days at his gold-bearing stream. He had given a lot of thought to the gold that he had found and to where he had found it. As the pond had a lot of large nuggets in it and those nuggets were quite obviously larger towards the head of the pool, he reasoned that the source of the gold could not be too far upstream. He also reasoned that the fast--

flowing water above the pool would have, over the years, moved the smaller nuggets and smaller particles of gold downstream much further than it would have any really large nuggets. He concluded that the weight of any really large pieces of gold would cause them to settle down and into the bottom of the stream, and that they would be able to withstand the strong currents much better than would the smaller pieces that he had already recovered.

Wanting to prove or disprove this theory, Caylen followed the gold-bearing stream up about one-half mile to where it had, over the ages, carved its way through a rocky canyon. Skirting wide around the rough rocky sides of the stream he finally came to where it began its rushing journey into the steep canyon. He spent about an hour panning the streams bottom upstream of this location with no luck whatsoever. Realizing that the lack of any gold signs above the canyon meant that the source had to be somewhere in the canyon itself, he began to work his way downstream through the high, rocky walls of the canyon, doing test panning every fifty feet or so.

When he had reached what he estimated was about the halfway mark through the canyon, he came to an area where the stream had made its way through a very narrow section of solid rock about one hundred feet long, cutting nearly vertical walls in the rock. This made it quite impossible for him to reach the streams banks. Caylen took only a few moments to make his way to the tiny, swirling pool at the base of this section of the stream. He was about to scoop up some of the course bottom materials with his pan when he realized that the boiling, turbulent water held just too many large boulders for him to be able to scoop out the bottom materials with his gold pan.

Thinking that he would pick out enough of the boulders so that he could scoop up the bottom sands, he reached in and began to remove some of the larger pieces by hand.

As he lifted out the first large, water-worn boulder, he thought that it felt rather heavy for its size, so he looked closer at what he held in his hand. It took him only about fifteen minutes to remove seventeen additional rounded, solid-gold boulders, the smallest being about five pounds in weight and the largest weighing twelve pounds.

When he had cleared the little pool of all the boulders that he could easily reach, Caylen estimated that he had one hundred and twenty or so pounds of gold heaped on the stream's shore.

A test panning of the fines that he had exposed revealed quite clearly that this little pools bottom was almost pure gold.

Over the next few days, Caylen gradually worked his way downstream to the larger pool where he had first discovered his gold. His finds diminished in size as he came lower in the stream, but the number of the smaller nuggets increased. When he felt, after four days of handpicking the stream's bottom that anything smaller would require panning or digging, he stopped and consolidated his find in a large heap by his shelter.

"Now, just what am I to do with all this?" he asked Warrior, who, in response, stood, walked over to the pile of gold, and in utter disdain, lifted his leg and urinated on one of the larger nuggets.

"Well, is that what you really think, boy? Do you really feel that's all it's really good for?" Caylen asked his pet, in as serious a tone as he could muster.

The next morning, Caylen had an early breakfast and then, taking his shovel, walked about fifty feet from his camp and dug a deep hole in the gravelly soil under a tall spruce tree. He then took the gold nuggets that he estimated weighed close to six hundred pounds and buried all save the largest, which he placed in his pack. When he was finished covering his treasure, he fashioned a small cross and placed it atop the mound of gravel that hid the gold from sight.

"There!" he said to Warrior. "If we ever need it, we can return and dig it up. There's probably another two or three thousand pounds of gold still in this stream and probably more than that in the rocks of that canyon. Still, but we have more than we can ever use, so it's about time to stop."

Warrior just sat and looked happily at Caylen, his head tilted slightly to one side and his tongue lolling out one side of his mouth, as it always did when Caylen addressed him in a friendly manner.

~*~

Caylen returned to his cabin and spent the next few days lazing about, doing a little fishing and repairing the tools and equipment that he had been neglecting while mining his gold. While trying to decide when to make his next visit to his mother and Fariss, he suddenly realized that his fifteenth birthday was only a few days away and that his mother would be angry with him if he didn't celebrate it with her. He left the following day and had a nice three-day visit with Lora and Fariss.

Fariss, as Lora told Caylen, was still behaving quite nicely, with only occasional recurrence of his angry and mean spells. She thought these recurrences might have been due to the fact that his finds at the mine had apparently given out once again.

She and Caylen discussed at length the idea of revealing the location of Caylen's mine to Fariss, so that he could extract whatever gold remained. They decided that they would wait for the time being and see what happened during the upcoming winter months. Caylen prepared a detailed map that showed the route and the exact location of his mine, and gave the map to Lora for her safekeeping, telling her that if she wished, she could give it to Fariss, at her discretion. Caylen also revealed to her that he had placed his gold with the Whitehorse bank in exchange for over two hundred and sixty thousand dollars and still had over six hundred pounds of gold buried in various places. Lora didn't really believe him until he showed her his twelve-pound nugget and the receipt from the bank, which he also asked her to keep in a safe place for him.

Caylen told Lora of the strange dream he recently had, and about possibly being summoned by the old Indian. They explored at length the many similar dreams that Caylen had dreamt over the years and their seeming similarities, but reached no obvious conclusions other than that they would just have to wait and see what happened next.

Lora did express to Caylen that she was a little frightened by the frequency and the similarity of his dreams but she also assured him that she was certain that he was mature enough to cope with whatever lay in store for him.

"I really do have an odd feeling that something unusual is going to happen to me very soon." Caylen said to Lora, as he was about to depart.

"Well, my son. Whatever happens, I'm sure you'll do the right thing." Lora responded. "I'm feeling kind of odd also.: she continued "It's as though you're going to go away for a long time."

"If anything does happen, Mom. " I'll come back here and I'll try to let you know what's going on until I can come back." Caylen said, as he suddenly felt the same thoughts enter his mind. "What'll you do if the police come for Fariss? You can't stay here by yourself and I'll not know if that does happen."

"I'll just have to go along out to Carcross or Whitehorse with them." Lora replied.

"Well, Mom. If you do have to leave here, you know where I buried that gold just outside of Carcross, so you should be okay for money." Caylen said.

With that comment, he went out and buried the twelve-pound nugget behind the cabin and then left, followed by Warrior, to return to his own cabin.

~*~

It was nearly two a.m. three nights later that Caylen woke again in a cold sweat from a deep sleep. He had, again been dreaming one of his realistic dreams about the old Indian. In this dream, the old wrinkled Indian had said to him,

"Adahy, my son. It is time. It is time for you to come to me. You must come to me now before it is too late for me. I grow weary of this place and I will soon be called by my master." He then added, " I will send Abhaya, my Tohopka, to guide you to me; he will come to you this night. You must not fear him. I will be with him as he leads you and your Cheveyo to me."

Coming fully awake, Caylen heard the eerie, long drawn-out howl of a mature timber wolf. The sound seemed to come from right outside his cabin door, so he immediately rose and, going to the door with Warrior padding silently by his side, threw it open wide. There, sitting no more than five feet from the open door was the huge black wolf of his dreams, with emerald glowing eyes staring fixedly at him. As soon as Warrior saw the big replica of himself, he rushed out in obvious joy, to lick the strange wolf's face, and to prance about him as though meeting a long lost friend.

Seeing the two animals side by side caused a sudden realization to dawn on Caylen. It was now obvious to him that the big strange wolf was, in all probability, Warrior's father. The strange wolf had exactly the same coloring and the same glowing, emerald green eyes as had his Warrior. The only difference that he could see, besides the much greater size of the strange wolf, was a definite graying around its muzzle that told Caylen this animal was probably much older than Warrior.

As he stared, wide eyed, at this huge wolf, it turned and walked slowly off towards the lake, with Warrior prancing along beside him. After going a few feet, it stopped and looked back at Caylen as if to say, *Well, are you coming or not?*

It took Caylen only a few minutes to dress and throw his already packed haversack over his shoulders. He also strapped Warriors loaded packs on the excited wolf. Then grabbing his big rifle, he followed the huge animal into the thick dark evergreen forest.

For the remainder of that night and all of the following day, the big wolf led Caylen and Warrior steadily Northwards. They were forced to wade the river that drained the lake on which he had found his gold mine and passed by his mine in the early hours of the morning. Without stopping, they continued ever Northwards until Caylen, exhausted, was forced to stop for a rest and a snack of some dried moose meat. The big wolf simply lay and waited for him to complete his lunch before standing and again heading North. It was late in the afternoon when they came to a small lake hidden in as pretty a mountain valley as Caylen had ever seen.

The big wolf led Caylen and Warrior around the lake to the banks of a small shallow creek that drained the lake and flowed off to the West. Hesitating for only a brief moment, the wolf led them across the stream to where a small, domed, low mud covered hut stood.

Standing in front of the caribou skin door flap, leaning on a long mountain ash staff, stood the old Indian man of Caylen's dreams. As Caylen approached, the old man threw his arms open in a wide, welcoming gesture and said,

"I bid you greetings, Adahy. I welcome you to my land, my home and my food."

"Who are you?" Caylen asked, amazed at seeing, live and in reality, the man of his dreams. "And what do you want of me?"

"I am Whakan Powwow. In your whiteskins' words, I am called a 'Sacred Priest'." the old man replied. "But you shall be permitted to call me 'Sania' and you shall know my Tohopka by the name 'Abhaya'."

" What do the words 'Sania' and 'Tohopka' mean in my tongue? Caylen asked.

"Sania means the 'old one'. Is that not a fitting name for one as old as I?" The old man replied. "Tohopka means wild beast and your wolf's father's name is Abhaya, meaning 'Has no fear'. Are those not good names?" The old man continued, with a smile. "Now come, young Adahy. Come into my home and sit and eat with me and we shall speak to each other of things that have been and of things that are yet to be. Now come quickly into my house, as this old man has many things to say that will fill the young Adahy's head with many questions that I will attempt to answer before this day is over."

Chapter 15

Introduction

Caylen followed the old man through the caribou skin door flap into his little oval-shaped, mud-covered hut. He was quite surprised at how large the hut was once one was inside. In the middle, towards the rear was an open stone fire pit that was obviously used for both heat and cooking and that now held only a small, warming fire, with a pot of simmering water suspended over it. At each end of the oval room were wooden sleeping platforms that stood about two feet high and were covered with warm caribou-skin robes. The walls beside and opposite the fire pit had shelves on them that stood out about eight inches and held small oil lamps and many other small, carved items that to Caylen were interesting, but unidentifiable.

The floor of the hut was covered with numerous animal skins that had been taken from bears, moose and caribou. The interior of the hut had a peculiar smoky odor that Caylen found to be quite pleasant to breathe.

The old man sat down on the floor beside the small fire and gestured to Caylen to do likewise.

"Sit, and ask your many questions of me, for I am to be your teacher, and I have many things that I must teach the young Adahy." said the old man.

"Has it been you and Abhaya that I have been seeing in my dreams all of these years?" Caylen asked.

"Yes, it has been I. You were chosen by the Great Spirit many years past to be my disciple. I have been selected by the Great Spirit to instruct you in the ways of the People before I am taken by Him into the afterlife. I am very, very old and my time on this world is now nearly gone." The old man said. "As I have said, you are to call me Sania and I shall call you Adahy from this time forth, until you receive your man name from the Great Spirit."

"Was it you who gave me Warrior?" Caylen asked.

"No, It was my Tohopka, my Abhaya, who did as the Great Spirit directed him, and he brought to you his own son, Cheveyo, to aid you and to be your brother for as long as the Great Spirit wills it. He will stay with you and aid you as you look for and find your true self and your rightful place in this world."

"But...I still can't understand why I'm here and what you're going to teach me." said Caylen. "I don't understand who or what you are and who the Great Spirit is."

"First of all, I shall tell you of the Great Spirit." Sania said. "In the world that you have lived in and have come from, your people call the Great Spirit that they believe in by the name, 'God', and you speak to him in your own special ways, do you not?"

"Yes, we pray to him and we ask him to help and guide us." Caylen answered.

"We also speak to our God, but we have given to him the name 'Great Spirit'," said Sania. "We speak to him in many ways, and in turn—if he so chooses—he speaks to us, guiding us, showing us what is to be, and asking, at times, that we serve him."

"Is that why you came to me?" asked Caylen.

"Yes, the Great Spirit told me to bring you here and to teach you the ways of our people and of our beliefs and to make you into a Whakan Powwaw as am I. A Whakan Powwaw is, in my tribe, the most sacred of medicine men or 'priest', as you white-eyes call your medicine men. We have been given many powers by the Great Spirit that enable us to do such things that you could only dream of doing. That is how I was able to visit you in your sleep, and to see you through the eyes of my wolf, Abhaya."

" But why?" Caylen asked. "Why would your Great Spirit select me to become a priest or as you say, a Whakan Powwaw?"

"I do not question the Great Spirit's wishes or his commands. I cannot tell you of his reasons for what he does. All I can tell you is that he is all wise and must be obeyed by those of us who can hear his voice. If you wish to know the Great Spirit's reasons for what he does, you must ask only him, for only he knows the answers you seek."

"But, what if I don't want to become a Whakan Powwaw?" asked Caylen.

"Why would you come here to me if you did not wish to learn?

Who do you think showed you the path to the heavy yellow stones that the white-eyes love so much? And why? Who do you think made the bullets fired at you by the white-eyes called Fariss Lubak miss striking you, and why? When you know the answers to these many questions, you shall know why you wanted to become a Whakan Powwaw as am I."

"How on earth could you know all about those things?" Caylen queried. "You were not there!"

"You are wrong, young Adahy. I have much to teach you, I have been with you and watching over you now for more than five snows, just as the Great Spirit has asked of me. And now, I must obey his further wishes and teach you the ways of a Whakan Powwaw." Sania sad. "Would you not wish to have these same powers? Would you not wish to be able to see far-away people, things and places? Would you not wish to be able to see what is to be? Would you not wish to be able to enter your Cheveyo's mind and travel with him over the lands, to see through his eyes as your own, to control his every action? Would you not wish to be able to see the essence of others and be able to sense their goodness or their evil? Would you not wish all these things?"

"It would be great to be able to do all of those things." Caylen agreed, eagerly. "What do I have to do?"

"You must first find out who you are, and if you are truly worthy of these many things, by going on a Vision Quest to a place that is sacred, and known to the Great Spirit. If you are to be chosen by him, he will come to you while you are on this Vision Quest and guide you on the path to your destiny. Only then can I teach you, and show you how you may use all these things that the Great Spirit shall bestow upon you if he so chooses."

"Well, how do I go about this Vision Quest?" questioned Caylen.

"We must first prepare you, for this is no easy thing that you plan to do," the old man said. "This Vision Quest will test every fiber of your existence and may even cause you to cease to exist on this earth. It is a very dangerous thing you are about to undertake and once you begin, there is no turning back. We shall rest now and begin your preparations at first light, should you still wish to continue."

When Caylen awoke early the following morning, the old man was already up and preparing the morning meal. Caylen quickly dressed and ate the piece of dried fish and drank the hot, pungent tea that Sania handed him.

Sania only spoke after they had both completely consumed their breakfasts.

"We must now begin to prepare you. Come and sit before me," he said.

Caylen sat on the floor in front of the old man as he shaved Caylen's hair so that he was completely bald. He then made him take off all of his clothing and gave him just a blanket to wrap around himself before leading him outside and over to a small, round mud-covered hut that was emitting smoke from a roof vent. Throwing back the caribou skin door flap caused a huge cloud of hot steam to billow out into the cool morning air.

"Enter." Sania ordered, following Caylen into the hot, dark, steamy interior of the little sauna. "We must cleanse and purify our bodies before we go to meet the Great Spirit."

The only light in the hot sauna was given off by a little fire that was centered amidst a circle of round black rocks. As he sat, the old man shed his blanket and bade Caylen do the same. When they were both sitting, naked, across from each other beside the fire, Sania took a little bucket of water and splashed some of the water onto the hot rocks. A heavy cloud of steam sputtered forth, causing the hut's temperature to rise even more. He continued, every few minutes, to splash more water on the rocks and created so much steam that Caylen soon could see nothing save a small glimmer of light from the fire. Just as he began to think that his body could stand no more, the old man began to chant, in a monotone voice, words that Caylen couldn't begin to understand.

Within a few seconds of Sania beginning his chanting, Caylen could feel a weird, icy-cold chilling that seemed to begin in the soles of his feet and then gradually rise throughout his entire body, until he began to shiver uncontrollably in the now steamy, hot, wet environment of the sauna.

"What's happening?" he exclaimed. "How can I be so cold with all this hot steam around me?"

The old man said nothing, but continued his chanting as Caylen, naked and shivering with cold, began to get really frightened by what was happening. As the old man continued with his chant, he also continued to create more hot steam by throwing water on the hot rocks surrounding the little fire. As the steam grew ever thicker, the hut grew hotter and hotter with Caylen growing even colder, until his teeth were loudly chattering and his whole body was shaking.

Determined to suffer through whatever the old man did to him, Caylen could feel his consciousness beginning to fade and a black darkness begin to fall over his wide open, staring eyes. Just as he felt himself begin to topple over in an unconscious state, the chanting stopped and his entire body was suddenly, nearly unbearably hot in the sauna's steamy interior.

The old man rose and, opening the sauna's door said to the now totally confused, heavily-sweating Caylen.

"Come."

The old Indian led the overheated and still naked Caylen down to, and directly out into the lake until the icy cold water completely covered him. Then, he led Caylen back to the shore and, handing him his blanket, said.

"Now, young Adahy. Tell me what you felt as your body was cleansed."

Caylen looked up at the sun, which indicated that it was now late afternoon and said.

"I thought we were only in the steam for a few minutes and then suddenly I felt colder than I have ever felt before. And then I was hot again. What just happened to me?" he asked.

"We were in the steam for nearly eight hands of time, or eight of your hours," said Sania. "When you felt the cold enter your body, the Great Spirit was showing you his powers and greeting you as is his way. In future times, whenever you feel that same coldness coming over you, you shall know that the Great Spirit is with you and watching over you. Now come, we must begin your Quest as your body is now purified and ready. Bring only your blanket and some water."

Sania picked up his staff and led Caylen up a narrow trail that meandered off towards a rocky cliff about one-half mile distant. Caylen was quite surprised to see Warrior simply lift his big head from where he lay and watch his master leave, without following him as he would normally have done.

It took nearly an hour of trudging over the rocky trail in his bare feet in the failing afternoon light before they reached what appeared to be a flat, rocky point high above the pretty valley where Sania's cabin was located. The view was spectacular, with snowcapped mountains surrounding them, save for a large lake-filled gap to the East. The rock they were standing on was about thirty feet across, with a number of round rocks placed in a circle with a ten-feet diameter at the flat rock's very center. Leading Caylen to the center of this circle, the old man said to him.

"Sit here until I return for you. You will eat nothing, but you may drink of your water. If the Great Spirit wishes, he will give you a sign that will be yours for your life's journeys; but you must not move from this sacred place until I return. Now sit and reflect on your past, the present, and your destiny."

"But, what of the cold? And what do I do about my body wastes?" asked Caylen.

"You have your robe and you may only leave this circle once each day for your body functions. You must not soil this sacred place or anywhere nearby with you body wastes." Sania said, as he walked off down the trail. "I go now to wait a sign from the Great Spirit that he has come to you."

Chapter 16

Visions

Searching around, Caylen found himself a flat rock about four inches thick and about fourteen inches in diameter and placed it in the center of the ring of boulders. He placed a corner of his blanket over the flat rock and made himself comfortable on his padded seat, with his legs crossed and the remainder of the blanket draped over his naked shoulders. He had no idea as to how long he was expected to remain in this particular place, or when Sania would return for him. All he really knew about what he was doing what was Sania had told him. He had said that the experience could be very dangerous for him and that the Great Spirit, who was apparently a God to Sania and his people, would come to him if Caylen were favored by this Great Spirit, and show him what his future was to be.

Caylen had, until his experiences in the sauna, been very skeptical of all that the old native had said to him. He thought that the old man likely had considerable knowledge of forest lore and native traditions, and could probably teach him much about these things. He also found himself liking the old man very much, and thought his seemingly simplistic way of life very interesting and intriguing. He recalled what the old man had said to him about potential powers that might be given to Caylen by the Great Spirit when suddenly, with a start, he realized that the old man was already in possession of at least some of those powers. Looking back over the past few years, he thought,

How else could he have known all those things about me? I was hundreds of miles away from here when I first dreamt about him and that big wolf. When we moved up here, I did see that big wolf more than once, and I even saw moccasin tracks appear on the snow that time, even though no one was there. None of those things are possible, he though. Only in a dream could those things happen.

Caylen found himself replying to his own questions as he formulated, in his subconscious, all of these questions.

"But I wasn't dreaming when I saw the wolf the first time outside of my tent, and I wasn't dreaming when I saw his tracks and the moccasin tracks on the snow. And I was definitely not dreaming when I observed those same moccasin tracks just disappear as I watched.

That old man does have some really good tricks that he might be willing to teach me so I had best do as he asks and see what happens. He said aloud to himself.

Soon after he had met the old man, Sania had told Caylen of his own background. He explained that he was a Hopi Indian from a tribe that lived far to the South and had been a Sacred Medicine Man in the tribe for many years. He went on to explain that some members of his tribe had become jealous and frightened of his seemingly extraordinary powers and that those tribe members eventually convinced the tribal elders that he, Sania, was an evil medicine man and should be killed or banished forever from the tribe. The tribal elders had met for three days to contemplate Sania's fate before they finally decided to banish him from the tribe for the remainder of his life. Sania told Caylen that he had only seen forty-five snows when his banishment had taken place and that it was seven more snows before he found his way North to where he now lived. When Caylen asked him how old he was now, the old man had smiled and said to Caylen,

"I have seen seventy-eight snows since my people told me to leave my home. My Abhaya has chosen to be with me for fifty-three of those snows. My time and my Abhaya's time left on this world is nearly gone, so I must pass on my knowledge to another. That is why you have been summoned to me, young Adahy. You have been chosen by the Great Spirit, who is so very wise, to take, and to use wisely these things and these powers that I alone, now possess. You must, though, be aware that you shall be given these gifts only if the Great Spirit finds through a Vision Quest, that you are worthy of such gifts."

Caylen hadn't, at first, really believed this part of the old man's story, but he was now, after all that had since occurred, not quite so sure of just what to believe. What he didn't, and couldn't know, was that he, by reflecting on all that had happened in the past, was doing exactly what was intended by his Vision Quest, and that his internal discussions were really just preparations for what was about to happen to him on this, his personal Vision Quest.

Caylen's position on top of the flat rock gave him a spectacular view, as he was quite high above the lake and the valley in which the old man's cabin was situated. While he couldn't quite see Sania's cabin, he could see a tiny wisp of smoke wafting up through the tall spruce trees that surrounded the aqua-blue waters of the lake. As he gazed out over the beautiful scenery, his thoughts drifted back to his early childhood and his long dead father.

I wonder if he saw all of this when he lived up here, he thought to himself. *I wish he were alive and here with Mom and me. I bet he really loved it up here.*

His thoughts then went forward to his mother's current situation with Fariss and all of his problems. He searched himself and his thoughts and decided that in some ways he liked Fariss, but in many other ways he knew that Fariss was only as good as the moment, and that his behavior could go from benevolence to being dangerously evil in just a heartbeat of time.

Caylen wondered if Kosumi and Lokni would ever return with the police to investigate Wildflower's death and if they would ever find out what Fariss's involvement was in her death that night.

Caylen's thoughts were suddenly interrupted by the eerie howling of a pack of timber wolves on a nearby hunt. The chorus of their howls caused him to look about himself and to realize that it was now nearly dark. Thinking that Sania would soon be there to bring him back to the cabin, he rose, stretched his kinked arms and legs and walked over far to one side to make his evening toilet. After standing and waiting a few minutes for the old man to appear, Caylen finally came to the conclusion that he was on his own and would have to spend the night perched on his lonely, cold rock. Sitting back down, he pulled his blanket up over his head, closed his eyes and listened closely to the intense silence of the cool northern night.

After about an hour in this state, he opened his eyes to watch the most spectacular, mind-boggling display of Northern Lights that he had ever seen. The multi-colored lights raced across the night sky in blazing patterns and dazzling designs that could only be described as a beautiful piece of moving artwork that made Caylen say out loud,

"That can only be the inspiration and work of an extraordinary intelligence, with powers that I can't even imagine."

~*~

Dawn breaking over the eastern mountains caused Caylen to realize that he had spent a full day and night sitting on his little rock, waiting for whatever was supposed to happen, to happen. His stomach told him that it wanted nourishment and was very unhappy about not receiving any. Caylen satisfied it for the moment with a swallow or two of his water before settling down to wait for whatever was supposed to happen to occur. He sat, motionless for nearly eight hours, standing only once to relieve his bladder and to stretch his aching legs. Absolutely nothing happened this day with the exception being a noisy raven that landed on the edge of his rocky ledge, harassing him with raucous squawking for nearly an hour before flying off. Caylen even thought, for a few minutes that the big bird's squawking was an attempt by the bird to tell him something, nearly asking it to repeat what it had just said.

As the sun began to slide behind the Westerly mountains, Caylen could feel himself beginning to drowse off on occasion. This tiredness lasted only until the chilly evening breezes began their downward slide into the valley below, causing him to wrap himself even tighter in his warm blanket. This second night was also uneventful, with only the sky's bright starlight to keep him company. He did hear the howling of the wolves again and wondered if his Warrior was enjoying the company of his canine father. At this thought, he wondered what it would be like to experience, as a wolf, a hunt for, and the bringing down of a large herbivore such as a caribou or a moose with only one's teeth as a weapon. He found that he was thinking of such weird and unusual things more and more as he sat waiting for something unusual to occur to him as the old Indian had suggested might happen.

He wondered again just what the danger could be that Sania had said he might be facing, as absolutely nothing even remotely resembling anything dangerous had appeared to him, or had occurred since he had begun his Vision Quest on this cold lonely rock.

~*~

It was late afternoon of Caylen's third day of his Vision Quest when something of significance finally did happen. He was watching a huge bald eagle circling about far overhead; imagining what it would be like to be soaring high above the earth, when it suddenly swooped down and landed heavily on the rock directly in front of him. It stood looking at him for a few moments, and then Caylen heard it say, quite clearly and without actually speaking,

"Adahy, why do you look at me so? Have you never seen an eagle before now?"

"How can you be talking to me?" Caylen asked, aloud and suddenly afraid. "Am I going crazy?"

"No, you're not crazy, Adahy, but you did summon me to come down to you. I heard your voice clearly ask me what it was like to be soaring high above you in the heavens," said the eagle.

"I admit that I was thinking you must have a wonderful view from up there, but I didn't ask you to come to me." Caylen said, beginning to feel foolish.

"You did not have to ask," replied the eagle. "All you had to do was think the thought and I could plainly hear your voice."

"Well, I didn't know that," said Caylen. "I am sorry, I really didn't mean to interrupt your flight."

With that the big eagle flew off, leaving Caylen sitting stunned and unbelieving of what had just taken place.

~*~

It was about two hours later and completely dark, with Caylen almost fully satisfied that the eagle episode had been just a silly dream, when he suddenly felt himself being lifted from his perch on the cold rock. Opening his eyes wide, he looked about, expecting to see Sania helping him to his feet. What he saw caused him to gasp in fear and reach out in an attempt to steady himself. He opened and closed his eyes two or three times, and then actually pinched himself before he came to fully realize that he was not in the midst of a dream, but was, in fact, hovering in the air some twenty feet above where he could see himself still sitting on the rocky edge.

" What on earth is happening to me?" he asked of no one in particular.

As he spoke aloud, Caylen looked closely at his unmoving physical body sitting below him on the rock. Coming from the centre of his unmoving bowed head, he could see a long, curly, golden thread that spiraled up and across the twenty or so feet that separated his physical body to where he was now suspended.

"What you now see connecting your earthly body to your Essence is your thread of life. Should you break that thread, your earthly body shall surely cease to exist and you will never be able to return to it." said a loud, clear voice.

"Who and what are you?" asked Caylen, in a terrified voice.

"I am what your earthly teacher calls, the 'Great Spirit', and I am He who all earthly beings must respect and obey." The voice said.

"But, why are you doing this to me?" Caylen was becoming a little less afraid, as he realized that he was not about to fall from the sky.

"Because your Whakan Powwaw has spoken to me in your favor, asking that I bestow on you the ability to attain such powers as he decides that you deserve and need, in order for you to carry out your life's destiny." the voice said.

"Are you God?" asked Caylen. "And if you are, is my father with you, and if he is, may I see and speak with him?"

"I am Qaletaka, Sacred Guardian of the People. I am the creator of all things, large and small. And, yes, your father is with me, and no, you cannot see or speak with him until your thread of life has been broken and your essence has joined with his."

" So, what now?" Caylen asked. "How do you figure out if I should be given these powers, and what powers do you mean?"

"I am, as I have spoken, the Guardian of the People, all powerful, and I have already seen that you possess a good spirit and are deserving. I shall hereafter call you by the name 'Mato Honi', or in your words Brave Wolf. You shall first be given the power to place a part of your essence into the essence of any of the creatures of the earth that swim, walk, crawl or fly, to see through their eyes what they see and to guide their every movement. You shall also be give the power to move your essence alone and from your earth body to within the distance that your thread of life permits."

"But, how do I get these powers?" asked Caylen.

"I, Qaletaka, have already bestowed these and other powers upon you." said the voice, "Your Whakan Powwaw must now instruct you on how you may call upon and use these powers safely. You must always remember to use them wisely or you shall surely lose them."

"May I return my essence now to my mortal body?" Caylen asked.

"Go." the voice commanded. "Return to your earth body and remember always what I have said. Go now, Mato Honi, go to your Whakan Powwaw. Your Vision Quest is now over."

Chapter 17

Sania's Teachings

Caylen came fully awake with a start. His last recollection of being aware had been that of being pulled upwards and out of his body, as his tired eyes were closing in the darkness of his third night on the rock. He could recall his conversation with the big eagle late in the afternoon and then while he was still trying to figure out whether it had been a real conversation or just a hallucination, darkness had fallen and he was suddenly being pulled upwards and out of his body. Everything that had happened after that moment was perfectly vivid and clear in his mind. As he now looked about, he realized that it was late in the afternoon and that his conversation with Qaletaka, the Sacred Guardian of the People and his 'out-of-body' experience had lasted for approximately twenty hours and that he was now completely exhausted from the experience that had occurred to him.

Unable, in his exhausted state, to stop himself, Caylen wrapped his wool blanket tightly around his body and lay back on the hard surface of the rock. His last conscious thought before sleep took him was to wonder what his friend Warrior was doing at that moment.

~*~

Caylen's sleep lasted until the following morning when he was rudely wakened by a warm liquid tongue that was slathering wolf saliva over his entire face. Opening his eyes, he saw, about one foot from his face, the happy, grinning features of Warrior. Behind him, standing just outside the rock ring, leaning on his staff, stood Sania, also smiling broadly at him.

"Well, young Mato Honi, are you rested sufficiently to return now to my home and to begin your future?" he asked.

" What did you just call me?" asked Caylen, still drugged from his long sleep.

"I called you by the name that you now are to be called. I called you 'Mato Honi', as Qaletaka has said you are to be known hereafter." Sania answered.

"I remember that," Caylen murmured. "I remember everything that he said. Was it just a dream?"

"Do you think it was but a dream? Do you think that the Great Spirit would waste his time to give you nothing but a dream? You have much to learn, young Mato Honi."

"But, how could you know that he named me Mato Honi? I was asleep when he named me and you were back at your house." Caylen said.

"The Great Spirit has instructed me to now give you the knowledge that you need to use those powers that he has bestowed upon you." Sania replied. "Do you think that, having asked that of me, he would not tell me of his name for you? Now rise and come, we must feed you and begin your teachings."

Sania led Caylen back to his cabin. Fortunately for Caylen, Sania had brought his moccasins with him so Caylen would have some protection for his feet on the return journey. Sania neither said or asked Caylen anything until after he had eaten some dried fish and some pemmican, washed down with copious quantities of warm tea.

"We shall begin your learnings with talk of our people's beliefs and of our traditions." Sania said. "If you are to use our powers, you must know of these things or you may fall prey to the many evils that travel this world."

"What evils do you mean?" Caylen asked.

"There are many evils on this earth that may tempt you and try to lead you to where you may not wish to go. These evils may also try to get you to do things that a good man would never do." said Sania.

"I don't really understand just what you mean." Caylen replied. "Please explain more to me about these evils."

"You have seen what the yellow stones can do to the minds of humans, have you not? Have you not seen how your Kachada, Fariss Lubak, acts when he finds the yellow stones? Have you not seen how he acts when he cannot find more of those yellow stones when he so wishes?"

"Yes, I have." Caylen said. "He acts really crazy when he does find gold and even crazier when he doesn't find it."

"That is one example of an evil that can enter a man's essence and cause him to, in turn, do evil things." Sania said. "And how did the young Adahy himself act when he found the yellow stones?"

"I'll not ask how you know of my gold find." Caylen responded. "But my thoughts as well as my actions were to be thankful that I could now give my mother the good life she deserves, and the many things that she requires for a good life. I also thought to provide myself with further learnings so as to permit me to be of assistance to others when I become a man."

"You have given me the correct reply, Mato Honi, as I knew you would. For if you had not, Qaletaka, the Great Spirit would not have chosen you and you would not be here with me at this time. Further, you shall now understand that you are no longer the young boy called Adahy but are now the man called Mato Honi. You have been greatly favored by Qaletaka and you have been given many things that I must teach you to use as they were intended."

"Is it the intention of the Great Spirit that I use these powers to fight evil?" asked Caylen.

"That is what he wishes, and that is what I must teach you." Sania replied.

"You shall be able to see evil and to know when evil is present. There is much evil in this world. Evil can only exist when good men permit it to exist. You are a good man, Mato Honi, and you will be unable to permit evil to exist."

"And just how am I to do that?" Caylen asked.

"You have been give this power, you shall, henceforth, be able to look at any earthly man and, if that man is evil, you shall be able to see, surrounding his head, the dark colors of evil. If he is a good man, his colors shall be those of a rainbow in the sky. You will also know when evil spirits are present. The worst of all these evil spirits shall be clearly visible to your eyes, this evil spirit is known by my people as a 'Wendigo'. A Wendigo is an evil so terrible and so ugly that ordinary men's eyes cannot see him. Only those men who are truly evil or whom, like you, the Great Spirit has blessed, are able to see him. Evil men can also feel him, as he consumes their very flesh and bone."

"That's awful." Caylen shuddered. "But, if he is invisible, how does he consume them?"

"The Wendigo has many powers," Sania responded. "He knows when a man becomes evil and he will only watch and enjoy that man's evil doings until he tires of this game; he will then make himself visible to that evil man and will tear him apart, eating him piece by piece, until the man and all his evil are part of the Wendigo.

"But, what does he look like?" Caylen asked.

"He looks like evil, he looks like the most evilest thing that a man can imagine but he only becomes visible to those who he is about to consume The Wendigo must consume evil men in order that he can survive. Evil men are the only food that he can consume. He cannot exist on this world for more than one hundred snows without consuming this evil food. He becomes stronger and even more evil when he consumes his evil food."

"Have you ever seen him?" asked Caylen.

"I have seen him many times, as shall you." Sania replied. "Your future has been written by Qaletaka and you will have no choice but to do as is written. You will, as I have said, be able to see and possibly even speak to the Wendigo, but you must never permit him to enter your essence or you shall be forever lost to the Great Spirit."

"Why would I permit him into my essence?" Caylen asked, somewhat bewildered.

"The Wendigo has many powers, he can, at times, make himself look as a good thing to an ordinary man; but as you are not an ordinary man, he can never hide his true self from your eyes. Fortunately for all men, a Wendigo has been limited by Qaletaka to living in only in specific, distant and remote forests."

"Well, that's good to know." said Caylen. "Is Fariss an evil man for what he did to Wildflower?"

"The Kachada, Fariss Lubak, is, at present, neither good nor evil. The Wendigo has tried and is still trying to make him into pure evil so that he can consume him, but has not yet fully succeeded."

"Will the Wendigo eventually consume him?" Caylen queried.

"That is for the Great Spirit to decide, he only permits us to see of the future what he wishes. There is good and evil present in all men and only men can decide the path of life that they will follow. Each man chooses his own life's path and his own destiny while he dwells on this world. It is only after a man ceases to exist on this world that the Gods of good or evil will rule over him forever." Sania instructed.

"Another thing I must tell to you is that we, in our beliefs, do not speak aloud the names of our dead until seven snows have passed, for those essences of our dead might think that we are calling to them and trying to keep them from going to the hereafter to reside in the lands of the Great Spirit. Now, Mato Honi, we must rest for three days before we begin to learn how to use those powers that have been given you."

~*~

Caylen enjoyed himself immensely over the next three days. He and Warrior explored the little valley in its entirety, looking up the many side canyons and sampling the fishing in the numerous little streams that drained the snow-covered mountains surrounding them. He contemplated going back to visit his mother, but decided that doing so would take up time that he wanted to himself. He found that he was spending more and more time thinking about what had occurred to him on his Vision Quest, attempting to determine just what it all meant. Sania was of little help to him as he refused to answer any of his many queries. He would only say to Caylen that the answers would soon be clear to him and that he needed only to listen to the many voices of the Great Spirit for guidance and for the answers to his many questions. This only served to arouse Caylen's curiosity even more, and to cause him to sit and think for hours at a time about all that had happened.

The fourth day following the conclusion of his Vision Quest began with Caylen's usual early morning awakening by the loud, liquid slurp of Warrior's wet tongue on his face as he slept. Quickly dressing in anticipation of the start of his lessons, he prepared breakfast for himself, Sania, Warrior and Abhaya. Sania had already been up and about, doing what Caylen thought were preparations for his lessons. During the time the foursome consumed their breakfast of hot Salal-leaf tea and dried smoked lake trout, Caylen decided to ask the old man about his lessons.

"Are we going to start my lessons today?" he asked.

"Your lessons are already underway, Mato Honi. Have you not

been musing over what you have become? Have you not been thinking about how your essence could possibly mix with the essence of your Warrior or any other of the forest's beasts and birds? Have you not been wondering how your essence could possibly control the essences of others? Have you not wondered about how you could possibly see through the eyes of others? Have you not been thinking about these many things?"

"Well, yes, that's about all I've been able to think about since we came back from the mountain. " said Caylen.

" Then you should also know that your lessons began the instant you accepted your gifts from the Great Spirit. Your lessons for the next two moons are to continue wondering about all these gifts you have been given and to ask of me the correct questions so that I may give you the correct answers and guide you through what must be." Sania stated.

"Also, as you are now a man with the name of Mato Honi, you must have a medicine bag to bear around your neck. This medicine bag shall contain things that are known only to you. These things shall be of no value to anyone other than to Mato Honi and shall, when looked upon by you, fill your heart, your body and your essence with much happiness or much sadness for all things that your life has seen and done. This is what you must now do, Mato Honi, before I next speak to you of things to be."

Caylen had seen the small leather pouch that Sania always carried with him on a leather thong about his neck. When he had asked him what it was, the old man had said that it was his medicine bag, which only he alone knew its contents, and that Caylen should not ask about it ever again.

Caylen then began to think about small things that he was greatly impressed with, that he cared about and that he knew would remind him of the past. As he considered these things, he realized that he already had many of the objects that Sania had mentioned might be a part of a medicine bag.

He first removed the medal from around his neck that his father had been awarded for valor in the Great War. He took the tiny locket that contained a small lock of his mother's hair from his pocket. In another pocket, he found one of the dewclaws that he had cut from Warriors paws and saved for no apparent reason. He placed all of these items in a small pile on the table and studied them intently for about ten minutes.

Examining his thoughts in detail, he knew that something was missing from the pile. After a few minutes more, he realized what the missing object was, so he went outside and clambered back up the mountain to where he had spent his four days on his Vision Quest. After looking about, he soon spotted what he was looking for. He picked up the small feather that had fallen from the bald eagle that had visited him while he was on his Vision Quest and, returning to the cabin, he added the feather to the little pile of objects that was to be included in his medicine bag

Caylen then spent the next few hours fashioning a small leather pouch that would hold all of the collected items he wished to include in his medicine bag. He cut a long leather thong from a scrap piece of moose hide that he wove into the neck of the little pouch, serving both as a closer and as a loop that fitted neatly around his neck and held the pouch close to his chest. When completed, he placed all of his objects into the pouch, closed it tightly and placed the loop over his head. He then found Sania and showed him what he had done. He was about to tell him what he had placed in the pouch when Sania said.

"No! You must tell no one of what you have placed in your medicine bag. Not even I must know what another man's medicine bag contains. Those things are now sacred objects that are to be known only by you. When you have the need to ask the Great Spirit for advise, you must hold your sacred medicine bag tightly in your hands, as it is your connection, and only yours, to the Great Spirit.

"I have another question that I would like you to answer." Caylen said.

"You now wish to know what gives you power over the creatures of the forest? I have been waiting for this question from you." replied Sania.

"How is it you always know what's in my thoughts and what it is that I'm about to say?" Caylen asked.

"I am a Whakan Powwow, I am a Sacred priest and a servant of the Great Spirit who has given to me such powers that no mortal man should be cursed with. This unwelcome power enables me to perceive the very thoughts of other beings, even as they form such thoughts. You should ask the Great Spirit to not bless you with this gift, for it is not a gift that any mortal man should ever possess." Sania replied.

"Now I will reply to your question of what gives a man powers over the forest creatures. The Great Spirit Qaletaka, the Creator of the people has given to all of his people the powers of '*concern* and *caring*'. The power of *concern* means that all of the people's actions are ruled, or should be ruled, by this power that we call *concern.* The Creator also, along with this power, gave the people another power called *caring.* These two things, concern and caring must always be used together. The Great Spirit gave powers only to the people, he did not give these powers to any of the other creatures of this land, only to the people. These powers are what gives the people of the land power over all other creatures that live. Only one who cares about and has concern for others is able to have power over the creatures of the land."

"Why would he give those powers only to the people and not to other creatures?" asked Caylen. "Why would he not give such powers to all of the earth's creatures?"

"Are you not filled with *concern* about what happens to your birth mother at the hands of Fariss Lubak?" asked Sania. "Are you not *caring* enough to be *concerned* about her well being?"

"I think I'm beginning to understand all of this." Caylen said. "But, again, why did the Whakan Powwow not give other creatures of the forest these same great powers?"

"How long do you think the wild wolf would live to prowl about on this earth if he was concerned and cared about the life of the caribou as he tore out the animal's throat before consuming his flesh?" Sania asked. "How long do you think that the fox would live to roam about the fields and the forests if he cared about and was concerned for the young who will surely perish when he, the fox, consumes the young rabbit's mother?" Sania added. "How long do you think that the bear would continue to exist on this land if he was to be concerned or cared about the unborn young of the salmon he is consuming?" Sania continued.

He ended the discussion by adding, "It is only the people who have the powers of *caring and concern* for if they did not, they would be no more than the other creatures of this land, they would not be people but would only be simple creatures caring for nothing save their own existence. The Great Spirit, Qaletaka has given these powers only to man as he wishes that only man have power over all creatures of this land. Do you now understand why you have been favored by the Great Spirit and given these special powers, Mato Honi?"

"Yes, I think I do. I shall think much about these things that you've said to me." Caylen replied.

"Go then, and ponder these things until you are ready to move forward with your learning for I have given you much to think about." Sania instructed.

~*~

With all this on his mind, Caylen decided to do some fishing in the lake where the stream entered it. This location usually gave up some nice Arctic grayling and the occasional lake trout that perceived his lure as a tasty little grayling. Landing his first fish, he noticed that it was a female grayling and that it was full of ripe roe that would never, should he kill this magnificently colored fish, become young grayling, never to be able to swim freely about in the cold water of this lake.

Caylen gently removed the barbed hook from the mouth of the fish and placed the fish back into the cold lake waters, saying as he released it,

"Go with the Great Spirit, little fish, for I am concerned about your children, I care about you and I wish for your young to survive and to be free to swim about in this lake.

Caylen spent the next two weeks thinking about all that had happened to him since he had been summoned to the old Indian's home. While he was not initially sure of the old man's honesty in all that he had told him, he now, after his Vision Quest, believed without any doubt whatsoever, in everything Sania said and told him. He knew from what he had seen himself, that what the old man said and did was completely and unequivocally based on the truth and on what he believed in. While Caylen had never been a religious person, he had been taught by his mother to believe in powers that were much greater than his or any other ordinary man's.

Now confronted by this old Indian who claimed to be a Sacred Priest with powers beyond comprehension, he was more than a little confused. His own experiences while on his Vision Quest served only to add to his confusion about everything the old man said. Sania's methods of instruction also added to the difficulties that he had in absorbing the quantity of information that he had been given. He found that the old man's unorthodox method of using questions as a teaching tool, only served to initiate, in his mind, more questions, questions that he found extremely difficult to answer. He did find, however, that as the days passed the answers to his many unasked questions simply and suddenly would come to him with great clarity.

After the two weeks were up, Caylen went to Sania and said to him.

"Sania, I have given much thought to what has happened to me on my Vision Quest. I know now that a power much greater than I has decided that I am worthy of his attention and that he also finds me worthy of receiving your teachings. I know also that what you have told me and what you will teach me may give me power that I could only ever dream of possessing. I know that what you have told me and what you will teach me in the future will be the truth and that I have been blessed by the Great Spirit to be able to call you my friend."

"I thank you, Mato Honi, you honor me by calling me your friend. A man who hopes to live a full and useful life on this world must have at least one person that he can call 'friend'. If you will permit me I would also be honored to call you my friend. I would even be more honored if you would permit me to become your brother as well as your friend." Sania said.

"Thank you for all you've done for me and all that you are still to do for me. I am pleased that you have agreed to become my friend as well as my teacher." Caylen said. "I would also be honored and pleased to call you my brother as well.

"We must then perform the sacred rites that will bind us together as brothers for all eternity." said Sania, drawing his belt knife. Give me your hand," he added, "so that we may cause our blood to flow together and to permit us to think and act as one." Taking Caylen's hand, Sania drew the keen edge of his knife across the base of both Caylen's and his own thumbs. Then he, with his bloody hand, grasped Caylen's bleeding hand in such a way that caused their blood to mix together, before it dripped to the ground.

"Thank you, Mato Honi, for becoming my friend and my brother. We are now as one for all of time." Sania said.

"And I thank you, Sania, for allowing me this special honor. I shall now ask you for one more thing."

"Ask what you will, but before you ask this thing of me, I would ask the same of you." said Sania, as he sliced off a lock of both his and Caylen's hair. He then mixed the two clumps of hair together before separating it into two separate locks that now held the combined hair of both Caylen and Sania. Giving one of them to Caylen, both he and Caylen placed the little clumps of their mingled hair in the medicine bags that they each wore around their necks.

"By placing these pieces of ourselves together and by allowing our blood to flow together, we have become as one. As long as we both still breathe the air of this world, we shall each have power to call to each other even if we are far apart from each other." Sania said. "It is now time, my brother, for you to begin to learn how to use the powers that the Great Spirit has given to you

Chapter 18

Power

Caylen didn't quite know just how Sania was going to teach him to use the powers that the Great Spirit had apparently blessed him with. All he knew for certain was that whatever instruction methods Sania used, they would be unexpected and unusual. While he felt quite good about the blood-brother rituals and the sharing of each other's mingled locks of hair, he didn't really share Sania's beliefs in the powers that the rituals had theoretically given him.

It was two days later, and the warm sun shining down on the sandy shores of the lake had lured Caylen into stretching out on the warm beach sand. He was lazily watching a bald eagle circling high above. Watching the seemingly effortless movements of the big bird, Caylen thought, *Wow! If only I really did have the power to see through another creature's eyes! That would really be great. I bet that eagle has a grand view from way up there."*

Caylen then closed his eyes and lay back on the warm sand thinking about what it would be like to be the eagle, soaring high above the lake and the pretty little valley, just enjoying the view, with only the occasionally flap of a wing.

Suddenly he was jolted into reality by a gust of cold air that seemed to penetrate clear through his breast feathers and chilled his entire body. He opened his eyes and saw, far below himself, a man and a black wolf lying on the sandy shore of the lake. He pivoted about and went into a long, shallow dive that took him down to within two hundred feet of the small, still figures. As he wheeled around the resting man, he angled his tail feathers and slightly tilted his body, so as to change his flight direction to where he could see the man's features more clearly. What he saw caused him to lose his balance entirely and to tumble, over and over, down toward the lake. His binocular-like vision had observed the face of the person lying on the beach, and that face was his very own.

As he fell, he finally came to the terrifying realization that he was now, somehow, inside the eagle, and was now seeing, through the eagle's eyes, himself and Warrior lying on the beach.

Suddenly afraid, he opened his eyes wide and found himself back on the beach, looking up at a large bald eagle that was obviously just recovering from a near crash landing into the icy cold lake. Shaking with fright, Caylen jumped to his feet and rushed back to the cabin to ask Sania if he could explain to him what he had just experienced. He realized that he probably had just experienced an out-of-body trip, which the old Indian had said he would eventually be able to control, and to perform at will.

What he didn't know was how or why it had occurred at that very moment, and how he was supposed to control the very frightening experience. *Well, I guess all those things that Sania said about powers and being able to see through other creature's eyes are really true. Up until now, I wasn't positive, but after that experience, I sure am a believer now.*

Caylen approached Sania, who was sitting just outside his cabin, enjoying the warm afternoon sun. As he grew near, Sania said to him,

"You are now ready to undertake the learning that is needed for you to understand and control your essence. If you are to use this power that Qaletaka has bestowed upon you, you must know these things well, as your trip in the sky nearly caused the death or serious injury to the eagle that you chose to use for your first attempt."

"But I didn't chose that eagle, I was not even aware of what was about to happen." Caylen protested. "And how do you know what happened? I haven't told you about it yet."

"As I have told you many times, I am a Whakan Powwaw. I am also your blood-brother. My essence can become one with your essence, as long as I have the talisman that we shared in my medicine bag. You also have this power, should you wish to use it." Sania said.

"Just how do I use this power of mixing my essence with yours?" Caylen asked.

"You must take your medicine bag to the sacred place on the

mountain where you experienced your meeting with the Great Spirit and put it on the very place where you sat. You must then ask the Great Spirit to honor you by giving this ability to your medicine bag in such a way that you can use it as you require. Only if the Great Spirit so wishes shall you then have this power. You shall receive a sign from the Great Spirit if he favors you with this power."

"But what about the power to travel with and see through the eyes of other creatures?" Caylen asked.

"You must show patience, Mato Honi. You cannot expect to learn all of these things in one passing of the sun. Besides, you already possess the power you speak of. It is only that you do not know how to use it that troubles you. Before I instruct you in the traveling of you essence, you must prepare your earthly body in the ways of our people. This is not an easy thing that you will have to do, as it may cause your body much pain, pain that you may think is unbearable and not worthwhile."

"So, should I first see if the Great Spirit is going to grant me powers to mix our essences?" Caylen asked.

"That would be wise of you, Mato Honi, my brother. Now go, for I grow weary and I have much to do to prepare myself for your teachings."

~*~

Caylen left early the following morning for the site of his Vision Quest. When he arrived, he removed his medicine bag from around his neck and placed it upon the small rock that he had sat on for four days and nights. Not knowing just how he was supposed to go about asking the Great Spirit for the power to blend his essence with Sania's, he decided to ask as though he were in prayer. Kneeling down he lowered his head until his forehead touched the stone on which he had placed the little medicine bag. he then stretched out his arms to his front and embraced the stone by clasping his hands together around it. He then uttered aloud, a short prayer to the Great Spirit.

"Oh, Great One, Great Spirit who has chosen to favor me with all these many things, Great Qaletaka, please favor me once more by granting me the powers needed so that I may blend my essence with the essence of my brother Sania, your Whakan Powwaw. I wish now, to be able to speak with my brother from great distances and without words from my lips."

Caylen remained in his prayer position for a few moments before standing. He wondered if he would even know or if he would be shown a sign that he had been granted these additional powers. After a few more moments had elapsed, he picked up his medicine bag and replaced it around his neck. As he did so, the bright, cloudless sky began to darken overhead until, within a very few minutes, it was as dark as night. Looking skyward, Caylen could see that a total solar eclipse was occurring at that very moment. As he watched, trembling in fear, he suddenly heard, emanating from the nearby forest, a loud chorus of eerie howls from a pack of passing timber wolves. He stood waiting for another few moments, until the sun had returned to its full, bright self and he had regained his composure, before musing,

Well, if that wasn't a sign from the Great Spirit, then I don't know what it was!

He then took his medicine bag in both hands and said, in his mind and to himself.

"Sania, my friend and my brother, are you able to hear me?

"Of course I can hear you, brother Mato Honi, but why are you speaking so loudly? I may be very old, but my ears still hear as a young man's do."

"Is that really you, Sania? Am I really speaking to you?" Caylen asked excitedly, speaking aloud now.

"It is I, Sania, to whom you are now yelling at. You must learn that you do not have to speak the words for me to hear what you are saying. You need only think what you wish to say and I shall hear your words, if you so wish it."

So this means that the Great Spirit has granted me the power to mix my essence with yours. Caylen thought, stating the obvious.

"You are now ready to prepare for your next teaching, that of traveling with and seeing through the eyes of other creatures. You must also know that the power just given you shall only be of use between you and me. This power cannot be used with others. Go now and rest for three suns as I prepare for your next teachings."

~*~

Caylen enjoyed the next three days immensely. He lazed about in the warm sun, did a little fishing and on three occasions practiced his new skill of speaking with Sania through his mind. The first two times he sent his thoughts to Sania, Sania replied to him using the same means. The third time, however, when Caylen sent his question to Sania, Sania didn't reply with his own thoughts as he had on both previous occasions. Instead, he came out of the cabin and strode down to the lake where Caylen, quite pleased with himself over his two successful communications with Sania, sat waiting for a response.

"Mato Honi, my brother, why do you continue to disturb my thoughts with your essence? Do you not think that your new power will stay with you? Do you think that this power will suddenly leave you? I have many things to do so that I may assist you to gain your remaining powers. Now go, and do not use your powers for such unworthy reasons. This new power you have been given should only be used when it is essential and you have no other means by which to speak."

Chastised, Caylen apologized to Sania and took Warrior and his fishing gear down along the lakeshore to a stream that held many large, hungry Arctic grayling. On the fourth day, Sania awakened Caylen well before the sun had risen.

"We must now prepare your earthly body for this teaching." Sania said. "Come now to the steam house so that your body may be cleansed of all physical things."

"But what of eating? My stomach is asking for food." Caylen replied.

"You must not consume any earthly foods on this day." Sania stated. Your body shall soon be filled with foods that the Great Spirit has provided for the nourishment of your essence. This food will sustain you during this teaching."

Caylen followed Sania into the already steaming little sauna. Sitting cross-legged in front of the small fire, Sania motioned for Caylen to sit across from him and then splashed more cold water onto the red-hot rocks and, through the billowing steam, handed Caylen a dried cylindrical yellow root of some plant unknown to Caylen.

"Take this food, Mato Honi, that Qaletaka has provided. Bite into it until it is liquid before you permit it to enter your body, and consume all, leaving nothing, so that your earthly body's hunger will be satisfied. Only then can I teach you what you must next know of the powers that the Great Spirit has granted you."

Saying nothing in response, Caylen bit into the dry root. It was quite bitter at first but he found that the longer he chewed on it the sweeter it became, until it had dissolved completely in his mouth. Swallowing it, he then bit off another piece, repeating the process until he had eaten the entire root.

Within a few moments of swallowing the last of the dissolved root, Caylen's hunger had completely disappeared, only to be replaced with a feeling of euphoria that grew more and more intense as he sat, waiting, cross-legged in the hot steamy sauna.

"Tell me what you now feel, Mato Honi. Is your essence now floating loosely about in your earthly body? Is it now ready to be led out and shown the path to other creatures' physical bodies? Are you able to hear the voice of my essence as I speak to you without speaking?"

My essence hears your essence speaking very clearly, Whakan Powwaw. What has happened to make my body feel in this way?

"You have consumed the food of the Great Spirit. This food shall free your essence so that I may teach you the ways in which you may mix your essence with the essence of the creatures of the land. If you do not learn these ways, your essence may become trapped within the essence of another. If this should happen, your earthly body would surely, before long, cease to exist on this earth. Therefore you must be able to, as you please, remove your essence from another's and return it to your own earthly body. You must also be able to leave a small part of your essence within your earthly body at all times so that you may protect it from harm as you are traveling within a creature.

Well, I would say that from the way I now feel, I'm about ready for anything that might happen. Caylen thoughts expressed his feeling.

"We must first ensure that your essence will permit this thing to happen, Mato Honi. Take this thing that I give you and hold it to the back of your main hand." Sania's thoughts echoed in Caylen's head, as the old Indian handed Caylen a wooden-handled steel stamp that he had heated in the fire until it glowed red.

Caylen took the hot metal stamp in his left hand and held the hot iron to the back of his right hand. He felt absolutely nothing but could see smoke rising from his burning flesh. After a moment or two, Sania reached over and, taking the hot iron from Caylen, sent

"Enough, Mato Honi, it is clear that you now have the sign of the Great Spirit upon you, and you now may be shown the way of moving your essence from yourself to other creatures, and the controlling of such moves."

How do I do these things, Whakan Powwaw? How is it that I may move my essence to a creature, control that creature and see through that creature's eyes? Caylen's mind asked.

"You must close your essence to all other things and think only of the very creature that you wish to send your essence to." Sania's thoughts rang in Caylen's mind. "Then you must command only part of your essence to mix with the essence of your chosen creature. You must do only this that I say, before you do more."

I will think only of my wolf dog, Warrior, and I will then, as you say, command part of my essence to join with his. Caylen sent his thoughts even as he did so. In the next instant, it was as though he could see two different scenes in front of him. He could still see Sania across the fire from him as though through a haze, but he could also see a view of the outside of the steam hut that he instinctively knew was the very view that Warrior had from where he was, just outside the hut.

He could also, for some surprising reason, suddenly detect many unfamiliar odors and sounds that had not been present a moment earlier. He quickly realized that what he smelled and was hearing were odors and sounds that Warrior's nostrils and ears were detecting. And that in addition to being able to see through Warrior's eyes, he could also now smell and hear what Warrior was smelling and hearing.

Sensing that Caylen had been successful in entering Warrior's mind, Sania sent his thoughts to Caylen.

"Now that you are with your Warrior, you must command him with you essence to do as you wish him to do"

Caylen thought for a moment and then silently sent,

Warrior, come to the steam house and take Sania's walking staff over to the cabin and place it there by the door.

As he watched through Warrior's eyes, he felt the animal rise and look about for the staff. Seeing it, he then walked over, picked the staff up in his mouth, and carried it over to the cabin, where he laid it against the caribou skin door before walking back and flopping down where he could watch the steam house.

As all this was occurring, Caylen could still, at the same time, see and sense Sania's presence with him in the steam house. Caylen also felt as though it had been he, and not his Warrior that had moved the staff. He felt himself looking again at the door of the steam house, waiting patiently for himself to emerge. Becoming quite confused about what was happening, Caylen then commanded his essence to return in its entirety in his own body.

The next thing that Caylen saw was only Sania looking quite pleased with both Caylen and himself, as he observed and sensed Caylen's actions.

"You have done well, Mato Honi. You are already skilled in the methods and uses of essence moving." Sania's thoughts said. "We will rest now so that you may ponder upon and practice these powers that the Great Spirit has bestowed upon you."

"Thank you, Sania, for blessing me with the knowledge and means to use these powers. I shall be forever your friend and your brother." Caylen said aloud.

"You are welcome, young brother. Now go and bring me back my walking staff that you commanded your wolf pet to steal!" Sania said, grinning broadly.

~*~

Caylen spent the next three weeks practicing his new skills. He found that he required less and less of the powerfully bitter root each time he attempted to transfer to a forest creature. Before long he was able to transfer to, and control birds, rabbits, moose, and even, with lesser success, the fish that swam in the stream and the lake without the use of the yellow root.

He soon found that it was much easier to transfer his control to a creature if it were nearby and clearly visible to him. The one exception to this seemed to be his pet wolf, Warrior. It seemed not to matter where Warrior was or what he was doing at the time. He could transfer to and control Warrior as he wished and whenever he wished.

Warrior didn't appear to be aware or care that anything unusual was happening, and showed no adverse reactions whatsoever to anything that he was made to do by Caylen while he was under his master' control.

Chapter 19

Sad Goodbyes

Caylen spent the next six months receiving more detailed instructions from Sania on how to use his new powers. Each day he practiced his new skills on different creatures that he saw around the cabin, in the forest, flying overhead or swimming on, or in, the lake. He found that he really enjoyed soaring high in the sky, with his essence implanted in a bald eagle or a falcon's brain. He also loved getting inside Warrior's head and racing through the forest on the scent of some prey animal. What he didn't like was the overtaking of some unfortunate animal and then killing it for food. He usually broke off his connection with Warrior just prior to his catching and killing the animal, as he didn't want Warrior to grow to dislike the presence of Caylen's essence within him, controlling his actions. By breaking the mind connection, he was not party to the slaying, if Warrior decided to kill and consume the animal he was pursuing.

It took considerable practice on his part before Caylen finally reached the stage in his training where he could transfer just enough of his essence to another creature so that he still had sufficient remaining in his own body so he could retain awareness and control of both the physical bodies his spirit occupied. Eventually, he was able to manage his own body and that of another creature with reasonable, if not considerable success. He did find, however, that any detailed mental work that he attempted within his own body at the same time he was also occupying another creature's mind left him extremely fatigued and mentally drained.

The snow had begun to melt when Sania asked Caylen to go into the steam house with him. Caylen was, by now, well aware that such an invitation meant that Sania had something that he considered important and serious to tell him. They sat in the hot lodge for at least an hour before the old man finally spoke.

"Mato Honi, I ask you to say to me how many snows that you have seen since the Great Spirit granted you life on this land?"

"I shall have seen seventeen snows when the next cold snow arrives." said Caylen. "Why does the Whakan Powwaw wish to know this thing?"

"You have studied your skills well, Mato Honi, and you have completed your Vision Quest as the Great Spirit has asked, and he is pleased that I have instructed you in the proper use of these Powers. He now asks that you undergo one more thing before you leave this place to begin your life's quest."

"What is this thing that he asks of me?"

"It shall be a happy thing for me but a not so happy thing for you, Mato Honi. It will, I am sure, cause you much pain and sorrow."

"But, what is it?" asked Caylen again; beginning to feel a little uneasy about the way the conversation seemed to be going.

"Qaletaka, The Great Spirit, has decided that he wishes me to embark on a great journey that will take me to his side. When I have taken my place there, he has said that he shall give me powers that no mortal man could ever perceive of. When I have become familiar with these new powers, the Great Spirit has said that I am to forever assist him in the many tasks that he must perform in the afterlife."

"But, when do you go? And what am I supposed to do when you go?" Caylen asked.

"I must leave when the Great Spirit calls for me. It is not for any mortal man to know of this time but it shall be soon. I know this thing that my mortal body is, even as I speak, growing cold and weak. This coldness is a sign from the Great Spirit that my time of leaving is near." Sania responded. "I must ask you, Mato Honi, my brother, to assist me to prepare myself for this long journey that I must soon travel to meet with the Great Spirit."

Caylen, with a sudden realization, finally grasped what the old man was trying to tell him.

"Oh! Now I understand." he said, with a trembling voice, tears beginning to well up in his eyes. "You're telling me that you think you are going to die soon! But, you can't die! I have so much more to learn from you before you die!" he exclaimed." I care too much for you. You just cannot die!"

"Ha!" Sania said. As I have said, the time of our leaving of this earth is not of our choosing. I have given all that I can to your wisdom and I now must do as Qaletaka demands of me." He continued. "You, Mato Honi, have blessed me by becoming my brother and as one with my essence. I now ask of you that I be permitted to forever call you my son. If you grant me this thing, I will, in the afterlife, speak well of you to your birth father. I will tell him many stories of the young man that his son has become, I will tell him also that his son, now a man, will do many great things with his life; things that he, your natural birth father, will take great pride in. I will ask also of the Great Spirit that he permit me to share these things that you do, and have done, with your birth father so that he may rejoice with me in your deeds."

"I would consider it a great honor to be called your son, now and for all of eternity, and I am sure that my father would be pleased to share this with you also." Caylen said, filled with emotion and with tears running freely down his cheeks.

"Then that is as it shall be, my son. Now you must take my cold mortal body to the place of your Vision Quest after washing it clean of all earthly substances. You shall then wrap it tightly in my favorite caribou robe and leave my mortal flesh in that very place. You must do all of these things that I ask when my essence has forever abandoned this weak old body."

"I shall do as you ask." Caylen sobbed.

"Do not weep for me, my son. I go to live with the Great Spirit. It is a happy time for me." Sania said, rising. "I have one more thing to ask of you before I leave this earth."

" Anything, Father. Ask of me anything."

"I have told you of where I have come from. This place, far away from here to the South, is the land of the Hopi, a proud people who I, long ago, so frightened with my powers that they sent me away from them. I now know that these things that happened so long ago were all plans of Qaletaka, the Great Spirit, who needed me in this place so that I would find Mato Honi, a young white-eyes that would become my son. The Great Spirit demanded that I be here in this place at this time to guide and teach the young Mato Honi the ways of our people before he would take me to be with him forever."

"What I have not told you, my son, is that in my home, in the land of the Hopi, I left my young wife and my small daughter

Kele, alone to mourn my leaving. I now must ask of you a great thing. I ask that, when I have gone to be with the Great Spirit, that you travel to the land of my birth, the land of my daughter and of her daughters. I have, many times, traveled with the birds of the air to this, my homeland of long ago, and have seen that some of my children and their children, still live and wonder what has become of the Sania who left them alone so long ago. I have seen that my daughter Kele, her daughter Sihu and her young daughter Aponi still question others about their ancestor Sania, who was banished so long ago, never to return. I ask that you go to them and tell them of my deeds, and of my life so that their lives may also be full and complete as has mine. I also ask that you take from me, after I join the Great Spirit, my medicine bag from my neck, and give it to my children's children, so that they will have something of their father's father to cherish, for they now have nothing of Sania, save the passed-down stories of my life. Without this knowledge that you shall give to them, of their blood father's life, my daughter and her daughters lives can never be fully complete, for how are they to then tell their children and their children's children of their ancestor's life and deeds if they have no knowledge of these things themselves?"

"Of course I will do these things that you ask. I will tell your children proudly of the great man that you are, and of how favored you are to the Great Spirit. And I will also tell them proudly of how you chose me to be your blood-brother and your son. But where do I begin this search in the Southern lands for your daughter and her daughter?"

"This place where I lived, and where they now live is on a white man's reservation and is called Oraibi. Oraibi is located on The Third Mesa, in a land far to the South, known to the white man as Arizona. I must go now to my sleeping robes, for I am very tired."

~*~

It was just before dawn when Caylen suddenly woke early the next morning. Something had woken him but the only sound he could hear was his own slow, even breathing. It took a moment for him to realize that he could not hear Sania's usual loud snores, and that what had woken him was the eerie wailing of Abhaya, the old man's wolf pet and Warrior, both of whom slept just outside the hut's door and who now resumed their mournful howls. Listening closely, he finally rose and in the dim light of the still glowing embers of last night's warming fire made his way over to Sania's bedroll. Watching his teacher's still form for a few minutes, the realization finally came to him that the old man had passed away during the night, just as he had said he would.

The still spring night was suddenly again filled with the eerie wailing of Abhaya, the old man's wolf pet from just outside the hut. An instant later Warrior joined in, with the pair continuing to howl and wail until the warming sun of the early morning finally broke over the eastern mountain range.

Caylen, with tears streaming down his face, fetched a clean cloth and a pail of warm water from the large kettle that Sania kept by the fire. Pulling back the old man's robe, he washed Sania's cold body from head to toe, before rolling him over and wiping down his back. His task completed, he took the old man's favorite sheared caribou robe from where it was hanging on the wall and wrapped his thin body tightly inside. He then lashed the robe in place with some of the leather lacing that was always kept handy.

He then went out into the forest and found two long slender poles that he fashioned, with the help of some shorter cross-members and more lacing, into a travois, onto while he placed the cold, stiffening body of Sania.

It took the rest of the afternoon for Caylen to drag the travois carrying Sania's body up the slopes to the sacred place of his Vision Quest. He placed the stiff, cold corpse in the very center of the circle of rocks where he had sat for four long days. After saying a short prayer, Caylen turned his face upwards and, holding his arms high with palms towards the sky, he chanted.

"Oh, Great Spirit Qaletaka, Whakan Powwaw, my brother, my father, and my friend has now departed from this place that he so loved. His Essence is now yours to take and to use as you wish. Please, Sacred Guardian, take this soul who has for his entire life, ever loved and obeyed your every wish and keep him in your house and by your side forever."

With that action accomplished, Caylen returned, weeping, to the cabin and prepared his evening meal, his first food of the day. As the sun set, he again heard, coming from the direction of where he had taken Sania's body, the mournful, sad howling of Abhaya, whom he had not seen since early that morning.

~*~

Caylen spent the next week simply moping about the cabin and thinking about the nearly eight months that he had spent with Sania. He had been just six years old when his father had gone off to fight the Germans and could only remember vague highlights about him. His real memories of his long-dead father were, for the most part, based on the stories that his mother had told him about her life with him.

Caylen felt as though he had lost a big part of himself with Sania's sudden death. He mourned him much as a son would mourn his father. Actually, in a kind of way, Sania served as a stand-in for his birth father.

Caylen experimented a few times with moving his spirit out of his body on its golden thread in an effort to locate Sania's spirit, but after failing to encounter him on these out-of-body trips, he eventually gave up and simply prayed to the Great Spirit for relief from the emotional pain that he was suffering over Sania's death.

On the seventh day, he decided to visit the Sacred place where he had taken Sania's body. As he approached the spot he could see the brightly colored robe he had wrapped the old man in was still as he had left it but beside it lay Abhaya, the old man's pet wolf. It was not difficult for Caylen to see that the wolf had been dead for at least five or six days. The faithful old wolf's eyes were closed tightly in death, and his front paws were lying across the still, cold body of the master he had loved and served for so long. At the sight of this total dedication and final display of love by a faithful pet for his dead master, Caylen could contain him no longer. He sat just outside the ring of stones that surrounded his dead friend and his dead pet and sobbed for over an hour. Finally calming himself, he stood and was turning to leave when he heard a familiar voice,

"Mato Honi, my friend, my brother, my son, why are you so sad?"

"Is that you, Sania? " How can this be, you speaking to me? Are you not dead?" Caylen asked, turning back to see where the voice had come from.

What he saw caused Caylen to gasp out loud. Hovering in the

air about ten feet above his body and the dead body of his pet wolf was Sania. The Sania that Caylen was now seeing was not, however, the Sania that had recently died. The Sania before him was now a young, strong, handsome Sania, standing tall and straight, and clothed in his brightly colored favorite caribou skin robe, with his beloved Abhaya standing beside him.

"It is I, my brother, my son, and I am now with the Great Spirit Qaletaka. He has granted me this last visit with you so that I might ease your pain at my departure from the land of the living. You must now go back to your mother, Mato Honi. She is in much danger and thinks that you also are with the Great Spirit. You must now go to her and see to her before the Evil One, Fariss Lubak, does harm to her and the one she now protects. You must go now, my friend, for your Quest has just begun."

"I hear you, brother Sania, my father, I shall leave at once, but shall I ever see you again?" Caylen asked.

"I shall leave with you, for all time, a small piece of my essence so that you may never forget of me and so that, if need be, you may speak to me, but you shall only see me again when the Great Spirit finally brings you before him." Sania said. "I must go now, for the Great Spirit again calls." said the spirit of Sania, as he slowly faded from sight.

"Goodbye old friend." whispered Caylen. "Goodbye my father."

~*~

Early the next morning, Caylen packed up his gear and set off for home. It took him the best part of the day to reach his own little cabin, where he spent that night and the following day. He cleaned up his cabin and did some minor repairs to the roof and to a drafty door. The winter's snows had nearly all melted, with the lakes, rivers and streams beginning to open up under the warm spring sun. Caylen also had to spend some time letting out his summer clothes so that they would fit him a little better. He hadn't realized that his body had bulked up considerably over the many months that he had spent with Sania.

He was no longer the gangly youth that spoke with a high-pitched tone in his voice. He was now a tall, well-proportioned, handsome young man of nearly seventeen years, who was showing the beginnings of a beard on his wind-tanned cheeks. Gazing at his reflection in the shard of a mirror that he had hanging on his cabin's wall, Caylen was unsure that even his mother would now recognize him. He wondered just what the spirit of Sania had meant when he had said that his mother, as well as the one she was protecting were in danger.

He took the trail, with Warrior at his side, before daylight the next day. Knowing that the warning of danger that had been given to him by Sania's spirit was to be believed, he kept his big rifle loaded and ready during the long journey home. Warrior seemed to sense where they were going and kept racing ahead until Caylen ordered him to stay beside him as he traveled.

They began to see familiar areas at about noon and soon after that, they broke out of the forest and onto the shore of the big lake that the cabin was built beside. After a few moments of trotting along the lakeshore, Caylen could see the familiar lines of his mother and Fariss Lubak's log home.

Chapter 20

Homecoming

Lora had given up all hope of ever seeing her son alive again. The last time she had seen him had been in early September of the previous year, more than eight months before he disappeared. Caylen often told her of the recurring weird dreams that he had been having about the old Indian and the huge black wolf, but she dismissed them as simply the overactive imagination of a teen-aged boy who was inventing his own kind of entertainment. When Caylen had not visited her by Christmas, however, she began to get worried enough to ask Fariss if he would attempt to track him back to his cabin.

Fariss, at first, refused, saying,

"He be nearly a man now. He's be living on his own and knows how to lives in the bush, so's we's should just lets him be, he's be okay."

It was not until another month passed that she was able to persuade him to look for Caylen. By this time, the winter snows were too deep for him to be able to find any signs of Caylen, even if he had known where to look.

"I'se will have to wait now fer the spring thaws and all this here snows to go." was Fariss's excuse now. Sides, less he be holed ups someplace, he's probably wolf food by now and I'se gots lots better ting's to do."

This last comment served its intended purpose. Lora began having terrible nightmares of Caylen being devoured by wolves, of falling through thin ice and drowning, of freezing to death and one vivid dream in which she watched Fariss stab Caylen to death and then throw him into a fast-moving river. Before spring arrived, she stopped asking Fariss to search for him and had begun to believe that he probably had some kind of accident that had killed him. She knew that if he were still alive that he would make contact with her, but after eight months and still no sign of her son, she was left with little hope of ever seeing him again.

To make a bad situation worse, Fariss had begun to revert back to the mean, miserable dictator that he had been when Wildflower's body was still buried under the cabin's floor. He was constantly berating her for no apparent reason, and was now even holding her responsible for the worsening yields from his placer mine.

"It's only been since I'se brought you's up here to lives that the golds been gone," he yelled. "I'se don't has any luck at all wit you bein round here. I'se was better off when you's weren't here. Maybe I'se should jest gits rid of you's altogether."

~*~

In early May, Lora was happy to see that spring was once again nearing. The big lakes were nearly free of ice and the days were lengthening under the warm northern sun. She was sitting, one fine warm day, on the shore of the lake near where the big stream entered it, enjoying the warm sunshine, when suddenly a canoe carrying two men rounded the point of the lake just to the East of where she sat.

Lora was quite surprised, as these were the first people other than Fariss, Caylen, Kosumi and Lokni that she had ever observed on this lake. Standing for a better look, she suddenly realized, from the clothes that the two men were wearing, that they were policemen and they were probably here to investigate Wildflower's death and to speak to Fariss.

The two men had also spotted Lora on the lakeshore and were soon pulling their canoe up onto the sandy shore.

"Good day, ma'm, I am Sergeant Bill Tomkins of the Northwest Mounted Police and this is Constable James Brookes. Are you Mrs. Lora Lubak?"

With her heart pounding, Lora replied,

"Yes, I am Lora Lubak.." replied Lora.

"Well, ma'm, we are here to speak to Mr. Fariss Lubak about a dead Indian girl called Wildflower. We also want to speak to him about the wounding of a Carcross man called Kosumi and the knifing of another man in Atlin." Sgt. Tompkins said. "Do you know where Mr. Lubak is at present?"

"He's up at his place mine, and won't be home until late

tonight. He usually doesn't get home until just before dark." Lora said. "Would you care to come up to our cabin and have a hot cup of tea and some warm bread rolls?"

"We would love to, Mrs. Lubak." Sgt. Tompkins said. "But before we do that, we'll hide our canoe in the bushes. We don't want to frighten Mr. Lubak away if he comes by here."

"Please call me Lora," Lora said. "I cannot get used to being called Mrs. Lubak."

"We need to speak to you about that also," the sergeant said, as they approached the cabin.

"Whatever do you mean?" asked Lora.

"Well, ma'm. I'm sorry to have to tell you this, but when we were asked to investigate Mr. Lubak, we did a background check on everything we could about him, yourself and your son. By the way, Mrs. Lubak, where is your son Caylen?"

It took Lora nearly two hours to tell the two policemen about everything that had occurred to her and Caylen since she had first met Fariss. She told how she had met him, about the journey North, of the promise of a big house near Whitehorse, of her marriage in Carcross, the canoe trips to the remote cabin, the shooting of Kosumi, the digging up of Wildflower and everything else she could think of. She decided, during her relating of her story, to not tell them, at least for the present, of Caylen's gold strike or of his mysterious dreams.

She did tell them of Fariss's attempted killing of Caylen and of how Caylen had then come forward and cowed her mean, arrogant, abusive husband. She found herself opening up to the police Sergeant, and felt quite comfortable telling him all the details of nearly everything that occurred in their remote home over the past four years.

"Thank you for telling us all that, Mrs. Lubak." Sgt. Tompkins said, beginning to really like and admire this attractive woman, who seemed to be completely open and honest. " Now, I'll tell you what we know of Mr. Lubak."

With that the Sgt. told Lora of Fariss's past life. He told her of the stabbing in Atlin and of the sordid past of drunken fights and thefts perpetrated by Fariss in years gone by. He explained that Fariss had been on their wanted list for years, but that, until the stabbing and the shooting, they hadn't considered his lawbreaking serious enough to warrant the two-week long trip to search for

Lubak and take him into custody.

"We also have one more thing that we must tell you about, Lora" Sgt. Tompkins said softly, using Lora's first name. "This is something very personal and I'm not sure you will want to hear it, but I think you must."

The reluctance in his words and the somber tone of his voice caused Lora's heart to plummet. She was sure that this nice policeman was about to tell her that her son was dead.

" Is Caylen dead?" she asked, without hesitation. "Did Fariss finally manage to kill him?"

"It's not about your son, Lora, it's about why I'm now calling you Lora, instead of Mrs. Lubak." Sgt. Tompkins said. "I'm really sorry to be the one to have to tell you this but the Justice of the Peace who married you was an imposter and not a real Justice of the Peace at all."

It took a few minutes for this information to sink in. When she finally realized what the Sgt. had said, Lora's face turned a pale white and she asked, "What on earth do you mean?"

"I mean that Fariss Lubak paid one of his drinking friends five dollars to pretend to be a Justice of the Peace and to marry you. I mean that you have never been legally married to Fariss Lubak." The policeman explained.

~*~

It took Lora only a few minutes to regain her composure after hearing this. The meaning of her next words were quite plain to all.

"Thank you, God! I thought you had forgotten about me. Now," she addressed the silent Sergeant. "Will you please get me out of this wilderness, Sgt. Tompkins? I will pay you if need be but please take me away from this place and this madman."

"We'll take you out with us, ma'm, and you don't have to pay us anything, but we must first get Fariss and take him in custody so that he can stand trial for all he has done." said the Sgt.

The two police officers questioned Lora about Fariss and Caylen for the remainder of the day. She told them, in detail, how her young son had matured and protected her and himself from Fariss's abuses. She expressed to them, her concerns for Caylen's safety and that now, after nearly nine months absence, she felt that he may have perished in the wilds, or that Fariss may have finally killed him.

"Once we take Mr. Lubak into custody, we can spend a few days looking for him. Do you have any idea where he may have built his cabin?" Sgt. Tompkins asked.

"Only that it's northwest of here and about four hours travel. I helped him build it but I'm afraid that I could never find it." Lora replied. "He told me that he usually came here using different routes each time so as not to leave a trail that Fariss could easily follow."

"It sounds as though your son is one smart boy, Lora. Now, about what time does Mr. Lubak normally come home?" asked the Constable. "It is beginning to get dark."

"He's usually home about this time of the day, unless he finds more gold than normal in his sluice way. If he does, he will sometimes not come home until much later." Lora answered.

"Then we had best get prepared," said Sgt. Tompkins. "Where did you leave your rifle, Constable Brookes?"

"Oh, I just leaned it against the outside wall, right by the door." replied Constable Brookes.

"Damn!" exclaimed Sgt. Tompkins. "He'll most likely see it and know that someone is here. Go and get it right now, before he gets here."

Constable Brookes rose and crossed over to the door. Opening it wide, he reached over in the fading, late afternoon light and picked up his rifle. As he turned back inside, he was silhouetted for just a moment in the doorway by the light from the oil lamp that Lora had lit and placed on the table. As he reached for the door's handle to close it, the roar of a heavy rifle that was fired from just outside the cabin shattered the evening's quiet stillness. Constable Brooke's tunic front suddenly blossomed red as Fariss's big 38/55 bullet penetrated the Constable's body, entering through his back and exiting his chest front. The tremendous impact of the heavy expanding lead bullet blew his heart and both lungs into small pieces, killing him instantly. Constable Brookes collapsed where he stood; his eyes open wide with shock, dead before his body struck the floor.

Sgt. Tompkins jumped to his feet and, in what seemed to Lora to be one quick motion, blew out the lamp, threw Lora to the floor and dropped beside her. Saying nothing, he crawled over to his partner and, observing that there was nothing that could be done for him, dragged his limp body aside, and pushed the door closed. Even as he did so, another heavy lead slug splintered the wood door at about waist level, crossing the cabin's interior before sloughing into the rear wall of the cabin just above Caylen's bunk.

Lora and the police sergeant remained huddled beside each other and the dead body of Constable Brookes until dawn of the following day. As they had heard nothing after the second shot, Sgt. Tomkins cautiously exited the cabin, rifle at the ready, to scout quietly about for any signs of Fariss.

Determining that they were indeed alone, Tomkins returned and, with Lora's help, removed the dead police officer's body from the cabin. It took them until noon to prepare and bury Constable Brookes' body at the edge of the small clearing. Sgt. Tompkins then said a short prayer over the newly dug grave as Lora stood with head bowed, saying her own silent prayer for the young man who had just died so far from his home and family.

~*~

Fariss had decided to return home early that day. His take of gold that day was as low as it had ever been and he was in a terrible rage. Everything seemed to be going wrong as of late. His sluice box had broken that morning. He had cut his hand on a sharp rock in the early afternoon. He had forgotten his lunch that morning and was, as a result, very hungry. To really make things worse, a raven had spent the entire afternoon noisily squawking and chirping at him from a nearby spruce tree.

About mid afternoon, he finally threw down his shovel, picked up his rifle and, for a moment, contemplated shooting the irritating bird. Cooling off just a little, he decided not to waste a bullet on the noisy pest and just go home instead.

As he broke out of the forest and into the clearing where his cabin stood, his eyes immediately noted that something was out of place. He stopped abruptly at the edge of the clearing and studied the cabin carefully in an effort to ascertain just what it was that looked different enough to cause him concern. It took only a few minutes before he saw the unfamiliar lever-action Winchester rifle leaning against the wall by the door. Stepping quietly back into the thickness of the evergreen forest, he waited silently for some indication of who had left the carbine by his door. He knew that the rifle was not Caylen's, so he immediately thought that it might just be what he had feared would eventually happen: other prospectors were finding and exploring his area. He stayed where he was, silently waiting as the day began to grow dark. He saw the light suddenly appear through the small window of the cabin when Lora lit the lamp. A few minutes later, he watched the door swing wide open and saw the tall, uniformed police constable reach over to pick up his carbine.

Fariss, with all of the day's frustrations still fresh in his mind, was now faced with possible arrest. Thinking no further than he had already done, nor even pausing to consider his next action, he simply raised his big rifle and, without further contemplation, triggered off a shot at the policeman in the doorway as he turned with his rifle to re-enter the cabin. When the man fell, Fariss could see, through the now clear doorway, another uniformed man leap to his feet and quickly extinguish the lamp. He waited for a moment with his rifle aimed at the now darkened opening of the cabin's door, hoping for a clear shot at the second policeman. When he observed the door closing, he quickly triggered off another shot, hoping to hit whoever might be behind it. Fariss then turned and ran back up the trail that led to his gold claim. He knew that whatever the police came here for no longer mattered, as he had just shot, and probably killed, a Northwest Mounted policeman in front of his partner and Lora.

He also knew that the Mounted Policemen's policy of never giving up the chase meant that the other officer would now pursue him until either he, Fariss, killed him or the policeman killed or captured him.

Certain that the policeman he had seen inside the cabin wouldn't likely pursue him until at least the following day, Fariss stopped at the steep, rocky part of the trail and, by the bright full moon, set the trigger to his trap. He had, some years back, prepared a log and rock-fall trap on the trail, just after his first gold discovery. The rock-fall trap consisted of a dam of logs holding back some very heavy rocks that he had levered into place behind the logs, on an almost vertical section of the trail.

Camouflaged behind some low-growing small willows, the logs and rocks would look—to the casual observer—quite natural and would probably be ignored. The trigger that released this deadly pile of boulders was comprised of a simple wood wedge inserted at the midpoint of the lowest log, between that log and the underlying solid rock.

A long length of wire had one end fastened to the wedge with the other end placed in a loose coil alongside the trail. This loose wire, once fastened tightly to a tree on the opposite side of the trail, would be about five inches above the trail and nearly invisible. Once pulled or stepped upon by anyone climbing the trail, the taut wire would pull the wedge out from under the bottom log. When the wedge was pulled out, the logs, followed closely by the huge boulders, would come tumbling down onto anyone on the trail, killing or badly injuring them.

Setting the trap was now easily done. Fariss soon located the end of the loose coil of wire that he had hidden in the brush; then pulled it taut and secured it to a tree that he had previously decided was in the best location. His death trap was now set and ready for anyone who might follow him up the trail.

Fariss then went directly to that small cave where he had hidden his gold. He had also stored an emergency pack of dried foods, some spare ammunition, a bedroll, a small tarp and other items that he might need in this type of situation. Grabbing his pack, he thought for a moment about what he had just done and then departed, taking his stash of cash and the bag of gold dust. Once out of the cave, he looked about for a moment at the surrounding hills and mountains before striking off at a fast pace back towards the lake and his canoes. Swinging wide, he bypassed his cabin by a wide margin. Arriving at his canoes, he dragged the smaller one down to the lake and threw his pack and rifle into the canoe before climbing in himself and paddling off eastward along the shore. His immediate plans were to go down to the larger Fantail Lake and then turn west toward that lake's headwaters and an even more remote wilderness area that he had never before explored.

~*~

Sgt. Tompkins, after burying his deceased partner, returned to his canoe and prepared a travel pack. He knew that he was now on his own, with an extremely dangerous fugitive on the loose who wouldn't hesitate to kill him if he had the opportunity. He deeply regretted the loss of his partner and old friend, but he knew that the longer he delayed pursuing Fariss, the less chance he would have in overtaking and apprehending him.

His long discussions with Mrs. Helms and his prior knowledge of Fariss led him to believe that Fariss, for all his belligerence and angry displays, was really just a coward and that he would probably, if given the opportunity, run rather than fight. He also knew from long police experience that even a lowly coward, once cornered, might just decide to fight rather than to give up to a pursuer. Returning to the cabin, he approached Lora who was sobbing softly, as she quietly worked at cleaning Constable Brookes' blood from the cabins floor and walls.

"Did Constable Brookes have a family, Sgt.? Lora asked.

"His given name was Jim and yes, he did—or does—have a family. They live in Whitehorse. His wife's name is Sarah and his four-year-old son's name is William. William was named after me and I'm his Godfather. Jim and Sarah were my best friends, and now I'll have to take his body back to his wife for her to bury.

" Oh, I'm so sorry, Bill," Lora said, putting her arms around the sergeant, noting the unashamed tears that were streaking his cheeks.

" I'll be leaving at first light tomorrow, Mrs. Helms" he said. "I must get after him before his trail gets washed away by rain."

"You're going to leave me here by myself?" asked Lora, fear in her voice.

"I need to do this on my own." Sgt. Tompkins said. "It will be very dangerous for anyone who goes after this madman, and I'll not risk taking you with me, so you must stay here until I return."

"That's if you do return," Lora said. "That's if Fariss doesn't kill you, too. He knows this land very well, and you do not."

"I think he'll probably go up to his gold mine or to wherever he has his emergency stash stored and get supplies before he leaves, so if you were to show me where his claim is and tell me if you know where he keeps his emergency stuff, that would help get me started and save some valuable time." the police sergeant said.

"I can do that," Lora agreed. "I can show you the trail to his mine but I don't know where he keeps any emergency supplies. But you must, Bill, before you leave, promise me that you will return, as I will surely perish here if I'm left here by myself."

"Let's go up tomorrow and see what there is to see at his claim before we decide on our next move." Bill Tompkins said, his mind busy.

She's right, if I leave her here alone and don't return, she'll eventually die of starvation. I'd better think this over a little more before I do anything that might cause her harm.

~*~

Early the following morning, Sgt. Tomkins, led by Lora, headed up the heavily defined trail that led up to Fariss's claim. In a few minutes they were at a steep, rocky section that slowed their ascent, and necessitated frequent rest stops. When they were about half way up the steepest section, Lora, in the lead, felt her right foot catch onto something that tripped her, causing her to fall flat on her face, forward onto the rocky trail. An instant later she heard a loud rumble and a crashing sound coming from directly on her right. She raised her head in just enough time to see a mix of logs and boulders come crashing by her and directly into Sgt. Tompkins, who was about fifteen feet behind her. In a few moments, all was quiet save for the loud beating of her heart. Lora got to her feet and looked back over the trail to where the policeman had, just a moment earlier, stood. Seeing nothing of him, Lora yelled.

"Sgt. Tompkins! Bill! Are you okay? Where are you?"

Getting no response, she climbed down over the pile of logs and boulders to finally discover Sgt. Tompkins. He was lying as though dead, with a large log across his chest and his left leg skewed over to one side. She clambered down to where she could examine him in more detail.

Grasping a small pole, she managed to lever the log free of his body before feeling his wrist for a pulse, holding her breath. Finding a strong, steady pulse, she noticed that in addition to the obviously broken leg, he had a large, bleeding lump on his forehead. She also suspected, from his rough and labored breathing, that he might have suffered a broken rib or two.

Knowing that she had to get him back to the cabin, Lora thought for a only a few moments before removing the sergeant's hatchet from his pack. Within a very few minutes, she had fashioned a small, crude travois. It took her only a few moments more for her to get the now groaning, semi-conscious Sgt.

Tompkins lashed to the travois so she could begin dragging him back down the trail to her cabin. Thankfully, it was downhill all the way.

In less than an hour, Lora had the badly injured and semi-conscious, moaning policeman flat on his back on Caylen's long-unused bunk, and was busily tending to his injuries. She stripped him down to his undergarments, and then bound his badly bruised chest tightly, before placing a cool, damp cloth across the big lump on his forehead. She then straightened his obviously broken leg and thinking that she should attempt to set it before he woke, began to tie a length of rope around his ankle so she could yank the broken leg bone into place before splinting it.

"I beg pardon, Mrs. Helms, but just why are you tying me to your bed, and why do I hurt all over?"

"I was not tying you up, Sgt. Tompkins! And you've just been badly hurt by some falling logs and rocks. And further, for your information, Sergeant, I just dragged you down off that mountain and lifted you onto that bed so that I could tend to your injuries." Lora said, slightly offended and not realizing that the injured Tompkins was, through his pain, actually joking.

"I did realize all that, Mrs. Helms. I was just trying to be funny. It's not very often I get a real pretty lady like you undressing me and pulling on my leg!"

"Well, Sgt. Tompkins, I don't think that what has happened is very funny, but I do appreciate your attempt at humor, and, by the way, just what do you think your wife would say if she knew you were flirting with me?" Lora said, her cheeks beginning to redden at her own boldness.

"I don't suppose she'd be too happy about it. That is, if I were married. But then again, if I were married, I would definitely not be flirting with another woman." Sgt. Tompkins said, with a smile. "Now, Mrs. Helms, would you care to pull my leg some more and set that broken bone. Owwwch! That really hurts! I think you may have gotten it that time, but let's give it one more good hard yank to make sure."

"Ouch! I'm sure you got it that time. Now we need some splints tied onto that leg and then I need some rest. These bruised ribs and this headache is really bad. Do you have any pain medication?"

"I'm really sorry, Sergeant. But I have nothing except some

herbal willow tea that might help a little." Lora replied.

"Anything will help, Mrs. Helms, and please, call me Bill. Anyone who can pull a man's leg like you do is entitled to call that man by his first name." the sergeant said, with a little smile.

"Sgt. Tompkins, I mean Bill, you're beginning to really embarrass me! Lora exclaimed, her cheeks getting even redder.

"Well, I certainly don't wish to embarrass you any further, Mrs. Helms. Because if I do, I'm afraid that those pretty red cheeks just might catch on fire!"

"Is it that obvious, Bill? And please, call me Lora from now on."

"Thank you, Lora. Thank you for all you have done for me. I would probably have died out there if it hadn't been for you. Now, I must get some sleep, I'm terribly tired. But, before I do, please bring me my revolver and some cartridges. We must be prepared in the event Fariss returns."

~*~

While the injured Mountie slept, Lora went outside and found four dry poles about one and one-half inches in diameter that she could fashion into a splint and bind to his broken leg. She also went back up the mountain trail to the site of the trap and retrieved the sergeant's rifle, pistol belt and pack that she'd placed to one side as she was tending to the injured man.

Returning to the cabin, she began to prepare a hot supper for herself and the injured policeman. She sat for some time, gazing at the sleeping, man who was occasionally still moaning from the pain of his injuries. Sgt. Tompkins was, she thought, quite a handsome man and probably in his late thirties or early forties. His actions following the accident had already shown her that he had quite a sense humor, even while he was suffering from considerable pain. She wondered, just for a moment, why a good-looking man with such an interesting sense of humor wasn't married, but then quickly changed her thoughts as she felt her cheeks begin to redden again.

What on earth is wrong with me? She thought. *Here I am, a thirty-six year old woman, living in a log and mud cabin in the middle nowhere, having the thoughts of a teenage girl*! She tried to refocus her thoughts. *But, he is really such a handsome man!*

~*~

Lora's next two weeks were spent looking after the recovering Sgt. Tompkins. These two weeks, even though she was busy constantly tending to the injured sergeant needs, and despite the impending threat, were the among the most pleasant that she had experienced in years. She found herself liking everything there was about Bill Tompkins. He was constantly regaling her with humorous stories of his past adventures with the Northwest Mounted Police. She discovered that she could speak to him in a serious or humorous fashion about any subject she chose and that he was always very attentive and interested in hearing of her past life as well. She dedicated many hours telling him of her son Caylen, his dreams and the sudden appearance of the wolf pup and of the messages he claimed to have received in his dreams from the old native.

"It has been my experience in dealing with native Shaman and Medicine Men that many of them have powers that would amaze and even terrify normal people such as you and I." Bill said. "I definitely believe that some of those men really do posses abilities and skills that they commonly use in ways that most of us cannot even imagine. Perhaps your Caylen has some quality in his 'essence', as the aboriginal natives call it, that drew one of these powerful Shaman to really speak to him in his dreams."

"What do you mean by essence?" Lora asked.

"Essence is the native Indian term for 'spirit' or 'soul'." Bill replied.

"I don't enjoy speaking of Caylen like this." Lora stated. "I know he's probably dead, but I'm still holding out hope that he might still appear one day. He would now be nearly seventeen years old, and I miss him very much."

"I would never give up hope, Lora, he may just show up at any time. If he was as skilled in the wilds as you say, he could live for years out there on his own."

"My heart tells me that he is still alive and well, but it has been almost a year since I last saw him and I don't know how he could live out there this long." Lora said, sadly. "I just don't know what to do."

"When I'm well enough to travel I will take you back out to

Carcross and then come back to hunt down Fariss, he has killed one of ours and we cannot allow him to get away with that.

"I will never leave here until I am sure of Caylen's fate." Lora insisted. "What if he suddenly came home and no one was here?"

"As I said before, it sounds as though he's a very capable woodsman and is quite able to care for himself. If he did come back and there was no one here he would probably go out to Carcross." Bill said, reassuringly.

~*~

It was only two days later that Caylen, as he approached Fariss and his mother's cabin, saw, under a large spruce tree, what appeared to be a recently dug grave. Approaching cautiously, he could make out some scratched printing on a small wooden cross that had been placed at one end of the freshly turned soil. The printing said: *Constable J. Brookes, NWMP.*

Assuming the worst, Caylen quietly slipped back into the dense underbrush, with Warrior close beside him. He soon located a good hiding spot from which he could watch the cabin without being seen. He waited until the sun had set and the bright moonlight was casting long, dark shadows over the little clearing. Only then did he decide that he had waited long enough. Leaning back against the rough tree trunk, he closed his eyes and, as Sania had instructed him, concentrated on the golden life thread. In the next instant, he could feel his spirit leaving his inert body. Looking back, he could easily see his golden thread of life curling away from his essence and going back into his physical body. Willing his spirit to obey, he soared across the little clearing and through the cabin's closed door. As his spirit entered the small room, he saw his mother look up as though suddenly startled by something.

"Who's there?" Lora asked, with a frightened look towards the door.

"Did you hear something, Lora?" Bill reached out and took hold of his loaded revolver.

"No, I didn't hear anything, but I thought I felt a sudden cold draft as though the door had just opened." Lora replied.

"It's me, Mom. It's Caylen." Caylen sent, forgetting, for the moment, that he was only thinking the words and not actually

speaking.

"Probably just a cool night wind coming in off the lake." Bill reassured her.

"Yes, I guess that's what it was, alright." Lora said, uncertainly. "But it certainly startled me."

Caylen, seeing through his spirit's eyes that there was an injured policeman in his bed, returned to his physical body and sat for a time, digesting and analyzing all he had seen. Realizing that his mother was safe, Fariss was absent, that one policeman was dead, another injured and lying in his old bunk, he reasoned, correctly, that somehow Fariss had killed one policeman and badly injured the other, before making his escape. Returning his essence to his physical body, he decided that it was probably safe to reveal his presence. He picked up his pack and, instructing stay Warrior to stay, walked boldly up to the cabin door and knocked loudly.

"Oh My God!" Lora shrieked, "Fariss is back!
Get your gun, Bill! Hurry!"

With that, the cabin door swung wide open and standing there before her, was her son Caylen, no longer the gangly youth that she had last seen, but now a nearly-grown, well-proportioned, handsome young man with a shadow of a beard on his face.

Chapter 21

Recovery & Romance

"Oh, my God! It's Caylen! It's Caylen. He's alive and he's back!" Lora screamed, rushing over to the doorway and wrapping her arms around her son tightly.

"I felt you would eventually come home, I just prayed you were okay. My gosh, but how you have grown. Where have you been? Why were you gone for so long? Tell me how you are. Is everything okay? Where is your Warrior?"

"Stop, Mom! Slow down. Stop asking everything at the same time. I'll explain everything to you but first will you please tell me, what's going on here? Who was Constable Brookes, who is this man and where is Fariss?"

Sgt. Bill Tompkins introduced himself to Caylen, and then told him how Lokni and Kosumi had filed a complaint about Fariss to the visiting Constable Brookes, whose home base had also been Whitehorse. Alone at the time he received the complaint, all that Constable Brookes could do was conduct an investigation into Fariss's doings in and about the Carcross area.

During this investigation he ascertained how Fariss had purchased Wildflower and taken her away. He also found out about how he had wounded and nearly killed her brother, Kosumi. He further heard rumors of a 'really good-looking' lady, and her young son; who had supposedly married Fariss and left Carcross with him. His questions of the Carcross locals soon revealed that the marriage of Fariss to this good-looking lady had indeed taken place, but was actually performed by a local drunk who, for a drink or a few dollars, would do just about anything that anyone asked, even pretending, at times, to be a Justice of the Peace and illegally conduct marriages.

After he had related all this information to Caylen, the sergeant waited for Caylen's comments.

"Well, Mom, I guess you're probably really happy to hear that you aren't married to Fariss." Caylen.

"Oh, God! Yes, I am. I really am." Lora's reply was emotional "But, I am also ashamed that I believed in what Fariss said, and that I was so easily deceived by him. I know now that just about everything he told us was a lie."

"He's fooled a lot of people in the past, Lora, but no more. We'll catch him soon, and he'll likely pay the price for all he has done at the lower end of a hangman's noose." Bill said. He went on with the story of how he had become involved in searching for Fariss.

Unable and unwilling to undertake the long, hard journey alone that would be necessary if he were to pursue the dangerous Fariss into the wilds, Constable Brookes had reported his findings and his recommendations regarding Fariss to his superior, Sgt. Tompkins, when the sergeant returned to Whitehorse. Thinking that the name Fariss Lubak sounded familiar, Sgt. Tompkins looked through his unresolved case files and found they contained a lengthy report of a stabbing that a prospector named Fariss Lubak had been involved in, from the Atlin area. After reading Sgt. Tompkins's report about Fariss's criminal behavior and his recommendations, the regional Police Superintendent in Whitehorse decided that his crimes warranted his immediate arrest for trial. He directed Sgt. Tompkins to accompany Constable Brookes out into the wild countryside as soon as the ice on the lakes melted, and to bring Fariss back to stand trial for assault, and for questioning regarding the disappearance of the native girl Wildflower.

Sgt. Tompkins described to Caylen the events that had occurred after he and Brookes had found the cabin. He grew quite emotional as he related the details of his friend's death, and his subsequent injuries from Fariss's log and rock trap. Caylen could easily see how the sergeant's mannerism seemed to change as he then described how Lora had dragged him down the steep, rough mountain trail from the site of his injuries and into the cabin, where she had been caring for him ever since. The policeman kept looking at Lora, and smiling at her, as he related this part of the story to Caylen.

Caylen could easily see that Sgt. Bill Tompkins had begun to care for his mother and that, from her pleasant reactions to the injured man's smiles, she felt the same way about him.

"So, Sgt. Tompkins, how badly hurt are you and how long ago did all this happen?" Caylen asked.

"I have a broken leg, several cracked ribs and a pretty good sized lump on the top of my head. I certainly would now be dead if your mom hadn't been with me." Bill answered. "This all happened about two weeks ago and I'm trying to get used to these nice crutches that your mother made for me."

"Bill's been a really good patient, and he should be able to get around better in a few more weeks. He's really lucky that he wasn't even more seriously injured." Lora chipped in.

"As soon as I can travel, we need to get your mother out to Carcross, and then I need to report to Whitehorse so I can get back here and get after Fariss before he kills someone else." Sgt. Tompkins said.

"Do you know where he went or in what direction he went?" Caylen asked.

"No, but Lora says that one of his canoes is now missing, so we can safely assume he left by water. What we don't know for sure is what direction he went in or how far. There are lots of lakes and rivers out here and some of these lakes are really big."

"I know this area really well, and I insist that I come with you. Fariss has done enough damage, and I want to see him punished." Caylen stated.

"Enough of Fariss and us, Caylen." Lora interrupted. "Tell us where've you been and what you've been doing all this time. You certainly look fit and well, it's quite obvious that you haven't been going hungry. Doesn't he look good, Bill? He's has grown into such a good-looking young man!"

"Yes, he does look quite fit Lora. But, as for his looks. I don't think that his appearance will ever scare the pretty young girls away. In fact, I think he looks very much like that handsome fellow in that there picture." Bill answered, pointing to a small, framed photo of Lora's dead husband.

"Yes, he certainly does, doesn't he? Now, tell us about yourself Caylen." Lora repeated.

Unsure of just how much he should say with the l Canadian Northwest Mounted Policeman present, Caylen said.

"Can you remember, Mom, what I told you about my gold strike?"

"Of course," his mother replied. "How could I forget?"

"Well, after the last time I saw you, I went back to my claim and found some more." Caylen said.

"So you found yourself some gold, did you?" Sgt. Tompkins asked, in a joking manner, not realizing that Caylen had made a very rich find. "Are you rich enough to buy a nice house for your Mom and yourself out in Whitehorse? Or, maybe in Florida?"

"I think you can trust Bill enough to tell him the whole story." Lora said.

"Tell me what whole story?" Bill asked.

"Can I show him that receipt you asked me to keep for you?" Lora asked.

"Just wait a minute, Mom. I'll be right back." Caylen said. Leaving the cabin, Caylen went behind it and dug up the big nugget he had buried. Picking it up, he returned to the cabin and placed it on the table in front of the policeman.

"My God! Is this what I think it is?" Bill asked, picking up the nugget.

"What do you think now? Show him the receipt, Mom. Caylen said.

Tompkins took the receipt and studied it carefully for a few moments before whispering.

"This is unbelievable! Do you realize just how much money this is?"

"Of course we do, Bill." Lora said, in a matter of fact way. "Now, do you suppose my son could manage to purchase me a nice house if he really wanted to?"

"With this kind of money he could buy you a hundred houses if he wanted to!" Bill exclaimed.

"Actually, since I banked that amount, I have another seven hundred pounds or so, that I buried at my mine and near Carcross." Caylen said, with a grin at the stunned policeman.

"This is beyond belief! You are probably one of the wealthiest people in this country!"

"The banker in Whitehorse said much the same thing." Caylen admitted. "Now all I have to do is decide what to do with it. Besides, unless I'm badly mistaken, the gold that I've so far taken out from my mine is nothing compared to what is still there."

"You're young and still have lots of time to decide what you should do with it." Sgt. Tompkins said. "But I would recommend that you get the rest of your gold into a bank before too long. I would also recommend that you register your claim before someone else finds it and jumps it."

"That all does sound like good ideas, Caylen." Lora agreed.

"Yes, I suppose I should at least get the rest of the gold into a bank, but I really don't care if someone else finds my mine. I have more gold than I'll ever need." Caylen commented.

At this point, Caylen decided to change the topic of the discussion by saying.

" Mom, do you remember me telling you about my dreams of the old Indian and the big black wolf?"

"Yes, of course I do. You had them, off and on, for more than four years. I remember you had one of them even before we left Greenwood."

"Well, about a year ago, just after I dug out the last bunch of gold, the old Indian man sent the big black wolf that he called Abhaya to lead me to his cabin. I went there with him," Caylen related, "And I've been living with him ever since then."

"Thank goodness you had someone to talk to, son. It has been over a year since I saw you last. I thought you were surely dead or hurt when I didn't hear from you, or see you." Lora said. "What did you do with yourself all that time?"

Unsure of exactly what he should tell his mother, especially with the police sergeant present, and equally unsure if she would even believe him, Caylen decided to, at least for the present, tell them only part of what he had done during his long stay with Sania.

~*~

"I got to the old man's cabin late last summer." he began. "He told me that his name was Sania and that he was a Whakan Powwaw from a tribe far to the south. A Whakan Powwaw is a Sacred Priest, with many strange powers. His tribe was afraid of him and his powers, so they banished him from the tribe and he decided to move up here. He had to leave his wife and daughter behind, as the tribal elders would not allow them depart with him. He, Sania, then led me through what is called by the natives, a 'Vision Quest'. This Vision Quest took place in a Sacred place on top of a mountain. It took four days to perform and, once my vision quest was over, Sania instructed me in how to use some of the powers that the Great Spirit Qaletaka bestowed upon me during my Vision Ques."

" I'vc heard of this old medicine man, the Whakan Powwaw that you call Sania." Bill said. "Some of the natives living in the Carcross and Atlin areas tell stories of a powerful old Shaman who has lived on his own in these Northern woods for many years. These same native stories also say that he has a huge black wolf with bright green eyes that he can control with his mind. I'm not sure I believe all these stories, as you can't always believe everything these native people say."

"You obviously haven't met Warrior yet, Bill." Lora said. "Caylen, why don't you bring him in, and introduce him to the good Sergeant."

Following his mother's mirth-filled suggestion, Caylen went to the door, opened it and said,

"Warrior, come!"

A second later, Bill saw a huge, jet-black timber wolf with glowing emerald-green eyes bound into the cabin. The animal nearly knocked Lora over, as he greeted her with tail wagging and his long red tongue lapping at her face.

"Down, Warrior. Down." laughed Lora. "Does this wolf perhaps resemble the one you just described, Bill?"

Sgt. Tompkins could scarcely believe what he was now seeing. Sitting on the floor, looking at him with glowing emerald-green eyes, was the biggest, friendliest wolf that he had ever seen.

Now a fully-grown and mature northern timber wolf weighing in at slightly more than two hundred pounds, Warrior could easily have been a clone of his now dead sire, Abhaya.

"My God!" Sgt. Tompkins exclaimed. "What a magnificent animal! Would it be safe for me if I were to pet him, Caylen?"

"Of course, pet away. He loves to have his head scratched just behind his ears. If he permits you to do that, he will be your friend for life." Caylen replied, knowing from Warrior's actions that his pet had already decided that Bill was a friend and could be trusted.

"This Sania sounds like a very nice man," Lora said. "Why don't you ask him to come and visit us?"

"He and Abhaya both died a few weeks ago." Caylen explained. "They were both really old."

"Oh, I'm sorry." Lora said. "It sounds as though he was a good friend to you."

"He was the best friend and teacher that I have ever had, and I really miss him a lot." Caylen said. "But he and Abhaya are both quite happy now."

"What were these special powers that he taught you to use?" asked Sgt. Tompkins, ignoring, for the moment, Caylen's statement about the old man and his wolf pet being happy now.

"If I told you and Mom about them, you wouldn't believe me." Caylen replied. "Someday soon I'll show them to you. I will only tell you that I knew that Sgt. Tompkins was here before I came in, and I also know that Mom felt a sudden, cold draft just before I knocked on the door."

"That's right, but how could you possibly know all those things?" His mother asked, with a puzzled look at Bill.

"As I've said, I have special powers that I'll show you at some other time." Caylen responded.

Changing the subject, Caylen then said.

"Would it be possible to get something to eat, Mom? Warrior and I haven't eaten anything since early this morning."

"Of course, son. I'll get something ready for all of us. This has been a very long and tiring, and most unusual, day."

~*~

Caylen, his mother and Sgt Tompkins spent the next four weeks doing nothing but waiting for Bill's leg and ribs to mend They discussed, at length, what their next course of action would be with regards the pursuit and capture of Fariss. The decision was made that Bill and Caylen would escort Lora out to Whitehorse and establish her in a comfortable hotel, while the sergeant reported the death of Constable Brookes, and the subsequent escape of Fariss, to his Regional Superintendent. Only then would they find out if Tompkins would be permitted to further search for and, hopefully, apprehend the fugitive Fariss Lubak.

As Sgt. Tompkins's leg grew stronger, he and Caylen spent many hours fishing in both the stream and the lake. Caylen found himself liking the man more and more each day. Bill seemed to have an easy-going manner about him that made him very easy to like and to respect. Caylen couldn't fail to see that his mother was also finding the good-looking Sergeant very easy to like. He even found them, on two separate occasions, walking along the lakeshore, holding each other's hands. His reaction to this sight was to simply smile to himself and whisper softly to Warrior.

"Do you see that, Warrior? Good for you, Mom! I'm really happy for you. Bill strikes me to be a good man."

During the third week, Caylen took Warrior and, deciding to heed Bill's advice, struck off on a five-day trip to fetch his big eighteen-foot canoe and the remaining buried gold from his mine site. Upon his return, he could see that his mother and Bill were still quite happy to be in each other's constant company. This was even further revealed when the police sergeant spoke to Caylen of his growing affection towards Lora, and that his intentions were entirely honorable towards her.

"I know that, Bill. Caylen said. "Mom seems to be so much happier now than I've ever seen her. Just don't hurt her, she's had enough hurt in her life."

"I'd never, ever hurt her. I just hope that she feels about me as I feel about her." Bill said.

"Between just you and me, Bill, I don't think you have anything to worry about in that respect. " Caylen said, with a grin.

~*~

It was five weeks before the Sergeant felt he was capable of undertaking the long canoe trip back to Carcross. He still required the use of a cane to get about but he thought that he could, with the assistance of Caylen and Lora, make the trip without causing further harm to himself.

Lora, knowing that she would never be returning to her unhappy wilderness home, packed all of her meager personal belongings, as Caylen and Bill readied the two canoes.

They left early one morning, just as the sun rose over the snowcapped easterly range of mountains.

"I will not, not for one moment, miss this place. Lora stated, as she glanced back at the little cabin that had been her home for so long. "But, I shall always remember the beautiful scenery and the magnificent views of those mountains."

"Yes, it certainly is a beautiful country." Bill agreed. "But if you don't know how to live in it, it can be a very cruel country as well."

"How long have you lived up here?" asked Caylen, as he

hoisted his little sail.

"I've served with the Police up here for almost seven years." Bill replied. "Before that, I prospected here until I went overseas in the Big War. When I came back, I joined the Northwest Mounted Police force, and they sent me up here. I've been here ever since. I love it up here. This country can really grow on you after a while."

" My husband used to say those very words." Lora said. "I did tell you that he was a prospector in the Whitehorse area before the war, didn't I?"

"I don't thinks so. Just what was your husband's name, Lora? I may have known him back then." Bill asked.

"My husbands name was George Helms." Lora answered. "We were married in nineteen hundred and seven, and Caylen was born in nineteen ought eight. Caylen and I came up here in nineteen-nineteen, so we've been here nearly five years."

"Well! This is quite a coincidence." Bill said. "Because I knew a fellow by that name. We prospected together for about a year. I can even remember him telling me that he had a beautiful wife and a young son somewhere in the south. Was your George a tall, slim man with blondish hair?"

"That was George, alright. He was killed in France near the end of the Big War." Lora said. "I still miss him very much at times."

"It's no wonder I thought that picture you have of him looked kind of familiar."

Bill was about to say more, but then he realized that the talk of her dead husband had brought forth old memories to Lora and that it was best that he now change the subject.

"If this southwesterly wind keeps blowing like this, we should make good time to Carcross"

Caylen, sensing Bill's anguish, agreed. "At this time of year it usually blows pretty good from that direction."

~*~

The trip to Carcross took them five days. They were forced to use the paddles for the entire third day, as the winds turned and blew down lightly from the North.

As they neared Carcross, Caylen pointed out the spot where he had buried the hundred pounds of gold. It took him only a few moments, after beaching the canoes, to excavate the small fortune and stow it onboard with the other gold from his mine. The small train to Whitehorse conveniently arrived in Carcross soon after they had heaped all their supplies and Caylen's heavy bags of gold on the station platform.

The trio, weary from the strenuous trip, were all comfortably bedded down, and fast asleep, in the Whitehorse hotel by nine o'clock that night.

~*~

The following day, Sgt. Tompkins reported in to the region's Police Superintendent and submitted his report on Constable Brookes murder, his own injuries, and the subsequent escape into the wilderness by Fariss.

Caylen, at the same time, was overwhelming the stupefied bank manager with his new deposit of what turned out to be seven hundred and forty-six pounds of gold, with a value of one hundred and four thousand, four hundred and forty dollars. Added to his already banked gold, he now had over three hundred and seventy thousand dollars in the bank.

As he walked out of the bank, Caylen's thought,

When one considers that a very good wage at this time is fifteen hundred dollars per year, it's no wonder that the bank manager had been speechless!

Sgt. Tomkins' Superintendent agreed with him that a pursuit of the murderous Fariss Lubak had to be undertaken. In as much as the Sergeant was the only surviving police officer familiar with the location and details of the crime, the Superintendent issued a warrant for the arrest of Fariss Lubak for the murder of Constable Brookes. He then gave the arrest warrant to Sgt. Tompkins and ordered that Tompkins immediately begin the search for the wanted man and to pursue and take Fariss into custody, wherever he may be, and return to Whitehorse with him so that Lubak could stand trial for the murder of Constable Brookes, the wounding of Kosumi and the injuries he had caused to Sgt. Tompkins.

The Superintendent also ordered that Sgt. Tompkins rest up for two more weeks before leaving on his pursuit of Fariss. He then, at the Sergeant's request, granted him permission to utilize the two brothers of Wildflower, Kosumi and Lokni, as assistants during his pursuit of Fariss.

Knowing that his Superintendent would refuse him permission, the sergeant made no mention of the fact that he also planned to ask Caylen to accompany him on his search.

~*~

The next two weeks went by quickly. Caylen, with his mother's assistance, purchased some new clothing, new tents and canvas tarpaulins, a new sleeping bag and many other useful articles that he, and she, thought he could use on the pursuit of Fariss. He also purchased a new thirty-ought-six, bolt-action, Winchester rifle and fifteen boxes of one hundred and eighty grain, soft-point bullets.

After a few hours of practice and sight adjustments, he found that he could, with this new rifle, easily keep all his shots within a three-inch circle at a range of over two hundred yards.

It came as no surprise to Caylen that Sgt. Tompkins was a nearly constant visitor and companion to Lora during these two weeks. They visited together nearly every shop in Whitehorse, sightseeing for the most part, but with Lora also purchasing herself much needed clothing and other small sundries.

Not knowing what she and Caylen were going to do or where they were going to live, Lora was a little hesitant to discuss her awkward status with either Caylen or Bill.

The sergeant resolved this problem, when, on the ninth day, he sought out Caylen and asked if he could, as he put it, "discuss a matter of some great importance "with him."

Suspecting that Bill was about to ask him if he would accompany him on his pursuit of Fariss, Caylen was just a little surprised, and pleased, when Bill said,

"I'm sure, Caylen, that you've noticed that your mother and I have been spending a lot of time in each other's company since we arrived here in Whitehorse."

"Yes, it's been rather obvious to everyone, Bill. I know Mom likes you lot, and it is pretty plain that you like her a lot, too." Caylen smiled. "In fact, I don't think that I've ever seen her happier than she's been since she met you."

"It's a little more than just 'like'." Bill admitted. "I've grown to love your Mom, and she feels the same way about me. We would like your blessing and approval to get married after I get Fariss back here."

"I must admit, Bill, that I like you, too. And, if it'll make Mom happy, it'll make me happy. Besides, you don't need my permission. Have you asked her yet?"

"I plan to do that tonight after we have supper at the Whitehorse Grill." Bill said. "I have a ring all ready to give her if she'll agree to become my wife."

"I really don't think that you have anything to worry about in that respect, Dad." said Caylen, smiling as he clasped Bill's strong hand in his. "I also want you to know that I insist that you allow me to accompany you when you go after Fariss."

"I was going to ask you if you wanted to come along. I just hope that we can catch up with him. He knows that country extremely well, and he has a good start on us." Bill said.

"Well, I've got a few tricks up my sleeve that may just give us a better chance than you think." Caylen said.

"Do you know where he went?" Sgt. Tompkins asked.

"No, not really. But I may have ways of finding out." Caylen answered. "I'm not ready to tell you about them just yet but someday I will."

Lora informed Caylen the next day that she had accepted Bill's offer of marriage and asked if he would like to give her away at her wedding.

"I'll gladly do that for you, Mom. I'm glad you are so happy, and I don't think that I have to tell you that I think Bill is one great guy!"

The next day, Caylen asked Bill and Lora if they would accompany him to the claims registry office so that he could record his rich claim. At the registrar's request, Caylen was required to complete and sign the papers that recorded the claim.

Caylen filled out all the mine location details as best he could, but when he reached the signature block, he turned to Bill and Lora and said, as he handed over the pen,

"Here, Bill, you and Mom sign this thing."

"What are you saying, Caylen? We can't sign this, it's your claim, not ours."

"Wrong, Bill. It's your and Mom's. It's my wedding present to you both." Caylen replied.

"You can't do this Caylen! That claim could be worth millions, once it's developed!" exclaimed Bill.

" I have all I will ever need, and I want you two to have the rest." Caylen insisted.

"Okay. We'll accept, but only if you sign as a third partner." Lora said. "That will make us equal partners, and give you a share in whatever the claim eventually produces."

Caylen could see that, unless he agreed to sign the register as a third partner, Bill and Lora were going to refuse his generous gift, so he finally relented and signed beside their signatures.

It was only a few days later when Sgt. Tompkins and Caylen boarded the train for Carcross and the beginning of their manhunt for Fariss.

Chapter 22

Manhunt

Kosumi and Lokni readily agreed to accompany the Sergeant, Caylen and Warrior in their search for Fariss. They knew, as did Sergeant Tompkins. and Caylen, that Fariss would probably not allow himself to be taken alive but they also knew that for Wildflower's sake that they had to be involved in whatever happened.

After two days of preparations in Carcross, the three men, Caylen and Warrior left the village in traveling in three canoes for the wild remote areas that lay to the south where they suspected that Fariss was now in hiding and awaiting their arrival with his big rifle loaded and ready.

It took them seventeen days of canoeing down the big lake and up the many navigable rivers and smaller lakes that drained into Tagish Lake before they received any indication of where Fariss might have gone. On one of their side trips they paddled right past the little stream that marked Caylens gold claim. Caylen pointed it out to Sgt. Tompkins as they passed, but, as Kosumi and Lokni were directly behind them, they decided not to stop as stopping would surely give away the mine's location to the two brothers. They then decided to swing eastward and travel through Graham Inlet towards the big Atlin Lake before searching the southern portion of Taku Arm. They knew that Fariss was familiar with this route that led over to the village of Atlin on the eastern shore of the big lake that carried the same name. They suspected that he just might head into familiar territory.

The posse had almost reached the short river at the East end of Graham Inlet when they spotted two bearded prospectors, who were attempting to pan powder gold from a small stream that flowed into Graham Inlet from the north. Pulling into shore, they beached their canoes and walked over to where the two men were watching them carefully, with rifles close at hand. It wasn't unusual for lazy claim jumpers to canoe about on these gold rich lakes, searching, not for gold, but for unwary gold miners. These claim jumpers would then, at gunpoint, take any gold or supplies that they desired from any unfortunate miner who allowed the claim jumpers the opportunity.

Holding his arms out to indicate that he was unarmed, Sgt. Tompkins introduced himself and then told the two miners who and what they were after and why they were after him. After he had described Fariss to them, the two men looked at one another, and began to curse.

"Yes! We has seen that murderous damned devil." said the taller of the two. "We was up at the far end of Fantail Lake, camped at the mouth of the big river there, when he snuck up on us and caught us unawares. He took all our gold and most of our food stuffs. We's been eaten fish and beaver meat ever since."

"About when was this?" Sgt. Tompkins asked/ "How long ago did this happen?"

"I'd say was bout eight, nine weeks now." the other prospector chimed in. We's has been trying to gets enough gold so's we can git back to Atlin and buy's us some more supplies."

"Did you notice what direction he went after he left you?" The Sergeant asked.

"We's was pretty damn busy cleaning the muds out of our rifles that he puts in them so's we couldn't shoot that S.O.B." The taller man said. "We thinks he went up the river, but we looked for three days and couldn't find hide nor hair of him. So's we finally gives up lookin and started back this ways. Sides, they's sumpthin damn weird bout that there country. It just doesn't feels right up there."

"Okay, thanks, guys. And, if you need some food, we can spare some." Sgt. Tompkins said.

" We's could sure use a dab of salt." the shorter man said. "That dang crook took all ours, and them fish just don't taste so good without salt."

After giving the pair part of a sack of salt, the four men boarded their canoes and headed back to Taku Arm and the river leading to Fantail Lake.

~*~

Two days later they were nearing the smaller river that led to Fariss's home lake.

"We should take a day and check out the cabin, in case he has returned." Bill said. Turning to Kosumi and Lokni, he continued. "Why don't you and Lokni go ahead and look for any signs that he may have left around the shores of Fantail Lake, and we'll meet you at the mouth of the river in about five or six days time."

After dividing up their stores, Sgt. Tompkins and Caylen paddled north up the short river that led to Fariss's home lake, while Kosumi and Lokni continued west on Fantail Lake, scouring the shoreline as they traveled, looking for any indication of Fariss's passing.

Once they arrived at Fariss's cabin, it took Caylen and Bill only a few minutes to ascertain that if Fariss had returned to the cabin, he had left no signs of having done so. They decided to spend the night in the comfort of the cabin before heading back down the river to Fantail Lake and their rendezvous with Kosumi and Lokni.

After consuming a warm supper of broiled trout, Sgt. Tompkins voiced his opinion to Caylen that, unless Fariss was really stupid, it would be nearly impossible to locate, apprehend and arrest him, as Fariss knew the area much better than either of them.

"I can tell you that Fariss isn't the smartest of people, but he is also not stupid." Caylen said. "He's really good in the woods, Bill, but then I guess you already found that out."

"Well, my leg, my ribs, and my head sure did." Bill replied, with a smile. "You know, Caylen, if Fariss went up that feeder river at the west end of Fantail Lake, he is in unexplored, really rough country. I have never been up that river, so I really don't know much about it. I have heard that the area to the west of there is, according to the natives, the home of some evil spirits that roam about the forest. I am surprised that Kosumi and Lokni agreed to go up there. At any rate, you have to know that, as his pursuers, we are at a real disadvantage. He knows this country much better than we do and, as such, he could set up an ambush anywhere, killing us both before we had a chance, especially with us traveling out in the open on the water like we are. We'll have to keep well out on the water and out of rifle range from now on."

At this point, Caylen felt that it might be appropriate for him to reveal to the worried Sergeant some of the powers that had been given to him.

"Bill, do you remember me telling you and Mom about the old Shaman I was living with, and how he taught me how to use the powers that the Great Spirit gave to me on my Vision Quest?"

" Yes, I do remember." Bill responded." Are you wanting to tell me about them now?"

"I would like to, Bill, but I'm not too sure that you'll be able to believe what I will tell you."

"I've seen many unusual and sometimes even unbelievable things since I began working among the native Indians here in the North." Bill said. "I just about believe that anything is possible if one only wants to truly believe."

It took Caylen until nearly midnight to describe to Sgt. Tompkins the powers that he had. Caylen could see the skepticism in Bill's eyes and could hear the doubt in his voice as he told him of what he could do. He eventually realized that, in order to really convince the skeptical policeman that he did indeed possess these powers, he would have to demonstrate the powers to him. He first asked the Sergeant to go outside the cabin into the darkness and perform something odd while out of Caylens sight. Before Bill left, Caylen asked him to handcuff him on the floor in such a manner that he could not move.

"Why do you want me to do that?" Bill was puzzled.

"Because I'm going to tell you, when you return, in detail exactly where you went and exactly what you did while you are outside and out of my sight. I will be watching your every move from there on the floor and I don't want you to think that I was actually watching you from the window."

"No one can do that." Bill insisted.

"That's what I have been trying to tell you, Bill. I can do just that! Now cuff me, and go outside and do something strange."

Using two sets of handcuffs, Bill fastened Caylen's hands to his feet, behind his back. Then the still skeptical Bill went outside, leaving Caylen lying prone, on his side on the cabin's dirt floor, unable to move. He was gone for about ten minutes before he finally returned and removed Caylens restraints.

"Okay, now tell me. What did I do and where did I go?" he asked.

"Well," Caylen said. "You went outside and just stood there for a moment. Then you walked over to that big spruce tree by the outhouse and you peed up against it. Next, you walked down to the canoe and pulled it up a little higher on the beach before coming back here. Oh, and one more thing, Bill. That little jig you danced on the beach wasn't very good. You should get Mom to show you how it's really done, and then you should practice some more! A lot more.

"My God!" Bill exclaimed. "My God, you actually can do what you said! Now, what about this traveling in animals? How do you do that? How do you do any of these things?"

"I can't explain how I do them, Bill. I just concentrate on what I want to do and it happens. That's all I really know."

"Does your mother know that you can do all these things?"

"No, she doesn't. And I don't quite know how to tell her." Caylen said.

"I'm not sure that you should tell her. She'll probably think that you have gone completely bush crazy!" Bill objected. "Tell me what you are thinking when you do this traveling outside your body."

"Well," Caylen hesitated. "It's hard to explain, but only a part of my essence travels outside of my body and the rest just stays inside my physical body. I can still do some things with my body when part of my essence is outside of it, but I can't really concentrate very well, just yet, on two things at once. It's much easier if I just sit or lay still and do nothing with my physical self when my essence is not all in my body. Sania said that, as I did more traveling with my essence outside my body, it would get easier, but so far I still have some trouble trying to do two things at the same time."

"What animals can you put your mind into and travel in or with?" Bill was fascinated.

" At the present, anything that I can see I can enter and control with my essence." Caylen explained. "So far, I've mostly used Warrior, but I've also used eagles, ravens, moose and one time I even traveled in a fish!"

"No one is ever going to believe all this." Bill said. "I'm not sure that even I do, and I've seen you do these things!"

"I didn't believe it either at first. But now I know much better." Caylen responded. "After living with Sania and experiencing my Vision Quest, I now know that there are many things that are possible, but that are really beyond belief of the average person. For example I can move my essence outside my body without entering another creature's body, but only for very short distances. I can also look at another person and, from the colors that always surround each of us, tell if that person is evil or is having evil thoughts. Now, we had better get some sleep or we're going to be really tired tomorrow."

~*~

Three days later, Caylen and Bill, approaching the western end of Fantail Lake, spotted the canoe of Kosumi and Lokni on the sandy shore just to the North of the mouth of the large stream that drained into the lake. Kosumi and Lokni were sitting on a log by a small fire, drinking tea, as the pair pulled their canoe up and greeted them.

"Any signs of him?" asked Sgt. Tompkins.

"We have seen a camp upriver about two or three miles that could have been his. It looks like someone spent considerable time there, maybe eight, ten weeks." Lokni said. "But whoever it was has been gone about two, three weeks."

"Did you go any further upstream?" Bill asked.

"No, we figured it best to wait here for you." Lokni said.

"Well, we still have a few hours of daylight left so if you two are ready, we may as well go for another few miles before we camp. You two take the north bank and we'll go up the south shore." Bill said. "Let's stay near each other so we can signal back and forth, if we see any sign."

They managed to get about two additional miles upstream before coming to a fast-flowing narrow section of the river. Seeing the two native brothers pulling ashore, Caylen and Bill paddled across to join them in making camp for the night.

As they climbed out of their canoe, Kosumi and Lokni clambered hurriedly back into theirs, and made ready to push off.

"What are you two doing?" Bill asked. "I thought we were going to camp here for the night."

"We will go no further up this river." Kosumi said. "We have come too far even now. We will go back to the lake and wait there for your return."

"But, why will you not go any further?" Bill didn't understand.

"I think we just might be catching up with him."

"We will not go further, this is an evil place here. There is much evil living in these mountains and these forests. This is not a safe place for any man to be." Lokni responded.

"We know that Fariss is an evil man." Bill said. "But we are here to bring him back so that he can be punished by the white man's laws for all the evil that he has done."

"It is not the evil in Fariss Lubak that we speak of or fear." Lokni said. "It is the evil that lives here in these forests that we fear. This terrible evil can consume ordinary men such as us."

"I don't know what you're talking about." Bill stated. "What is this evil called and how do you know that this is an evil place?"

"This evil that lives here is like a starving bad wolf of the North. This evil spirit marks his territory with his urine just as the forest wolf does. This evil spirit is known to our people as a 'Wendigo'." Kosumi said, looking fearfully towards the thick spruce forest. "We have seen the marks of this Wendigo's passing here in this place. Do you not hear the lack of sound in these woods? There are no creatures of the forest other than the black ravens that will live in the home territory of a Wendigo."

"I have heard of this evil spirit that is called a Wendigo." Caylen injected. "I have heard that he lives and grows strong by consuming evil. I have also heard that a good man cannot be harmed by this evil being as long as he is truly a good man."

"Who amongst us can say that he himself is truly a good man? Kosumi asked. "Are we to be our own judges in this matter and are we alone able to decide if we are good enough to be safe in the presence of an eater of evil? I and my brother Lokni shall not dare to wager our lives with the Wendigo who claims this land. We go now to the big lake to await your return."

With those comments, Lokni and Kosumi turned their canoe and paddled off down the swiftly flowing river toward the lake, leaving Sgt. Tompkins and Caylen sitting on the bank, watching them go.

"I've heard that the natives do believe in a evil spirit that they call a Wendigo." Bill said. "But this is the first time I have ever heard anyone speak that much detail of it."

"That's because they're really afraid of it." Caylen said. "Apparently what they call a Wendigo is very similar to what we call the 'Devil'. My friend Sania told me quite a bit about the

Wendigo."

"And just what did he tell you?" asked Bill.

"A Wendigo is believed by many of the native people to be an evil being between fifteen and twenty feet tall. It is said that he was once a very bad man that, because of his evil nature and because he refused to give up his evil ways, was transformed into this devil monster by the Great Spirit. He is permitted to live only in remote areas of these northern forests. He can survive only by consuming raw, the flesh of a living human who is also very evil. His very appearance is said to be so horrible that a man cannot stand to look upon his face and still live. I have also heard it said that he is only visible to a mortal man if he faces that man. If he turns to the side, he is supposed to then become invisible."

"Is it possible to kill this Wendigo?" Bill asked.

"It is said that a Wendigo cannot be killed by any mortal man. It is said that he has only to find and feast on one evil man each one hundred years in order that he survive for a further one hundred years." Caylen said.

"So, if he doesn't eat at least one evil man for one hundred years, then he dies?"

"That's what native legends say. " Caylen replied.

"Well, if such a creature does exist in these woods, our friend Fariss is in good company. Fariss's making himself available will surely seal his fate and will also keep the Wendigo alive for another hundred or so years." Bill said, with a smile, not fully believing what he had just heard.

"I think that we should really be taking this seriously." Caylen rejoined. "Sania said that he saw a Wendigo that he said lived around these lakes at one time."

"Your Sania must have been a good man or else the Wendigo would have gotten him!" Bill said.

"My senses tell me there is definitely something odd about this area." Caylen remarked. "Kosumi was right about there only being ravens around here. I haven't seen any squirrels or any other wild animals or even birds since we got here."

"It certainly is quiet, alright." Bill said. "I suppose we had better move on now. We can make another mile or two before nightfall."

They paddled upstream against the ever-quickening current for another hour, stopping for the night at the base of a long, turbulent rapids. The level, sandy area beside a large, quiet pool at the base of the rapids looked, from the canoe, as though it would offer a good campsite.

As they walked about, looking for a good location to place their tent, Caylen's eyes were drawn to a small circle of rocks on the forest floor.

"Look at this, Bill. It seems that someone recently made a campfire on this spot. These ashes are dry and powdery, and it rained here just two days ago. That would mean that there was a fire here after that rain."

"So if it was Fariss, he's not far ahead of us, at the most a day and a half." Bill replied, "He must have been here for quite a spell. We may be getting really close, so we'd best keep our eyes and ears open."

"I'm sure that Warrior will let us know if he tries anything, or if he is anywhere nearby." Caylen said. "I'll send him upstream tonight to look around before we take off tomorrow. I'll also take one of those big ravens out to have a look around before dark."

"How will that help us?" Bill asked. "I know Warrior is good but I also know he can't talk, so how will he tell us if he does find something?"

"He won't have to tell us, because my essence will be with him and controlling him for the entire trip." Caylen answered.

"You mean you're going to put part of your essence into his mind and travel with him?" asked Bill.

"Yes, as soon as we set up camp and eat. I'll lie down and head off with a raven first to look for his tracks. If I don't spot him from the air, I'll take Warrior and see if I can track him down that way." Caylen said.

"I think I am going crazy," Bill mumbled. "No one will ever believe any of this."

About an hour passed before Caylen felt that he was ready to make his attempt at over-flying the forest in his search.

"I should be able to do this and still carry on talking to you, Bill, but I don't have too much experience at it so I'm going to completely relax as I attempt it." Caylen said.

" Go ahead. I'll just sit here and watch the action. Bill joked.

Caylen lay on his back and looked upwards to where two ravens were circling about far above them. Concentrating his mind intensely on the largest, he suddenly found himself looking down at himself, Warrior and the Sergeant sitting beside their small campfire.

Wheeling about on the ever-changing mountain air currents, he headed off in a northwesterly direction, following the general path of the fast-flowing stream that ran past their camp. In less than fifteen minutes, he concluded that his search path had taken him about ten miles up the valley. Since the thick evergreen forest prohibited him from seeing many parts of the forest floor, he soon realized that, unless Fariss were to foolishly show himself in one of the few openings, he was wasting time. Turning about, he was soon over their camp and, in a instant, back in his own body beside Warrior, who had flopped down by his legs. The big wolf was calm and looking at him in a expectant manner, as if he knew that something was about to happen.

"I'm back, and I saw nothing, so I'll take off with Warrior now," he said to Bill, who just sat, looking at him with a funny look on his face.

Caylen let his mind go blank for a moment before willing his essence to jump across and into the mind of Warrior. It was less than a second before he realized that he was now looking at himself through the eyes of Warrior, as he lay sprawled out on his bedroll. His next thought was to rise up and head upstream, ranging back and forth along the riverbank in an attempt to detect the distasteful strong odor of Fariss. As he did so, Caylen could also see and hear, although not clearly at first, Bill asking him if he was okay, and telling him that he looked 'kind of funny'.

"No, I'm really fine, Bill. I have to tell you though, that I can now sense whatever Warrior senses, and that he, as did Kosumi and Lokni, feels something bad about this place, something evil that makes him not like it here. He really wants to leave but he'll do as I wish, so now I should concentrate on trying to sniff out Fariss."

"You mean that Warrior should, don't you?" asked Bill.

"No, I meant me. Warrior and I are one and the same for now. We will be that way until I bring him back here and return my essence to myself." Caylen said.

"This is just to much for me to comprehend." Bill said. "Just let me know when you're all here!"

Warrior had only gone about two hundred feet when his sensitive nostrils detected the strong sour scent that told him Fariss had passed that spot in the not to distant past. Caylens essence then directed the wolf to follow the strong smell to see where Fariss had gone. It took only a moment for Warrior to locate the hiding place where Fariss had placed his canoe before striking off on foot along a small tributary stream that led off towards the northwestern mountains. Caylen again guided Warrior to follow Fariss's scent for about another two miles upstream before leaving his trail and returning to the camp and Sgt. Tompkins.

"Are you okay, Caylen?" Bill asked, as Warrior suddenly ran out of the forest and dropped to the ground by Caylen's side.

"Yes, I'm back, and I know what Fariss has done and where he has gone." Caylen. "He's hidden his canoe not far from here and headed up a small valley towards those mountains to the north. His scent was quite strong, so I think he just left here a day or so ago. If we get going, we may soon catch up with him."

"Well, I don't think he knows yet that we're after him. I wonder what he's up to." Bill said.

"Do you know what's in that direction, if he were to keep going that way?" Caylen asked.

"I think that if he were to swing a little to the west, he might eventually hit the rail line from Skagway." Bill replied. "But the maps of that area are not very good, so I don't know exactly what's between here and the railway tracks."

"As long as we have Warrior with us, we can track him down anywhere." Caylen stated. "Let's pack up and get going."

~*~

Fariss, once he had gotten down to the big Fantail Lake, had changed his mind. He went downstream to the huge Taku Arm of Tagish Lake. He entertained, for some time, the idea of heading across to Atlin, or even striking off up Tagish Lake and the Yukon River into the North Country of the Yukon. After he observed and spoke to a lone prospector camped on Taku Arm, he soon changed his mind about where he would go after he realized that, if seen by anyone at all, that person could tell whoever followed him which direction he had gone.

Fariss rose during the night that he spent with the solitary prospector and, taking his big rifle, struck the man across his forehead with its iron butt, killing the prospector instantly. After he had ransacked the man's belongings and taken what he wanted, Fariss dragged the dead man down to the lake and rolled him into the cold water.

"There you's be!" he muttered. "Now's you's can't be tellin nobody nothin bouts where's I'se been or where's I'se goin to." With that, he threw the dead man's remaining supplies into the lake and smashed his canoe, before heading back up the river toward Fantail Lake.

Fariss took his time traveling up to the head of Fantail Lake. He paddled only a few miles each day before pulling his canoe up into the forest far enough to conceal its presence from any passing eyes. He spent three or four days at some stops, just lazing about in the warm sun, fishing, sleeping and doing some panning in any creek that looked promising.

It took him nearly two months to reach the extreme western end of the large Fantail Lake, where he encountered two prospectors panning gold on the beach next to the point where the fast-flowing feeder stream exited the valley, draining into the lake. Surprising the two prospectors, he soon had all their gear and food stuffs in his possession. He decided not to kill the two men, but made them throw their weapons far out into the lake, and send them off in their canoe, with only the barest of supplies and no weapons.

Soon after the prospector's departure, Fariss established himself in a more or less permanent camp at a location near the base of some fast-flowing rapids, where he could easily see down toward the big lake. He found that wild game of any sort was rare in this area, even though there seemed to be plenty of the types of foods they liked to eat. As a result, he lived mostly on freshly-caught lake trout and grayling.

His one attempt at moving further up the fast-flowing river was to be thwarted by the steep rapids, where he would have had to portage at least three miles around before being able to launch his canoe into the river once more.

He did walk up the river's three miles of rapids to see if a portage was even possible, but the terrain was extremely steep, rocky and just too difficult to even attempt, while carrying a canoe and heavy packs. Even after he reached the top of the rapids, he could see that the river was flowing just to rapid for him to even contemplate attempting the long portage.

He also felt, for some unknown reason, very uncomfortable and uneasy whenever he ventured west of the base of these rapids. He found, during his exploratory trip upstream along the rapids, that he was constantly looking, around in expectation of something or someone appearing out of the forest. Twice during this hike, he thought that he saw a huge, shadowy figure darting silently from thicket to thicket, but he was never able to get a clear look at whatever it was.

Unable to explain the odd uncomfortable feelings that he had while passing this area, he decided to venture no further west and that, if he did have to leave the area where he was now located, he would go in a Northwest direction. He knew that if he went far enough to the North and West, he would eventually find the tracks of the Yukon and White Pass railway. He could then flag down the train and ride it into the port city of Skagway, and then seek passage on a steamer to some southern port, where he could, with his cash money and gold, begin a new life.

He had remained in this particular camp for almost two weeks when, as he stood one afternoon fishing at the river's mouth, he saw, far down on the lake, a canoe approaching, with two men in it. Waiting until they were closer, he recognized Kosumi and Lokni. He thought for a moment about shooting both of them, but suddenly and without further ado, he returned to his camp, packed his gear into his big backpack, dragged his canoe well into the forest, and then headed off to the northwest, following a small stream that made its way down from the nearby snow-clad mountains through a small narrow valley.

~*~

Sgt. Tompkins and Caylen, with Warrior's keen nose guiding them, knocked a large hole in Fariss's canoe. They found Fariss's trail, for the first few miles, quite easy to follow through the thick forest along a small stream. As the trail led them higher and higher into the mountains, the rocky terrain made traveling both difficult and dangerous. At one point, Fariss's scent led them along a steep narrow ledge that gave them no more than a foot of space between a vertical cliff on one side and a thousand foot drop on the other. This trail then brought the pursuers back down and into a pretty little valley that swung over and led to the west.

It soon became evident that they were once again in the seemingly dead zone that appeared to be devoid of all wildlife save the noisy ever-present ravens. The valley appeared to about two miles long and lightly treed, with many large grassy meadows dotting its expanse. It ended to the west, with a narrow pass that the men could see led much higher along a cliff towards the west.

~*~

Fariss could feel the icy cold fingers of extreme terror beginning to crawl up his spine. Ever since his travel route had taken its westward turn, his feelings of unease had begun to, once again, increase to the point where he felt sure that he was being closely watched and followed.

His overnight camp and soft, comfortable spruce-bough bed had not granted him any sleep whatsoever, nor any relief from this feeling that something terrible was about to happen to him. As a result, he decided that he would spend another day and night in this same camp, attempting to get some much needed rest, before tackling the next, obviously steep and narrow rocky mountain pass that rose just ahead.

He rose from his cold camp early on the second day and, after consuming a cold slab of fire-dried trout, strapped on his big pack, slung his rifle and struck off across a large meadow for the western slopes leading to the pass. As he was entering the low alder and spruce growth at the edge of where the pass began, he heard the loud yelp of what sounded like a wolf from behind him. Swinging around, he saw, at the far edge of the clearing, Caylen, Warrior and the easily recognizable uniformed figure of a Northwest Policeman.

Unslinging and shouldering his big rifle, he quickly triggered off two rifle shots at his pursuers, then turned and began to trot up the indistinct trail that appeared to lead up and through the pass.

~*~

Caylen and Bill had located Fariss's camp shortly after they themselves had resumed their pursuit that morning. From Warrior's reaction to the scent around the camp, Caylen knew that Fariss had just recently left.

"We are right behind him, Bill, we should be prepared for anything once we catch up with him because I'm sure he won't willingly just give himself up to us." Caylen said.

"I think you're right." Bill agreed, as he unslung his rifle and levered a cartridge into the chamber.

They had gone only a few hundred yards when the trail that Warrior was following led the group out of the woods and into a large open meadow. As they entered this clearing, both Caylen and Bill heard Warrior suddenly give out a loud yelp of discovery. Looking ahead they both could see, about four hundred yards away, at the other end of the clearing, Fariss aiming his rifle at them.

"Get down! Get down fast!" Bill yelled, as he shouldered Caylen off to the left, falling to the ground as he spoke.

Caylen immediately dropped down beside Bill and listened, as the angry buzz of the two heavy caliber bullets whirred by, directly over their heads.

The twosome remained prone on the ground for two or three minutes, with Bill triggering off three fast shots in the general direction of where they had last seen Fariss.

Fariss, after firing at his pursuers, turned, without waiting to see if his bullets had found their mark, and raced off, as fast as he was able, up the narrow trail that led toward the pass just ahead. As he hurried up through the pass, he found himself on a widening trail that led upward towards the opening in the rocky hills ahead. As he ran, his nostrils were suddenly assailed by the most horrible stench that completely surrounded him and seemed to be coming from every direction.

"Must be's some dead beasts round here," he said out loud to himself. "Sure stinks likes somethin rotten."

A short moment later, his ears were assaulted by what seemed to Fariss to be the loudest, most awful scream of utter rage that he had ever heard. The sound appeared to be coming from directly to his front, but he could see nothing. Thinking that he must have startled an eagle or a falcon, he continued on up the steep trail, noting that, just ahead, was a large, dark hole in the cliff's wall that looked as though it might be the opening to a cave.

This prompted the thought that he might possibly be able to ambush and kill his followers from this dark place, as they followed him up the trail. He had just come up to the opening when he saw a huge, black figure suddenly spring out of the opening to stand on the trail before him, completely blocking his ascent.

Coming to a sudden halt, it took Fariss the better part of a minute before his terrified brain could even begin to interpret what his eyes were now seeing standing in front of him.

No more than ten feet from him on the trail, was what could only be described as a monster. This naked, black creature stood about fifteen or sixteen feet tall, on long, spindly legs that ended in cloven feet that closely resembled moose's hooves. The creature had long, hairy, thin forearms, with big muscular biceps, huge, boney hands with long dirty fingers that were tipped with filthy torn, claw-like fingernails. The head and face of this thing that stood before him was unlike anything he could ever begin to imagine. It had small black beadlike pupils that were staring directly at him where he stood. These pupils were centered in large circular, whitish-colored eyes that had no eyelashes or eyebrows. The creature's head was completely devoid of hair of any sort. Its huge mouth and jaws could only be described as wolfish in shape, with a mouth and fangs that seemed totally out of proportion to its smallish head. These fangs were at least two inches in length, and projected well below the thing's lower crimson-dripping lips. What was even stranger was that the thing appeared to be as thin in depth as a piece of tissue paper. Its entire body seemed to be shimmering, like a mirage in the bright noonday sun, with the edges of its body seeming to appear and disappear before his very eyes.

As Fariss stood in speechless, frozen, abject horror, unable to move and gaping at this monster that had suddenly appeared before him, the creature began to shuffle slowly towards him. Now completely frozen in terror, Fariss wanted to turn and run back down the trail towards his pursuers, but found that he was unable to move any part of his body whatsoever. He could only stand, in frozen horror, where he was, as this huge black thing shuffled up to him and grasped him by his shoulders with its long, dirty, foul-smelling hands.

The last things that Fariss was aware of, before he died, was the monstrous creature picking him up as though he were a feather, the terrible stench, and the horrible, white pain as the two enormous fangs entered his neck and severed his head entirely from his body.

~*~

Caylen and Bill could clearly see Fariss as he raced up the steep trail. They had lain prone for only a brief moment before Bill had risen sufficiently to observe Fariss racing up the steep trail. He stood and beckoned to Caylen, watching Fariss carefully as they sped after him across the meadow's wide expanse. They had only traversed about half of the distance across the opening when Caylen, glancing up towards Fariss, saw the huge creature leap out of nowhere and confront Fariss on the trail, high above them.

"Bill! Quick! Look at that!" he exclaimed.

"What is it you see, Caylen? Oh, it looks like he's stopped for something." Bill replied.

"Don't you see that thing there in front of him? Oh my gosh! I've never seen anything like it." Caylen said.

"I can't see anything but Fariss just standing on the trail up there. My God! What's happening to him now?" Bill exclaimed, as Fariss seemed to rise up and float horizontally in the air.

"Can't you see that thing that's got hold of him? I think it's going to throw him off the cliff." Caylen said. "No! Oh, my God!"

"What just happened?" Did you see that? Fariss's head just disappeared from sight!" Bill shouted.

"I think I know what is happening now." Caylen said Caylen. "We may as well just watch and then we can go back home."

"What do you mean? What's happening to him? Look! His right arm just vanished!"

"I'll explain in a minute, Bill. Let's just wait until it's over with. I don't think it'll take much longer." Caylen said, a great sadness in his voice.

The pair watched as, over the next few moments, Fariss was totally consumed by the Wendigo. Caylen, with his powers, could quite easily see the creature, as it relished and slowly ate all of the unfortunate Fariss. When nothing remained of the human's body, the supposedly mythical creature spat out Fariss's indigestible clothes and his backpack onto the rocky trail. Then, he vanished from sight, returning to his cave.

"I think that the Wendigo who lives around here just ensured that he'll surely live for another hundred years." Caylen's voice was a whisper. "You couldn't see it, Bill, but Fariss was just eaten alive by a Wendigo. We can go up now, if you want, and retrieve his belongings as proof, or we can just leave everything and go home."

"Are you telling me that what I just saw was an invisible monster called a Wendigo eating Fariss?" Bill asked, unbelieving.

"That's exactly what you saw, Bill, except that the Wendigo was invisible to you because you are a good man. The only way you could have seen the Wendigo was if you had been a evil person, and then it probably would have came down here and eaten you, too."

~*~

Caylen and Sgt. Bill Tompkins left for home the following morning after recovering Fariss's clothing, rifle and pack. It took them a day and a half to reach the campsite of Lokni and Kosumi, at the mouth of the river on Fantail Lake. They explained in detail, what had happened and how Fariss had met his untimely, but well deserved end.

Kosumi and Lokni, upon hearing how Fariss had died, looked at one another briefly, and Lokni then said.

"It is done. Our Wildflower is avenged. She is now free to travel forever with the Great Spirit in the afterlife. That evil man has now been taken to another place, a place where he shall be made to suffer for all eternity for his sins."

Sgt. Tompkins, having earlier discussed with Caylen what to do with Fariss's rifle and the contents of his pack, gave them to the two brothers. Going through the pack's contents, the brothers soon found the bag of gold and the roll of cash.

"Did you know that this was in his pack?" Lokni asked.

"Yes, we did, and we both think that you and your brother should have it. You both have done much for us, and you have also lost much. So, please take it and use it for whatever you wish." Bill said.

"You are good men, we are proud to call both of you our friends. You are both welcome, at any time, to our houses and to partake of our food and our hospitality." Kosumi said.

"It is nothing but what you both truly deserve, and we thank you for all you've done." Bill responded. "Now we all must get back to our homes. This pursuit is over and justice has surely been done."

~*~

It was ten days later that Bill and Caylen stepped out of the rail car and onto the station platform at Whitehorse. Caylen was quite anxious to get back to his hotel room and get himself cleaned up, while Bill reported in to his superior officer at the Northwest Police detachment headquarters.

Caylen, about two hours later, was knocking on the door of his mother's hotel room, anxious to tell her of all that had occurred on their manhunt.

Lora, on answering the door and seeing Caylen standing before her, blurted out fearfully.

"Where is Bill? Is he hurt? Why isn't he with you? He's okay, isn't he? Please, Caylen! Please tell me he's okay!"

"Yes, Mom." laughed Caylen. "He's fine, he's just reporting in at his office, and then he will be right over. He can't wait to see you, either."

"You certainly frightened me when I saw you standing there all by yourself." Lora said. "Did you bring Fariss back with you?"

"No, Mom. He's dead. We both saw him get killed way back up in the mountains, west of Fantail Lake."

" Who killed him, Caylen? I hope it wasn't you or Bill."

"No, Mom. It wasn't either Bill or I, but let's wait until Bill gets here, and then we can both tell you what happened." Caylen said.

Bill arrived about an hour later. After the greetings were out of the way, Bill and Caylen gave Lora all the details of the chase, leaving none of the information out. Caylen also explained to his mother the details of all the powers that he had been given by the Great Spirit.

She was quite unbelieving at first, but Bill's adamant confirmation of what he had personally seen Caylen do finally convinced her. They broke for a late supper in the hotel dining room and then, around midnight, came to the part where Fariss had been killed and consumed by the Wendigo.

Both Bill and Caylen, having seen the death of Fariss differently, told Lora what they had each seen.

"But, why could you see this creature while Bill couldn't?" Lora asked.

"I really don't know for sure, Mom. I must have been given that power, also. I do know that Sania said that he also had once seen a Wendigo, so perhaps I can, too."

"What did you put in your report about his death?" Lora asked Bill.

"I said he fell over a cliff and was killed when trying to escape after he tried to shoot us." Bill replied.

"Caylen, you mustn't ever tell anyone of these powers that you have." Lora said Lora, as Bill nodded in agreement. "You may think that having them is a good thing but I don't think that's what others may think. They would probably have you put into a crazy house for the rest of your life, if they heard you speak of these things."

"I agree completely, Mom. It'll be our secret." Caylen nodded. "Now, Mom, Bill, just when are you guys planning to get married, and what're you going to do then?"

"If your Mom agrees, I would like to get married this week." Bill said, glancing sideways at the blushing Lora.

"Good. Then you two can spend the next few months on your honeymoon just resting up because I have to go visit Sania's grandchildren in a place called the First Mesa on a Hopi Reservation somewhere down in Arizona." Caylen said.

"We'll be right here when you return." Bill commented. "I have some plans concerning our mine that I want to discuss with Lora. If she agrees, we may have a big surprise for you when you return. Now go to your Arizona Reservation and meet your Hopi relatives."

"Have a good time, but fetch me back a nice Hopi blanket." Lora smiled, her blush fading.

Chapter 23

Deep South

Caylen spent the following week resting and discussing his proposed trip with Lora and Bill. He also went to the Whitehorse train station and discussed, at length, with the station's ticket attendant, the best possible route to take to get to Sania's homelands that lay far to the South. The station attendant was not really too helpful, in that all he knew for certain was that Arizona was in the far South, and that, in order to get there, Caylen would have to first get to the coastal city of San Francisco and then go east to Arizona. His searching of the maps that he had available showed no indications of any Hopi reservation whatsoever in the entire State of Arizona. His maps did, however, indicate that some kind of vehicle road and a railroad did exist that went from San Francisco to and across the state of Arizona.

Caylen decided to purchase a railway ticket to Skagway for himself and Warrior, and that once he reached San Francisco; he should be able to get further details from the locals about the route, and a mode of travel to Arizona and the Hopi reservation.

Bill and Lora were married two days later. Caylen had purchased himself travel clothes that included a custom-fitted, grey three-piece suit, suitable also for use at his mother's wedding.

The informal wedding was performed by a Whitehorse judge who had also presided over the trials of many of the culprits that Bill had apprehended at one time or another.

Following the marriage ceremony, Bill, Lora, Caylen and Bill's Superintendent, as well as the judge, had a more or less formal supper at the Whitehorse Hotel.

At the end of the sumptuous meal, as dessert was being served, Caylen, following a congratulatory speech by Bill's Superintendent, rose and asked the newly-wed couple if he could now say a few words.

" Of course, Son." Bill said, with a smile. "Do you mind if I now call you Son?"

"As long as you don't mind me calling you Dad." Caylen replied, also smiling. "Now, I'd like to congratulate Bill and Mom, and wish them a very long life and a very happy marriage. I would also like to ask my Mom and Bill—Dad—if they would like to celebrate with me, my seventeenth birthday, before I leave for Arizona."

"Oh, my gosh!" Lora exclaimed. "I'm so sorry, Caylen. I totally forgot about it in all the excitement. Bill, we must have a party for Caylen. His birthday is today!"

"Well, just a minute and I'll call the waiter over." Bill said. "There's no time like the present, so let's start to celebrate both of these happy events right now!"

The combined wedding reception and birthday party went on until dawn of the following day. Both Lora and Bill were more than just a little tipsy from the many bottles of wine that now stood empty on the big dining room table. The little three-piece band had also stayed, at the judge's request and expense, to play on until the wedding/birthday party finally broke up at dawn when everyone went home.

~*~

Before leaving on his southern journey, Caylen thought that he should discuss with his mother and Bill their plans for the future. Not sure of how long his journey would take, he thought that he should try to get some idea as to where they might be when he returned.

" We were going to keep it as a secret and surprise you when you returned." Lora said.

"From what you told us about your finds at your gold claim, we think that you may have only scratched the surface." Bill said. "We thought that we would see if Kosumi and Lokni would be interested in going back to the mine with us and doing a little more exploring. We would like to see if we can determine just how big the gold-bearing area is, and if it's worth establishing a real mine there."

"I think that's a great idea." Caylen quickly agreed. "I think if you offered Lokni and Kosumi a percentage of the take, that they would be happy to go. They both seem like good, dependable workers."

"We just don't want to let the word get out about your find any sooner than it has to. We thought that if we did it the right way, we could, if needed, get more claims registered around the property and the mine more or less established before the area is swamped with other prospectors."

"That all sounds good to me, it sounds as though you two have everything planned out. Will you be going with them, Mom?"

"We're going to purchase a big motor-powered boat to take us there. We'll have room on board for lots of supplies, so it'll be like a wilderness vacation. I think it'll be fun." Lora said.

"If we think it worthwhile, we may stay the summer, and then contract the mining out, or perhaps we will sell it and let someone else have all the headaches and the hard work." Bill said. "I have one other thing I would like to discuss with you, Caylen, before you leave."

"Anything, Bill. What is it?"

"Well, as you know, my partner for the past three years, Jim Brookes, left a young wife and a two-year-old son behind when Fariss killed him. The Police pension she'll get is only twenty-five dollars per month. That's not enough to do more than just feed them. I would like to give them a small percentage of our share in the mine.

"I think that's a great idea."" Caylen agreed. "In fact, I'll give you a bank draft in her name right now for twenty-five thousand dollars, as my contribution. Whatever else you decide on is fine with me. Just leave word here at the hotel as to where you go, so that I can find you when I get back from Arizona. Now, I have to get myself ready as the train to Carcross leaves here at six a.m. tomorrow."

~*~

Caylen and Warrior spent the next twelve days traveling, or waiting to travel, on trains and ships. He did encounter more than a few passing glances and questioning looks from the many other travelers who wondered about the good-looking young man with the huge jet-black wolf by his side.

His arrival, by steamship, at the port of San Francisco was a huge event for Caylen. The very size of the city, and the throngs of people milling about, terrified him, until a friendly African man driving a horse-drawn buggy approached him to enquire if he could be of service.

"I need to get to a place called Arizona." Caylen said.

" Well, you's got a long ways to go's! Arizona be's far aways east of here, over them there mountains." The man said, pointing to some cloud-covered mountain peaks far to the East.

"Do you know how far it is, and how I can get there?" asked Caylen.

"From the size of that there dog, I would guess that you could probably just ride him there!" joked the man.

"He's not a dog, he's a full-blooded Arctic timber wolf; and he is really hungry!" Caylen said. "Now, can you help me or should I be asking someone who can?"

"Don't be gettin yerself all lathered up, boy, I was jest joking you. Fer one dollar, I can takes you and yer wolfs east of town to a station where railroad trains travels East every day. Theys also a Hotel there fer you's to stay at."

"Here's your dollar and another dollar for you, so take me, there if you please, Sir." Caylen requested.

Caylen was amazed at the size of the city and even more amazed at the number of people that seemed to him to be just wandering aimlessly about the streets. His driver pointed out a few of the cities more prominent features but, for the most part, he was kept quite busy avoiding pedestrians and the noisy motorcars, whose drivers all seemed to be enamored by the raucous sound of their vehicles horns. It was nearly three hours before the buggy pulled into a driveway that fronted a two-story, wood-frame inn. To one side of the inn stood a long, rectangular wood-frame building with a wooden sign on the front that proclaimed that this was the Atlantic and Pacific's western-most railroad terminus.

Caylen could see at least two rows of train tracks behind this railroad station, but no trains were in view. Thanking his buggy driver, Caylen, after some discussions regarding Warrior's presence, was safely housed, with Warrior, in a small, ground level room to await the following day's early departure of the steam train for Arizona.

The next morning, after a greasy breakfast in the hotel

restaurant, Caylen boarded, with Warrior, the puffing and smoke-belching train that had pulled up in front of the station. It finally, after three or four long delays, puffed out and onto the main linc leading East towards the far distant mountains.

~*~

It took the train nearly three days of belching smoke and steam to reach the Arizona village of Flagstaff. The train's conductor had been a wealth of information for Caylen. He said that the majority of the natives seen in the Flagstaff area were from one of the Hopi reservations that lay somewhere to the northeast of Flagstaff.

Caylen soon found himself wandering aimlessly about the little town of Flagstaff. Primarily a logging and mining town with some sheep ranching, the town had recently grown to be quite famous, and had begun to grow rapidly after the famous Lowell Observatory had been built nearby. He saw numerous native Indians lounging about, but whenever he spoke to them, they either responded in their native tongue or simply ignored him.

After about two hours of finding out exactly nothing, he made his way to a small hotel at the edge of town and rented a room. The desk clerk, after much persuasion and a fifty-cent tip, informed Caylen of a small bar, about a block away, that prospectors often frequented and who might have some knowledge of the Hopi Reservation lands.

As he made his way up to this little bar, Caylen spotted, sitting on a bench in front of the bar, two native Indians of indeterminate ages, that were obviously interested in, and eyeing Warrior, as they approached.

" That there animal be one big wolf." said the one on the left.

" That there animal be a spirit wolf." said the other.

"You are both correct, Caylen said. " But how did you know these things about my pet wolf?"

"We are men of the Hopi. We have knowledge of these things. We live to the North of here and we come here to trade the white-eyes for seed for our lands."

"Do you know of a place called the Third Mesa?" Caylen asked.

"We know of this place, white-eyes. Why does the white-eyes

with a spirit wolf wish to know of this place?"

"I must go to the Third Mesa to find someone." Caylen answered.

"The people of the Third Mesa do not like strangers to walk on their lands. They guard their lands well against the white-eyes." the taller native spoke.

"Is there any way I can get there?" Caylen asked. "I will pay well, in gold, for any man who'll lead me to the Third Mesa."

"What Power is it that makes the young white-eyes who has a spirit wolf for a pet wish to travel to the pueblo of the People of the Third Mesa?" asked the tall native man.

Caylen, tiring of this back and forth bantering, said,

"I do so at the wishes of the great Whakan Powwaw that the People banned from the Third Mesa long ago because they feared his great powers. I cannot speak his name aloud as he has just recently gone to be with the Great Spirit, Qaletaka."

The two native men looked at each other, whispering back and forth for a few minutes as Caylen waited patiently. He knew from the expressions on the two men's faces that they recognized just who Caylen meant, and that the two likely knew of Sania's history with their people.

"How do you know of this Whakan Powwaw? He has been gone from this place now for nearly eighty snows. No man now knows the land where the great Whakan Powwaw lived, as he must have gone to be with the Great Spirit long ago."

"You are wrong; he has only been with Qaletaka now for less than five moons. Before he went to be with Qaletaka, he asked that I, his blood-brother and his adopted son, come to the Third Mesa to tell his people of his travels, and of his many mortal feats."

"From where on this land have you traveled to tell the People of the travels and feats of the great Whakan Powwaw?"

"I have come from a land far to the North of this land. I have been traveling by land and by water for more than fifteen suns so that I might fulfill my promise to my brother."

"It is good. We will take you to the Third Mesa at the rising of the next sun. It is a four day walk from this place, so the brother of the Whakan Powwaw should prepare well for this long walk to the North." The shorter Hopi native stated.

"I shall be here with the rising sun." Caylen said. "And I'll be ready."

~*~

The journey north to the Third Mesa was the most amazing trip that Caylen had ever undertaken. The terrain was near desert-like, with only an occasional tree, the wood of which was so hard it dulled his knife at his first cut, when he tried to cut shavings off a dried piece. He also discovered, to the amusement of the two native men, that a large dried log that he tried to pick up for firewood, was, in fact, a petrified tree of many different colors that probably weighed over a ton.

The many cacti, scorpions, rattlesnakes and coyotes were of great interest to Warrior, who soon discovered that the majority of the area's wildlife was best left alone.

The two natives enjoyed showing and explaining both the flora and fauna to Caylen, thankfully before he encountered them in an adverse manner.

Caylen could see the Third Mesa long before they reached it. The Mesa's Pueblo, with its prominent mud and stone buildings, stood high above the surrounding hills. His two guides informed him that the Third Mesa was one of three main pueblos of the Hopi People, and also one of the oldest. The pueblos had been constructed on the high mesas so that they could be easily defended against the Hopi people's warring neighborhood tribes.

As they entered the village, Caylen could see many of the residents standing outside their homes, watching as he and Warrior followed the two guides towards what appeared to be the largest stone and mud building in the village. He was then ushered in this structure to find nothing inside, save a few floor mats that lay scattered near the midpoint of the round structure.

" Wait." one of the native guides said. "Wait and we shall find the elders, who will hear you speak of the Whakan Powwaw who left this place so long ago."

"I really just wanted to speak to his children's children and their children." Caylen said. "Those are the people that I must speak with."

"We shall find all of these people." The second guide said.

"We shall find them all for you." His companion added,

Caylen waited for some time before ten older native men filed in, followed by three native woman, one quite old, another middle-aged, and the third that appeared to be about Caylen's age. The younger girl looked shyly at Caylen as she entered the big room.

Caylen looked back at her, and then gasped out loud, startling Warrior, who rose quickly to his feet with a loud snarl. Caylen's gasp had been the result of his having just looked at the prettiest girl he had ever seen.

She stood straight and slim, with raven black hair that reached just past her waist. She wore a fawn-colored buckskin dress with a frilly hem that brushed at her trim, shapely ankles and had, about her neck, a beaded turquoise necklace.

Caylen couldn't take his eyes from this young native girl that he could see bore some faint resemblance to Sania. He assumed that she was probably Sania's great-granddaughter. It wasn't until one of the native men began to speak that he could even remember the reason that he was here.

"We see the young white-eyes with the spirit wolf." one of the old men said. "We have been told that he wishes to speak with us of one of our people that, long ago, was banished from our pueblo. Speak now, white-eyes, of what you will."

Finally looking away from the girl, who was now looking at the floor with downcast eyes in embarrassment at his gawking, Caylen began to address the group.

~*~

"My birth name given me by my mother is Caylen Helms. My name given me by my Hopi blood-brother is Mato Honi, or Brave Wolf, and I have come to speak to the children of the children of the Whakan Powwaw that made me his blood-brother. This Whakan Powwaw is not long with the Great Spirit, so I must not speak his name."

"The people of this, the Third Mesa, however, would know this man as the Whakan Powwaw that they, nearly eighty snows past, banished forever from this place."

"How can this be?" asked one of the elders. "This Whakan Powwaw of whom you speak was indeed banished from this place some eighty snows past by our fathers' fathers. This man had already seen some forty-five snows when he was banished. This man you speak of would have had to live for least one hundred and twenty-five snows for him to be the Whakan Powwaw that was banished from this place."

"Actually, he had lived for only one hundred and twenty-four snows when the Great Spirit took him from before my very eyes." Caylen replied. "And if the Whakan Powwaw I speak of and knew is not the same one that your people banished long ago, then tell me how he would know of all these things. How would he know exactly what happened those many snows past? How would he have knowledge of the names of those who banished him? How would he know the name of his wife and daughter, if he were not the same man? How would my blood-brother, the great Hopi Whakan Powwaw, be able to tell me all these things, if he were not your Whakan Powwaw? How would this man, if he were not the same Whakan Powwaw of your people, be able to convince the Great Spirit to give me the same powers that he gave to your Whakan Powwaw so long ago? How would this man, if he were not the same man, be able to teach me the use of these powers if he were not the same man that you banished so long ago?"

The ten old men whispered back and forth to each other for about five minutes before one of them said to Caylen,

"If we are to believe what you have said to be true, the Whakan Powwaw that our fathers' fathers once banished from this place is now, after one hundred and twenty-four snows, gone to be with the Great Spirit. You say that he taught you the use of those same powers that caused him to be banished from this place. If this is so, you shall show us these powers that you say you now possess. If you do this thing that we ask, we shall believe your words from this day forth and you shall be recognized forever as the blood-brother of the great Whakan Powwaw that our fathers' fathers wrongly banished from this place. You will also, if you do these things, be forever welcome in the lands of the Hopi."

Caylen absorbed all that had been said for a few moments before saying,

"I shall, as you ask, demonstrate to you who are present, some of the powers that the Great Spirit has bestowed upon me. I shall sit here in this very place, in this house and send my essence to the outside world while my mortal body remains here. My essence will then return and I will speak to you of what my essence has seen. I will next mix my essence with the essence of my spirit wolf, Warrior, and go with him to the place that you chose, while my mortal body, again remains here. My Warrior will then return here and I will speak to you again of what my essence has seen. Will these things be sufficient?"

"They will." chorused the ten elders.

It took over an hour for Caylen to complete his power display for the elders. Their reaction to his display was to ask if he possessed any other powers that he hadn't told them about. He decided that he had best not tell them any further details of his other powers, as they were already showing some signs of being afraid of him, and he didn't want to be banished as had Sania. He then spoke to the group for about two more hours, describing to them Sania's life in the North, and how he had missed his family and his life on the Third Mesa with his people.

They questioned him at length until their leader finally stood and said,

"Enough! We are satisfied that this man Brave Wolf is who he says he is. We are satisfied that our banished Whakan Powwaw has taught this Brave Wolf in the use of his many powers. We are satisfied that this young Brave Wolf speaks the truth in all these things. We now say that he is forever welcome to our house, and to the lands of our people."

"I thank you for these things that you have said to me." Caylen said. "Now, may I speak to the children of the children of my brother?"

"My mother's mother cannot speak in the language of the white man, so she has asked that I speak for her," the young native girl said, causing Caylen's heart to again skip a beat, just at the sound of her voice.

"She wishes that I tell you this. You shall come now to our home to eat and sleep, and speak to us of our father's father. We, his children and the children of his children, are greatly in need of our family's life stories that have been for so long missing from our lives. Perhaps by knowing these things about our past, our lives can now be made complete, and we can tell to our children, stories about the deeds of our fathers' lives."

~*~

Caylen spent the next three days at the pueblo of Sania's daughter, Kele, who was in her mid nineties and could barely remember her father. What she could remember, however, was the uproar about the reservation when the tribal elders announced his permanent banishment from the reservation lands.

She remembered her mother's sorrow, and her own bewilderment, at her father's tribal dishonoring and his sudden departure from their lives. She also could recall her mother's inability and unwillingness to even speak to her about her father and his banishment. She had no way of knowing, at her young age, that ancient tribal laws forbade anyone, even her mother, from speaking, for ten snows, the name of a person who had been banished from the tribe.

Caylen sat and spoke to Sania's daughter Kele, his granddaughter Sihu and his great-granddaughter Aponi for two full days, stopping only to eat and sleep. He told them of all that had happened to him while he was living with Sania. He told them of his dreams before meeting him. He told them of Sania's gift to him of Abhaya's puppy. He told them of his Vision Quest and of how he had, with Sania's blessings, obtained his powers from the Great Spirit, and of Sania teaching him how to use those powers.

He told them, with tears streaming down his face, of Sania's and Abhayas death, and of their final resting place. He told them how Sania had, knowing of his impending demise, asked Caylen to go to his birth place in Arizona, to seek out his descendents, give them his medicine bag and tell them of his life and his many exploits in the Northern wilderness.

When Caylen finally finished telling the family of Sania's life story and of his life in the North, Sania's old daughter rose and, coming before Caylen, placed one hand on each of his shoulders, and, translated by Aponi, said,

"I have seen more than ninety snows come upon this land of my people. I shall also, as was my father, soon be summoned by the Great Spirit to be with him, and to stand at the side of my father in the lands of the Great Spirit. You have given me great comfort by what you have told us here. We now know that our father was a great Whakan Powwaw who was wrongly banished from the lands of his people. We now know that he was greatly favored by the Great Spirit, who protected him from all of life's evils, and who finally took him to be by his side with him for all of eternity."

She went on.

"We can see, from the tears that have stained your cheeks for these two days, that you, Mato Honi, loved our father as though he were of your own blood. We have seen that even from the lands of the Great Spirit, our father is still able to place his mark on your very essence so as to make the waters drain from your eyes. We see these things, Mato Honi, blood-brother of our Father, and we welcome you into our house for as long as you chose."

With those final words, the old woman gave Caylen a hug and kissed him, first on his left cheek and then on his right, before relinquishing her hold to her daughter, Sihu, who did the same, as she said,

"We welcome you to our house, also."

It was then the turn of Aponi, Sania's pretty young great-granddaughter, to hug and kiss Caylen's cheeks in a similar manner. As she did so, Caylen nearly swooned at the very aroma of her body, which reminded him of wild sage, cedar, pine and wood-smoke.

Sensing his shy awkwardness at her nearness, Aponi pulled him even closer, before finally releasing him and saying, with a beautiful, mischievous teasing smile.,

"What seems to be troubling you, Mato Honi? Are you not the brave blood-brother of my father's father? Are you so brave that the kiss of little Aponi now frightens you?"

"Aponi!, Stop teasing the young Mato Honi. Can you not see that you have caused much redness to appear on his face? You have now even made him unable to speak!" said Aponi's mother, who had already noted that her young daughter was quite taken with this handsome young man, who obviously was also quite attracted to her daughter. "Why do you not ask him to come to our pueblo this night to eat his evening meal with us?"

~*~

Caylen remained at the Third Mesa for over a month. He stayed at the pueblo of Sania's daughter during this period, but the majority of his time was spent in the company of the young Aponi, who seemed, from the start, to have Caylen completely under her control. She fascinated Caylen with her freshness and her eagerness to know everything she could about her great-grandfather's history. She was also extraordinarily interested in Caylen's background, and in how he had lived in the far North with his mother and Fariss. She loved to play with Warrior, who also seemed to have been taken in completely by this pretty young Hopi girl.

Aponi also attempted to get Caylen to demonstrate for her alone, how he could use his powers to travel about in the body of Warrior, or other creatures on and about the reservation. Caylen would do nearly anything that the beautiful Aponi asked except openly show her his powers. He simply refused, telling her that he had promised Sania that he would never use his powers in any frivolous manner. He also, after much consideration, decided not to tell her, or anyone else on the reservation, about his gold mine and of his personal wealth.

As September drew to an end, Caylen knew that he must soon return to Whitehorse. He knew that his mother and Bill were probably already much concerned about his two-month absence, and likely expecting him back at any time. He informed Kele that he would be leaving for Flagstaff in two days time. Kele openly wept at this news and hugged him tightly as she asked,

"Have you told Aponi that you are now about to abandon her? Do you not know that she cares for you much as a wife would care for her husband? Do you not know that if you leave here, her young heart shall surely be broken, and she shall shed many tears for you?"

"I didn't realize all of that." Caylen said. "I knew she liked me as a friend, but I didn't know she felt that way about me."

"You are a foolish young man! Aponi has shown us all that she cares much for you. She cares for you even as a wife for a husband. You must speak to her of this and tell her of your own thoughts about these matters of the heart."

"Thank you, Kele. I shall think much on what you have said, and I'll also speak to Aponi of my plans on this very day."

Caylen told no one else about his plans to leave the reservation until later that day when he and Aponi were out, holding hands and walking with Warrior. Not quite knowing how to break the news to her, he finally said,

"Aponi, winter will soon be here, and my mother will be quite concerned about me. I must now return to my home in Whitehorse, far to the North of these lands. I shall leave in two suns time, but I'll write to you often if you promise me that you'll write back."

Aponi stood quite still for just a moment, saying nothing but looking intently into Caylens eyes as he spoke. Her face suddenly turned a pale white as she burst into tears. Dropping Caylen's hand, she then turned and still saying nothing, ran back down the trail towards her mother's pueblo.

Heartsick, Caylen shouted after her.

"Wait, Aponi! Please wait and let me explain what my plans are. Wait!"

Aponi didn't stop but continued on, her sobs tearing at Caylen's heart as she ran down the trail and away from him.

Caylen tried in vain to see and to speak to Aponi that day and the next. Every time he knocked on her pueblo door, her mother would answer and tell him that Aponi did not wish to see him or even speak to him. He sadly prepared his and Warrior's packs for the long journey home and went about the reservation with a heavy heart, saying his goodbyes to his many new-found friends. Nearly everyone he spoke to that day asked him the same question.

"But what are you going to do about Aponi?"

As the day went on, his heart grew heavier and heavier. He had not seen Aponi for less than two days and he terribly missed her already. As the sun set behind the Western hills, he tried one last time to see her.

Again her mother answered, saying that Aponi would not see him. Aponi's mother, at this time noting his grief, then spoke to Caylen, saying softly,

" You are a good man Mato Honi, but you have broken the heart and spirit of my little Aponi. Did you not know that she loves you and that, even now as we speak, her very soul weeps for you? Did you not know that she cares for you in the same way a wife would care for her husband? Did you not know that my Aponi expected that you would soon ask for her father's permission to take her for your wife? Did you not realize these many things, as you walked and talked with her these many days? Could you not see, in her eyes, her love for you?"

By the time Sihu had finished telling Caylen of her daughter's love for him, he too was weeping softly.

" No, I didn't know she felt that way about me." he said. " I knew that I loved her, but I didn't dare to even think that she might love me."

"You are a foolish, unseeing young man, Mato Honi. Now, go to the place where you and my Aponi sat and spoke so often to each other, and I shall attempt to convince my daughter that she should come and speak to you one last time before you leave our lives and this land of ours forever."

Caylen went immediately to the place that Aponi's mother had meant. It was a rocky ledge in a secluded nook on the trail down from the Third Mesa, where they often sat and just talked of things that they liked to do, and of things they wanted to do together. They had never spoke, or even mentioned the possibility of one day getting married, but Caylen now knew, from what her mother and her grandmother had said, that Aponi must have just taken for granted that he would one day ask for her hand and that they would marry.

He had, himself, given a great deal of thought to that very idea, but never for a moment thought that she had felt the same way, as she had never given him even the slightest sign of her feelings. He was now elated beyond belief. The very thought that the beautiful Aponi could like him that much sent his mind spinning. He had no idea of what he would say to her if she did show up. All he could think of was that he no longer wanted to leave this land, and that he had to find some way of showing her how he felt. An idea finally came to him, so he raced back to Kele's pueblo and retrieved a heavy object from his pack before returning to the rocky ledge.

He sat on that rock ledge, waiting, until nearly dawn. The Eastern sky was just turning pink when Caylen heard someone coming slowly down the trail. His heart pounding wildly, Caylen stood, as Aponi came around the corner to stand before him.

"You have waited through the entire night for me?" She asked, in a whisper.

"I would have waited here forever for my one true love." Caylen said, as grateful tears streamed down his cheeks.

"But, why do you now weep, I am here."

"I was so afraid that I would not see you again." Caylen said.

"But, why would you wish to see me, when you are leaving this place to never return?"

Caylen thought for only a moment before finally deciding that he should just say what felt to her.

"Because you did not, the other night, permit me to say to you what I now say to you."

"And, just what is it you further wanted to say to me that night? Was it more of your goodbyes?"

"No Aponi, my little Butterfly. I wanted to tell you that my heart sings when I am with you. I wanted to tell you that my love for you causes my whole being to ache when I am away from you. I wanted to tell you that if you wanted me to stay in this place forever, that I would do so. I wanted to tell you that my love for you is so deep and so strong that I fear that I shall soon die, if I leave you in this place. Those are the words that I wanted to say to you, my love."

Aponi took Caylen's tear-soaked cheeks in her tender hands and said softly,

"Then why do you weep, my Mato Honi, my Brave Wolf? You have now spoken to me with your heart and your very essence. I now speak to you the truth, with my heart and my essence. I have loved this Brave Wolf, this Mato Honi, from the first moment you spoke at the meeting with the Elders. I have loved you in such a way that my heart also aches when I am apart from you. I do not wish you to leave this place, but I know you must. I know also that if your love for me is as mine for you, that you will return for me one day, so that we may wed and become as one. Now, my oh so loved Brave Wolf, kiss this little Butterfly so that she will know the taste of her love before he leaves this land."

With that, Aponi placed her arms around Caylen's neck and kissed him squarely on the lips. Caylen's thoughts were in total turmoil as he held her tightly to him and returned her passionate kisses, kiss for kiss.

Finally, reluctantly breaking away, he reached over to pick up, off the ledge, the three-pound gold nugget that he had placed there earlier. Placing it in her hand, Caylen said,

"I want you to take this golden symbol of my love for you and keep it close to you until I return. I make this promise to you. I shall return here to this land, and to you, before you have seen more than two snows pass. I shall then ask you, on that very day, to become my wife, if you so still wish. Until that day comes, I would ask only that my Butterfly wait for me and give to me her permission to tell the world that we are now forever promised to each other."

~*~

Caylen left the Third Mesa with Warrior early the following day. The entire trip back to Whitehorse was without incident, and took him fifteen days. When he stepped down off the train from Skagway, a light snow was falling on the frozen ground, and the cold North winds were sweeping over the bustling little city.

Chapter 24

Glory Hole

Four days after Caylen's departure for Arizona, Bill and Lora rode the train to Carcross, where they, after first finding accommodations for themselves, inquired as to the location of Kosumi and Lokni. Bill had, prior to leaving Whitehorse, obtained approval to take a four-month leave of absence from his police duties, telling the Regional Superintendent that he needed more time to completely heal from his wounds, and to also consider his future with the police force.

Kosumi and Lokni found them at their hotel during the evening of that first day. It took Bill and Lora only about an hour to tell the two brothers of their proposal for the mine. Both the brothers expressed open astonishment at finding out that Caylen had made such a rich discovery while on his own in the wild North country. They indicated that it was even more surprising that he had been able to keep his find a secret for so long a time. At Bill and Lora's offer of a ten percent interest in whatever was found, they quickly agreed to accompany Bill and Lora on a trip to the mine site in order to conduct some exploratory work and to determine fully the size and potential of Caylen's find.

~*~

A week later, the four explorers were on board a forty-five foot motorized workboat that Bill had purchased from an about-to-become-bankrupt mining company in Carcross. The company's president was quite happy to sell the sturdy little ship to Bill for twelve hundred dollars, as he knew that no one else would take it off his hands, except for his creditors.

The foursome purchased, and loaded, foodstuffs, sleeping goods, lumber, spades, nails, gold-pans and, optimistically, many wooden kegs and burlap bags, in which to store their find. They also towed two eighteen-foot freighter canoes behind the workboat, as they were not overly confident that the bigger boat would be able to navigate the shallow river that led to the lake where the mine site was located.

It took them the best part of four days to reach the mouth of the little stream that Caylen had shown Bill and where they had stopped to dig up Caylen's buried gold. They had been able to navigate the stream up to the lake without causing any damage to their boat. The lakeshore dropped off so quickly that they were also able to tie the boat to the shore, with its bow nestled into the sandy shore.

Bill and Lora decided that they would sleep on board the boat, while Lokni and Kosumi elected to construct a small lean-to on shore and sleep on a thick bed of aromatic cedar boughs.

Bill and Lokni soon verified what Caylen had told Bill. Panning on both sides of the stream showed extremely good quantities of nuggets and gold dust below the steep-walled little canyon, but absolutely nothing above that area.

"This means that all of this gold and the gold that Caylen took out originated somewhere in this little rock canyon." Bill said. "We need to wait until later in the summer for low water, and then wade up into this canyon and see just what's up there. Until the water level drops, we'll construct a good sluice box and see what the stream bottom and a few exploratory holes along the lower reaches will give up."

They spent the next four days constructing a sluice box about thirty feet in length and about eighteen inches in width alongside the stream. The bottom of the sluice box was covered with four-foot long, loose-fitting sections of boards, to which had been nailed, at four-inch intervals, one-inch thick by one-inch wide wooden slats. The top end of the sluice box was positioned just below a small pool that was about three feet higher in elevation than was the lower end. The natural changes in the area's elevation meant that the sluice box, with its top end supported well above the lower end, had about a fifteen to twenty degree slope down to its outfall.

Bill had designed the sluice box and its supports in such a manner that it could easily be disassembled and moved further upstream, if and when desired. He had also designed a smaller vshaped wooden trough that would carry some of the streams water from just below the steep-walled canyon to then dump into the sluice box's upper end .The bottom end of the sluice box terminated in a flatter, removable board to which was secured a heavy woolen blanket.

Bill explained, in detail, to Lora just how this method of gold extraction worked. She had seen Fariss's sluice box in operation, but he had never completely explained its operation to her.

Bill had designed and built the water supply trough so that, by placing a section of board across the trough, the water's flow into it could easily be diverted and controlled. He took Lora up to this, the upper end of his sluice box system and began to explain.

"We first get the amount of water that we want flowing through the trough and into the sluice box before we start to shovel the gold-bearing gravels into it. The fast-flowing water pushes and carries the gravels down the sluice box and over these wooden slats. As the gold nuggets and gold sands are much heavier than the gravel and rock sand, the gold settles down to the bottom, where it is caught and held by the slats on the riffle boards. The wool blanket at the bottom catches some of the really fine gold in its fibers the same way. Every so often, depending on how much gold we find in the gravel, we divert the flow of water away from the sluice box and take out the boards with the slats on them that are holding back the gold. We then scrape off the gold and black sand from behind the slats and then put the boards back in the sluice box. Then, we take off the wool blanket and wash all the very fine gold out of it. Then we start all over." he concluded.

"But, how do you find the really big nuggets?" Lora asked. "And how do you get the gold out of the black sand?"

"That's where you come in." Bill said. "We will set you up at the pile of gravel at the top of the sluice box where you can examine the sand and gravel mix as it is being shoveled into the saucebox. You should be able to spot and pick out most of the bigger ones, before they get shoveled. At the end of the day, we take all the black sand and gold dust and with, a magnet, remove the black sand, as it is magnetic."

"It actually sounds like quite a simple process." Lora said.

"There are other methods, but for this place, a sluice box is probably the best method." Bill told her. "From what I've seen so far, I think we're going to be very rich, very soon. We'll do a test run first thing tomorrow morning."

~*~

The next day, Bill, Kosumi and Lokni spent the entire morning dredging the bottom of the big pool with buckets; dragging the buckets across the gravelly bottom until they were nearly full. They then poured the heavy buckets of gravels into a heap at the upper end of the sluice box, where Lora stood, scratching through the wet pile and picking out the yellow nuggets that gleamed wetly at her from the growing heap. After a hurried lunch, Bill removed the board that held the creek's water from entering the upper end of the sluice box. The three men spent the next three hours shoveling the wet pile of gravels into the sluice box, while Lora rushed back and forth the entire length of the sluice box picking out even more of the gleaming little nuggets of solid gold, and she then placed them into her pail.

When the pile of gravels had been completely run through the sluice box, Bill diverted the water's flow and the three men removed the riffle boards that were now silted up completely with tiny golden nuggets, gold sand, gold fines, as well as the heavy black sand. They scraped the boards clean, and ran a little water through the sluice box to clean it out completely, before replacing the riffle boards. It then took them only a few minutes to remove the wool blanket and wash the gold fines out of the wool fibers and into the steel washtub they had brought for that very purpose.

The sun was beginning to fall behind the snowcapped peaks to their West when the four finally finished panning their first day's take. Adding in the nuggets that Lora had previously scavenged from the wet pile of gravels before it was shoveled into the sluice box, Bill did a few rapid weight estimations and a few calculations and said to the eagerly waiting others,

"Well, folks. I would estimate that we have in front of us, approximately eighty pounds—or eleven hundred and twenty ounces—of gold. At ten dollars per ounce we, just today, made ourselves over eleven thousand dollars! I also think that we have just scratched the surface. I believe that, in all likelihood, the stream has been eroding gold out of that little canyon for thousands of years, and that the deeper we dig, the more we'll find. I'm positive that we have a 'glory hole' here and that we are all now unbelievably rich!"

None of the four slept that night. They sat about a bonfire on the bank of the stream, drinking coffee and deciding on their next course of action. Kosumi and Lokni wanted to continue working the pool itself, while Bill wanted to dig and analyze some exploratory holes at evenly spaced intervals away from the stream.

"This stream is thousands of years old and has probably changed course many times over the years. We may find even richer beds of gold where the stream once ran." he explained.

It was finally agreed that Bill and Lora would spend the next five days digging small, deep test holes in an attempt to determine the extent of the gold field, while Lokni and Kosumi would continue to work the pool's bottom. Bill and Lora were to test their holes' richness using just their gold pans, while the two brothers would continue to use the sluice box.

Bill decided to dig his first hole about two hundred feet to the west of the creek. They had dug down only about four feet when they hit bedrock. Scraping about two pans full of the moist sand into a bucket, he and Lora took the bucket of gravel and their gold pans back to the creek and panned the gravels without speaking. Finally completed, they were looking at about five ounces of gold in each of their pans.

In disbelief, they returned and began to dig their second hole about twenty feet closer to the stream. Again hitting bedrock at about four feet, Bill decided to widen the base of the hole. As he pulled the larger boulders away from the outer edge, Lora, standing atop the little pile of excavated gravels, shouted,

"Bill! There! At your left foot! I just saw something yellow. See what it is."

A moment later, Bill handed her a solid gold nugget that she estimated would weigh seven or eight pounds. Two more pans of gravels gave up another ten or so ounces of gold to the pair.

"I think I need to go and sit down somewhere, before I fall over with a heart attack." Bill said. "Do you realize that we have just, in less than two hours, dug up and panned about twelve hundred dollars worth of gold?"

~*~

Bill and Lora dug and tested another sixteen holes to the East and the West of the little stream during the next four days. Taking only two pans of gravels from the bottom of each hole gave them a total of three hundred and fifty ounces of fine gold plus another seventy or so ounces of nuggets for a total weight of four hundred and twenty ounces or so of gold for their four days work. Adding this to the twelve hundred or so dollars worth that they had gotten the first day gave them over fifty-five hundred dollars worth of gold.

Meanwhile Kosumi and Lokni had sluiced another three hundred pounds of gold from the pool. The estimated value of their entire take over the first six days was nearly sixty thousand dollars and, from all indications, they had barely scratched the surface.

~*~

Once Bill and Lora had completed their initial exploratory survey of the immediate area, Bill decided that they should excavate a larger area at the point where he had found the large nugget. The three men scraped clean the top two feet of an area about twenty feet in diameter and ran these materials through the sluice box. While not nearly as rich as the lower gravels that lay just above bedrock, the results of four hours work proved to have a monetary value of slightly more than seven hundred dollars. The next day they stockpiled the lower gravels beside the sluice box and then, for four hours, and after Lora had picked out the obvious larger nuggets, put these lower materials through the sluice box. Their estimated take at the end of this day was roughly seventy-five pounds of nuggets that varied in size from a grain of rice up to two pounds. The sluice box gave up another one hundred pounds of finer gold and smaller nuggets. Monetary value of this day's take was in the area of twenty eight thousand dollars.

"This is beyond belief." Bill said. "Do you realize that in less than one week of work, we have dug up nearly ninety-one thousand dollars worth of gold? I'm too excited to even think about what we should do next."

"We seem to have had better luck away from the stream." Lora said. "Perhaps we should continue that way until the water goes down and we can get further upstream and into the canyon."

They all agreed that Lora's idea seemed to be the most

reasonable and would give up the most gold. For the next month, they spent all of their time digging, sluicing, picking up nuggets and panning out the sluice box's trapped fines. Their average daily take was about one hundred and seventy pounds of nuggets and gold fines.

Bill calculated, at the end of the thirty days, that they had in their possession over eight hundred thousand dollars worth of gold.

Having dug and sluiced an eight-foot wide trench that ran to the West, about three hundred feet from the stream, Bill decided to begin a trench that ran parallel to the stream at about one hundred feet to the West of the first. Lora was keeping track of each day's take, so they were easily able to monitor the richness of the gravels that they processed each day. What they found was that the gravels' gold content increased considerably as they worked their way upstream. What they also noted was that the numbers and the size of the gold nuggets that they found also increased as they proceeded. Their second month's take was nearly double the first month.

~*~

By the end of September, the four miners had about eighteen troy tons of gold nuggets, gold gravel and gold dust stored around the camp. Bill and Lora estimated that they had mined over five million dollars worth of gold out of the little stream and its surrounding gravel beds. Bill's cursorily survey indicated that they had, at best, only processed about ten percent of the gold-bearing gravels, and had yet to enter the canyon.

Deciding that they had better get out to Whitehorse before the onset of winter and freeze-up, they loaded almost four tons of the gold onto the work boat and one of the towed freighter canoes. Leaving Lokni to guard the mine site, Bill, Lora and Kosumi headed back to Carcross.

~*~

At Carcross, Kosumi arranged for security guards to assist in the gold's transfer, while Bill chartered a steam engine and a boxcar to transport their gold to Whitehorse. Three days later Bill and Kosumi, accompanied by two trained security guards, were on their way back to the mine site, towing a small barge while Lora remained in Whitehorse.

The news of such an enormous gold find soon spread like wildfire among the many miners in Whitehorse and Carcross. Fortunately, the quickness in which Bill and Kosumi had transported and banked their gold provided very few clues as to the mine's whereabouts to the rabid gold-rush miners, who were soon left far behind on Tagish Lake by the much faster motorized workboat.

~*~

The four men had all the remaining gold on board the barge and the workboat in two days. Cleaning up the lakes shoreline, they concealed all evidence of their four months presence from any passing boats. Six days later, they had all the gold safely stowed in the Whitehorse bank. The division of their summer's take gave Kosumi and Lokni a savings account of over five hundred thousand dollars each, with Bill, Lora and Caylen each receiving a bank statement that showed that Caylen's account had over one million, nine hundred thousand dollars in it, with Lora and Bill's showing just over one and one-half million dollars each.

Chapter 25

A New Career

Caylen arrived back in Whitehorse in mid October. Winter snow had yet to arrive on a permanent basis, but most mornings revealed frost on the rooftops and roads in and around the town. Lodging space was, as usual for this time of year, at a premium, as hundreds of prospectors gathered in the town to cash in their summer's take of gold nuggets and dust, and to hole up for the long, cold winter.

Fortunately for Caylen, he had paid the Hotel sufficiently, well in advance, to keep his room reserved for him while he was away. Unpacking his gear and bathing was the first thing on his mind, as even Warrior seemed to find his long journey's accumulation of body grime hard on his sensitive nose.

Finally, clean and dressed in fresh clothes, he wandered down to Lora and Bill's room and knocked loudly.

"Come in," Bill yelled through the door.

After all greetings were over and done with, Caylen didn't give Bill or Lora a chance to say much about anything before he regaled them with the story of his long journey to the Third Mesa and of meeting all of the Hopi people, especially Sania's descendents.

Both Bill and Lora quickly noticed that Caylen's stories seemed to contain a lot of references to some unknown person named Aponi. This person's name seemed to be coming up in just about every sentence that Caylen spoke until Bill finally said,

"Hold on there a minute, Caylen. Before you go much further, you should tell us just who some of these people are. Who is this Kele and Sihu? And, most especially, who is this 'Aponi' that you seem to mention in just about every sentence."

Lora and Bill both saw at once how Caylen's face reddened at hearing the reference to Aponi. He was suddenly at a loss for words, with his face growing even redder when his mother said,

"Oh, I think I know, Bill. Our young man has found himself a lady friend in Arizona and her name is Aponi. What does the name Aponi mean, Caylen? Please, don't be embarrassed and tell us all about her."

"Aponi means Butterfly, Mom. She is the same age as I am, and she's Sania's great-granddaughter. She's the prettiest girl that I've ever seen, and she told me that she loves me." Caylen blurted.

"And how do you feel about her?" Bill had a wide grin on his face. "Does she know how rich you are?"

" No, I didn't tell her about the gold mine, but I did give her a big nugget to keep as a present from me, before I left. I also love her and promised to return within two years."

Caylen found that he couldn't stop talking about Aponi. Bill and Lora were more than a little concerned about how infatuated Caylen seemed to be with Aponi, but they both knew that he was much too intelligent to do anything really stupid. This assessment was confirmed when Caylen told them of his plans to continue to communicate with her but to not return to see her for about two years, as he wanted to advance his education and prepare for a career.

Once Caylen had pretty much completed telling Bill and Lora of his trip, they filled him in on their exploits at the mine, and gave him his adjusted bankbook.

"My God! I had no idea there was that much gold there. I knew it was rich, but this is amazing! What's next?"

"We don't know. We wanted to wait and discuss it with you, as it's really your mine." Bill said. "What do you want to do?"

"I really don't know. Any suggestions?"

"Well, as you know, we brought Kosumi and Lokni in with a ten percent share, so maybe we should see what they have to say before we decide." Bill answered.

"Why don't we ask them to come up here for a few days to talk with us. Then, we can figure out what to do." Caylen suggested.

~*~

A week later, the two brothers met with Bill, Lora and Caylen to discuss the mine's future. It took only a day and one-half for the group to make a decision.

A Whitehorse lawyer drew up a agreement that gave the two

native brothers forty percent of the mine, with the remaining sixty percent being split equally three ways between Bill, Lora and Caylen.

In return for their share of the mine, Kosumi and Lokni agreed to fully finance and operate the mine in the future. They agreed to meet with each other every fall, after freeze-up, to discuss the mine's operation and its future.

Bill, Lora and Caylen reserved the right to inspect the mine, or have the mine's accounts audited at any time they so chose.

After all the legalities had been taken care of, Caylen sought out Bill in private to discuss a matter of some importance to him.

"Bill, I've been trying to think of some way that I can use my powers to benefit everyone and I think I may have the answer."

"Well, tell me what you have in mind."

"I think that my powers would be very useful in police work. Just think what Warrior and I could do to help the Northwest Mounted Police." Caylen said excitedly.

"I agree, but you're just seventeen years old and convincing the big brass in the police force of your potential benefit to them might not be all that easy." Bill replied.

"I could demonstrate my powers to them. They would be foolish not to want to use me in some of their investigations."

"All they can do is say no." Bill laughed. "So, let's go and speak to the Regional Superintendent."

~*~

The Regional Superintendent agreed, at Bill's request to meet and speak with Caylen about a possible career for him in the Force.

A two-hour meeting was soon arranged for the following Monday at nine a.m. Bill had decided to not inform the Superintendent of Caylen's special powers or of his wolf dog Warrior. He felt that the best qualified person to explain the powers that Caylen possessed would be Caylen himself and that if he, Bill tried to explain them, the Superintendent would probably throw both him and Caylen out of his office. He did ask, however, and was granted permission, to be present at the interview when it took place. He also advised the Superintendent that he should have a second senior member of the Force present as a witness, and that he should be prepared for the surprise of his life.

Bill then advised Caylen to think up some really good ways of demonstrating to the Senior Force members his extraordinary powers. He thought that if Caylen could demonstrate just how his powers worked and how they could be useful to the Force, the Superintendent would not only support Caylens application, but might even sponsor him.

At eight-thirty a.m. Monday morning, a very nervous young Caylen, with Warrior and an equally nervous Bill Tompkins, was pacing back and forth on the boardwalk that fronted the Whitehorse offices of the Northwest Mounted Police Force Superintendent. At precisely nine a.m., the Constable who served as the Superintendent's aide opened the door and beckoned to Bill.

"Good morning Sgt. Tompkins. Is this the young man who wants to join the Force?"

"Yes, Constable Akins. This young man is called Caylen Helms, and this is his dog Warrior. Is Superintendent Simons ready to see us?"

"He asked me to come out and let you know that he has asked Sgt. Britton to attend the meeting but that Sgt. Britton is a little late, so he asked if you would wait just a little longer."

"We don't mind." Caylen said. "We'll wait here until he is ready to see us."

They waited for another thirty minutes before Sgt. Britton appeared. Sgt. Britton was an old friend of Bill, so they exchanged pleasantries for a few minutes before entering the Superintendant's office. Once inside, Bill introduced Caylen formally to Superintendent Simons and Sgt. Britton. He said nothing about Caylen's powers or of Caylen's relationship with Warrior, even though he saw the Superintendent looking at Warrior with a puzzled expression.

"So you're the young man that Bill's been telling me about. He says that you were instrumental and a great help in chasing down that killer Fariss Lubak. He has also told me that you are interested in pursuing a career as a member of the Mounted Police Force."

"Yes, Sir. I've seen the good things that the Mounted Police do, and I, as well as Warrior, my dog, would like to become a part of your Force."

"Did Bill tell you that the training is really tough and it takes place a long way from here. You would have to leave your family and your dog behind as you trained. By the way," he asked, "is that animal a dog or is it a wolf? I've never seen a dog that big. He must weigh two hundred pounds!"

"He's a wolf and he weighs two hundred and twenty-five pounds at the moment, but he's a little out of shape. When he is fit and in prime shape, he weighs about two hundred even." Caylen replied.

"Is he vicious?" Sgt. Britton asked.

"If anyone tried to harm me, he would tear their throats out. Caylen responded. "He wouldn't harm anyone else, unless I told him to do so. He will do whatever I tell him to do."

With a smile, the Superintendent said,

"I suppose you would even tell us that he understands everything you say. Or, do you think perhaps that he can read your mind?"

Smiling back at this near-truth, Caylen said,

"No, he does not understand quite everything I say, but he does understand most things that I say. And, no, he doesn't read my mind, but he does have the ability to sense what I'm thinking, especially during stressful times. For example, he knows that you are making fun of him right now. That's why his ears went back a moment ago."

"Do you think that if I continued to make fun of him that he would attack me?" the Superintendent asked.

"No, as I said, he wouldn't attack you unless I ordered him to." Caylen repeated, beginning to get a little frustrated with the conversation. "I thought this meeting was about my possibly becoming a member of the Force, but all you seem to be interested in is Warrior. Don't you wish to ask about me, and what I have to offer?

Aggravated and irritated at Caylen's sudden outburst, Superintendent Simons said, despairingly,

"Well, just what do you think that you, a seventeen-year-old boy, can do for the Force that would possibly impress me? The only thing that I have seen so far that is impressive is the size of your dog and the sharpness of your young tongue. Does he do tricks or does he just lay there looking stupid."

"Why don't I just show you what this stupid dog and this seventeen-year-old boy can do?" the frustrated Caylen said, as he walked over to the closed office door with Warrior at his heels.

Opening the door he said to Warrior,

"Warrior, go see who's in the Bank right now. Sgt. Briton, please go with him to confirm what he tells me when he comes back."

As the bank was just around the corner from the Superintendent's office, Sgt. Briton and Warrior were back in only a few moments. The Sergeant whispered to the Superintendent the names of the three people he had seen in the bank, as Caylen recovered his essence from Warrior's.

"Warrior has told me that the only person in the bank other than the two clerks, Mr. Smyth and Mr. Albany, was your wife, Mrs. Simons." Caylen informed the Superintendent.

"You must have heard the Sergeant telling me who was there." the Superintendent said. "There's no other way you could know."

"Yes, there is," Caylen responded. "Especially if I accompanied Warrior when he went to the bank."

"But, you didn't go with him, you were here with me all the time." the Superintendent rebutted.

"Most of me was here." Caylen said. "But I sent a little piece of my mind with Warrior and I saw, through his eyes who was at the bank."

"That is ridiculous!" Sgt. Britton said. "Let me throw this fool out of your office, Sir."

" Just a moment, Sergeant. Caylen, can you explain to us just how you did that trick you just did so that we can understand you?"

It took Caylen the entire remainder of that day and the next morning to explain. and further demonstrate, his extraordinary powers to Superintendent Simons and Sgt. Britton. It was only after he used a passing raven to show the two police officers his complete control by making it land on the Superintendent's shoulder and then scout the nearby Yukon River for passing boaters that they began to realize and partially believe the extent of his power and control over the birds and animals. When Caylen informed the officers that the bird had seen three canoes, each with two paddlers, the Superintendent himself confirmed the accuracy of his observations. What really convinced the Sergeant was when Caylen made, at Sergeant's request, a large Chinook salmon beach itself in front of the officer as he stood on the bank of the large river.

Caylen did not reveal to the two police officers his ability to separate his essence from his body and travel short distances while still connected to his physical body. He felt that he should always keep something back, at least for the time being.

Sgt. Tompkins decided, at that point, to tell the Superintendent about how Caylen had been the only reason they were able to catch up with Fariss Lubak. He did not reveal, however, what had really happened to Fariss, as he knew that his superiors would never believe him. He simply reiterated that Fariss had fallen over a cliff and had died as a result of this fall.

The Superintendent and Sgt. Britton then met in private with the retired Sgt. Bill Tompkins for over two hours, discussing at length Caylen and his unusual powers. The decision to recommend Caylen for police training was relayed to Caylen late that afternoon.

The Superintendent, with the other two officers agreeing, felt that Caylen's powers should not be made common knowledge, and that only Caylen should be the one who decided who was to know of them.

He was required to undergo the complete police-training program in Regina, Saskatchewan, that all Mounted Police recruits underwent. He was also to be permitted to have Warrior accompany him during his twelve-month training period. Upon completion of his training, Caylen was to be stationed in Whitehorse, under the command of Superintendent Simons as a Special Constable, and utilized in law enforcement duties where and as the Superintendent saw fit.

Caylen readily agreed and was soon issued a travel warrant and orders that took him first, to Ottawa for additional assessment, and then back to the Regina training establishment

~*~

It was nearly two years later when Special Northwest Mounted Police Constable Caylen Helms boarded the ship that was out of Vancouver and bound for California. He and Warrior had finally finished their yearlong training course in investigative and general policing procedures at the Northwest Mounted Police training facility in Regina, Saskatchewan.

When he had finished demonstrating his and Warrior's powers

to the Northwest Mounted Police Superintendent in Whitehorse, the Police Superintendent wired his supervisors in Ottawa, Ontario, who then requested that Caylen and Warrior attend a further four-day assessment in Ottawa, to determine the extent and possible usefulness of his powers. Caylen agreed, with the stipulation that he alone was to be the sole decider of who, in the future, was to know about his extraordinary powers. Again, Caylen didn't reveal to the Ottawa examiners his, as he called it, "separation power."

Following this assessment and the signing of all the appropriate documents, Caylen was still required to attend the yearlong training course in Regina. Once he had completed this course, he was granted the rank of Special Constable with the Force. He was to only be utilized on cases anywhere in or out of Canada, where it was felt that he could use his unique and extraordinary powers to apprehend, or help to apprehend, wanted criminals.

He was also given the authority to decide for himself just what cases that he would attend.

~*~

Kosumi and Lokni, over these two years, moved a small crew of miners onto Caylen's mine, where they removed over nine million dollars worth of gold, adding substantially to Caylen's, Bill's and Lora's fortune.

They were, for another twelve years, to take a minimum of two million dollars worth of gold per year out of the mine, before the gold eventually ran out, forcing the closure of the mine.

Chapter 26

Impatience

The reservation bus from Flagstaff dropped Caylen off at the base of one of the main trails leading up to the pueblos that were located on the top of the Third Mesa. Caylen could see the little nook hideaway where he had frequently went with Aponi to look out over the desolate but beautiful desert lands below. His heart began to beat rapidly at the sight of a tiny, buckskin-clad figure of a beautiful Indian maiden that he knew had to be Aponi, sitting on the little rock ledge, patiently awaiting his arrival.

Growing ever more impatient to see her, he suddenly recalled something that Sania had once told him,

"Mato Honi, your impatience is that of a youth. You must learn that a man's patience is much more fulfilling to him than is impatience. Impatience is only ever justified in our lives on two occasions."

"And what are those two occasions, Sania?"

"A man may become impatient when he is very, very hungry, and his nostrils are quite suddenly assailed by the powerful aromas given off by a roast of spring lamb being barbecued over an open fire of hot sagebrush coals." Sania had replied.

"And when else may a man become impatient?" Caylen had asked.

"A man may also become impatient when he has not, for many suns, felt the warm embraces and the sweet kisses of the woman he loves and adores and who also loves and adores him."

Recalling this conversation with Sania, and the broad, warm smile on Sania's old and wrinkled face as he spoke, Caylen suddenly knew exactly what he needed to do next.

He quickly threw his pack to the ground and then raced as fast as his legs would carry him up the steep trail to where his beloved Aponi and his future waited.

~*~

Watch your local bookstores for Caylen's Journey, the exciting sequel to Caylens Quest soon to be released.

3232889

Made in the USA